SECRETS OF THE DEAD

THE MINDHUNTERS

KYLIE BRANT

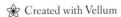

For Regan Aidrick, my newest love

ACKNOWLEDGMENTS

Once again I stumbled into unknown territory while writing this book (which, as it happens, is easily done!) A special thank you to all who facilitated with the language assistance necessary for me to write a book about a hyper-polyglot! Special appreciation to Bodhi DuBin, Loreth Anne White Beswetherick, Nicola Brooks, Eve Gaddy, Jill Welter, Junliu Zhang, and Tomaz Bester. Couldn't have done it without you guys!

"YOU HAVE BECOME EXPENDABLE."

The man stared unflinching at the weapon aimed at him. He'd been known by many names in his life, but none of them mattered now. Just as the names of his soon-to-be killers were meaningless. All except the one whispered only with furtive looks from dark corners. *Èmó*. Demon.

Staring down the barrel of a gun brought a startling clarity to life. Complications had a way of dropping away. Priorities shifted. Survival trumped all else.

"Your business will fail without me."

"There are other suppliers. Cheaper."

"But none who can get you what you most want." It was almost painful to utter the words, even though they were the only ones that might stay his execution. "I have found the boy."

Èmó's expression was inscrutable, but the man saw the signs of interest. The sudden stillness. A flare of a nostril. No other explanation was needed. There was one boy whose birth nine years ago had altered both of their fates.

The discovery of the child's whereabouts could alter them again, in a much more advantageous way.

"I don't believe you."

"The evidence is on my phone." At least there were photos of the proof he kept hidden away.

The weapon never wavered as Èmó reached into the pocket the man indicated to draw out the cell and thrust it at him in unspoken command. Swiftly he unlocked it and brought up the slideshow of evidence he'd been painstakingly collecting for the past few years. All on his own time. At his own expense. Finding the boy was to be his big payoff, one that would have him out of the business and retiring in peace. Sharing the knowledge meant splitting the cash. Or being cut out of the operation altogether.

But a loaded weapon trained on him meant certain death.

Èmó studied each photo, each note, for a long time before handing the phone back to him. "His parentage must be verified, or he is useless to us."

Us. The word was a stay of execution, perhaps uttered unwittingly, but the man breathed a bit easier. Another supplier could be found, but no one else had put together the puzzle of the child who had vanished nine years earlier. "First we must get the boy. The rest comes later. His father will still be interested, I think. He has only become more powerful over the years, and he has no other sons. I have heard this."

The weapon lowered. "Tell me everything you know."

CHAPTER ONE

THE SCHOOL DOORS burst open and spewed children from various exits in crowded tangles that had started as straight lines and immediately snarled with the addition of sunlight. Teachers in neon-green vests were stationed at the school's exits, directing the human traffic in a semi-orderly fashion. One exit for bus riders. Another for the walkers. The most crowded area was reserved for those children waiting on rides.

Catching sight of his friend, Danny, Royce hung back, jostled by the swell of children behind him rushing toward the front of the steps. Vehicles snaked along the curb bordering the property and a block to the west in the daily routine of pick-up. Some drivers would be parents. Many more would be nannies or *au pairs*.

And a few—like Royce's—would be manned by a personal security detail.

"Oh man, you shoulda seen." Danny laughed as Royce reached his side. "Bentley Cordron blew chunks all over Mr. Griffin in art class."

Momentarily forgetting the reason for their meeting, Royce said, "No way! You mean like on his shoes?"

"And his shirt and his hands...I think maybe some on his face. Definitely on his face." In the spirit of artistic license, the embellishment became truth the moment it was uttered. "Mr. Griffin had to call the office, and Mrs. Heckleman had to sub so he could go home and change his clothes." As an afterthought he added, "Bentley went home, too. Do you have it?"

At the *non-sequitur*, Royce turned his head in feigned nonchalance. His ride, a white Suburban, was parked down the street. No green vests were nearby. He let his backpack slip off one shoulder, unfastened the top, then reached inside the inner compartment and unzipped it.

"Here it is."

Danny huddled closer to take the pocketknife from Royce. "Whoa!"

His friend's exclamation of awe made up for Royce missing out on Mr. Griffin getting puked on.

"This is totally bad ass." Danny pulled out the larger of the two blades to admire it. "How sharp is it?" He immediately tested the edge. Blood welled on his finger.

"That was dumb."

His friend popped his finger into his mouth to salve the wound while Royce showed him the screwdriver, tweezers and scissors attachments. "It has my name engraved on it."

Danny was far less impressed with the lettering than he was with the gadgets. "Did you get it for Christmas?"

"No. My Uncle Paulie—he's not really my uncle. He works with Adam, my dad. He's..." Royce tried to remember how his mom explained it. "He's my honorary uncle. He gave it to me for my adoption last summer."

The other boy's gaze finally settled on the engraving. *Royce Raiker.* "Does it seem weird? To have a new name?"

Royce jerked a shoulder. Danny wouldn't get it. He'd always had a dad. Royce had never had one until his mom had gotten married last year. It was a little weird, yeah. But mostly cool.

"Royce Raiker!"

He froze at the sound of the voice. Danny, more adept in such matters, put the hand carrying the knife down against his jeans-clad leg, pressing the attachments back in place one at a time while he arranged his expression into a mask of artful innocence. As they turned to fully face Mrs. Cleveland, the handoff was accomplished with an adroitness matched only by the most practiced of criminals. Royce slipped the knife into his front jeans pocket with one hand as he wrestled his backpack into place with the other.

"Ma'am?"

"Royce, you're on inside pick-up only this year, remember?" The young teacher put a hand on his shoulder and began guiding him toward the school door. "And your ride is going to be a little late today anyway. They just called a couple of minutes ago."

After the sun and warmth outside, the school felt like a dungeon. Royce trudged down the nearly empty hallway toward the school office where a small group of other students waited. He hadn't been happy with the new pick-up arrangement, but he hadn't wanted to change schools like Adam had suggested either. His mom said this was a compromise, which meant he had to suck it up.

Taking a book from his backpack, he opened the office door. Great. The chairs were all taken by the other kids waiting. "Royce. You're late." Mrs. Gonzalez looked up from her computer across the counter and smiled at him. "¿*Cómo te fue hoy?*"

He grinned at the secretary. She was teaching him a little Spanish. "*Muy bueno.*" The blue light flashed on her headset and she turned away to take a phone call. He sat on the floor next to the counter and was halfway through a chapter of the new *Captain Underpants* book when he heard, "Hey there, Royce. Eddie was delayed today. My name is Marlin."

He lifted his gaze to look at the stranger crouched in front of him. "I've got your snack." The man handed him a small bag of crunchy Cheetos.

Cheetos, because it was Tuesday. Royce reached out hesitantly for the package. Eddie and Cliff were the drivers, and one or both of them usually came. But every once in a while, there was someone else, and instead of the secret code Royce had suggested, Mom had decided the snacks would be their code. Monday was pretzels. Tuesdays, Cheetos. Fridays were best, because then the snack was popcorn. Royce could eat popcorn every day, twenty-four seven.

"Sir!" Mrs. Gonzalez's voice was firm. "I'll need to see your ID."

"Sorry, ma'am." Marlin got up and went to the counter. He was really tall. And he talked a little like the guy on TV who used to wrestle crocodiles.

Royce saw him take off his ID badge and hand it to the woman. She studied it carefully and then shook her head. "I'm sorry. You're not on the permitted pick up list, nor have I gotten a call from Mr. or Mrs. Raiker." She looked up at the man, her lack of height not diminishing the note of finality in her voice. "I did receive notification several minutes ago saying Royce's ride would be late."

"Eddie discovered he'd be held up longer than he

expected, so he called me." Marlin didn't seem upset by the delay, sending Royce a wink as he spoke. "Could you check your list of people approved to pick up Royce again? I was told I'd been added recently."

The secretary sat in her chair in front of her laptop. Her fingers tapped the keys rapidly, then she held the man's badge up next to the computer screen, her gaze darting back and forth between the two.

"I apologize, Mr. Hobart." Rising, she handed the ID back to the man. "Someone else must have been at the desk when Jaid Raiker added you yesterday. I wasn't notified of the change."

"No problem." Marlin clipped his Raiker Security ID back onto his front pocket. "We all want to keep Royce safe." Turning, the man looked at him. "You ready, buddy?"

Clutching his snack in one hand, Royce shrugged into his pack and accompanied Marlin out of the office. He wondered when his mom had had time to stop in and make the change on his pick-up list. FBI agents didn't usually have flexible work schedules. She'd had to plan vacation time just to make sure she'd be at his school plays.

"I hear you're an Orioles fan."

Royce nodded enthusiastically as he ripped open the bag.

They went down the brightly lit hallway, passed only by the occasional teacher and other kids waiting on rides. The parking lot was on the side of the building facing the playground. "Me, I like the Braves," Marlin said as he pressed the bar on the door to open it. Royce walked out into the bright sun again, snorting in disgust while he shoved Cheetos into his mouth.

"You don't like the Braves?" Marlin took a pair of

sunglasses out of his pocket and put them on as he strolled along beside Royce.

Swallowing, Royce said, "They kinda su—um, they're not very good." Charitably he added, "Maybe they'll be better next year. But there's no way they'll get into the play-offs, not even as a wild card. What do you think?"

But Marlin didn't answer. Instead he took a phone out of his pocket and began texting a message even as they approached the white Suburban. It was now parked in the second row of the lot. They had to walk across the playground's blacktop area to reach it, and he used the intervening time to shovel more Cheetos into his mouth. Lunch had been hours earlier, and he was starved.

Tipping the bag to his mouth, he finished off the crumbs, crumpled up the sack with one hand and proceeded to suck the orange powder off his fingers. They drew parallel to the vehicle which Royce saw now was running with someone behind the wheel. His steps slowed. "Is Cliff with you?"

"No, Parker is driving today." Hobart opened the door to the back passenger seat and said, "In with you. We're going to take a different route home and see if we can avoid the mess Eddie ran into on the way here."

"Why was there a mess?" Royce climbed up into the seat and took off his pack to set on the floor beside him before fastening the seatbelt. "Was there an accident?"

"Yep." Marlin got into the front passenger seat and slammed the door.

"All buckled in?" The driver was already backing out of the parking spot as he spoke.

"Yeah." Royce shoved the empty bag in his backpack then considered its contents. He had math and spelling to do, and he could easily get the problems done in the car.

Mom said he had to stop trying to write his spelling words on the way home because the ride made his penmanship *atrocious*. He pulled out his math folder and withdrew the sheet before returning to the bag to dig for a pencil. He'd told her Adam's penmanship was atrocious all the time, but she'd just smiled and said when he owned his own forensics company, Royce could have bad handwriting, but not until then.

He figured Adam must've had crappy handwriting way before he'd started The Mindhunters Agency, but maybe not. Royce found a pencil with a decent amount of lead and turned his attention to the worksheet. Maybe Adam had gotten atrocious handwriting after that bad guy had cut him up a long time ago. He even had scars on the backs of his hands.

The radio was turned on, louder than Eddie ever had it. Royce worked through all ten problems and then rechecked them. Math could be hard sometimes when they were learning something new, but this was just review of three and four-digit addition and subtraction, so it was pretty easy. He bent to drop the pencil in his pack, but as he straightened Royce noticed the driver's hands on the wheel.

Bandages were wrapped around each finger and thumb, just below the knuckles. How could the man have hurt himself in exactly the same spot on every finger? Intrigued, Royce scooted to the edge of his seat to look closer. There was another smaller circular bandage below his right eye.

He settled back on his seat, studying the driver. Marlin was big and blond, but the other man was shorter and sort of square, with dark hair. The black shirt he wore had long sleeves despite the temperature. It was warm for late September in DC. They'd played soccer at recess today, and it'd been hot enough to make Royce sweat.

There was a weird feeling in his stomach. At the base of his neck. He looked out the window and didn't recognize the street. They were going a different way, Marlin had said. Royce wanted to ask when they'd get to the highway but hesitated. If he was going to convince Mom and Adam to stop treating him like a baby, he couldn't get freaked out every time there was a little change in pick-up. Marlin had the ID. He had the white Suburban. So what if the driver looked different from anyone else Royce had met at Adam's company? There were a lot more people there he hadn't met.

Feeling slightly better, he settled back and took his book out of the bag and began reading about the adventures of George and Harold defeating the dastardly Mr. Krump. He'd only gotten through a couple of pages, however, when something had him raising his gaze again. The guys in the front seat were talking. At first he'd thought it was the radio, but music was still blaring from it.

The sick feeling in his belly intensified. He couldn't understand what they were saying, but he could hear enough to be certain of one thing.

They weren't speaking English.

"Sorry I'm late. The detour took a little longer than I expected." Eddie DeBower scanned the private school's office, which was devoid of students, before his gaze settled on Mrs. Gonzalez. "Where's Royce?"

"He's already left with your colleague. A Mr. Hobart. About..." The secretary glanced at the clock on the wall. "Fifteen minutes ago, I'd say."

DeBower went still. "Hobart. Never heard of him. I

called." His tone was even, giving no clue to the sudden suspicion churning through him. "I told you I'd be late, and you agreed to keep Royce here until I arrived."

Unease flickered across the woman's expression. Swiveling her chair toward her computer screen, she said, "I hadn't seen the man before, but he had an ID exactly like yours. He said you'd sent him." She began to type rapidly, bringing up the screen she'd consulted earlier. "And he'd recently been added to the computer list of okayed pick-ups —" Her voice abruptly broke off as she stared at the monitor in disbelief. "It's gone." Stricken, she lifted her gaze. "I assure you, I double-checked his ID against the computerized likenesses of each person on Royce's list."

Eddie was no longer listening. He strode away several steps and pulled out his cell, punching the speed dial number he'd never wanted to have to use. When he heard Raiker's voice on the other end, he swallowed hard before forcing out the words. "Unless you or your wife sent someone else to get Royce today, it looks like we've got a code red."

Royce's heart was tripping hard and furious as he turned the pages in the book without really seeing them. This was stupid. He was overreacting. Mom used to say that when he'd throw a fit about getting a shot when he was a little kid. Not a big deal. So someone else had picked him up today. Marlin had the right ID. Mrs. Gonzalez had said so. He'd been in her computer, and so he must be okay.

But then his gaze snuck back to the driver. The guy Marlin had called Parker. He didn't look like a Parker. And something about those bandages... The man jerked his shoulder at something Marlin was saying in the different language, and Royce caught sight of the skin beneath the collar of the man's shirt. It had something black on it like...

He caught his breath. Like ink. Like a tattoo. Paulie had a tattoo of a royal flush on his arm. He'd shown it to Royce once. Lead settled in his stomach as he realized the significance of the bandages on every knuckle. Below the man's eye. They covered tattoos.

The Suburban wasn't even going in the direction of the Interstate. Royce had a feeling it had nothing to do with avoiding an accident scene. His chest hollowed out as he studied the passing scenery. They'd gone through lots of streets with old tumbledown houses, but now there were more apartments and stores than homes. He didn't recognize the neighborhood. Neither Eddie nor Cliff had ever driven this way before.

Maybe because this wasn't the way home.

Adam's voice sounded in his head then. They'd had a long talk when they'd decided to change pick-up at school. *Your mom and I aren't trying to scare you. We're trying to keep you safe. Be aware of what's going on around you. Assess the situation. Safety starts in your head, but sometimes you have to listen to your gut.*

They slowed for a stoplight. Royce looked at the door. He could tell by the red button the child safety lock was on. That wasn't unusual; the drivers always engaged them. But it meant he couldn't open the door, either.

Listen to your gut. Right now his was doing flips. The driver glanced at him in the rearview mirror, then said something to Marlin in the strange language. The blond man twisted around his seat to look at Royce.

"Something bothering you? It takes a little longer to get

to your place this way, but believe me, it'll be faster than going by the accident Eddie got stuck behind."

Royce shook his head. "I'm getting carsick." The lie sounded in his ears before he even knew he was going to utter it. "Can I lay down in the backseat?" The bench seat would put some distance between him and the two men. It was also closer to the back gate, which wouldn't lock automatically when the child safety feature was on.

The man stared at him, his eyes hard. He didn't seem friendly like he had when they'd been talking about baseball.

"Stay put. Take deep breaths. You'll be fine."

"Can I at least lower the window?" Maybe he could yell for help if he needed to. The thought seemed crazy, like the antics of the boys in the book he'd been reading. But his gut didn't feel like it was crazy at all.

Marlin leaned forward and fiddled with a knob on the dash. "How 'bout I turn up the air conditioning for you. Better?"

"My head kinda hurts. And my stomach. Bentley Cordron hurled all over the art teacher today. It was gross. Maybe I got her germs." No need to mention he'd been halfway across the building in science class at the time. He slouched in his seat, head back, eyes half-closed, taking deep breaths and swallowing a lot, like he did when he really was going to puke.

"Think about something else," the man advised.

Suddenly Royce bolted upright in his seat, bent over and clutched his stomach. "I think I'm gonna throw up." He tried a dry heave. Impressed with the result, he managed another, this one louder.

The driver yelled something at Marlin who turned around again. "Jesus. If you're going to throw up, don't do it in the vehicle." In the next moment, Royce's window buzzed down.

He leaned his head as far outside as his seatbelt would allow, drawing in deep breaths under the man's watchful gaze.

"Feel better now?"

"Maybe," he muttered. He attempted to look pathetic, crooking an elbow on the opened window and resting his head on it. "I think I need the fresh air, though."

Again the driver released a spate of words in some foreign tongue. And Royce stopped trying to convince himself everything was okay. These two guys weren't normal. The only question was how he was going to get away from them.

"WE'VE GOT a BOLO out for a white Suburban within a thirty mile radius of Royce's school." Jaid Raiker burst through her husband's office door, his secretary trailing behind her. "Vienna Police Department and two FBI special agents are on their way. His picture has been shared with transit police as well as airport and port security. Do you have the forensic artist at his school yet?"

At her entry, the small cluster of people in Adam Raiker's office looked up, expressions solemn. Adam rose, his laser-blue gaze fixed on hers. She didn't go to his side. Didn't dare. One touch from him, one sympathetic glance, and she feared she'd crumple like a twig in a windstorm.

"The artist will arrive there within minutes. DeBower is taking statements from the school personnel now and will bring the police and feds up to date." He surveyed the others gathered in the room. "You know what to do. Stay in constant contact." As one they got to their feet and departed. When the door closed behind them, Adam walked over to her and slipped an arm around her waist. Pulled her close. For an instant, just one, Jaid let herself lean against him.

"I should have insisted he change schools when you brought up the security." Self-recrimination was a fanged beast raking at her insides. Making arrangements and pulling strings could keep it and thoughts of Royce at bay only momentarily. If she let it, fear for her son could cripple her. "I should have realized..."

She felt his lips brush her hair. "We don't know whether that would have changed anything, so we aren't going to dwell on it. We focus on the now." Gently he turned her in the direction of the large digital screen behind his desk. Picked up a remote and clicked it on. It was a jolt to see the picture of Royce she'd given to the police next to a solemn-faced news anchor.

"....subject of the Amber Alert is ten-year-old Royce Raiker. He was picked up from St. Mark's Academy by a man described as six foot four inches, two hundred pounds, blond and blue-eyed. Royce was last seen getting in to a white Suburban with this man and an unknown driver in the school parking lot before the vehicle headed east on Montrose Avenue." A number flashed on the screen then, one Jaid recognized.

"I still have contacts myself." Under different circumstances, his understatement would have been amusing. Eight years ago Adam had been Quantico's top profiler. Now his was the most renowned forensics agency in the country. Jaid had the resources of the FBI and the local police at her disposal. But all her faith, every fragile remnant of hope, rested with her husband.

"Vienna PD agreed for the tip line to be managed by my people." Adam's voice was gravelly. It'd been ruined nearly a decade ago by a knife-wielding maniac who'd attempted to cut his throat. She found its familiar rumble reassuring. "Between my teams and the PD, we'll check out every viable lead as it comes in. We will find him, Jaid."

She gave a jerky nod, her fist clutching reflexively against her thigh until he took her hand, smoothing each finger out one by one before lacing them with his. They stood there, hands clasped, staring blindly at the screen for a moment.

They'd acted fast, but would it be quick enough to erase the head start the kidnappers had gotten? She had to believe it was. Had to, because the alternative was too terrifying to contemplate.

The neighborhood was the kind Eddie always called *wayor* or walk-at-your-own-risk. Royce watched it crawl by as the Suburban slowly rolled down its streets. The shops had bars on the windows and big metal gates pushed back from the doors. Small groups of young men collected in small clusters playing loud music, shouting and laughing. In the Mall area, there were cops on every corner, but Royce didn't see any police now. Maybe they didn't come here. Maybe they were too scared.

His eyes were only half open, and he concentrated on looking pathetic, because every now and then, Marlin turned around to stare at him. He dry-heaved occasionally to keep up the pretense. But he was watching the streets. The people. Because *wayor* or not, Royce knew if he was going to try to escape, his time was running out.

One hand went to where his seatbelt was buckled. Parker was slowing the Suburban for a red light. Royce would wait until the light turned green again before making his move.

Marlin muttered something to the driver as a small group of guys at the corner noticed them. One of them pointed at their vehicle, and the rest turned to look. Three split away to walk toward them. Marlin said, "Royce, move back so I can put your window up." He didn't look away from the approaching men to make sure Royce obeyed, which was a good thing because he didn't. Instead, he tucked his feet under him on the seat, so he was on his knees, as if he wanted to see better.

The guys drew closer to the car. Hobart's attention was on them. The light was still red, but Royce knew he couldn't wait until it switched. With his left hand, he quietly pressed the button to release his seat belt and eased it back. He slipped his other hand into his front jeans pocket, closing it around the knife.

"Hey, man, you lost?" This from the leader of the group. He was skinny with skin the color of iced coffee and a snake tattoo wound over one cheekbone. "You must be lost, man. Don't he look lost?"

"Move, so I can put the fucking window up!" Marlin snapped.

But Royce was already diving through the opening, one hand on the roof for balance, as he drew his other leg out before jumping to the ground. One of the strange men shouted something, but he didn't catch it. He got to his feet and ran.

He wasn't the fastest runner in fourth grade—Amber Hadley was— but he was the fastest boy. He sprinted toward the sidewalk. Pulling the knife from his pocket, he fumbled to draw out the blade without daring to look down. He heard the car door opening behind him. Hobart's shouts mingled with those of the men who had neared the Suburban.

"Grab the kid!"

He ran like he never had before, his breath sawing in and out of his lungs. He ran like his life depended on it. It did. He knew it. If Marlin caught him, he'd never get another chance.

Spotting a group of teens loitering in the middle of a sidewalk, Royce put on a burst of speed and barreled through them. He heard their shouts and calls behind him as he darted into a small market. They'd hassle Marlin when he followed. Maybe slow him down long enough.

The man behind the counter was waiting on a customer. Royce ran up to them, his words coming in short, choppy spurts. "Help me. Please, help. Call 9-1-1."

"No kids! You come back with your mama. No kids allowed in here alone." The man jerked a thumb at a sign tacked up on the wall behind him.

Royce risked a glance outside. Marlin had taken the street around the guys on the walk and was angling back toward the sidewalk. "Please. Please help," he implored the man. "Call 9-1-1. He's trying to kill me!"

"Go off with your games!" the man thundered, looking up from the change he was counting to glower at Royce. "Or I'll call the police."

"Do it!" He dropped to the floor and crawled frantically around the counter, crouching at the man's feet as the door burst open.

"A boy came in here." Marlin's voice was breathless. But the edge of mean in it had Royce shuddering. "He stole from me. Did you see him?"

The next seconds stretched interminably as Royce trembled near the shop owner's ankles. One. Two. Another. Then, "Out the back. The little thief ran in, then out."

There was the sound of running footsteps. Then a hand gripped him by the shoulder and pulled him up. "I will call the police," the old man declared, keeping a death grip on Royce's shoulder. "They can figure it out."

"Call them." Isn't that what he'd been asking him to do? "But first hide me. Because he'll be back. And maybe his friend, too."

The shopkeeper bent low to look into Royce's eyes. He was old. Way older than Royce's grandma, with a beak nose protruding from the folds and creases in his skin. Finally he gave a short nod and looked at his customer. "Rita, lock the back door. Then the front. You, with me." He marched Royce through a curtain into a tiny room with an overflowing desk.

An old-fashioned square phone sat in the midst of the clutter and he snatched up the receiver now, his gnarled fingers going to the keypad. "And what should I tell the police, hmm? That I have a boy here. A runaway? A thief?"

Royce tried to answer, but his teeth were chattering too hard. He was shaking all over, although he didn't feel cold. He wrapped his arms around himself and squeezed to make it stop. Fearfully, he threw a glance over his shoulder, half expecting to hear the outside door break open. Imagining in the next instant he'd see Marlin standing there. "Tell them... tell them to call Adam Raiker."

CHAPTER TWO

TEN WEEKS Later

Declan Gallagher had the blood of warriors pulsing through his veins. Seven centuries earlier his ancestors had fought to the death beside William Wallace. In more recent times, his relatives did their fighting in the Scottish Parliament, where the lack of bloodletting didn't equate to less carnage. He was second-generation American, but had been raised to believe a person's worth was measured by love of family and unfailing commitment to a righteous cause. In a manner of speaking, the man before him epitomized both.

The similarities between Adam Raiker and him had nothing to do with bloodline and everything to do with priorities. In Raiker, Declan recognized a kindred spirit who mirrored his own strict sense of honor. Which was why his agreement to the man's request—whatever it was—would be immediate and sincere.

"I invited you here because I've developed a strategy. And I want you to carry it out."

Declan straightened in his chair, adrenaline spiking. The family code that had been drilled into him as a child was coupled with an unflagging sense of adventure. When he'd been called to Raiker's office, he'd figured on seeing several other team members here. The regular briefing sessions over the past couple of months had been a vehicle for the operatives to share the intelligence gathered on each prong of the investigation into Royce's attempted kidnapping. But there was no one else in the room, which should have been a tip off. This meeting was going to be different.

"Whatever you want."

Raiker's smile was grim. "Better wait until you hear what I have in mind for you. Then if you opt out, there will be no hard feelings. I have a plan B."

Declan didn't doubt it. In his experience the hype surrounding powerful personalities far dwarfed the men themselves. But not in Raiker's case. His reputation when he'd been a profiler at Quantico had reached legendary status. His torture at the hands of the serial child murderer he'd eventually captured had capped his career, and the results of his final case could be seen in the patch he wore over the eye he'd lost— the scar tracing down his jaw and another across his throat. Raiker was a survivor. He'd been a canny agent. But despite the path he'd taken, his international renown, at his core, the man was a brilliant cop.

They had that, too, in common. Although Declan's career track had led him to the DC Police Department. Then to the streets for years as an undercover vice officer before rising in the ranks to homicide detective. Few opportunities would have enticed him to leave the DCPD. A chance to work for Raiker Forensics was one of them.

His path had crossed with Adam's when they'd both worked the assassination of Supreme Court Justice Byron Reinbeck a year and a half ago. The job offer tendered later had been an unexpected honor. And too good to pass up. As a member of the elite team of investigators working for Raiker Forensics, Declan investigated some of the most high-profile and complex cases in the country, while also utilizing his strength in computer forensics. A strike against Adam's stepson was a strike against the whole agency.

"Like I said. I'm in."

Raiker gave a curt nod, seemingly satisfied, then rose and—forgoing the use of the cane leaning against his desk—walked with a perceptible limp to a door leading off his office and opened it. "Please join us, Ms. Larrison."

Interest mounting, Declan watched as a pixie-like blonde entered the space. Not an agent, he instantly surmised. He didn't recognize the name or the face. Maybe she worked in the labs. Although...he narrowed his eyes slightly as he watched her smile sunnily up at Adam as the two approached. She didn't look old enough to have acquired an advanced degree. Despite the muted sophistication of her sleek, black fitted coat and matching pants, she appeared young enough to require a curfew.

She sat in the empty chair next to Declan, setting her black purse on the floor and crossing her legs before beaming a thousand kilowatt smile in his direction. "Declan Gallagher. Adam told me he was expecting you. I'm Eve Larrison." She paused a beat. "Your new wife."

His brow winged up. "My new one? I don't even have an old one yet."

"He agreed before I got to the details." Adam dropped back into his chair to survey them both across his desk. "Let's back up a bit."

Wife? The very real wariness with which he'd always considered the word had him casting a sidelong glance at the woman beside him before Declan focused on his boss.

Trepidation had made an appearance when Larrison had walked in and abruptly gelled at her introduction. *Wife?*

"I didn't get a chance to finish filling Eve in on all the backstory." Adam's chair creaked as he leaned back in it, his gaze on the woman. "Shortly after the foiled kidnapping of my stepson, the Vienna Police Department caught two men responsible for the murder of a police officer. They delayed Eddie's arrival at the school, and so are considered accomplices. However, they aren't talking. Not a word from either of them. It's thought they're foreigners, but since they won't answer questions, we can't be sure where they're from."

Declan stretched out his legs and crossed them at the ankle, adding, "No tags in their clothes, no ID in their wallets. They likely had cells. Had to, in order to communicate with the other suspects. But the phones weren't on them when they were found. Possibly destroyed."

The woman next to him leaned forward, seemingly fascinated. "Do you want me to speak to them?"

Declan's words were tinged with surprise. "Why would you do that?"

"Eve has...a unique skill set. But right now, I have other plans for it."

Her teeth flashed. And again, Declan thought she'd look right at home in a high school cheerleader outfit. She was... perky. The way some people were before life slapped them around a bit and dulled their beatific glow. She certainly didn't seem like anyone familiar with interrogation techniques. "They're the FBI's problem now."

"Their photos have been all over the news, but there have been no solid leads about their identity. Although something could still turn up, they're currently a dead end for us."

Raiker had focused elsewhere, Declan knew. He'd been

part of those efforts. With the cop killers in custody, police resources had dried up fast, especially since Royce had been returned home safely.

"The forensic sketch of the would-be abductors was a tentative match for this man." Picking up the remote from his desk, Adam pointed it in the direction of the screen on the wall. Declan's interest sharpened. This was news to him. And quite possibly the lead from which Adam's plan of action had blossomed. "Royce's description of his tattoos helped us get a hit on the sketch when we ran it through the international databases. The kid's observant."

"Not to mention resourceful," Eve murmured, staring hard at the picture. "To get away from two of them."

The stranger in the photo sported teardrop tattoos beneath his right eye. Even without the markings, there was a palpable danger emanating from the one-dimension likeness. Declan asked, "Does he have a name?"

"Several, as it happens." Adam clicked the remote, and what looked like a booking sheet was shown. "Lafka Malsovic, Sergei Peterol, Liam Nesche. No match to any of those on incoming airline manifests, so who knows what name he's using here. He's Serbian. Wanted in multiple countries for charges including gun running, murder and sex trafficking."

It was a sobering list of crimes, but how did it fit with the plot to kidnap Royce? Perhaps he was a hitman. The possibility sent a chill through Declan. But he couldn't figure a reason for going outside the country for wet work when there were plenty of hired killers right here. Nor could he guess why anyone would want a young boy dead. "Doesn't really help us narrow down motive, does it?" The endless possibilities had stymied the investigation.

Declan ticked them off on his fingers from memory.

"Money's still the most likely. Greed's a powerful motivator. Revenge. You and Jaid have plenty of people lining up to take a swing at you. Or leverage. Maybe by grabbing Royce, they expected something of you in return. Or, equally likely, Malsovic might have his fingers in pies Interpol knows nothing about, and one of those sidelines is the reason for his appearance here."

"Whatever it is would be high stakes, wouldn't it?" Eve's voice was tentative. "Four people involved, at a minimum. And killing a police officer guaranteed a massive manhunt."

Raiker shot her an approving look, and Declan wondered again what the hell she was doing here. A unique skill set could mean anything. A martial arts expert. Or a contortionist adept at eating with her feet. Although the latter thought was intriguing, it didn't answer the question of where the woman fit in.

"Motive continues to elude us. Malsovic's trafficking record reveals he's a mid-level player, a grunt who supplies women for large trafficking networks, although the rings have also been known to take money by smuggling males out of the country and then selling them into servitude. Same with the guns...he's strictly a muscle man. Brutality is his trademark." Raiker's mouth tightened for a moment, and Declan knew he was considering how close Royce had come to falling into the man's hands. The moment passed, and he continued, "Whether he's working on something similar here or was hired because of his penchant for violence is uncertain. At any rate, a manhunt is underway to find him, but we've got no solid leads on his whereabouts at this time."

With a click of the remote he brought up another photo. "Unlike the man who called himself Marlin Hobart."

Declan's blood simmered just at the sight of the smiling

bastard. If Royce had been a little less clever... The IT agents had been able to retrieve the phony ID picture that appeared then vanished from the school's computer. The forensic sketches drawn with the help of Royce and the school secretary had been uncannily accurate. They'd plastered Hobart's photo all over the news. None of the resulting tips had led to his location. And the cyber trail had fizzled. The computer twice used to infiltrate the school's server had been in a large WiFi café downtown without security cameras.

"We dead-ended on finding signs of him anywhere." Declan lifted a shoulder. "Name's a fake, of course, but nothing came up in the databases. No match with Homeland Security and Border Customs. We're still going through airport security and border crossing tapes. At this point, we have nothing to suggest they left the country." He cocked a brow at Adam. Unless..."

Raiker clicked to another photo, and Eve gave a strangled gasp. Declan couldn't blame her. A close up of a decomposing corpse was off-putting regardless of one's skill set. "Eight days ago, a jogger ventured off a trail in the C&O Canal National Park near Georgetown and went into the woods to relieve himself. He stumbled upon this body, partially buried in the leaves. The coroner estimates the man had been killed within the last ten to twelve weeks. The timeline, and the victim's general physical description, had the homicide detective alerting us."

He leaned forward, a thrum of adrenaline in his veins. "Impossible to match a description to the sketch." The face —what was left of it—was partially mummified, with areas covered by mold and adiopocere. Much of the skin had been eaten away.

"Caitlin Fleming is assisting the coroner's office and will

construct a forensic sculpture we can compare to the sketch. This is all preliminary until then." Fleming was one of Raiker's forensic anthropologists. "But the height and weight fit. Sandy blond hair. Nothing left of the eyes, of course. But these were convincing." He switched to the next picture.

Declan paused a beat. "His shoes?"

Raiker gave a flicker of a smile. "Royce did a good job working with the forensic artist describing the two men. But the boy has uncanny powers of observation when it comes to sneakers. He's got a closet full, because he wheedles a new pair from his mother every month or so. From his description, we were able to nail the style."

"Puma GV Specials," Declan recalled. The information had been impossible to trace. The brand was widely distributed in stores and online. Another dead end. Until, at least, their match had shown up on a dead body.

"How did he die?"

It was the first time Eve had spoken since Adam had shown the most recent pictures. "Two shots, center mass. It was a body dump. He wasn't killed on scene."

Looking at the other man speculatively, Declan mused, "Maybe he got the blame for the kidnapping going wrong. Or whoever ordered it just wanted to tidy up loose ends. With the two cop killers in jail, only Malsovic is still unaccounted for. He might be responsible for the hit. Or else he took off, figuring he'd be next in line."

"The feds are focusing on the two in custody." Adam shut off the digital screen. For Eve's benefit, he added, "By examining earlier crime incidents in the surrounding area around the same time, we learned there was an attempted carjacking of a street maintenance truck in Vienna that morning. The driver managed to get away, and he ID'd the men as the two who killed the cop."

She nodded her understanding. "Their job was to supply a diversion, and they needed an official vehicle to tie up traffic and delay Royce's real driver."

Declan was impressed anew with the truck driver's deed. Less than a half hour later the pair had somehow overpowered the policeman.

"And now we come to the part involving the two of you." It was always a bit uncomfortable being pinned by Adam's laser-blue gaze, summoning distant memories of Declan's misspent youth in elementary school. Although even Sister Juanita's penetrating stare paled compared to the man before him. "After two and a half months, we're no closer to discovering why Royce was kidnapped, much less the identity of those in charge. Which means we have to consider he's still a target. Still in danger."

"Where is he now?"

"Safe." Adam's response to Eve's question was clipped.

Undeterred, she gave him an understanding look. "Keeping a ten-year-old boy corralled indefinitely under high security can't be easy."

He grimaced. "You have no idea. Jaid has taken a leave of absence from the bureau, so she's with him around the clock, but he wants his life back. His friends, his freedom, his school, and he wants it sooner rather than later. That's where you two come in. Your cover will necessarily be part truth, part fabrication."

Eve's earlier words began to make sense to Declan now. "As a married couple."

Adam gave a nod. "Exactly." There a flicker of amusement in his expression for an instant before it vanished. "Meet the new Mrs. Gallagher. You got married in Scotland, which alleviates the need to falsify records here. Your names appear on a piece of property—a house the two of you own."

"I'm sure we have excellent taste."

Declan slanted the woman at his side a quelling look. Undercover work wasn't a damn lark. And he wasn't anxious to go into deep cover with someone by his side he didn't know. Had no reason to trust.

"As it happens, it's quite nice." A note in his employer's voice made Declan think the man was enjoying this. "Too expensive for you now, though, since Gallagher got himself fired from Raiker Forensics, so you're renting it out while you live in a much cheaper place in downtown D.C. 'Cheap' being the operative word."

Forgetting his trepidation for a moment, Declan said, "So I'm a disgruntled ex-employee with an ax to grind? Hope you aren't type casting."

Raiker ignored the comment. "I have an extensive web of contacts on the street, and for the past couple of weeks, we've been seeding them with your phony backstory while you wrapped up your last case. There's definitely been interest. The story is you were canned four months ago, which should be safe enough, since you were working in Vancouver at the time. You've been turned down by every agency where you've applied for employment, and you blame me. I figure the botched snatching had to involve more than the four men we know of. They probably planted a kid in Royce's school, so everything about our routine could be noted. Then they hacked the school's computer, copied our ID and inserted Hobart's picture there. If there are accomplices who haven't scattered, they'll try again, and with your background, you'll present an irresistible opportunity. I'm betting they'll reach out to you."

The pieces were falling into place. "So, I got fired, I'm

pissed and looking for payback." Declan hooked an ankle over a knee, intrigued at the prospect. "What exactly do I bring to the table?"

"You have extensive knowledge of my security systems."

He snorted. Like Raiker would ever be so careless. No one person, hell, no one company possessed more than a splinter of that knowledge. It'd be nearly impossible to piece together all the elements comprising the security layers protecting his agency and home. "We're counting on them to grossly underestimate you?"

The man's grin was feral. "They already have if they don't think I'll come after them with everything I've got."

"Okay." He was more comfortable now with a blueprint of the plan. "I'm going to give them information to entrap them?"

"In a nutshell. All the while, providing us with inside evidence about who's behind this whole thing and what they want. After you provide them with the phony details, we'll do the rest of the investigation from afar. And we'll be ready for them when they act."

"That sounds like something I can do on my own. No offense to Ms. Larrison..."

"...none taken." Amusement laced her voice.

"...but I've done deep cover before." He went on as if she hadn't spoken, his attention on Adam. "I'm not sure what Eve can add to the op."

"More than your undercover experience will be needed on this case. I'm hoping you'll get a chance to use your computer know-how, as well, if the opportunity presents itself. As for Eve... Malsovic's network includes a number of central European and Asian organizations, so we're not quite sure where this will lead. He's Serbian. We haven't yet determined the nationalities of the two accomplices downtown. But there may be more foreigners involved. You're bi-lingual, and your second language is somewhat obscure. You and Eve will be able to converse freely without fear of being understood."

Declan's mouth quirked. "You don't believe the kidnappers will be speaking Scottish Gaelic?"

"I'm hoping not." Raiker set the remote on his polished cherry desk. "But Eve does. She speaks several other languages…well." He corrected himself. "Several is a massive understatement. She's a hyper-polyglot. How many languages, Eve?"

"Sixty-seven, including dialects."

Stunned, Declan swiveled his head to gape at her. "Fluently?"

Looking vaguely insulted, she replied tartly, "What's the point of learning a language if fluency isn't the goal? Currently I'm able to read and write in about fifty of them. I'm working on expanding the number."

Belatedly aware his jaw was hanging open, he shut it. Over sixty languages. Yeah, that'd qualify as a special skill set.

"Eve is on loan to us from the Department of State. She's qualified to not only identify the language used by the people who reach out to you but to also translate anything they might say in your presence." Adam's voice was satisfied. "Consider her your secret weapon."

~

DECLAN'S secret weapon was currently plowing her way through a plate heaped with an open-face hot turkey sandwich, gravy and mashed potatoes. He paused in the midst of eating his hamburger, half in awe at the systematic battle she was waging on the meal. They'd been living their cover for three days, and he still couldn't get used to her appetite. He gauged her at about five five, a hundred and ten pounds. Where the hell did she put all that food?

Eve looked up then, fork paused on the way to her mouth. "What?"

"Nothing." Resuming eating, he took a bite of the burger. Chewed reflectively. Swallowing, he added, "You should sign up for clinical studies at Johns Hopkins. I'm sure they'd jump at the chance to study your metabolism."

She shrugged, seeming unabashed. "It's been a while since we've eaten."

"Breakfast. Today, not last week."

She set down the silverware long enough to sip from her water glass, her gaze unflinching over the rim. "You're probably used to the kind of women perpetually on a diet who nibble rabbit food and complain about their weight."

As it happened, he was. And the trait had long baffled and frustrated him. "I have a large extended family. Only my niece, Sadie, eats like you. Of course, she's four."

"And headed for a positive body image. Good for her." She picked up her fork again and resumed eating.

They spoke in Scottish Gaelic whenever they conversed, at his insistence. It was never too early to take safety precautions. "Assuming the kidnappers' accomplices eventually make contact, and Adam appears certain they will, we need to finalize our strategy." He polished off the burger well before she finished her meal.

She rolled her eyes. "We've been over it. Daily, in fact." Her response was made between bites. "We already memorized the background Adam arranged for us. My job is mostly listening for a foreign language and interpreting what's said even as I pretend I don't understand a word they're saying. I've had practice. Don't worry about it."

He was dubious about the type of "practice" she might have gotten, but when he tried to probe she always shut him down. Despite living in close quarters with the woman for nearly seventy-two hours, in most ways, she was still an enigma.

Which had all his instincts quivering. She wasn't a cop or an agent, but she was damn well versed at speaking without giving away anything personal. It wouldn't normally bother him, but he didn't like walking into danger with a partner who was as much of a question mark as the situation he was sent to assess. "Deep cover isn't like the safe surroundings of the State Department. One slip up and we're both screwed. It isn't a matter of *if* this can go bad, it's how."

He'd managed to snare her attention. "What's the worst-case scenario?"

"The worst?" He snagged a fry off his plate and contemplated it. "Not having them take the bait," he decided, before taking a bite. "Then we're blown before we ever start. Raiker has a backup plan, but this one is pretty damn fine." And he might not be selected to have the starring role in Plan B, a scenario he wouldn't be at all happy about. "Fastest way to burn us inside is if someone recognizes us. I put away my share of scumbags when I was working the streets. Scum attracts scum. Believe me, I've been in the middle of high-stake deals and then some assh—guy," he amended quickly, "from my past walks in and calls me by a different name. Things can go south fast, and it's impossible to predict just how or when it's going to nosedive. Just take your cue from me."

There was a thin line between convincing her of the

possible dangers and scaring the hell out of her, so Declan subsided. He didn't know why he had such a bad feeling about the case. He'd usually worked alone undercover, but had often partnered after he'd made detective, or on the job for Raiker. Maybe that was the source of his foreboding. He knew nothing about his "wife" except she looked like a high schooler, and she could give the Rosetta Stone a run for its money. But book smarts didn't necessarily translate to common sense.

"When were you working the streets?" Eve swiped a fry as she asked the question. "You mean before you were employed by the Mindhunters?"

"I should probably warn you Adam isn't fond of the nickname his agency got tagged with, but yeah. I was with DCPD before joining his agency." Given the interest she was showing in his fries, he probably should consider himself lucky he'd finished the hamburger when he did. "It's an intriguing job. The agency is called in at the request of other law enforcement entities, so we partner on the most complicated cases. And of course, Raiker's private lab facilities are second to none, and many agencies contract just for them to avoid the backlog in their state labs." He stopped then, aware she'd neatly extracted information without providing any in return. She was too skilled for it to be accidental.

"How long have you been working at DOS?"

"A few years." She smiled slightly. "You're guarding your plate like a goalie defends the net. Wise choice, if a little late."

He wouldn't be distracted. "Do you have family in the area?"

Her eyes, a pure and cerulean blue, went immediately wary. "Why?"

"It's a normal enough question." He picked up his napkin and wiped his lips. He could count the things he knew about her on one hand, even after living with her for the past few days. The apartment had only a single cramped bedroom, but after one look at the double bed in it, Eve had opted to make up a bed on the couch each evening before putting the evidence of their sleeping arrangements away the next morning. Still, one usually learned more than they wanted to in such close quarters, especially sharing a bathroom. It wasn't that she didn't talk. She did. Incessantly. She just rarely revealed anything about herself when she spoke, and Declan had come to believe it was by design.

Mentally he ticked off what he'd learned about her since leaving Adam's office. She was neat. And quicker than any female he'd ever spent time waiting on, which was a plus. He'd also discovered the soft waves falling to her shoulders were the result of some very determined time spent taming her curls with a straightener.

He ate another fry, smiling as he recalled he'd learned she had a deep and abiding fear of cockroaches.

"My family all live within twenty miles of DC. I have the requisite parents. Still married. A sister and a brother, both older. Two nieces and a nephew whom I adore. And you?"

The waitress appeared silently beside them and refilled Declan's water glass. They were done with the meal, but it wasn't like they were in a hurry. Picking it up, he took a sip, aware of how little her revelation really divulged. "Parents, not still together. A maternal gran and grandda who are. Paternal grandfather. An eclectic collection of half-siblings and ex-stepparents and stepsiblings, all of whom seem incapable of managing their affairs properly for any length of time."

She eyed him knowingly. "So they call you in to do it for them."

Her guess was uncomfortably spot-on. "How do you know?"

"You seem supremely competent. Plus, you have a bossy I-know-best air."

He set the glass down with a bit more force than he'd meant to. Not for the life of him would he reveal just how often he'd had something similar hurled at him by a spiteful relative who'd only hours earlier called him sobbing and pleading for advice, before he'd wised up. "I'll admit to being a fixer. But I've learned most people asking for help only want me to mitigate the consequences of their actions and aren't actually interested in changing the things about themselves causing the problem to begin with."

Finally she lowered her fork and pushed the plate away with a satisfied sigh. "Speaking as someone who has been on the receiving end of a truckload of unsolicited advice, I can understand the sentiment. But if they call and ask, they can't cry about getting exactly what they requested." Sneaky as a snake, she reached across the table and stole some more fries from his plate before he had time to react. She sat back to eat them, appearing supremely pleased with herself. "How much longer do you think we'll have to wait for the failed abductors to make a move?"

"Getting edgy? Almost three months is long enough for them to have recovered from their first failed attempt. Plenty of time to regroup. Maybe they decided it was too dangerous, in which case we're likely to have very long and boring days ahead of us. But if they've been planning to make another try...then we'd likely hear from them soon."

"I hope you're right."

He hoped he was, too. They'd maintained high visibility, coming and going from the dive of an apartment. Browsing in markets, loitering in parks, and spending several eye-bleeding hours in museums, he'd tried to keep them accessible. Raiker's contacts had made certain the information about their story was spreading on the street. But he hadn't seen a sign anyone gave a damn about it.

It wasn't that they hadn't seen some questionable strangers in the neighborhood they were residing in. *All* the residents there seemed questionable.

She plucked the menu from behind the napkin holder and began to peruse it.

"What are you doing?"

"We're not ordering dessert?"

He stared to make sure she wasn't messing with him. "We're not. Because I don't want to have to roll you down the sidewalk when we leave."

Snapping the menu shut, she replaced it. "You're right. We can always stop at a street vendor and get a pretzel later this afternoon." He knew she would, too, despite the bone-chilling December temperatures. Declan was beginning to think Eve's gift of languages was secondary to her staggering metabolism. Calories seemed to have no effect on her, as if consumed in a vacuum.

Sliding carefully out of the cracked vinyl seat, she shrugged into her thigh-length bright red wool coat and pulled on black gloves from her pocket that matched her leather boots. He got up and shrugged into his own coat before accompanying her to the register. It was second nature to maneuver his body to keep her between him and the counter as he glanced at the street outside the diner. The occasional car. Passersby. The neighborhood was seedy but fairly quiet each day until mid-afternoon.

Turning back toward the clerk, he paid the bill, and

they walked out into the sharp wind. Fall had surrendered early this year, crumpling in the face of an unseasonably early arctic blast of air that had gripped the city in its icy fist a couple of weeks ago and had only sporadically loosened since. At least there had been no measurable snowfall yet. The apartment they were staying in had a love-hate relationship with heat, which meant they were either stifling or shivering with no in between.

They turned right out of the restaurant and moved in a silent orchestrated dance they'd developed. Declan was between Eve and the curb, dividing his focus between the people heading toward them on the sidewalk and the street. After a moment, he whispered in an undertone, "Black sedan parked on my left. Two car lengths ahead of us."

She didn't visibly react, maybe because he'd issued too many similar warnings in the past. Like every time he saw more than one individual heading toward them, or a parked car with two or more occupants. But they'd only gone a few more steps when the front passenger door opened, and a tall, dark-haired man exited to open the back door of the vehicle.

He felt Eve tense beside him.

"Gallagher." The stranger was an inch or so shorter than Declan's six feet, dark haired with pockmarked skin partially covered by a beard.

"Don't know 'em." He nudged Eve toward the right to angle around the man. The stranger straightened to take one long stride onto the walk, his hand slipping into his open coat. With a quick flip, open-close, he flashed the gun in his hand where he held it inside the jacket. "We take ride." His voice was heavily accented, but his English was understandable.

Declan slowed to a stop. "To where?"

As an answer, the man grasped his arm and shoved him against the car, doing a quick one-handed frisk of his body, coming away with the weapon kept in a shoulder harness beneath his ski jacket. The guy jammed it into his own waistband and straightened, turning toward Eve. As he reached for her, she gave a scream that could shatter windows.

"*Pohiti!*" This from the driver.

Keeping his weapon trained on them, their accoster replied, "*Najprej se moram...*"

"*Zdaj!*"

Seeming to have lost the verbal battle, the stranger sent a look up and down the street and gestured with the gun. "Get in." When Declan made no move to obey, the man swung the weapon toward Eve. "I shoot her now. Get in."

She'd gone silent, her eyes huge in a pale face. Declan jerked his head. "In the car." She obeyed immediately, shrinking away from the man holding the weapon to slide across the seat. Declan followed her.

"Give me purse."

Eve shoved her bag at the man. He slammed the car door and got in the front seat.

"Where are you taking us?"

There was no answer, and despite the adrenaline spiking in his veins, he was content to watch the passing streets. Eve's scream hadn't summoned help, which was unsurprising, given the area of town. But after a few blocks, they entered an even more unsavory neighborhood. He watched for landmarks, mentally noting street signs. At least those still standing.

"*Tha sgian nam brog.*" Eve whimpered the words in Scottish Gaelic. It took everything he had to avoid a double take.

Learning she had a knife in her boot instantly re-shifted the odds in their favor. "It's all right," he said soothingly in English. "I've got this. Just follow my lead, and we'll be fine."

The man with the gun turned more fully in his seat to look at them. "Shut up."

"She's scared. Tell us what the hell is going on."

"Later. No more talk." He wagged the weapon threateningly, and Declan showed his palms.

"Okay. Fine."

Eve raised her knees chest level and clutched them with her arms. The man in front eyed them suspiciously. Declan looked out the window, everything inside him coiled tight.

"Posrkbel bom za žensko."

The gunman glanced at the driver for a moment. *"Pogumni mož."*

The exchange provided the opening Declan had been waiting for. But as quickly as he struck, Eve was quicker. Her movements a blur, she straightened, knife in hand and was on the edge of her seat with the blade against the side of the driver's neck even as Declan clamped his fingers around the gunman's wrist. The man tried to jerk away violently, to no avail.

"Easy there, dobber, unless you want to see your buddy shanked. Give me the weapon."

The gunman stilled, his gaze settling on the knife. Eve exerted enough pressure that a thin line of blood welled above the blade. The driver shouted. *"Daj mu pištolo!"*

But it took another moment before the other man loosened his grip. Declan took the weapon and turned it on him. "Now I want mine back. Two fingers. Slow and easy. I'd hate to blow your head off because you got stupid."

Jaw clenched, the passenger did as he was told. Declan

retrieved it with his free hand. "Now the purse." The man handed it back, and Declan tossed it next to Eve on the seat. "Good lad. Here's a message to take back to whoever sent you. Are you listening? Nod if you are." The man in front of him gave a jerk of his head. "The next time I see you, you're a dead man. Got it?" Another nod. "I figure you're working for someone else, because you lack the brains and finesse for it to be otherwise. And I don't deal with lackeys. Now tell your buddy to pull over."

"*Ustavi avto.*"

The driver eased the vehicle toward a curb. "Open the locks." A click signified the man had obeyed. "When we get out of the car, you have two seconds to get gone before I start shooting." Only then did Eve withdraw the blade from the driver's throat, leaning back to grab her purse before opening the door with her free hand. Simultaneously, they burst from the car, both bolting toward its rear. Declan raised both guns, but the driver wasted no time. With a screech of tires, the sedan barreled away.

CHAPTER THREE

"SHITHOLE, SWEET SHITHOLE." Declan closed and locked the apartment door behind them. The original had been replaced prior to their arrival with a steel model, complete with matching frame and reinforced surrounding plaster. The likelihood of someone breaking through the door was slim, although Eve wasn't sure what would stop a determined burglar from moving down the hallway and simply kicking a hole through the crumbling plaster wall. The visual image of someone performing the act wasn't difficult to summon after the scene earlier.

"Dirty Harry." Spoken in Scottish Gaelic, the words lost a bit in translation. But the image of Declan standing in the street, feet splayed, a weapon in each hand had vividly reminded her of the Clint Eastwood character. "Would you really have made their day?"

Ignoring the question, he locked the door behind them before answering her in the same language. "You made *my* day when you said you had a knife in your boot. Which leads to the question of why."

"The answer seems self-explanatory, given the circumstances." Eve slipped out of her coat and shoved her gloves in its pockets before crossing to the postage-stamp closet to hang it up. "We went over it often enough. Both of us would be armed at all times. You were quite adamant."

"Yes. I figured you had your gun in your purse and screamed to avoid being frisked."

"I *was* trying to avoid a frisk. But guns aren't my first choice of weapon." She turned, then cocked a brow at him. "If I had been searched, there's a better chance they would have missed the knife than a gun."

His expression was bemused. "You're probably right. I'm not sure if I was more surprised you were carrying a hidden knife or that you seemed so adept with it."

Her mouth twisted wryly. "It's always a mistake to underestimate people." Their attempted abductors had made an error with her. She was certain Declan had done the same. Eve knew exactly what people saw when they looked at her. She'd spent her life fighting the perception before she'd learned to use it to her advantage.

His grin did intriguing things to a face that would border on pretty if not for the edge of hardness in his eyes. "I'm guessing those two are figuring the same thing about right now. Their boss won't be pleased to hear how the scene went down." His Scottish was flawless, although she knew it wasn't his first language. Earlier he'd mentioned a gran and grandda, and she'd bet they were the Scottish Gaelic native speakers who in turn had passed down that part of their culture to their grandson. "Our position is stronger than it would have been if they'd just hijacked us off the street. Had they succeeded, we would have lost all bargaining power. Now we've commanded a bit of respect. At least if we're correct and they were sent by someone else."

"Or we pissed off some very dangerous people if they aren't." But she tended to agree with him. She'd spent the past eight years working in close proximity to power. Those who wielded it and those who sought it. The two who'd attempted to kidnap them were no doubt dangerous. Just the thought of meeting them without Declan at her side sent cold waves of fear radiating through her. But in Eve's experience, those at the top tended to avoid getting their hands dirty.

Digging in her purse, she brought out the phone Raiker had supplied to replace her personal cell. Bringing up the notepad option, she quickly wrote the word "Slovenian" on the screen and walked over to show it to him.

Declan frowned at it for a moment. "Odd, isn't it, to have dirt balls from two different countries represented in this operation? Gangs and criminal networks tend to be homogenous. Same thing at the transnational level, except for cybercrime and its degree of anonymity."

Malsovic had been a Serb, she recalled, deleting the note she'd written. And according to what Declan had told her, the man had never spoken English in front of Royce. Either because he didn't know the language, or because he'd been taking the same precautions they were.

"They exchanged little else of interest in our presence." She moved toward the couch in an effort to put space between them. She should be used to him by now, but something about him still made her a bit edgy. His enigmatic gray eyes and raven hair would warrant a second glance from any female under ninety. But the faint sheen of danger surrounding him was her own personal kryptonite. "There were commands to get in, to take your weapon, to hurry. The two likely came from the southern region of their country, as they spoke with the same dialect."

Declan shrugged off his gray Columbia jacket, and hung it on the back of a dining room chair. Although that was perhaps a charitable way to describe the cramped area adjacent to the kitchen counter. The apartment was essentially one room with a kitchenette tucked into the corner. A miniscule bathroom and tiny bedroom opened off the main area. It was *small*. His presence always seemed to shrink it.

Dropping on the couch, Eve picked up the book she'd been reading earlier. But instead of opening it, she watched him draw his gloves on before handling the weapon he'd taken from their would-be kidnapper and unloading it. After scanning the space for a moment, he put the clip on the shelf of the closet where she'd hung her coat before disappearing into the bedroom. A moment later, he returned and jammed his gloves into the pocket of his jacket. "For future reference, I put my gun under the mattress. His is in the bedroom closet next to yours. I should have asked before, do you know how to load your weapon?"

"Yes."

His expression grew speculative, but he said only, "Good. First available chance, we'll have the one we took off our friend tested for prints, so I'll need to get it to..."

"Adhamh," she provided when he seemed to search for how to say Adam in Scottish. *Ah-guv*.

When his gaze didn't move away from her, Eve opened her book, pretended to read. Found herself staring blindly at the page. "What exactly do you do in the course of your job?"

Although she'd managed to dodge similar questions over the past couple of days, she knew he wouldn't be put off again. "Translate foreign documents. Provide interpreter services for diplomats as needed." She flashed him a smile. "Boring stuff." The explanation always satisfied her family.

But they were conditioned to expect the mundane from her. For some reason, Declan looked unconvinced.

"Uh-huh." His eyes were the color of dense impenetrable fog, a stark contrast to his dark hair. And his unblinking gaze was more than a little unnerving. "Boring stuff that requires you to know how to load a gun and to carry a knife in your boot?"

"Single woman, living alone." With effort she focused on her book again. Turned the page even though she hadn't read a word. "Just makes sense to take precautions."

"I suppose, although I can't imagine any of the females in my extended family having the fortitude to hold a knife to a stranger's throat, much less carrying one to begin with."

"Lucky for you, perhaps."

His dark brows rose.

"You said they get angry when you offer advice," she clarified, more than a little relieved the topic had shifted away from her. "Best they aren't armed."

He tapped an index finger against the corner of his right eye. "See this scar? Bella threw a ceramic elephant at me when we were eleven. I must have dodged into it, because athletic she's not. Split the skin and required four stitches."

Fascinated despite herself, Eve gave up the pretense of reading and stared. "Is she your sister?"

"Stepsister from my mother's third marriage." He unbuckled his shoulder harness and set it on the small table beside the leather recliner he favored. "She still has a hair-trigger temper." Amazingly, his tone was indulgent. "There are eighteen of us in all, step and half. Flotsam from my parents' serial marriages. We keep in touch. Habit, maybe. All of us spend a week together at my grandfather's home in Hyannis Port every July. With everyone's kids and spouses, the group numbers almost fifty. By midweek, my ears are ringing, and I'm looking for a quiet place to hide."

Eve tried but failed to think of a single time her family had ever taken a vacation together. There had been outings growing up, of course. Museums, opera and ballet, most with an *au pair* in attendance rather than her parents. Margaret and Ronald Harrison's lives revolved around their careers. Their research. Her siblings were enough older than her that they'd been away at private schools when she was growing up. And when she'd been old enough to follow in their footsteps, it had been with something akin to relief.

She could, however, heartily empathize with his wanting to hide from his family when they got together. Holidays often affected her the same way.

As usual, thoughts of her family had her slamming mental doors. "When do you think they'll reach out again?"

He went to the coat closet and took something off the shelf. The place had been equipped for this assignment prior to their arrival, and he regularly used the hand-held bug sweeper. He paced the small area now, holding the device in his outstretched hand as he scanned the place.

"Soon. They've obviously been watching us since they knew where we'd be. Probably split up, so as not to draw attention until they were ready to make their move. Now they have to go back to their boss and admit they failed. He won't be happy, but we still have something he wants. My guess is he'll ask nicer next time." Finishing with the small living area, he moved toward the kitchen.

She recognized sugar coating when she heard it. Eve slanted a look at the front door. It seemed just as likely they'd try again with more force the next time, but there was no sense debating the point with him. They'd find out soon enough.

Curling her feet up on the couch beside her, she tugged the coverlet over her lap and returned to her book. Patience had been a trait hard learned, but it had served her well throughout the long years at private academies. Eve lifted her gaze to study Declan as he moved into the bedroom with the detection device. She was less acquainted with faith, at least when it came to depending on another person.

As she'd told him, she carried the knife because she was unused to relying on others...for anything. But the most disconcerting part of the day was the realization that armed or not, she'd never doubted Declan Gallagher would have protected her. For a woman used to depending only on herself, it was more than a little alarming to discover she was beginning to trust a man who was for all intents and purposes a stranger.

JAID RAIKER ENTERED the room serving as her husband's home office, only to stop inside the door.

Adam was on his cell. There were times in the past few months when she'd imagined it was glued to his ear, which was unfortunate, since he detested speaking on the phone. More often than not, he insisted on video chats. He preferred to look in the face of whomever he was talking to if possible. She'd often considered him a human lie detector.

But he'd foregone his personal preference as a safety precaution. He hadn't wanted to allow any hints of Royce's new location, not even to those he trusted most. Because when it came to their son's safety—or hers—Adam trusted no one but himself. She couldn't fault him.

He gestured for her to stay, so she closed the door. She strolled about, the ornate trappings lost on her. The estate was luxurious, but it had been selected for its remote location and security. And though it was petty of her, Jaid thought it resembled a prison more than a home. Maybe Royce's complaints were rubbing off on her. More likely the constant restrictions on their lives were driving her a little mad. Almost three months of forced inactivity would be enough to get on anyone's nerves. And that wasn't taking into consideration the continued threat to her son.

"I assume Royce is otherwise occupied."

She jerked around. Finished with his call, he was regarding her with a knowing glint in his eye. "He's in the home theater watching Devlin and Ramsey's live stream as they visit the National Zoo. It will keep him occupied for hours. Thank you for arranging it."

"He's always been a fan of the Strykers. And the pandas." He watched her pace for a bit longer. "Gallagher hasn't checked in. That's not what I wanted to talk to you about."

The news had her shoulders slumping a fraction. "Oh. So, no contact has been attempted with them yet."

Adam shrugged. "I'll hear from them when they have something of note to report. I wanted to show you something else." He held out a hand, and it took little urging for her to go to his side. His arm slipped around her waist, and he walked her around the desk to face his computer screen. "I told you about the unidentified corpse matching Hobart's general physical description."

Pulse quickening, Jaid looked at him. "You said Caitlin Fleming and Aislynn Nichels were working together on the facial reconstruction. Have they finished?"

As an answer, he reached out with an index finger to tap some keys, bringing up a continuum of photos. "They tried superimposition first, and the match was close enough to compel them to make a full cast."

She nodded. The method would have had the women aligning Hobart's photo ID retrieved from the cyber trail on the school's server and then superimposing it over the skull of the corpse. The sketches would have been less helpful in the process, since they differed somewhat from each other.

Intrigued, Jaid peered more closely at the screen as Adam clicked through the pictures. The first several shots show 2D images of the skull before it had been cleaned and after. The next photos depicted the clay cast of the skull with the tissue depth markers in place. This type of forensic work had always fascinated her, but her focus now was on the possibility she was looking at her son's kidnapper. Quickly, she scanned the images of the model with prosthetic eyes, then progressed to the ones with the eyelids and brows blocked in. The final shots had the cheek area and nose approximations added.

She hissed in a breath, almost unaware of the reassuring hand Adam placed on her shoulder. "It's him."

"It would appear so. Uncanny, really, how closely it resembles the drawings."

"I don't want this shown to Royce." Jaid couldn't seem to tear her gaze away from the finished reconstruction. "There's no need, is there?"

"Probably not." They were both silent for a moment as they contemplated the 3D model of the man who would have taken their son from them. "Mrs. Gonzalez at school can make the ID. But there's no doubt in my mind. I've already alerted the homicide detective, who gave me a heads up about the body, that his John Doe is almost certainly one of Royce's kidnappers."

She'd been with the Bureau for over a decade. Had

always known, logically at least, why agents weren't allowed to work on cases with which they had personal ties. But she was still unprepared for the flood of emotion warring within her right now.

A primitive part of her—a part only a parent would recognize—was glad the man was dead. He'd never threaten Royce again.

But the agent in her realized they now had one less person who could provide details about why her son was targeted. And the need for those details trumped any visceral thirst she might have for revenge. In death, the man who had called himself "Hobart" gave them little real information. The prints on his corpse hadn't matched any in the AFIS database. Dental work was a dead end without the man's real name.

Adam's voice at her side interrupted her dark reverie. "Why don't you sit down?"

"I'm okay." This development was a step in the right direction. After weeks of more questions than answers, they'd finally found one.

"Jaid." Adam's tone, and the expression on his face had her stomach knotting.

"What is it? Just tell me." The man was capable of an almost brutal brusqueness, which made his uncharacteristic hesitancy doubly alarming. He only gestured to the desk chair silently. Without a word, she sank into it, mentally steeling herself.

"The ballistics evidence on the John Doe was unbelievably slow."

She smiled slightly. "Well, not everyone has the premiere forensics lab in the country at their disposal. State crime labs are notoriously backed up, and even at the bureau lab, evidence tests are prioritized."

"Exactly." His intense regard had all her instincts quivering. "And this case would have been low priority. An unidentified victim. No weapon retrieved. No brass. No leads. It's a wonder they went ahead with the detective's request for a ballistics report at all."

"I'm not a fan of your new kid gloves approach," Jaid said evenly. "What is it you're trying very hard not to tell me?"

"I just got off the phone with Detective Ramos who caught this case." With a slight inclination of his head, he indicated the images on the screen. "Both bullets were recovered from the body. By submitting the markings to the National Integrated Ballistics Information Network, they were able to match the weapon used on Hobart to a half-dozen unsolved homicides in the past decade. But a homicide from about nine years ago caught my attention. That body was never identified either. And it was found within a half mile of where Hobart was dumped."

He closed out of the window they'd been viewing and brought up an email. Clicked on the attached file. But Jaid didn't need to see the photo of the unidentified man to guess who would be pictured.

Even after the intervening years, seeing the lifeless face of her father again stabbed her with a relentless pain. It was a moment before she could speak. When she did, her voice was husky with unshed tears. "They buried him in a pauper's grave. No ID. No service. He warned me not to try to find him. Not to call attention to our relationship in any way."

"Because doing so would have led them to the child."

She nodded. After being absent from her life for fourteen years, it had required an act of sheer desperation for Royce Benning to seek her out and hand over a weeks old baby for safekeeping. He'd left her and her mother when Jaid had been eleven, and she hadn't seen him since. They'd no longer shared anything, not even a last name. But perhaps one could never really sever the familial bond.

"My father managed to convince me Royce's life depended on me keeping his identity secret." He'd claimed the boy's mother had already been killed. Her father's murder six days later seemed to have lent credence to his concern for Royce. She'd watched all the crime databases. Contacted the detective in charge of the case to make discreet inquiries. Her father had been tortured before his death. But Jaid knew he'd died without revealing the secret of the child he'd given his daughter for safekeeping.

She could do no less. So, an elaborate ruse had originated, one where she'd claimed the boy for her own. And he *was* hers, in every way that mattered. He'd been named for her father, although she'd had no real evidence he was the child's parent. It hadn't mattered. Despite all the unanswered questions about his birth, she was the boy's mother, and she'd do whatever it took to keep her son safe.

"You said you did a sibling DNA test."

She looked down at her lap, half surprised to see her fists clenched there. Deliberately, she loosened her fingers. "Twice. They've gotten more sophisticated. Now they compare a million markers. It's obvious Royce is mixed race, but I still thought...given Benning's involvement... Jaid shook her head. "There's almost no statistical possibility my father is also Royce's." The results had left her with more questions than answers. She and Royce were family, and their bond had been forged the moment he'd been handed over to her care.

She could feel Adam's gaze on her. "Being in the bureau, I had access to all the crime databases. There was no kidnapping reported at the time of a child matching Royce's description."

"Jaid." His voice had been ruined from injuries sustained on his last case for the bureau. But hearing the gentleness in it now nearly made her weep. "I've never judged you. Whatever the circumstances of his birth, Royce got lucky when your father put him in your care. But the ballistics report proves the deaths of your father and Hobart are linked."

Her stomach went leaden. "Which means his kidnapping had nothing to do with one of my old cases. Nothing to do with you."

"It appears to have everything to do with the mystery surrounding Royce's birth."

～

THE GAG in the man's mouth muffled his screams. Xie Shuang finally tired and lowered the whip, seemingly gratified by the bloody crisscross of welts and open wounds across the man's back. "You fucked up." The man nodded, his eyes rolling wildly although Malsovic knew he didn't speak a word of Chinese. But pain was a universal language.

"If you fail me again, you die. Nod if you understand." This was delivered in Slovenian, badly mangled as usual. But the man's head bobbed frantically. A boot to his backside sent him sprawling, and at Shuang's gesture, Malsovic moved forward to haul the man up and out of the room.

When he returned minutes later, his employer was seated behind the cheap polished desk, the laptop open. The printer next to it hummed. And when that flat, black gaze shifted from the computer screen to him, Malsovic felt a prickle of something very like fear.

Men—and women—had underestimated Xie Shuang in the past, and many had ended up dead. Malsovic had so far managed to evade a similar fate, but at times it felt like an orchestrated dance with the devil. *Èmó*. The nickname was spoken only in hushed tones, but it was apt.

"Those men were yours. You are responsible for their failure. Cretins, both of them."

He replied in Serbian. "Hobart was not my pick. Neither were the two who now sit in a cell." He stood, ready to dodge. Shuang was prone to throw whatever weapon was handy when angered.

But no missiles flew. "They will not talk. They know their families' fates depend on their silence. The plan must be changed. I will deal with Gallagher myself. You will arrange our meeting."

He swallowed the questions on his tongue. Shuang wasn't known for taking risks and dealing with Gallagher directly was a definite risk. Not for the first time, he mourned having to share his discovery about the boy. There hadn't been much choice.

He knew better than to voice his doubts. "As you wish. But what will be done with him and the woman once they've outlived their usefulness?"

Shuang shrugged carelessly. "That much has not changed. You will kill them."

By no stretch of the imagination could their apartment building ever be described as quiet. The walls were wafer thin, and the constant serenade of babies wailing, televisions blaring and music pumping bombarded them all day and well into the night. Eve's ability to sleep through a small explosion was as legendary in her family as was her appetite and considered just as indelicate. The talent seemed to have escaped her tonight.

Every new sound, every set of footsteps past their door, set her senses on high alert. Ears straining, she'd bolt upright on the couch and wait, barely breathing until they faded in the distance.

It didn't take much imagination to recognize the source of her newfound anxiety. Declan seemed certain there would be another contact soon. How did they know it would come in the daylight?

He'd gone to bed at midnight, hours earlier. If he lay awake similarly vigilant, she could hear no signs of it. Through the open door, Eve could barely make out his form beneath the covers on the mattress. It was unmoving. Maybe he was as adept as her at sleeping through a din.

Or maybe he had far more experience than she did at sleeping comfortably with a half-naked person of the opposite sex close by. One who was for all practical purposes a stranger.

The thought suffused her with heat. It wouldn't be hard to surpass her experience. Most of the men she came into contact with at work were decades older than her, which meant she had plenty of practice dodging unwanted male attention, but far less with men who actually interested her. Not that any of her work colleagues or acquaintances fell into the heartthrob category—a niche seemingly carved with Declan Gallagher in mind.

To be fair, he didn't seem to be one of those men cognizant of the potent combination of black hair, smoky eyes and sardonic grin, which made this situation bearable. If he seemed unaware of her as a woman, at least he wasn't acutely conscious of his own assets as a male.

Assets she shouldn't be wasting valuable sleep time considering.

Eve re-arranged the blanket and shifted on the couch. It was comfortable, as was all the furniture delivered to the cramped space. She was willing to bet it was of a much higher quality than had ever graced this area before. But the furnishings were in keeping with the supposed descent in their circumstances. The good pieces had presumably come from their fictional too expensive house.

She picked up her cell and checked the time. Blew out a breath. It was already two, and she'd already learned Declan was an early riser. Regardless of her usual ability to sleep through anything, somehow her senses went on high alert when he was in the room. That hyper-awareness of the man had her inner alarms shrilling.

Punching her pillow with a little more force than necessary, she turned over and pulled the coverlet up to her chin.

Thinking about Declan in the next room was no guarantee of summoning sleep, so she concentrated instead on mentally cataloguing the level of sound coming from the surrounding apartments. It had quieted somewhat, and she knew from the past few nights it would quiet even more over the next hour once the building's occupants had stumbled home from the bars and the prostitutes.

Her breathing slowed. Every random rattle of pipe or creak of the floor was familiar. The shuffle of footsteps in the apartment above. The baby's cry, which was just as quickly hushed. Nothing out of the ordinary.

One moment she was drifting off to sleep, and the next she was jerking to a sitting position, the pounding of her heart sounding in her ears. She scanned the interior shadows, trying to place the source of her sudden fear. Nothing moved. She could still see Declan on the bed. The footsteps overhead were absent. Even the baby's whimpers were silenced.

Then it came again—an almost imperceptible squeak. A shoe against the cracked tile floor outside their door. Hauling in a breath, she attempted to calm her breathing. Just another resident on his or her way home. She told herself that. And would have believed it, if it weren't for the flat white paper slipping under the door like an ethereal wisp of fog.

Frozen, she stared at it, her heart doing a tattoo beat in her chest. Try as she might, she could hear no other sound. Was the person still out there? Her limbs abruptly thawed, and she jumped from the couch, tiptoeing across the room to sidle along the wall. Feeling vaguely ridiculous, she reached out a bare foot and slid the paper toward her until she could pick it up. She heard nothing from the hallway. Eve took the note back to the couch and picked up her cell, using the screen's light to read the message.

The words on it had her scurrying into the bedroom, stopping just inside the doorway. "Declan!" she hissed. She threw another glance over her shoulder. Was there a sound in the hallway? The possibility had her crossing the steps to the bed and nudging the side of the mattress with her knee urgently. "Declan!"

One moment he was lying still. The next he was a blur of motion. He sat up and pulled her down on top of him in a smooth movement, one arm around her throat, a hand clapped over her mouth. With his free hand, he held a gun at her temple. For a moment, shock and fear shut down her body's responses. A silent scream welled inside her. Went unuttered. A second ticked by. Two. Then a well-trained sense of self-preservation kicked in.

She bit down hard on the hand covering her mouth and rammed her elbow into his chest with all her might.

"Dammit!" She was flipped to her back, pinned in place on the mattress by the full weight of his hard body stretched out over hers. It took a sluggish moment for him to make sense of the scene. He blinked. "Eve."

"Very astute, Captain Obvious," she snapped. "Your powers of observation are truly exemplary." Her body heaved under his. "Get *off* me!"

"Right." He shoved the gun under his pillow and rolled to the side. Since she certainly wasn't going to scramble over his body—his partially *nude* body—to get off the bed, she scooted toward the wall, putting as much distance between them as possible.

"Sorry." He jammed his free hand through his hair. "But I didn't expect... dammit. This probably isn't a great idea. I mean...I'm sure lots of guys would find you attractive, in a pint-size high school cheerleader type of way. But with the two of us working together...not smart. Sex clouds the senses. I think we can both agree we need to keep our wits during this thing."

Eve gaped at him, her mind sorting through the carelessly offensive remarks. Somehow, coming upon her uncomfortable earlier musings about him, high school cheerleader seemed the most insulting. "I know sixty-seven different ways to call you a jackass." She slapped the now wrinkled sheet of paper against his bare chest, tempted to pin it there with her knife. "None of them do you justice."

"What's this?" He smoothed it out, squinting at it in the shadows.

"The reason I came in here. That, and my overpowering, and yes—thanks for the clarification—*unrequited* state of lust." She turned on the flashlight app on her cell so he could read.

Mr. Gallagher,

I apologize for my assistant's over-enthusiasm this afternoon. He has been properly disciplined. I hope you will still consider listening to my business proposition. I will be available to discuss it over lunch tomorrow, 11:30 in the dining room of the Latifma Hotel on Fourth and Prospect.

Your humble servant.

His reaction was swift. "Shit. I mean..." He shot her a look. "This," he shook the paper, "is good news. At least it can be if Raiker has time to check out the location for the meet. The rest..." He went silent, and a part of Eve was gratified by the pained expression on his face. "Umm... I'm going to blame a brain muddled by sleep fog."

As apologies went, his didn't go far enough. Still stinging from his earlier remarks, her tone was caustic. "Uh-huh." Another woman might find him harmlessly adorable, with his hair all mussed and one cheek still bearing a crease from his pillow. Ten minutes ago, she might have thought the same.

Of course, that was before the man had, in the space of a second, held her immobilized with a gun to her temple. Had outraged her with his awkward refusal of a sexual encounter she hadn't even offered. The second act felt more insulting than the first.

Eve eyed him warily. His shoulders were much too broad to be considered harmless. And his torso was roped with muscle his clothes did a good job of hiding from the world. And she...she was spending way too much time contemplating a half nude man who had, intentionally or not, just disparaged her. Jackass.

It took more effort than it should have to drag her focus back to the note. "A little odd for it to be unsigned, isn't it?"

He shrugged. "We'll get a name soon enough." He was silent for a moment, studying the message. "'Your humble servant' sounds Asian, doesn't it? Chinese? Japanese?"

"Or someone attempting to sound Asian." Linguistically speaking, there was little of value in the message. If the author was bi-lingual, he or she had a good grasp of English. Declan reached for his cell, which was setting on a small nightstand next to the bed. "What are you doing?"

"Texting Raiker the details of the meet. Hopefully by tomorrow he can get us a scouting report of..." He consulted the message again. "The Latifma Hotel on Fourth and Prospect."

Concern shoved aside her irritation with him. "I'm still a bit leery of using cell phones to communicate, even if they did come from Raiker's labs. Nothing is untraceable."

"These are." He was already bent over his phone typing a message.

"Impossible. The technology doesn't exist." This much she was sure of.

"His innovation lab works on select contracts for...those in charge of the military. Believe me, for every new bit of technology in civilian hands, the military has had it for at least a decade."

The Pentagon he meant. There was no Scottish Gaelic word for it, so he was careful to avoid speaking the word aloud. She was fascinated in spite of herself. Moving over to sit beside him on the edge of the bed, she asked, "But how do they work?"

Finally, he raised his head to look at her. "I'm not going to bore you with talk of cryptographic algorithm options and transmission security functions. Suffice it to say, all sent or received messages are encrypted for secure transmission and decrypted for the receiver. Anything deleted from the phone is not recoverable, except back at the lab where the scientists can do unimaginable things to retrieve it. Can I finish this?"

She lifted a shoulder. "Be my guest." Obviously, he wasn't a multitasker.

Moments later, he straightened, set the cell down and looked at the message in his hand again. "How long since you found this?"

"It was passed under the door about six minutes ago. I... it took me about thirty seconds to pry myself from the couch. I brought it right in here."

His gaze sharpened. "You were awake when it was delivered?"

She couldn't resist needling him. "Yes, sleep was impossible. I was tossing and turning in a turmoil of longing for you."

He gave her an elbow nudge. "Okay, I deserve that."

"You really, really do."

Her sweet tone didn't seem to fool him. "You're a bit of a smartass. Who would have guessed?" He leaned forward to look at the couch. Then toward the door. "Did you hear anybody out there before it was delivered?"

Her skin chilled at the memory. "I thought I did. A slight sound of a footstep in the hall. Not much more." But enough to strike fear in her heart when the paper was slipped inside the apartment.

"Okay. They would have cased us thoroughly before approaching us today, so of course they'd know where we were staying. And security at this dump is a joke." He stifled a yawn. "I think it's best if we trade places. You take the bed, and I'll take the couch."

"It's at le

longer would

"I'll man

was wearing

thankfully, t

from the roo

Eve cont

indentation

been pound

lonely?" she

"Use you

equivalent is

She grir

erous dreams have me sleepwalking and coming out there to ravish you."

His voice sounded a little grim. "We're going to declare a statute of limitations on the episode. Any remarks about it are confined to the next hour. Tomorrow, it's off limits, got it?"

She waited a full five minutes before singing the chorus to "Simply Irresistible."

"Shut up, Eve."

Grinning, she stretched out on the bed and made herself comfortable. And before she fell asleep, she mentally congratulated herself for not agreeing to the statute of limitations.

CHAPTER FOUR

"WHY ARE WE GOING TO A BANK?"

An hour and a half before their lunch date with the mysterious messenger, Declan ushered Eve into the lobby of Citizen's Home Bank of DC. "Ostensibly it's handling the foreclosure on our fictional home. It's also the place where Raiker is storing a computer we can use to securely communicate with him."

His tone was a little brusquer than he'd meant it to be, a byproduct of too little sleep and a tinge of leftover discomfort from last night. A couple of mugs of coffee hadn't been able to completely alleviate the effects of either. Nor had they cleared his brain enough to figure out why his first conscious reaction to being awakened by her last night was to assume she'd had sex on the mind.

Jaw clenching, his step quickened. He hadn't thought of her that way. Not once. Declan could be exceedingly single-minded on the job, and sex—or the lack of it—had never even occurred to him. And this woman wouldn't have starred in an X-rated dream in any case. He liked his women stacked, long-legged and independent. His white knight instinct could wreak havoc if he let it. Coming to the rescue of his assorted family members was time consuming and exhausting. He didn't welcome emotional upheaval in his personal life, which was one of the reasons he'd skirted marriage the way others avoided quicksand.

But something had planted a steamy mental image of the diminutive Eve, with her wide blue eyes and tousled gold curls squarely in his subconscious, and recognition of the fact had him feeling just a bit edgy. A little surly. He was a man who prized control. Relinquishing it, whether due to sleep or hormones, was unacceptable.

His hand on the bank's polished beveled door handle, he heard a small sound and realized the woman at his side was humming beneath her breath. Declan stared hard at her. The wind had raked careless fingers through the casual waves she'd tamed her curls into. Her expression was guileless. If she'd suffered any ill effects from too little sleep and leftover embarrassment, it certainly didn't show.

Yanking the door open, he waited for her to enter. Of course, she wasn't the one who'd been embarrassed. Recalling the sarcastic remarks she'd aimed his way, she also wasn't completely defenseless. Not for the first time, Declan was reminded he really knew very little about the woman who was—like it or not—his partner for at least a few more days.

They'd no more stepped into the lobby before they were greeted by a tall, deeply tanned man sporting a mane of white hair and an exquisitely cut Brioni suit. Declan's grandfather favored the same tailor. "Mr. and Mrs. Gallagher." His handshake was firm. "I'm Bank President Irving Baltes. I'll be handling your affairs. Please." He gestured for them to precede him. "Let's go where we can be private."

Declan shoved his gloves in his coat pocket as he and Eve followed Baltes to a room lined with rows of safe deposit boxes. The bottom row in this one was comprised of boxes the size of small safes.

Once the door was shut behind them, the man lost his previously grave expression. His face was wreathed in a smile. "Mr. Raiker sent me excellent likenesses of you two. I must say, I'm gratified to have the chance to repay him in some small way." He went to one of the larger security boxes in the bottom row, unlocked it and withdrew a laptop, which he handed to Declan. "I'll show you to a place where you can be undisturbed." The key, he gave to Eve. "Feel free to come as often as necessary." They followed him to an adjoining private transaction room where he left them alone.

"Makes you sort of wonder what Adam Raiker did to elicit such gratitude."

Declan lost no time sitting down at the long table and powering up the laptop. "Baltes was alerted to irregularities in the bank's finances three years ago. Discretion is the name of the game when it comes to financial institutions." He quickly typed in a sequence of letters, numbers and symbols. "Raiker was hired by the bank board to bring in a team of forensic accountants each night to find where the money was going. They eventually nailed the chief financial officer for embezzling over four million dollars."

"Four million buys a lot of gratitude."

"Four million buys a lot of everything." He tapped a few more keys and sat back in his chair. Eve looked from him to the still dark screen.

"What are we waiting for?"

"Me, I assume." Adam Raiker appeared on the screen,

seated in a darkened room. The background was shrouded in shadows.

"Miss Larrison. I hope Gallagher has been treating you well."

It was as if he'd snatched Declan's brief mental aberration of the night before from the depths of his memory. With a mischievous glance at Declan, Eve said in a judicious voice, "For the most part. Other than this overwhelming hunger I seem to have acquired..."

"Eve..." Declan growled the warning.

"What?" She was all innocence. "You didn't feed me breakfast."

"Feed the poor woman, Gallagher. It's not like you don't have an expense account."

"Wait until you see it." Declan's gaze when it met hers promised retribution. "She eats enough to keep a small village alive for a week." And she apparently had no clear understanding of the term "statute of limitations".

"Let's hope the dining room in the Latifma Hotel is up to your standards," replied Raiker. "I found nothing about the quality of the food there, but the hotel itself has had a colorful history."

"By any chance are the owners of Asian descent?"

"Not currently, no. A group of Pakistani investors own it, and some of their people run it. But twenty-five years ago, a Malaysian by the name of Rizqi bin Osman bought it. Seven years ago, ICE raided the hotel, busting a drug operation and a prostitution ring peopled mainly with illegal immigrants. Before he could be scooped up, bin Osman fled the country. There's been no police activity at the property in the time since. Here's where you'll be going." The photos filling the screen depicted an aging structure in pale brick. The inside lobby was well kept. It looked like a moderately priced establishment. "It seems to cater mostly to foreign businessmen, but there are certainly American guests there," Raiker's voice continued. The next picture showed a rather unremarkable dining room. And then there were several shots of the exits of the building. "I've emailed you the blueprints of the hotel so you're not walking into the place cold."

"That might come in handy," Declan muttered. "Right now, we have no way of knowing if the location was chosen at random or whether our mystery messenger has a connection there."

"We'll learn soon enough." Raiker was back on screen. "I'll have a couple stationed in the dining room while you're present. They'll take photos of your host, and we'll run him through various international databases."

He nodded. "And we'll let you know just what his business proposition entails." He was clear on the parameters of the assignment. Adrenaline began to fire in his veins. And he was more than ready to get the waiting over and the mission underway.

Never one to linger over conversation, Raiker was nonetheless silent for a moment, as if choosing his next words carefully. "Some information has come to light leads me to believe neither Jaid nor I are the motivation behind Royce's kidnapping."

Declan paused a beat as he digested the new information. "If not money or revenge, we're back to square one."

"The motivation is Royce himself." His expression went fierce. "This information is need-to-know only. Jaid... adopted him when he was a few weeks old. She knows nothing about his parentage. But we have reason to believe the attempted kidnapping somehow stems from the mystery surrounding his birth."

"Surely she has details about where he came from. There have to be social workers who were involved. Birth records..."

"It's complicated." Raiker's terse reply stemmed Eve's flow of words. "And the only person we know of who had all the facts has been dead for nine years."

"Taking the secret to the grave," she murmured.

Her words were dramatic but true enough, Declan realized. It would have been easier to track someone who sought revenge, or even hoped to gain leverage over Jaid or Adam by snatching their son. Unraveling a mystery nearly a decade old might prove to be a bit more challenging.

"This information actually gives us a head start," Raiker said. "We already know Royce was the target, if not why. It's up to you to get us answers."

"And also to lead them into a trap in which they incriminate themselves," Declan said.

He inclined his head. "Any details you might acquire about the criminal activity these people may be involved in will have to be shared with the authorities. It would behoove us to gather facts as quickly as we can."

"In case one of the alphabet agencies swoops in and changes the focus of the investigation." Declan reached into his coat and withdrew a hand towel he'd wrapped around the weapon he'd taken off their would-be kidnapper. He held it up to the screen. "If I leave this gun here with the computer, can someone fetch it to run it for prints? I took it off one of the guys who tried to abduct us yesterday. Who knows, we might get lucky."

"An agent will come for it. I left you something else besides the computer."

Eve got up and opened the door to cross to the safe. She returned with a small, lightweight pouch and brought it back to the table in the adjoining room. From the bag, she withdrew an MP3 player and earphones. "I hope there's no country music on this."

"I can't make any promises," Raiker said. "It can play music. But it also acts as a receiver. There should be a small listening device in the pouch, as well." Reaching into the bag, Eve took out a small clear plastic box. Inside it was a tiny silver, square item.

"Nice," she said admiringly, turning it over to peer at it closer. "But it's not cell phone activated?" Her words had Declan sliding her a careful look before leaning over to examine it himself.

"It's a new prototype and virtually undetectable. Voice activated and fully charged. The receiver allows you to listen in without drawing undue attention, since there might be interested parties nearby. No distance limitations. It'll work for seventy-two hours on standby, with at least twenty hours of usage time. But," his face went grim, "don't take any unnecessary chances. FBI Agent Stillions got the warrant, and I just sent it along in case an opportunity presented itself. I'll let you know if we get a hit on the photos taken today. Until then watch your back." The screen abruptly went black.

"Well. That was an unceremonious sign off."

Declan didn't answer. He was opening the email Raiker had sent and studying the blueprint of the hotel.

"Dining room is left of center on the lobby floor." He tapped the indicated space on the screen. "Note the exits. The hallway to the restrooms is here."

"There should be a door leading outside from the kitchen. Likely toward an alley or the back of the building. They'd need a place to put their waste and Dumpsters are usually hidden in less public places."

He smiled. "Trust you to think of the kitchen." Checking the blueprint again, he said, "It wouldn't be considered a public exit, but yeah, here's a door." He surveyed the screen before closing out of the email and tapping in a series of code that wiped the computer screen completely clean. "It's likely to be a very low-key first meeting. An offer might not be made until later." Despite the matter-of-fact words, he couldn't deny the kick in his pulse. Their assignment had just broadened in scope. Identifying the people responsible for Royce's kidnapping attempt was as crucial as learning the circumstances of the boy's birth.

"The message mentioned a business proposition," Eve pointed out reasonably. "They've waited ten and a half weeks. I think they'll be in more of a hurry than you imagine."

"Either way, the meet will be perfectly safe. Raiker will have another couple of people in there as back up if things go wrong. I'm not expecting they will."

Her brows rose. "Excellent news, but I don't require handholding. Let's do this."

Closing the laptop, he sat for a moment surveying her. "You sounded familiar with the workings of listening devices."

Because he was watching so closely, he noted the way her expression subtly altered. Those blue eyes widened just a bit, perfecting the mask of innocence. "Trust is sometimes a commodity in short supply in the State Department, especially with emissaries from opaque regimes." She didn't flinch under his regard.

Plausible, of course. And yet...something about the woman didn't add up. He gave a mental headshake and pulled out his cell to check the time. His efforts would be better spent preparing for the upcoming meeting. He'd already devoted way too much energy considering the incongruities of Eve Larrison.

His chair scraped the floor as he pushed it back. "We've got time if we hurry."

She rose and fell in step beside him as he started for the door of the transaction room. "Time to get a look at where those hotel exits lead?"

"You read my mind."

"THOSE TWO LATINO gentlemen in the cheap suits."

It was Eve's third guess in the past ten minutes. And just like her other two predictions, Declan made no attempt to turn around and look at the people she indicated.

"Since he's unlikely to send agents who can be identified as his employees, I wouldn't recognize them anyway."

They spoke in Scottish Gaelic, as usual. "Our host is late."

"Ten minutes." He reached for his water glass. Took a sip. "We'll order in another five, whether the approach is made or not."

The restaurant wasn't overly large, with room for no more than sixty. They'd been led to a secluded table in the far corner, although only a third of the tables and booths were occupied. The wait staff were a mix of nationalities, but like the hostess posted at the door, they all spoke excellent English.

Eve smoothed the narrow wool skirt she'd worn and eyed the rest of the dining room's occupants surreptitiously. Besides the middle-aged males she'd just mentioned was a group of four German-speaking men two tables away. The hostess was conversing with an Asian woman inside the doorway, and an elderly couple drank tea at a booth across the room, neither exchanging a word. As Raiker had mentioned, the clientele was an eclectic mix of foreign and American guests. The couple who had come in directly after them was still her best guess for those reporting to Raiker. They'd chosen the booth closest to Declan's and Eve's table and sat next to each other. The woman was a great deal younger than the man. Maybe she was supposed to be his daughter. Or his trophy wife.

Even as she had the thought, Eve saw the woman rest her hand on the gentleman's thigh and slide it slowly upward to cup him intimately. Her cheeks heated, and she quickly averted her gaze. So...that couple was out. Unless they were devoted to taking their cover much further than duty required.

She focused on the menu. After studying it for a minute, she said, "Just to forgo any snide comments, I plan to order enough for breakfast *and* lunch."

His tone held a hint of indulgence. "I'd expect nothing less."

"I must apologize again, this time for my tardiness."

Eve's head jerked up. The Asian woman who had been conversing with the hostess stood beside the table. "Mr. Gallagher, I presume?" She offered her hand to Declan. "Please, do not get up. May I?"

"Yes, of course. Please join us." His tone was as polite as Eve had ever heard it, proving the man did have manners when he chose to use them. The shock she was experiencing wasn't mirrored in his voice. Of all the possibilities they'd considered, she didn't think even Adam Raiker had imagined their contact would be female.

Of course, the woman may only be a go between used by whomever had masterminded Royce's kidnapping.

"My name is Xie Shuang." The woman turned to Eve. "You must be Mr. Gallagher's lovely wife. Thank you for meeting with me today."

Eve sent her a vacuous smile. "Oh, it was our pleasure. You're Japanese, aren't you? We had a Japanese cook when I was little. She taught me to speak a little of the language. *Genki des ka.*" She purposely mangled the pronunciation.

Shuang's smile didn't reach her eyes. "Yes, I am from Tokyo. How clever you are to guess."

Eve beamed. "She made the best sushi, too. Do you know how to make sushi? I can't quite get the knack. I really don't like to touch raw fish. I only like to eat it." She gave a tinkling laugh. "I know it makes no sense, but there you go. Maybe that's what I'll order today, darling," she said to Declan. She scanned the menu again. "Oh." She made a moue of disappointment. "It's not on the menu here."

"We'll find a sushi restaurant another time. Hush now, while we discuss business."

"Okay." Eve hummed a little to herself as she looked over the menu in order to polish the pretense of complete vapidity. The woman dismissed her with the flick of an eye and turned her attention to Declan.

"I have heard you were once in the employ of a man I very much want to meet."

He set down his menu to regard the woman. "Since I've held a few jobs over the years, you'll have to be more specific."

"Of course. It is your most recent boss I am speaking of. Adam Raiker."

Declan bared his teeth. "Raiker and I aren't exactly on the best of terms these days. He cut me loose months ago and burned me for any decent job prospects in the future. Sorry. Can't help facilitate a meeting. Bastard wouldn't take my calls, much less make time to talk with anyone I recommended to him."

"How unfortunate. He sounds like a difficult man." Something about her intense regard made Eve second-guess her earlier prediction. This wasn't necessarily a woman who took orders from a higher up. "I, too, have found him difficult, at least to get close to. Perhaps you can help in another way. Why did Raiker, as you say, cut you loose?"

Declan drummed his fingers on the menu. "He's a suspicious SOB. Paranoid as hell. He was afraid I'd learned too much about his security. I was just trying to make myself indispensable." He lifted a shoulder. "He's not one to give the benefit of the doubt."

"I must say, I find your words surprising." Shuang reached for her water glass, fingers toying with the stem. Her nails were short, Eve noted. Not manicured. No polish. Nothing about the woman suggested she was overly concerned with looks. Her dark hair was worn straight to brush the tops of her shoulders, without bangs. She wore no makeup, and her simple white cotton blouse was tucked neatly into a pair of black tailored pants. Her face was unwrinkled, but there was a hardness in her expression. She could have been anywhere between her early thirties to mid-forties. "I heard you were caught in an area of his compound where you had no business."

Declan's brows skimmed upward. "Did you, now? Raiker's security consists of layers. I was fired because he thought I was taking too much of an interest in how those layers connected." He sat back in his chair indolently.

"And were you?"

He let her question hang for a long moment before flashing a feral smile. "Yes."

The woman couldn't quite hide the flicker of satisfaction on her face. "Then perhaps we can help each other."

Declan picked up his water glass and saluted her with it. "Perhaps we can."

The other woman slanted a glance toward Eve who quickly fell back into character. Twisting around in her seat, she scanned the room and asked plaintively, "What happened to our server? I'm *starving*."

With a quick wave of her hand, Shuang summoned a waitress who moved immediately in their direction. "Of course. I have been inconsiderate. Please order. Our business can wait."

Eve certainly hoped the irritated scowl Declan aimed in her direction was as much a farce as she was engaged in herself. She prattled on mindlessly to the young server who'd hurried over, dithering between menu options, all the while aware of Shuang's inscrutable gaze fixed on her with single-minded focus. She shot the woman a blinding smile. "I've already decided what dessert I'll order later. Declan absolutely abhors when I eat sweets. He's afraid I'll get fat."

"Please bring an assortment of cheese and crackers for Mrs. Gallagher to snack on immediately while her meal is prepared." There was command couched in the other woman's request. Declan ordered and looked expectantly at Xie Shuang who shook her head. "I'm afraid I cannot stay to eat. But I would like to continue our conversation while you wait for your lunch, if that meets with your approval."

"I'm interested in the specifics of your needs." He waited for the waitress to collect the menus and move swiftly toward the kitchen before continuing. "If it is to bring Raiker to you, I can't deliver. As I indicated earlier, I have no influence with the man, especially now. If, instead, you would like to go to him, my area of expertise would be helpful."

"Once I am able to reach the man, he will be persuaded to speak with me." There was something chilling in the other woman's smile. "Unfortunately, I am told his security had become even tighter in the past few months. How can you be certain your information remains current?"

The waitress returned with a small plate of assorted cheeses and crackers. Declan responded, "I still have friends in Raiker's employ. Friends who are...ah...as disenchanted as I was with the terms of my employment. I would, of course, use my contacts in Raiker's network to be certain I have the most up-to-date information."

Eve forced herself to enthusiastically choose some snacks, but her usual appetite had vanished. Whether Shuang worked for herself or was here on behalf of another, the woman's intent was obvious. And Declan played his part of a mercenary ex-employee harboring a grudge to perfection.

"Ah, but do you have similar information about the whereabouts of his family?" The words sent a chill trickling down Eve's spine. "I have always found a man becomes more reasonable when concerned with the welfare of his loved ones."

"No one knows for sure where Raiker hid his wife and son after the boy was almost kidnapped." Declan reached over to pluck a piece of cheese off the plate in front of Eve. Bit into it. Swallowing, he added, "But I do know the man doesn't trust any other security in the world like he does his own. He can't afford to rely on others to protect him—he has too many enemies. There's only one place he'd be holed up." His gaze did battle with Shuang's.

"You mean his home in Manassas?"

"You know he's not there." Unperturbed, he polished off the rest of the cheese. "You would have checked before ever approaching me."

The woman clenched her hands together on her lap. "So, he is at his compound?"

"It would be the most likely location, but it will take money to persuade my contacts to part with the knowledge. And once they have, I'm the only person who could get you inside." He quickly glanced at Eve, who was nibbling on a cracker. "Raiker would know exactly who had given him up, and he'd come after me with all his considerable resources. Eve and I would have to disappear abroad. As you can imagine, my assistance will be costly."

"SHE SEEMED SHOCKED." Eve huddled inside her coat as she walked beside Declan down the sidewalk, blocks away from the hotel. "I hope you didn't price yourself out of the market."

"Xie Shuang—if that's her real name—would expect to pay for the kind of help she's requesting. And she doesn't expect to meet the asking price. I'm sure she'll send an email shortly beginning the negotiation."

"She mentioned Royce only obliquely."

"On purpose, I'm sure." He led her to the curb and threw a quick look up and down the street. "She risks losing my sympathy if she brings the boy into it. I'm supposed to not give a damn what she might have in store for Raiker, but I might have a sudden attack of scruples if she mentions his son."

"Or you may be tempted to sell details of her interest to

the man she's hoping to find."

He gave her an approving nod. "Exactly." Grasping her elbow in his hand, he led her into the street once the light changed. "We've got an escort. Two blocks back, light-colored ski jacket. Jeans. Black boots. Recognize him?"

With only a slight turn of her head, she spotted the man he described. A ripple of recognition went through her. "One of our friends from yesterday. The driver."

"Yep."

She hurried to keep up with his stride. "They already know where we live, so what's the point of a tail?"

"To see where we stop. Whom we talk to." His smile was fierce. "He'll report back that we went directly home, speaking only to each other." They stepped up on the opposite curb and turned toward their apartment, thankfully away from the wind this time. "What did we learn? Do you really think she's Japanese?"

"No, she's almost certainly Chinese and not a native English speaker." She didn't know whether to be amused or offended at his double-take. "Her name, whether it's real or not, is Chinese, as is her accent, which is slight, but still barely noticeable on the short Is and Ns. I offered a simple Japanese phrase. How are you today? And she was unable to respond. If I could actually hear her speak in her native tongue, I'd be able to pinpoint a province or part of the country she grew up in. There are many dialects in China, despite the government's attempt at a unified language. I'm familiar with all of them."

"What's the first language you learned?" He steered her around a homeless man who was slouched against a building. Perhaps because he'd already learned she was prone to reach into her purse whenever she passed one. "Besides English, I mean."

"It really was Japanese, although we didn't have a cook. She was my *au pair* for a time. We went through several, and many of them were immigrants. I picked up a little from each of them."

"Is that when you learned your acting ability?"

"At least you realized I was acting," she muttered, shoving her gloved hands in her pockets as she walked. This cold snap was one for the record books. It was just her misfortune their assignment had her outside each day. "Shuang would certainly have heard about my using the knife yesterday, and I wanted to convince her I wasn't a threat."

"At first, I thought you were laying on the empty-headed blonde act too thick, but she bought it. Almost too easily. Wherever she's from, she doesn't have a high opinion of her own gender."

"I agree. People see what they want to. I've found it's sometimes easier to play on their preconceptions, especially if it gives me an advantage."

His regard was a little too intent to be entirely comfortable. "I'm beginning to realize you're more adept at that than I ever would have believed."

Because his words arrowed a little too near the truth for comfort, she shrugged. "Me? I'm an open book." But she knew he remained unconvinced. The problem with close proximity assignments was in what could be revealed without one even being aware of the disclosure. Eve was no newcomer to such tasks, but this case required a whole new degree of closeness.

And it was imperative she return to her job at the State Department with her cover firmly intact.

Only the frigid air outside could make Eve grateful to reach the shabby apartment. Heat greeted them when they stepped inside, which wasn't always the case, so she didn't take it for granted. She went directly to the vent next to the couch and stood over it for a couple of minutes, thawing out. Declan crossed to the closet and withdrew the detection device to begin the same methodical search he enacted each time they returned to the place.

Finally warming enough to take off her gloves, Eve removed them and crossed to hang up her coat, but halted in her tracks when Declan turned toward her, one finger to his lips.

The device in his hand had a small red light blinking rapidly. He took a couple of steps toward the bedroom and the flickering slowed. He turned and took a few strides toward the kitchen area and it sped up.

"Bug or camera?" she asked in Scottish Gaelic.

"This device would pick up either, but it's definitely a bug." He lowered the instrument to scan the small space with his gaze.

An icy finger traced down her spine. Someone had been busy today while they'd met with Shuang. Declan had told her the security measures taken with the door and windows would ensure no one could enter without them being alerted, which made her wonder how a listening device had been planted.

Declan moved toward the ancient stove and peered above it. Going to his side, the first thing Eve noticed was the light sprinkling of plaster dust on the appliance. Raising her gaze, she saw a small dime-sized area she might have thought was a water spot in the wall a few feet above the stove.

"How did they get in?"

"They didn't." She followed him to the door, which he'd unlocked, and they moved into the hallway. An electrical plate had been screwed into the wall, pinpointing how the bug had been planted. White plaster dust on the floor was as telling as a shout.

Declan surprised her by heading back into the apartment. Trailing after him, she shut the door behind her and relocked it. Somehow securing the multiple locks no longer made her feel safe. "Aren't you going to remove it?"

"Finding it gives us the advantage." He returned the surveillance detection device to the closet shelf. "It's almost certain the listener doesn't speak our language. There's no danger of us giving anything away. And the detector has jamming capabilities if there's ever a time we need more privacy." His grin was just a bit ruthless. "Our new business partner doesn't trust us, it seems. Which means she's smart and careful. So are we."

His words had a familiar adrenaline punching through Eve's trepidation. The game of cat and mouse had begun. And from the looks of Declan's smile, he was looking forward to the challenge. The recognition had her feeling a sort of affinity with the man, because she was more than ready start the assignment that would guarantee Royce Raiker's safety.

THE PROPERTY BOASTED two attached garages, each large enough to house half a dozen vehicles. Adam had deliberately left the one on the far end of the house empty, and Jaid had soon learned why when a truck full of lumber had arrived shortly after they had. The mini half-pipe ramp had taken less than a day to construct, but she'd often thought the structure had saved her—and Royce's—sanity numerous times over the past weeks.

She watched him now, her nine-year-old bundle of energy, doing dazzling spins, Ollies and stall combinations on his skateboard. He wore a helmet and protective pads, although they hadn't spared him a broken arm when he'd attempted a homemade ramp just over a year ago.

"Nice tail stall!" she called out as he executed a move he'd been practicing for weeks.

"You wanna try one?" came his response as he whizzed by again.

"I'm good on feet. Not necessarily on wheels." When her cell vibrated in her pocket, she drew it out of her jeans while keeping an eye on her son. Sarah, the tutor they'd brought along, was taking a much-needed break, and Royce was not above trying an aerial move if he thought no one was watching.

"When's Grandma gonna get here?"

"Soon." She had to pitch her voice above the sound his board made on the ramp. "A couple more days, probably." Jaid moved away as she brought the phone to her ear.

"I can tell from the background noise exactly where you're at."

"Adam." There was a quick clutch of pleasure at the sound of her husband's voice, despite the fact that they'd been married nearly a year after their relationship from a decade earlier had been rekindled. Given their history, the man knew her better than anyone else did. Perhaps too well. "You haven't even been gone six hours. We're really okay. I'm assuming you've made it to Atlanta all right."

"Just left the briefing." It had taken her days to convince him to accept the job consulting on a case for the Georgia Bureau of Investigation. He could fly back and forth as he wished, doing much of the work from this estate. There was no reason for both of them to stay here around the clock.

Being holed up for weeks was like being trapped in a state of suspended animation, which was very close to the trick Royce was attempting on the ramp. "Warning one," she called out to him. He shot her an irrepressible grin but did a quick kick turn and began to coast.

"It sounds like an intriguing case," she said into the cell. There was a black widow killer at work in Georgia, who had already left behind a trail of six dead men in her wake. From the little he'd told her about the case, she'd predicted two women might be working as a team. She could admit, at least to herself, how much she missed the constant mental stimulation of working intriguing investigations, even though there were none as critical as the one keeping her glued to her son's side.

"You may be correct about a pair of killers. There was something in the case files I'll have to dig deeper into. But I called for a different reason."

A layer of ice sheeted her stomach. "Gallagher made contact?"

"He did, yes. Their meeting was with a female. Xie Shuang. Chinese, according to Eve, although at this point, there's no way to know whom she may be working for. I was able to run photos two of my people took through the international databases. No matches. Prints might be a better bet, but they may come later when Eve and Declan actually begin working with the woman."

Jaid considered the information. Tiny steps toward the plan they'd put in place. She throttled back her impatience. She wanted her son safe. Their lives back. Before she'd get either, they needed to catch the people who would put him at risk.

"Well, at least things are moving forward. Thanks for

the update." Her tone was wry. "It's a special kind of hell to have to hear about the progress from afar."

"There should be more to report in the next few days. With any luck, they'll try to move on the compound within a couple weeks."

His hesitation then had all her instincts alerting. "What else?"

"Nothing about the case. I did hear from Stephen Mulder today."

"The man who owns this property." Adam had rescued Mulder's daughter from kidnappers not once, but twice in the past several years. No wonder all the man's homes had been turned into fortresses. "Don't tell me he has a hankering for the ocean?" Mulder's Virginia Beach property had been put at their disposal. It was located on a secluded, wooded peninsula with a private beach. Its large helicopter pad allowed Adam the freedom to move between here and the agency compound. Or further, as was the case this morning.

"I don't want to alarm you, but he's received some reliable intelligence about a threat against his family. He has no idea at this point in what manner it might present itself, but he's upping his security on all his properties. He advised me to take precautions."

She gave a humorless laugh. "It would be difficult to imagine this place with more security."

"Even so. Your mother will be joining you there soon, which will free up a couple more team members to join you there. It's a distant possibility, but I'm already looking into alternate sites to evacuate to if it becomes necessary."

The words hit her with the force of a left jab. "It all just keeps getting more complex." She couldn't prevent the bleakness from coloring her words. Her mother could be difficult under the best of circumstances, but the trials she'd been having with a hip replacement, then a subsequent fall and follow-up surgery would stretch anyone's patience. Patricia Marlowe's recovery and necessary therapy had caused constant delays in reuniting the woman with the rest of the family here. And her presence on the property would also complicate a rapid response if they were compelled to leave this compound quickly.

"Jaid." His voice softened a fraction. "At this point, it's merely a safeguard."

"Just another few weeks," she murmured, her gaze on her son. "Maybe three. We're so close."

"Keep thinking that way. And Stephen will update me as new intelligence comes in. If we need to clear out, we have options."

Of course, they did. They said their goodbyes, and she tucked the cell back into her pocket. But they'd spent a great deal of time discussing it and had thought *this* property had been the best choice. Royce slowed, and jumped off his skateboard. "I'm thirsty. Can I get a Gatorade?"

Jaid forced a smile. "You may."

"Sweet." He unstrapped his helmet and set it on the board. "By the time I get all this gear off, I'll probably need two."

"By 'two,' I assume you mean a Gatorade and a water." She trailed behind him as they entered the house. Surely the property could be secured for the next few weeks. Because as much as she was coming to hate the constant confinement, she was just as reluctant to change hiding places when this ordeal was so close to coming to an end.

～

"THERE'S BEEN AN INCIDENT."

Xie Shuang looked up from the computer she was using to communicate with Gallagher. Like most men, he believed his assistance was worth far more than what she was willing to pay. She pressed send to email her latest offer before focusing on Malsovic.

"Now what?"

"You need to come quickly." He stepped aside as she got up and rounded the desk, checking the clock on the wall. It was past twelve. If his tone hadn't been enough of a warning, the time would be. In her experience, nothing good happened in a hotel after midnight.

"Where are we going?" She spoke in English, her voice snappish. She followed him to the employee elevator, which was reserved for cargo.

"Eleventh floor. Room 1107." He stabbed the appropriate button impatiently with a forefinger. "It's Dajana. She's dead."

Xie said nothing more, even when the elevator doors closed behind them, and they were assured of privacy. There was nothing to say. She'd assess the situation, and then she'd take action, as she'd been doing for more than twenty years. Fix other people's messes. It was a job she'd become quite adept at, although it was frequently wearisome.

When they arrived at room 1107, she turned to the man next to her. "Film everything." She had to knock several times before the door was opened by Khalid, one of the assistant managers. "You must take care of this." He yanked her into the room with a hand on her arm. Malsovic followed them inside silently, pulling out his cell phone. "It is a police matter. The publicity. Very bad."

Ignoring him, Shuang looked at the overweight man

sitting on the small couch, his robe revealing far more than she wanted to see of his nudity beneath. He held his head in his hands, and another man sat nearby, murmuring to him in urgent tones.

She crossed toward the bed, tilting her head to survey the scene with clinical detachment. Dajana was most certainly dead. She lay on the floor next to the bed, on her back, wearing only a wisp of black panties. Her arms and legs were splayed, her neck twisted at an odd angle. Crouching next to the body, Shuang could see the tiny, ruptured capillaries in her wide, staring eyes. Strangled.

Rising, she turned to approach the man on the couch. One of the Germans, she recalled. He and his companions had been in the dining room this morning. "English?"

The man who'd killed Dajana didn't look up. The other one did the talking. "*Ja*. Yes."

"Your friend has done a bad thing. This girl..." She waved a hand toward the body on the floor. "Her family is very powerful. They will be angry. There will be police. Jail time."

"It was an accident. The whore...she liked to play rough. Begged for it. Hans would not hurt anyone on purpose."

Shuang's lip curled. But she only said, "It is a tragedy for all. I would like to assist, but only money helps in situations like this. It will be expensive."

Hans finally raised his head. He had thick lips set in a fleshy face. His thinning hair stood on end. "You can silence the family?"

Easy enough to promise since Dajana's people were halfway across the world. "For a price. And then there's this mess to clean up." She gave a wave of her hand. "But it can be done if you are willing."

The friend pointed at Malsovic, who was filming the scene. "What is he doing?"

"Protecting all of us. This agreement we have—it *is* an agreement, yes? Both sides are vulnerable. The one who killed the girl and the one who offers to cover it up." After a long moment, the German nodded and looked away.

Stupidity. It was all Shuang could do not to laugh at the man. Of course, when they were done with the recording, she would be cut from the frames. And all that would be left was the damning shots of the dead girl and the Germans begging for a cover up.

"How much?" This from Hans. Tears tracked down one pudgy cheek. Since they'd been absent until now, Shuang guessed they'd been elicited by the thought of parting with his money, and not the dead girl. How much to make this all go away?"

"Fifty thousand." The two men gaped and gasped, then jabbered together in German in hushed undertones. She walked to the window to give them time to confer. They'd agree, because they had no choice. Desperation always made for the best leverage.

Hooking a finger to pull the curtain back, she looked down at the street until she heard Hans speak. "Yes. All right. But it must be soon. No one can hear of this."

She allowed herself a satisfied smile before turning back toward them. "Of course. But first you make payment."

CHAPTER FIVE

"EVE. IT'S YOUR PHONE."

It wasn't the words that roused her. It was the touch on her arm. Tiny tendrils of heat traced beneath her skin. Instinct rather than consciousness identified the source. She sat straight up in bed, instantly alert in a way the ping of the cell hadn't been able to accomplish.

"What? What are you doing in here?" She looked around for the blanket. Found it and promptly drew it to her chin. "Why do you have my phone?" Eve grabbed it from him and checked the time. One AM.

"Because you weren't answering it yourself." His tone was amazingly patient, given the hour. "It was the alert Adam set for our answering services. Yours went off about three times in the past half hour. Didn't you hear it?"

Belatedly, comprehension filtered in. She hadn't heard the sound before, but she did recall Adam Raiker explaining that as an extra security precaution, calls to their personal cells wouldn't go through these phones. Instead, they'd set up an alert for voicemails.

Thumbing through the log, she saw four messages had

been left in the last forty-five minutes. It was odd he'd heard the small noises when she'd stood over him the night before and had barely been able to wake him. Maybe he wasn't sleeping especially well on the couch, which made this moment an odd sort of *déjà vu*.

She started to call her cell to access the voicemails. Stopped to look at him. "What about the bug?"

"I jammed it before coming in here. It's safe."

She lost no time completing the call. Since she was on leave from DOS, she doubted the messages were work related. Which left family. And phone calls in the middle of the night were never good news, regardless of who they were from.

Listening to the last voicemail first, she heard her sister, Leslie's, annoyed voice. "Eve, honestly. Where on earth are you? Mother has called twice. Vincent once, and now me. Father has been admitted to George Washington University Hospital. Meet us there immediately. Your tardiness is just going to upset Mother more than she already is."

Her feet were on the floor before the message ended, bringing her face to face with Declan, who hadn't moved. She elbowed her way past him in search of her clothes then belatedly checked to see what she'd worn to bed last night. Relief swept her. She was decently covered in the satin nightshirt. "My father's been taken to the hospital." Nerves jittered through her. If he'd ever had anything more serious than a cold, she hadn't known about it. Not that she would. Her family wasn't prone to share confidences.

Which made this message even more nerve-wracking. "I'll need to get a cab." A sudden thought struck her then, and she stopped in the midst of gathering up jeans and socks. "Do you think Shuang posted someone to watch the apartment?" They'd been followed back to it after their meeting with her yesterday but hadn't seen anyone when they'd ventured out for dinner.

"It's doubtful, but we'll slip out the back just in case. A cab would draw attention in this area, so we'll walk a bit before calling one."

She shook her head. "There's no reason for you to go. If you want to get a taxi for me, I'll be perfectly fine to..." Her words trailed off when he went to the small dresser and started digging through the drawers. "What are you doing?"

"Finding you a top. Unless you were going to wear the nightshirt over those jeans."

"Declan." A sense of urgency was whipping her pulse. She needed to listen to the rest of the messages then call her mother. Maybe once she got settled in a cab...

"Eve." He turned from the dresser and shoved a beige sweater on top of the pile of clothes she held. "I realize you're perfectly capable. But there's no way I'd send you out alone in the middle of the night, even if we weren't in this neighborhood. Now you can argue, or you can get your pretty butt in gear, because the quicker you get dressed, the quicker you can get to the hospital."

For the space of three seconds, she stared at him. "Have I mentioned my dislike for bossy men?"

His lips quirked a bit. "You've alluded to it. I'm sure you have a similar distaste for men who are right. And I am. Get dressed." He went to the small bedroom closet and gathered up his own clothes. "Last one ready has to spring for coffee."

IT WOULDN'T OCCUR to Declan until later that he'd witnessed a metamorphosis over the next few hours. At the time, he only noted Eve was ready quickly, although not soon enough to get out of having to buy him coffee at the all-night coffee shop where they'd stopped to call a cab.

Her demeanor had been calm as she'd listened to her messages and then returned calls to her family members. She hadn't been able to reach her mother, but Declan had eavesdropped unabashedly to her side of the conversation with her siblings. Both older, he recalled her saying once, which was odd, because she'd spent a great deal of her time on the phone making soothing noises and uttering reassurances.

"Has your father been sick?" The cab drew up to the emergency entrance of the hospital as he spoke.

"No. I mean..." She hesitated. "I'm not sure. My family isn't exactly forthcoming about such things."

She exited the cab, and he thrust money at the driver before following her to the entrance. Her family must be the polar opposite of his, since most of his relatives were guilty of over-sharing. Despite the time, he found himself a bit intrigued at the prospect of learning far more about Eve that night than she'd seen fit to share with him in the days since they'd been paired on this assignment.

He caught up with her at the door, only because she'd paused to wait for him there. "I'm going to tell my family we work together, but don't offer anything else."

"What if they press for more details?"

Her smile was wry. "They won't." Without further explanation, she pulled the door open and entered the hospital.

The emergency room waiting area housed nearly four dozen people, which was a little surprising, given the time. Declan had about ten seconds to guess whether any of them were related to Eve before she headed straight for a couple in the corner who'd risen at her approach. Studying them, he could see a familial resemblance between the two, but not to Eve.

He followed more slowly and drew close enough to hear the man say, "Honestly, Eve, it's unfathomable how Leslie and I beat you here. Why didn't you answer your phone?"

"I was asleep and didn't hear it. Has Mother been out yet? Has the doctor been in to see Father?"

"We have no idea where they've taken him. The help in this place is absolutely deplorable, isn't it, Vincent? Believe me, administration will hear about it when I...who's this?"

Eve's sister was tall and spare, towering over Eve by at least six inches. Her drab brown hair was pulled back off her face in a no-nonsense manner, and the imperious look she turned in Declan's direction immediately had him harboring an immature urge to do something shocking.

Instead, he stuck out his hand. "Declan Gallagher." The woman gave him a bone-crushing handshake.

"He and I work together. He lives nearby and offered to accompany me so I wouldn't have to come downtown by myself. Declan, my siblings, Leslie and Vincent." Declan shot Eve a considering glance. It was becoming apparent she had a gift for deception he'd previously only guessed at. She hadn't said anything untrue. She'd just given a purposefully false impression, and he couldn't help wonder how often she'd done the same to him. Wonder, hell. He *knew* she had.

"Well thank God you had the sense for that, Savvy." This from Vincent. "I can't count how many times I've told you to find a safer neighborhood. Georgetown is getting downright seedy, at least in the area where you live."

"Why don't I get you both some coffee?" Eve's tone was entirely pleasant as she ignored her brother's words. "I know they have a twenty-four hour kiosk around here somewhere. And then I'll see if I can't find someone to give us an update on Father's condition. Mother said it was his heart?"

"A heart attack, most likely," Leslie said darkly, sitting down again. "He eats entirely too much red meat. For a brilliant man, he can be absolutely pigheaded about his vices."

"Coffee would be excellent. Make mine black." Vincent retook his seat, as well. "But you aren't going to be able to find out more than we have. The doctor we did talk to in the emergency room was absolutely uncivil."

Eve merely smiled and left the area. Declan looked around, intent on putting a bit of distance between himself and Eve's family. His plans were disrupted by Eve's sister, Leslie. "There's an empty seat here, Mr. Gallagher. You may as well sit, at least until Eve gets back."

The alternative would make him look churlish. Hiding his reluctance, he sank into the unwelcoming, barely padded chair. Both of the siblings stared at him with unabashed curiosity.

Vincent spoke first. "How long have you known Eve?"

The interrogation had begun. Declan settled back, hooked one ankle across his knee and sipped at his coffee. "Not long. This is the first time I've worked with her."

"How did you come to be available to accompany her this evening?"

Comprehension dawned. Vincent Larrison was playing the heavy-handed big brother. In spite of Eve being... The thought fractured when it occurred to Declan he had no idea how old she was. But her age must be far beyond her high-schooler looks, given her occupation. Too old for this degree of meddling. He'd like to believe he'd refrain from a similar line of questioning in the man's place, although his stepsister, Eugenia, might disagree. "We live quite close to each other currently." The half-truth was oddly entertaining. "It was no inconvenience."

"Yes. Well." Obviously, the man wasn't satisfied. "It's unfortunate you had to be bothered. Eve can catch a cab from the hospital safely enough." His smile looked as though it pained him. "We appreciate your efforts, but there's no need for you to miss more sleep."

Holding up his to-go cup, Declan said, "Too late, I'm afraid. Once I've had caffeine I'm up for the duration. I may as well give her a ride back. I won't sleep anyway." It didn't escape him that Eve's older brother wasn't professing a desire to take her home later.

From then on, the two decided to ignore him and focused on conversing among themselves. Work talk, Declan surmised. And whatever their careers were, they sounded wearisomely boring. He listened with half an ear, grateful the short-lived interrogation had died without a whimper. The others in the waiting room proved to be more interesting than the couple at his side. Especially the drunk and bloody Santa Claus in the chair next to his who was nursing a head wound while loudly proclaiming he'd sustained the injury fighting off the thieving bastard who'd stolen his sleigh.

It was a good hour before Eve returned, and if anything, the ranks of those in the waiting room had swelled. Declan got to his feet as she arrived, more than a little grateful to have a reason to give up his seat.

Steam rolled off the cups she was holding. "Sorry to keep you waiting. I was able to speak to Mother and to the doctor overseeing Father's care."

"What?" Vincent took the cup she offered and took a cautious sip. "How did you manage that? Leslie and I met with nothing but obstacles when we asked to be taken to them. And the people manning this place," he gestured to the waiting room contemptuously, "either can't or won't update us."

Carefully, Eve handed the remaining cup to her sister. She must have finished her own earlier. To Declan's discerning eye, she looked like the past hour had been a trying one. "Father is likely suffering from some unstable angina..."

"I knew it." interrupted Leslie grimly. "As many times as I warned him about his dietary habits..."

"Oh for heaven's sakes, Leslie. Angina isn't the same as a heart attack," Vincent said wearily.

"It's symptomatic of underlying coronary heart disease," the woman disputed. When she looked down her nose, Declan thought rather uncharitably, she bore an unfortunate resemblance to a stork.

"Which is exactly why the doctor ordered an EKG," Eve put in smoothly. He was beginning to realize why she looked so tired. If her mother were as difficult to deal with as these two, it would explain the signs of strain in her expression.

Her sister took a large gulp of coffee. "Some people with angina have normal EKGs. I'm a doctor. I should speak to the consulting physician myself."

"You haven't practiced medicine for ten years," her brother scoffed.

"In my research—" the woman began.

"Cancer research, not cardio," he interrupted, his tone rising.

Declan looked on with something akin to awe. This was beginning to be every bit as entertaining as drunk Santa, at least since the costumed man had fallen asleep. Although, the two were not yet near as combative as his family could be whenever all of them were in close proximity. There had not yet been blows exchanged nor a bout of theatrical weeping.

"As it happens, Father's doctor said the exact same thing." Eve didn't pitch her voice above her siblings, but somehow her even tones got their attention. "He's also had a chest x-ray, and neither test will be interpreted until tomorrow. Then a full plan for treatment will be suggested. When I saw him, he was dozing, and Mother was preparing to sleep in his room. If you want to see them, I have the room number and can take you there. But we should go quickly."

Vincent rose, smoothing the creases from his trousers with his free hand. "We don't want to disturb Father if he's already resting. We'll come back after work today, depending of course on Nancy's schedule."

Leslie seemed less convinced, but she stood as well, turning to collect her purse. "I'll be speaking to the hospital board about ways they can improve communication with the patients' families. But yes, it would be best to return later. I know Frank has a late day planned, but perhaps we can do some rearranging. Or find a sitter." Nancy and Frank would be spouses, Declan deduced. He wondered briefly if they were any more interesting than Vincent and Leslie.

"Mother will leave messages for us as information becomes available." Was it Declan's imagination, or was Eve slowly guiding them in the direction of the hospital entrance? "You know how it is with test results. A lot of hurry up and wait. The doctor said Father appears in no immediate danger of a heart attack, but of course, he will be monitored closely."

They'd moved outside the waiting room. Leslie looked down the hallway, appearing torn. "Perhaps I should go and speak to the head nurse on his floor. It wouldn't hurt for them to be made aware whom they're taking care of."

"The doctor appeared to be fully apprised." No one else seemed to recognize the wryness in Eve's tone. "But, of course, you should do as you think best."

"We should go. Mother would likely be asleep before you even find the room." Vincent switched his attention to Eve. "Savvy, I certainly hope you'll stay available. We should probably arrange a schedule where we visit one at a time. We don't want to overwhelm Father with visitors."

"I'll keep my phone close," Eve promised. "Where did you leave your cars?" And with an ease that spoke of practice, she dispatched her siblings toward their vehicles. While she was saying her goodbyes, Declan summoned one of the cabs parked at the curb near the entrance and waited for her to rejoin him.

He waited until she slid into the vehicle. Noted the way she slumped against the seat, her head back, eyes closed. "Go ahead. Fire away."

Not for the life of him would Declan admit just how piqued his curiosity was. "Your brother called you something a couple of times. Savvy? Is it a nickname?"

The evasion in her expression was as easy to read as neon. "They were both quite upset. My family isn't known for managing well in a crisis."

"Then you must be the exception." He turned to more fully face in her in the shadowy back seat. "Because you managed *them*. It was a thing of beauty. A marvel in psychological warfare. I should have been taking notes. I thought I was adept at detonating potential family explosions. You..." He shook his head in admiration. "Your talents would come in handy as a battle strategist for the military."

Her eyes popped open then, and she looked at him, a

slight frown on her face. "What are you talking about? There were no battles."

Surer of himself now, he countered, "Only because you headed them off at every turn. How much younger are you?"

She blew out a breath. "Twelve years Vincent's junior. Ten years younger than Leslie. I was likely the only thing in my parents' lives they hadn't planned out to a tee."

He was silent for a moment. "They're nothing like you. Or you, them, I should say."

Eve's voice went flat. "No. Vincent is staggeringly intelligent, a mathematician with multiple PhDs and works at NASA's Goddard Space Flight Center in Maryland. Leslie is on staff at the National Cancer Institute in Bethesda. She's focused solely on research for the past decade. They are both clones of my parents. I'm the mutant in the family, disappointingly average."

He snorted before he saw from her expression she was deadly serious. "Fluent in over sixty languages is average? C'mon."

She looked out the window beside her. "I'm not curing cancer or devising ways to get astronauts into space faster and more safely. I haven't discovered genes associated with risks of Alzheimer's nor been a leading researcher on the human genome project. Believe me, in my family, anything short of brilliance is a disappointment."

Brilliance? Declan considered the word doubtfully. Certainly when her siblings had been talking about their jobs, he'd understood only the occasional word or phrase. But the two had seem completely inept at dealing with a situation that, while stressful, shouldn't have turned two adults into bickering incompetents. Comprehension dawned. "You're the peacemaker."

"Peacemaker seems a bit of a demotion from battle strategist, but whatever."

"The best strategist is one who can defuse the battle, hence the term." The more he considered it the more certain he became. "Brilliance doesn't necessarily equate to social acumen or dealing with life's ups and downs."

"My family hires people to limit the ups and downs life might deal them," she said dryly. "But, yes, okay. I'm the smoother when we're together. I find the lost items before they start a minor catastrophe. I divert the conversation when things grow heated and listen impartially when one sibling needs to vent about the other. Every family has roles. We've already ascertained yours is the bossy one."

He grunted. "Believe it or not, I find myself playing peacekeeper every time my family gets together, so we that have in common."

Nestling her head against the back of the seat again, her eyes fluttered closed. "Something else we have in common is lack of sleep. When do we have to be at the hotel tomorrow?"

The negotiation between him and Shuang had been drawn out. She'd eventually agreed to his demand for a quarter of a million dollars for his assistance but would only wire half of it up front to the account number Raiker had provided for just this purpose. Ostensibly, the final half would be paid at the end of his services. He wasn't naïve enough to believe she had any intention of following through with it. "She expects us at eight."

He grinned at the whimper he got in response. "Maybe you can order up breakfast from the hotel restaurant. It would give you a chance to wander around a bit." She didn't answer. While he was deceiving Shuang and her men, it would be Eve doing the actual poking around in the workings of the hotel. The thought brought a frown to his face. They needed to discuss what to look for and where. Not to mention the caution necessary to avoid alerting suspicions.

Glancing her way, he swallowed the words. If she wasn't already dozing, she was damn close, and she'd earned a bit of rest after dealing with her family. They could discuss strategy later.

He was silent until the driver pulled up in front of their apartment building. Reaching into his pocket, he withdrew some bills, adding a hefty tip as compensation for entering a neighborhood the man probably normally avoided. Getting out of the cab, he rounded the trunk and opened Eve's door.

She was sound asleep. Declan considered her for a moment. Not surprising. He could feel weariness creeping in, regardless of the caffeine he'd consumed. Without conscious thought, he reached down and lifted her out of the cab, cradling her body against his chest as he nudged the door shut with his hip. Eve woke only enough to slide her arms around his neck and cuddle closer. She didn't move when he jostled her to reach for the door. Nor on the three sets of stairs, or when he was juggling his keys to unlock both the door and deadbolt.

In fact, she was motionless for the entire time it took him to re-secure the door and stride to the bedroom. He sat down on the edge of the bed, reaching up to unlock her arms from his neck. When he settled her onto the mattress, she was still out like a light. He should follow her example because in less than three hours, they'd have to be up again. But still he lingered, taking the opportunity to study her as she slept.

His hand reached out without volition from his brain to brush a strand of her hair from the curve of her cheek. A curl wrapped around his forefinger, a silky golden ring. He rubbed it lightly with his thumb. While she could subdue the curls into waves in the morning, they began to take on a life of their own toward evening. A smile tilted his lips. Somehow, he knew she'd despise the observation.

Odd that he'd learned more about her personal life by accompanying her to the hospital tonight than she'd willingly revealed over the past several days. Odder still to find a number of similarities between her family dynamics and his own.

He didn't come from a family of intellectual eggheads. Far from it. But after his parents divorced, he'd been bounced between his mom's and dad's homes like a ping-pong ball, with stints spent at his gran and grandda's for good measure. He knew what it was like to sense you didn't belong, and likely Eve had grown up well-acquainted with the emotion. It was ridiculous to feel a pang of empathy for that alone.

Even more so to have an overwhelming urge to learn more about her. To push aside the evasions and smash through the half-truths to discover what else she hid from the world. Even from her own family.

She made a small sound then and rolled to her side, and Declan leaped from the bed as if his ass were on fire. There was something a bit creepy and more than a little out of character for him to linger over the woman watching her sleep. It smacked of an emotional relationship the two of them didn't have. Didn't want.

He remembered to unblock the listening device so anyone checking the receiver would have a clear signal again. Then he crossed to the couch and dropped down on it fully clothed, attempting to fold his long frame into a semi-comfortable position. Tomorrow—or later today—marked the beginning of this mission. He needed to minimize distractions, not multiply them. He had one last conscious thought before falling asleep—if he let her, Eve Larrison could become one hell of a distraction.

~

"I'M STILL NOT EXACTLY sure what was so important you had to wake both me and Mr. Baltes up for an early trip to the bank." Eve fished into the bakery sack to draw out a chocolate-filled pastry.

Declan didn't look up from the computer. He needed to work fast if they were going to get to the hotel on time, and the success of this particular task was completely dependent on Hotel Latifma's Internet security. Or the lack thereof. "I needed the blueprints of the compound." He nodded at the circular mailing containers on the table between them. "I did feed you," he pointed out. Baltes had proven to be much more amenable to their before-hours visit than Eve had been. Declan had collected the laptop from the security box and then found a bakery across the street from the hotel, where they were now sitting.

"The promise of which is the only thing saving you from serious physical harm."

He glanced up to see her sucking frosting from one finger. There was no reason, none at all, for the sight to lodge in his skull like a brand. With supreme effort, he forced his attention back to the computer screen before him and waited for the software to download. "Make sure you save me one of those."

"I will. If you tell me what you're doing."

"Getting us an edge, hopefully." He reached out and took the bag from her, dug around for a glazed donut. As pastries went, he wasn't too adventurous. "I can see the hotel's router online, and of course it's locked. I have software to predict the password. If I can get in it, I can take a look and see if their security is online, as well, which would be very, very fortunate for us."

Her eyes were wide. "You know how to hack into their router?"

"Hacking has such a negative connotation." He took a bite of the donut and waited impatiently for the download to complete. Negative was the exact reaction he'd get from Raiker if the man learned of his tactics. The agency worked consultatively, partnering with law enforcement on a request basis. As such, Raiker Forensics had to be above reproach.

But there was a lot riding on the success of their assignment. And Declan would like to go in armed with more intel on the workings of the hotel than a hotel diagram and knowledge of the exits.

"Where'd you learn those skills?"

A quiet ding alerted him the download was ready. He put down the pastry and took another napkin from the bag to wipe his hands. "I actually started at DCPD in the Cyber-crimes unit. Switched to vice after six months."

Swiftly, he tried first one suggested password and then another. If the router security had been set to shut down after a set number of attempts, he was screwed before he really got started.

"Why did you switch?"

He made the third try with bated breath. It wasn't correct, but neither was he shut out of the system. "Vice was more exciting. Give me a minute here." It was just under that, on the eighth suggested password before he was accessing the hotel router. "Okay, let's see what we've got." Minimal security, he saw at a glance. The encryption wouldn't deter a twelve-year-old. He didn't care about the server and wasn't interested in the workings of the front desk or reservations log. He just wanted to see if... "Bingo."

Her chair scraped on the floor as she moved it over to sit beside him. "They've got digital hotel security cameras, and they're accessible on the router." He shook his head. Sometimes when people made it too easy, it took the fun right out of it. He did a quick online search for the camera model's user manual and looked up the default username and password. Tried it and failed. He thought a minute and did a few variations of the router access ID and succeeded on the third try. "They've got eighteen cameras. Weird."

Eve peered more closely at the screen. "Having eighteen cameras is weird?"

"No, using fourteen of them on hotel floors is strange." He sent her a sideways glance. "I'm going to be unhappy if you drop filling on the keyboard."

She leaned back a little. "Not as unhappy as I'd be. How wasteful."

He stifled a smile and studied the screen. "Most hotels would have their cameras on the exits and the public areas. Some also have one on each floor, occasionally at every elevator, but discretion is key. They've got only the lobby exits covered, the front desk and another camera for the lobby itself, which makes me wonder if management is more concerned with monitoring their employees than they are with guest security."

"The usefulness of cameras depends on how often they're monitored and by whom," she observed before finishing off the pastry.

"True enough. The bad news is that if these were installed to monitor employee productivity, they are likely to be watched more regularly than cameras mounted for safety reasons." He changed the password on the cameras and—with a quick glance at the time on the computer—pulled up a full screen grid showing each of the devices. The only way anyone would know a camera wasn't behaving properly was if they tried to change an alteration he made to one of them. Hopefully, he'd have it back to normal before IT was alerted.

He scrolled through his emails and brought up a photo of Raiker's compound. It was more than one would see from the road, but the people who would see this weren't going to get close enough to the property for it to make a difference. He layered the picture over the camera display and stood, closing the lid and shoving the computer in the laptop sleeve before tucking it under his arm.

"Ready?" Eve rose and wadded the bag up in her palm.

"We are." Grabbing the donut he hadn't finished, he ushered her to the door of the bakery while he ate it. "We have to take precautions because we don't know how closely the cameras are watched. If you leave my side, text me the floor you're heading to. Spell out the number."

"You can read Scottish Gaelic?" Her tone sounded surprised as they walked outside into the single-degree temps.

"Not really. But I can handle numbers. I'm serious, Eve." When they reached the curb, he halted her progress with a hand on her elbow. "I want to know where you are in the hotel at all times. I can turn off the cameras or at least change the angle to give you protection."

"We're walking into enemy territory without a clear idea of what we're getting into." She pulled her gloves from her pocket, drew them on. "Don't worry. I'm all for taking any edge we can get."

They proceeded across the street toward the hotel,

adrenaline firing through his veins. He'd gotten them some advantages. Only time would tell if they would be enough.

～

"I THINK we should agree to a no weapons policy for the duration of our business relationship." Xie Shuang gave them a thin smile as she unlocked a hotel room door and ushered them inside. "We must be able to trust each other."

Declan didn't return her smile. "Trust has to be reciprocated. If I'm unarmed, your men must be."

After a moment's thought, she shrugged. "But of course." She turned to the three dark-haired men lounging in the room. It had been divested of the bed and dresser and was furnished instead with two long tables, a desk and a laptop. "I will collect all weapons. Now."

No one moved to obey. Declan recognized one of the guys as the driver of the car during their botched kidnapping attempt. Another who had followed them from the dining room yesterday. He glowered at Eve and fingered a visible scab on the side of his neck. Apparently, he wasn't the forgiving sort.

The woman snapped out an order in another language. There was a general shuffling of feet, but one by one, each of the men gave up a weapon. Setting each one on a table with a clatter, which was bullshit, of course. Declan took his time placing the computer in its sleeve on one end of a table along with the blueprints. Removing his coat, he hung it on the back of the chair and withdrew his gun from his shoulder harness. Any of them could have another weapon concealed somewhere on his body. He certainly did.

The driver said something quickly to Shuang, his gaze never leaving Eve. The other woman's face darkened, and her response had his expression flickering. But she turned to Eve and said, "My man says you have a knife. You held it on him two days ago."

"I thought he and his friend were trying to kidnap us!" Eve's tone was indignant. "I had a right to protect myself." Her skills were wasted at the State Department, Declan decided. She should have been on the stage.

"Yes. But today is a new day, and we are all friends here. So...your weapon."

With visible reluctance Eve drew the knife from what Declan could now see was a sheath cleverly sewn into the inside of her left boot. And since she was wearing brown boots today, rather than the black ones she'd worn before, he could only surmise she'd had every pair she owned custom-made to hold a weapon.

It was another puzzle piece about the woman. Declan had a lot of pieces—enough to intrigue—but no clear picture of who she was yet. And no idea why all of a sudden that seemed to matter so much.

She made a production of crossing to the table and slamming her knife on it, all the while returning the driver's glare with one of her own.

"Good." Shuang walked toward the table, indicating each man as she made introductions. "Harris, Taufik and Amin. Declan and Eve." She gathered up the weapons. "My office is on the seventh floor. One of my men can show you at the end of the day if you want to collect your weapons before leaving." She headed for the door, her arms full. Declan had to wonder what a hotel guest might think if one happened to pass her on the way to her office. But she didn't seem concerned about the possibility.

Declan went to the sheaf of phony blueprints he'd brought from the bank and took them out of the container, attempting to roll out the first one. Finally, one of the men—Harris, he thought it was—came to help with a stapler to hold down a corner. One by one, each of the others joined him to grasp an edge so the blueprint was flat.

"The most secure area Adam Raiker owns is the property containing his headquarters. His lab facility is there, as well as his office complex," Declan began. "Beneath the space is a large, underground compound capable of withstanding everything short of a high blast explosive. I believe you'll find him there. And I can get you in." He stabbed an index finger at the area housing the front gate. "This will be the first security you'll have to clear." The other men leaned in to see the spot he indicated.

"Before you guys get too involved in your work," Eve interrupted brightly. "Who wants breakfast?"

INSISTING she wanted to examine the menu herself, Eve went down to the restaurant. But she spent very little time making her selection. Ordering all of it to be delivered to the room on the third floor where she'd left the men, she exited the area and took the stairs to the fifteenth floor, texting Declan as promised. The journey had her mentally vowing to add more cardio to her exercise routine. She peeked into the hallway but saw no one. A maid's cart was parked outside one of the rooms. Figuring there was no better way to get to know the workings of this hotel than to speak to its workers, she headed down the empty hallway toward the cart, ignoring the camera mounted near the ceiling at the opposite end. If not for Declan's warning, she likely wouldn't have given it a thought. Now, however, her heart was doing double time as she wondered if he'd managed to get to the cameras in time.

She loitered in the area until a dark-haired maid came out of the room for towels. "Good morning."

"Good morning." The woman repeated the words but didn't make eye contact. When she would have scurried back into the room she was cleaning, Eve halted her. "Could you tell me if there's a restaurant in this hotel?"

The maid backtracked. "Restaurant. First floor."

"Is the coffee good there?" Eve pressed. It was clear the woman wanted nothing more than to return to her job. The glance she shot up and down the hall was almost fearful. "I mean, if it isn't, I'll go to the nearest Starbucks. There is a Starbucks close by, isn't there?"

The woman—whose nametag read Lin—gave a helpless shrug. "My English. No good."

"How is the restaurant's coffee?" Eve tried again, this time in Korean. When the same confusion appeared on the woman's face, she repeated it in Chinese. Saw surprise and a bit of pleasure in the woman's expression.

"I hear people say it is very good. You will like it," she replied shyly in the same language before scurrying back into the room she was cleaning.

Interesting, Eve thought as she headed back toward the elevator. Xie Shuang hailed from China, as well. Did she have anything to do with providing this young woman a job here? Shuang didn't strike Eve as the altruistic type.

She went to the elevator. She texted Declan as she impatiently waited for it to arrive. When it did, she descended to the next floor. The doors buzzed open almost silently. She stepped out into the hallway and lingered until the couple approaching the elevator had gotten on before heading toward the cleaning cart parked in the hallway.

Again, she attempted to engage the maid in conversation, with less success this time. But after several tries, Eve had learned one thing. The woman's native language was Slovenian—just like the duo who had attempted to force her and Declan into their car a couple days ago.

Her instincts were humming as she rode down to the next floor, messaging Declan of her intent. She stepped off the elevator and started down the hallway to the now familiar cleaning cart. Prepared for a wait, she loitered outside the room being cleaned, pretending to search in her purse for something. But the sound of quiet sobbing inside the space changed her plans.

Cautiously, she approached the door. It was propped partially open. The weeping had grown more muffled. The sound would no longer reach further than a few feet. Looking around, Eve saw no one who was paying her any attention. Dodging around the cart, she ducked inside.

The maid was leaning against the wall next to the bed, bent at the waist, a towel pressed to her face. At Eve's entrance, she whirled around, mopped at her eyes and lowered the towel. "No ready. Later."

Eve made a quick assessment. Not Chinese. She tried in Slovenian, "Can I help?" When there was no immediate response, she attempted again, this time in Serbian. "*Mogu li da pomognem?*"

The woman gasped a little even as she shook her head and replied in the same language, "No one can help. My friend..." She seemed to crumple then, sinking to the floor. The silent sobs racking her body were somehow more gut wrenching than her audible weeping.

"Tell me." Eve crouched beside her, sympathy uppermost. "Is your friend ill?"

The housekeeper shook her head vehemently. But it

was a long moment before she could catch her breath to answer. "Not sick. Dead. Someone killed Dajana last night."

A sick feeling settled in Eve's chest. "Oh my God. How horrible. The police..."

"There will be no police. There is never police for people like us." The woman's words came as fast and violent as rifle shots. "We are disposable. They do what they wish with us."

Eve had the foreboding feeling there was far more here than a senseless death. "What do you mean? Who does what they wish with you?"

A voice sounded in the hallway. The woman's eyes widened, and she leapt to her feet. "You must go! You cannot be found here!"

The urgency in her tone couldn't be ignored. Eve rose and strode toward the door but heard a voice right outside it. "Brina!"

Impulse had her dodging into the bathroom, which appeared to be freshly cleaned. Pulling back the shower curtain, she stepped in the tub and yanked the curtain closed moments before the voice sounded closer. "You are behind schedule! What the hell is wrong with you?"

"Soon done. Soon."

There was the unmistakable sound of flesh meeting flesh. "Move faster. You do not have time to cry."

"I cry for Dajana." This was uttered in Serbian.

"Do your job, or I will make sure you end up just like her. Hurry!"

There was no more talk, but Eve stayed where she was, frozen in place as long minutes crawled by. Then the curtain slid back. Brina stood before her, eyes wide and frightened. "You must go," she whispered in her native tongue. A palm print still showed red against her cheek. "Please. *Èmó* will kill me."

Eve had rarely felt more impotent. "I can help." The words tumbled from her mouth before she'd considered them. "An employer can't treat you that way. Not even if you're in the country illegally." The woman had to be, didn't she? Everything Brina had said led her to believe the woman operated in the shadowy world of illegal aliens. Exploited by an unscrupulous employer, with nowhere to turn, not even law enforcement, for fear of being deported.

"Please." The beseeching expression on Brina's face was difficult to withstand. "She will come back."

Eve stepped out of the tub. Followed the woman to the doorway while Brina looked up and down the hall again and then stepped aside. Before she left, Eve said, "We will talk again." And she hurried out of the room.

Wanting to avoid the elevator, she headed to the stairway, angling around a couple in the hallway arguing about the weight of their luggage. She was beginning to understand just how dangerous Brina's attacker was. Eve had recognized the voice berating her, the woman she'd called *Èmó*. Demon.

It belonged to Xie Shuang.

CHAPTER SIX

"I'M GOING to get some bottled water." The remains from breakfast had been cleared away hours ago by housekeeping. Eve had carefully watched the young woman who cleaned up, but the server didn't speak or raise her gaze from her task as she bundled the dishes onto a tray from the cart she'd brought to the room. Was she another person like Brina? One who felt she had no voice, no choices? There were subtle differences between those who worked in the dining room and the few Eve had spoken to in housekeeping. In the service industry, it wasn't unusual for people with the best command of English to serve in jobs where they'd be meeting the public. But she thought there was more at play here. Brina's words from earlier came back to her.

We are disposable. They do what they wish with us.

Given the way she'd been mistreated by Xie Shuang, the woman was obviously a part of the 'they' Brina had mentioned. But who else was included in the group? If Eve could get the maid to talk to her again, perhaps she could begin to get answers to the questions flooding her mind. But she had to be sure she didn't endanger the housekeeper by seeking her out.

"Why don't you bring some for all of us?" Declan suggested. Eve rose, sliding the strap of her large purse over the shoulder and smiled at him as she walked from the room. *"Dhá dheug."* Closing the door, she first made sure there were no eyes on her before walking directly to the elevator.

She'd told Declan which floor she'd be heading to and went to the twelfth, where she'd left off. Although there was a housekeeping cart on the floor, the maid who was pushing it was unfamiliar to her. There were people coming and going in the hallway, and Eve didn't dare try to engage the housekeeper in conversation. A feel of urgency was fueling her. Maybe she should find Brina again. Perhaps the woman could be compelled to be a bit more forthcoming this time.

Her efforts paid off on the ninth floor. She positioned herself where she had partial vision into the room being cleaned. When she saw a familiar face, Eve checked the hallway again to be sure she was alone and slipped inside.

"I have something for you," she said in Serbian. Brina was stripping the two beds. When she whirled around, her expression was surprised.

"You again."

Eve reached into her purse to remove her wallet. Took out the largest bills she had and walked toward the woman, her hand outstretched. "Take this. Maybe it will help."

Brina looked at the two one hundred dollar bills uncomprehendingly but made no move to reach for them. "We must give all our tips to Xie Shuang."

"This is not a tip." She thrust her hand forward. "Do you have a place to hide it?"

The woman's eyes grew wide, but her hand came up to

take the money and fold it, slipping it into her bra. "Yes. But why do you do this?"

"I want you to tell me more. About how you came to be here. Who brought you?" They were speaking in hushed tones.

The maid glanced toward the door. "We cannot talk now. You come to the laundry room in an hour. It is below the first floor. I must work there soon." Her mouth was a grim line. "It is my punishment for being behind today. After cleaning, I must wash the sheets and towels for the rest of the day."

"I'll meet you there," Eve promised, and lost no time going to the door and slipping out when she saw the hallway was vacant. Adrenaline had been kicking in her veins ever since speaking to the woman earlier. Rather than spending hours trying to find another of the beleaguered maids to talk to, it seemed she might learn all she needed to with one more conversation with Brina where there was no chance to be overheard.

She used the stairway again and looked for a vending machine on the next floor. Quickly selecting a half dozen bottles of water, Eve slid half in her purse and carried the other three toward the elevator. A man came out of a room down the hallway. When he turned toward her, it took effort to keep the jolt of shock from slowing her step. From showing in her expression.

Eve recognized him from the photos Raiker had shown them. It was the second kidnapper. The driver. She watched him without seeming to as she slowed to a stop before the elevators, aware he'd noticed her, too. A thread of ice skated down her spine as she felt his dark gaze on her.

Lafka Malsovic hadn't left the country at all. It took

little imagination to figure out what was keeping him here, despite the manhunt after him.

Royce Raiker.

Forty-five minutes later, Eve pulled off the earbuds and tucked them with the mock MP3 player into her purse. As Raiker had promised, the listening device did also hold music, and she hadn't found much to quibble about in the choices loaded on it. She rose, strolled toward the men crowded around one of the tables and leaned over behind Declan, her arms looping carelessly around his neck. "How much longer do you think you'll be?"

The look he aimed over his shoulder held just the right amount of irritation. "This is going to take two or three days, Eve. I told you."

With a theatrical sigh, she dropped her arms and stepped away. "I'm going to go look for a snack. *Tráigh.*"

"Take your time."

There was a snicker from two of the men as she turned toward the door. "That one is always hungry," one man muttered to the other in Slovenian.

"If I had some privacy, I would give her something to *eat*. Something she would choke on," the other responded crudely in the same language. They exploded into laughter.

Eve continued to the door as if she hadn't understood a word they'd uttered. In the hallway, she looked around carefully before heading to the stairwell. She'd get the snacks first, before she forgot about the excuse she'd used to escape the room again. But she was a little more skittish this time as she wandered the floors hunting for vending machines. She didn't want to run into Malsovic again.

Although she'd alerted Declan about her destination, he hadn't mentioned a camera outside the entrances or lobby area. Her movements furtive, she made her way toward the laundry room. She wouldn't have been certain the metal door on the ground floor marked "Employees Only" was the entry she wanted if there hadn't been a small wooden wedge between the door and jamb to keep it from closing all the way. Sending a cautious look around, Eve opened the door and bent to retrieve the wedge before moving inside to find herself on the first step of a cement stairwell. Setting the wooden piece on the stairway, she descended slowly, until the din below assured her she was in the right place.

There was a line of large canvas-sided, wheeled laundry hampers parked haphazardly across the space. They were situated several feet in front of a row of industrial washers and dryers, all of which seemed to be running.

She didn't see Brina until the woman straightened from where she'd been bent over a large canvas cart. She turned, the pile of sheets she was carrying nearly obscuring her face. Eve saw the woman's feet stop moving and knew she'd been sighted. The load of linens lowered. Brina.

The noise from the machines would make anything other than a close conversation impossible. Eve closed the space between them, half grateful for the sound level. Even if someone happened into the vicinity, there was no way they'd be overheard.

"Did anyone see you come down here?"

The Serbian woman's expression looked guarded, and Eve wondered if she were regretting her earlier decision to continue their discussion. Shaking her head, Eve said, "I closed the door behind me."

The words had something in the woman's face easing, but she dropped her load of laundry and gestured for Eve to follow her.

She did so, slowly. The place was poorly lit, a cavernous concrete pit with a spider's web of old ductwork crisscrossing overhead. There was a distinct odor of mildew in the space. Brina stopped by the last of the laundry carts, and Eve realized the location would obscure them from the view of anyone descending the stairs.

"I saw a man earlier today I recognized. A bad man. The name I know him by is Lafka Malsovic. He has…" She was about to describe his tattoos, but the other woman's reaction told her it was unnecessary.

One hand to her throat, Brina replied in Serbian, "He has many names, but the only one that matters is *monster*." A shudder racked her body, punctuating the words. "He is dangerous. A liar and a brutal man. I wouldn't be surprised to hear he is the one who killed my friend. He threatens us often. Hurts us. I put nothing past him."

The information matched with what Eve had heard about the man from Raiker, but she was more concerned about the experiences responsible for the fear and loathing on the woman's face. "Why is he here? Do you know?"

Brina studied her, as if for the first time considering the ramifications of talking to her. "You are…police?"

Eve shook her head. "But I can help you," she assured the woman. "If you tell me what is happening here, I can get help."

Mouth twisting, the woman said fatalistically, "There is no help. Police will send me back to my home country, and my family would still owe Malsovic a debt for bringing me to America. They cannot pay, and there are no jobs for me there, or marriage. No man wants to marry a woman who has been forced to…" Her features hardened. "But I do not care for me. Dajana. Someone must pay for what was done to her. And if that someone is Malsovic, all the better."

Eve glanced over her shoulder to be sure they were still

alone and then angled her body for a better view of the stairway. "How did you get to America?"

Brina looked away. "I answered an ad," she muttered in such a low voice Eve had to strain to hear her. "I could pay four thousand dollars, or he would have a job for me when I got here, working in a hotel for three hundred American dollars a week. I would give him half my wages for the first year to repay him for his troubles. I would have paid even more for the chance he was promising. He showed me pictures of other girls he had helped. I knew it was a risk, but the risk I thought was in getting caught. Being sent back." An expressionless mask came over the woman's face. "But the reality was far worse than I feared. I have been here more than two years. We are prisoners, all of us. We do not leave the hotel, and we are not allowed to keep any money."

Eve swallowed hard. The situation was as bad as she'd feared, but somehow hearing those fears put into words made it harsher. "What about Xie Shuang? You said earlier she keeps all your tips."

A flash of fright flickered over Brina's face, and she sent an uneasy glance at the stairwell. "Malsovic works for her. She pays him to bring her workers, and we work here for nothing. There were thirty of us. One less now." The words were tinged with grief.

Eve studied Brina for a moment. With the man's reputation for brutality and the housecleaner's reaction to the mention of him, there was more here than had yet been revealed. An ugly suspicion bloomed. "What else does Malsovic do?"

Brina ducked her head. "He...he finds men. Almost every night, there are several for each of us." The woman refused to meet her gaze. "He shares the money with Shuang, but he keeps most of it, I think."

"Oh my God, you're living a nightmare." Sympathy twisted in Eve's chest. The horror of the women's plight was almost too much to contemplate. But she was too familiar with stories much like the one Brina was telling to doubt the woman's truthfulness.

The housekeeper bent and rolled down one of the white cotton socks she wore to reveal a thick black bracelet around her ankle. "If we get even a few feet outside of the hotel, an alarm goes off. They can track us through this bracelet. We are brought back. Beaten. Nearly killed." She bit her lip. "No one has tried to leave more than once."

"Where do you stay?" Eve asked. There was a helpless sort of desolation welling up inside her just thinking of what Brina and the others were going through. It couldn't come close to the impotence and violation the women experienced every day and the knowledge made her physically ill.

"There are two rooms on the fifteenth floor filled with bunk beds. We sleep there, and one of the men stands guard all night." Brina slid an uneasy glance at the stairwell again before returning her gaze to Eve. "I must get to work, or I will be beaten. You say you want to help." She dug into the pocket of her apron and came up with a hotel key card. Handed it to Eve. "It is a master. It will open all the rooms." Her gaze were dark and intense. "You can see I tell the truth. Our rooms are 1501 and 1502. Shuang is in 701 and Malsovic is in 823."

Eve hesitated but didn't reach for the card. "What will happen to you when they find you've lost your master key?"

"It is Dajana's." Brina's lips quivered for a moment before she tightened them. "She will not be using it anymore."

Eve took the key card and dropped it into her purse. It was too good an opportunity to pass up, but she prayed it didn't end up costing the woman far more than she expected. She reached out and grabbed Brina's hand. "I am going to get help for you, but it might take a few days." She wasn't sure how they would coordinate their mission here with a rescue op for the women trapped in virtual slavery, but she was damn sure going to make it happened. And if Adam Raiker couldn't facilitate it, she had contacts who could. "Can you hang on for a little while longer?"

The woman's laugh was bitter. "What are days compared to years? I want to believe, but I will not let myself hope. Hope has died inside me. Now you must go before you are caught here, and then it will be too late for both of us."

As difficult as it was to allow the Serbian woman to turn away and pick up the load of sheets she'd dropped earlier, Eve knew she'd already stayed longer than she should.

But it was hard to walk toward the staircase and make her ascent, knowing Brina wasn't free to do the same.

At the top, Eve put her ear against the door, one hand on the knob, but of course could hear nothing from the outside. Dragging in a breath, she eased the door open until she could put an eye to the crack she'd created. Her view was limited, but no one appeared to be around. She hurried out the door and down the hallway. As she turned the corner, she heard voices. She dug in her purse and pulled out her cell, holding it to her ear as she slowed to a stroll.

"I know, can you believe it? I took a wrong turn and ended up in a housekeeping closet," she exclaimed as she walked behind two men who were speaking in low tones. "I just can't get my bearings in a hotel." With a jolt, she recognized one of them as the bearded man who'd forced her and

Declan into the car at gunpoint a day earlier. "I went to get snacks and ended up lost." She pretended to prattle on as she passed the two. "I'm hopeless, aren't I? Okay. See you soon."

The men's conversation had stopped as she walked by. Eve halted before the ground floor elevators and stabbed blindly at the up button. She felt like a penetrating laser was stabbing in her back, and she knew precisely the cause. The second man—the one talking to her abductor—was Lafka Malsovic.

A hot ball of anger settled in the pit of her stomach. She'd heard about his past from Raiker. Knew what he was suspected of. But Brina had brought the man's violence to vivid Technicolor. And with every fiber of her being, she resolved the man would pay for even more than his attempted kidnap of Royce Raiker.

He'd pay for ruining the lives of every woman he'd brought here.

ZUPAN WAS SPEAKING AGAIN, but Malsovic wasn't listening. He stared after the woman who'd walked into the elevators. "That female," he interrupted the other man in broken Slovenian. "Have you seen her before?"

The other man turned around. "The blonde who went by? Of course. She is the bitch who was with Gallagher. The one with the knife who caused Shuang to nearly kill me."

"You failed your task," Malsovic said flatly, finally bringing his focus back to Zupan. "You let a mere woman outwit you." Seeing the other man's thunderous expression, he recalled the reason he'd had for speaking with him to begin with. He might need him later, and it paid to have allies. "But Shuang was too hard on you. I told her so myself." He'd done nothing of the kind, but Zupan didn't know that. "You did not deserve such a beating. Especially at the hands of a woman."

Agreement was written on the other man's face, but he wouldn't dare speak of it aloud. Malsovic was in business with Shuang. Everyone knew. And no one could be sure how deep his loyalties ran. Malsovic was careful to keep it so.

He took a wad of crumpled bills from his pocket and shoved it at Zupan. "Take this for your suffering. It is too little, but all I have right now."

His largesse clearly took the man by surprise, but he reached for the bills and put them in his pocket. "Thank you, Lafka."

When Malsovic clapped him on the shoulder, Zupan winced. "Your time will come soon. Until then, stay away from Shuang if you can." It was the first he'd seen the man up and around since his beating two days ago. Zupan was weak and not always smart, but his computer skills had come in handy once already. Loyalty could always be bought.

"Take care, my friend." Finished with the man he headed toward the lower floor to the laundry room to check on the disobedient Brina. Shuang had told him about the woman's slowness today, which he cared nothing about. But she'd been asking about Dajana, which was of far greater concern. It was his task to make sure the woman knew to keep her mouth closed about Dajana's fate or risk sharing it.

But Brina was not on his mind as he made his way down the hallway. It was on the woman with the bright hair. The one he would be charged with disposing of when Shuang was done with Gallagher.

He had no problem killing women, but he did have a problem with waste. Reaching the entrance to the laundry room, he opened the door—immediately heard the hum of machines coming from below. Killing the small blonde *would* be wasteful. He began to descend the stairs. She looked younger than their research had reported, which could be an advantage. Women were a commodity to be sold and traded, and in many countries, a blue-eyed blonde would fetch a handsome price. Especially one who appeared so fresh.

He wasn't sure yet what that meant for him but knew he'd have to give it thought. Just as he'd been giving thought on exactly how he could double-cross Xie Shuang.

THE HOURS PASSED with excruciating slowness. The men had fallen ravenously on the snacks Eve had brought back and handed out with accompanying empty-headed chatter about how long it had taken her to find the floors with vending machines, and how she'd visited them all to get the best selection. Then she settled into a chair, earphones in place. But she wasn't thinking about the music.

Shuang was on the seventh floor. Malsovic on the eighth. It didn't require much thought to be certain the receiver Raiker had given them should go in the woman's offices. According to Brina, Malsovic worked for Xie. Any meetings between the two of them would most likely take place in her territory.

And Eve was keenly interested in just what the two might have to say to each other. She debated the point mentally, her gaze going to Declan. His sleeves were rolled up showing strong forearms as he explained the security at Raiker's checkpoints. She knew what his reaction would be if she planted the device without discussing the location with him first. But she also didn't want to risk a conversation about it here, even in a language the other men surely weren't familiar with.

They both had jobs to do, she thought mutinously. And Declan Gallagher was going to have to get used to the fact they had an equal say in how those jobs would be done.

She made herself wait for an hour before rising and wandering over to him. "I'm going to find a bathroom."

He looked at her, and then at the adjoining door. "There's one right over there."

It was incredibly difficult to summon a vacant smile. "Oh, darling, you realize I'm not going potty with a room full of men next door. Don't you know me by now?"

His enigmatic, gray gaze seemed to bore straight into her mind and pluck out her intention. "I do, indeed." She heard the warning layering his tone. "Be careful. I don't want you getting lost again."

"I can't make any promises. *Cóig deug. Seachd.*" The words trailed behind her on a laugh, but once she had the door closed, the smile faded from her lips. Their time was running out for the day. The thought propelled her to the stairway exit and up the flights of stairs to the fifteenth floor. There were enough people in the hallway to keep her ducked inside the stairway doorway for several minutes, which gave her some much-needed time to catch her breath. She'd told Declan the floors she'd be visiting, if not the reason. Hopefully, he'd be able to work his magic with the cameras.

It was check-in time, which explained the luggage carts

and people looking for their rooms. Minutes ticked by with excruciating slowness before Eve decided she didn't have the luxury of time. Drawing in a deep breath, she pushed the door open and—with a glance at the signs on the wall— headed for 1501, the pass card in her hand.

No one seemed to pay her any mind as she slid her card into the door and pushed it open to step inside. A quick glance showed it was empty, and for a moment, Eve slumped against the door, all the strength streaming out of her.

Then she took a cursory walk through the room and into the next one via an open adjoining door. Each was the size of a regular hotel room but devoid of all furniture except for rows of metal bunkbeds. Counting them, Eve noted there were eight bunks per room, with only inches separating each set from the next. Thirty-two beds. Beneath each bottom bunk were two pillowcases. Checking those closest to her, she found in each an extra uniform and a few personal items.

The paltry stash was as chilling as the room itself. The cold utilitarian bunks, all as precisely made as those in military barracks. The metal sheet of bars bolted to each window frame. The rooms were a prison.

It was exactly what Brina had described, but somehow worse. The space resonated with despair.

The thought had her setting her jaw. Taking her phone out, she took pictures of both rooms. Returning her cell to her purse, she went to the door and opened it a crack, looking out carefully before strolling down the hall to the stairway. She descended to the seventh floor, her stomach a tight tangle of nerves and entered the hallway. An elderly couple was closing the door of a room behind them halfway down the hall. The woman's large, oversized tapestry purse had perhaps been in fashion when Truman was president, and the man's only remaining hair was a walrus style mustache. Still there was something endearing about the way he patted the woman's free hand where it was tucked into the crook of his elbow as they tottered toward the elevator.

Eve waited until the open elevator swallowed them before walking swiftly to the room in the now deserted hall and letting herself inside.

The phone was sitting on the desk and she bee-lined for it. Lifting the receiver, she studied the message on how to make a room-to-room call. And then dialed 701.

The thudding in her chest seemed to echo in the empty room. The call jangled once. Twice. And then...

"Yes?"

"In the kitchen." Eve used a breathless whisper, English with a Korean accent. "They said not to bother you, but you should come. Hurry!" Then she dropped the phone back in the cradle. Blew out a shuddering breath and strode to the door to press an eye against the peephole.

There was no telling if her farce would work, but Eve had a second plan ready in case it didn't. She waited, scarcely daring to breathe as the moments ticked by. Finally, the door to the room four down from this one opened. An irritated Xie Shuang marched out, her pace swift. Her back ramrod straight. Eschewing the elevators, she moved instead in the direction of the stairway exit. By the time Eve pulled the door open to make certain, the woman was out of sight.

Speeding out of the room, she had her key out and was inside 701 in seconds, her heart heaving as though she'd sprinted a marathon. A quick glance showed the space was used primarily as an office. A rollaway bed was shoved into the corner under the window. Two armchairs faced the desk. Skirting both, Eve dropped to her knees to examine the face of the desk.

It was a cheaply made piece. Particle board stained and polished to look like oak. The front panel in the middle stopped four inches shy of the floor. Crawling to look at it from the other side, Eve found the two pedestals held three drawers each with a wide center drawer. At the bottom of the pedestals, the edges bore decorative cutouts a couple of inches from the floor. Eve was able to slip her fingers into them.

A sense of desperation filled her, although logically she knew it had only been a couple of minutes since she'd entered the room. Her imagination was busy painting all sorts of scenarios that would have Shuang returning unex-pectedly. Meeting someone on the stairs and abruptly changing priorities. Using her cell to call the kitchen and discovering there was no emergency. Forgetting something in her room...

Elbowing the doubts aside, she set her purse on the floor and dug in the zippered pocket for the plastic box holding the receiver. Her hands fumbled a bit when she took it out. Nerves were ridiculous. It wasn't as if she'd never bugged a room before. Turning the small device over in her hands to examine it, she discovered a round disk on one side. Scraping at it with her thumbnail, she peeled off the metal colored paper to expose an adhesive area. Wedging her hand under the right pedestal, she blindly affixed the trans-mitter to one interior side where it'd be undetected.

Unless, she thought, wincing as she scraped the back of her hand on the edge and drawing it out from beneath the desk, it happened to loosen and fall to the floor. Because it was useless to worry about what-ifs, she heaved herself to her feet and strode quickly toward the door. Stopped for a moment before retracing her steps. The desktop was tidy with a laptop computer, its lid closed, a pen and a box of Kleenex. Eve tried each of the drawers and found them locked. Snatching a tissue, she wrapped it around the pen and tucked it into a pocket in her purse before heading toward the door. She would have been in the room for under five minutes. Mentally congratulating herself, she reached for the knob just as a loud knock sounded on the other side of it.

Her hand froze in mid-air. She risked a glance at the peephole and a jagged blade of fear pierced her. Malsovic.

Whirling, her gaze skated around the area, looking for a hiding place in case she needed it. Surely he wouldn't come in. The knock sounded again, louder, and Eve wasted no more time. She chose the closet, feeling slightly foolish as she slid the door back as quietly as she could to step inside and close it again. He would likely go away once it became apparent Shuang wasn't here, but his presence was slowing her escape. Eve couldn't be sure how long she had before the woman returned.

Under no circumstances did she want to be here when Shuang came back.

The thought froze in her mind as a knock sounded a third time followed by the sound of a lock releasing. Eve shrank back in the corner of the closet, her purse clutched to her chest, wishing frantically for her weapon. But since she'd given up the knife, she had nothing more lethal than the pen she'd just stolen off Shuang's desktop.

Barely daring to breathe, she strained to decipher the small sounds she heard. If he meant to wait for his boss, Eve was screwed. The knowledge stabbed at her like sharp little daggers. She couldn't hope to evade both of them.

Minutes ticked by. She heard fingers tapping on a

keyboard. Then a vicious curse in Serbian. More tapping. He was trying to get into the woman's computer, Eve realized. Unsuccessfully.

Despite the danger, she found herself intrigued. There was no honor among scumbags. No surprise there. But she couldn't help wondering what the man was looking for. Surely Shuang would demand a full accounting of the day's events from her employees holed up for the day with Declan, and Malsovic would be included in the briefing, wouldn't he? He'd been a part of the first attempt to abduct Royce. It made sense he'd figure into the next plan, as well.

There was a small noise. Then footsteps scuffed on the carpet. Eve pressed herself back against the wall of the closet, scarcely daring to breathe. The man hesitated at the door for a long moment. Then there was the slight sound of the knob turning. Of the door closing.

Her breath rushed out of her, a silent stream. Still, it took another few moments ticking by before she could bring herself to slide the door back. Eve looked out the peephole. No one was in sight, but the view was limited to almost directly in front of the door. Urgency rapping at the base of her skull, she gave it another thirty seconds before she eased the door open a bit, glanced out and stepped into the hallway.

Her heart thundering in her ears, she strode to the stairway exit and pulled open the door, racing down the stairs as though a monster were chasing her. Malsovic was all of that. And Eve had come much too close to being discovered by him.

She descended to the sixth floor and then the fifth. She heard someone in the stairwell before coming face to face with the other person.

Xie Shuang.

"Mrs. Gallagher." The woman's face was impassive. Eve knew she didn't imagine the sudden flare of suspicion in her eyes. "You are a long way from the third floor."

"Am I?" Eve twisted around, as if trying to get a look at the sign on the landing above the woman. "It's easy to lose my bearings when I take the stairs." She blinked and tried for a guileless expression. "Actually, I just came from trying to find you on the seventh floor."

"Come." The word was more demand than request as the woman took her by the arm and turned her around to make the ascent again. "Walk with me, and you can tell me what is so important you felt you must see me."

"Well, because you told us to, of course." Every muscle in her body tensed as she fell into step beside the woman. "You said to come up at the end of the day and collect our weapons. Our apartment isn't the greatest these days. Or our neighborhood. It's just temporary, I know, but I wouldn't feel safe if we weren't armed before we left the hotel."

"I didn't realize the men were finished for the day." Their steps echoed hollowly in the area as they climbed.

"Well, I think they're close. Declan and I have an appointment at the bank before closing time, and it's imperative we aren't late. They really aren't very understanding about such things. It's about our house, you see, and it's just been unpleasantness all around ever since we put it up for sale." She launched into a monologue about shifty buyers and unreasonable realtors until the other woman's gaze went glassy.

"Here we are." There might have been a tinge of relief in Shuang's voice when she reached the door leading to the seventh floor. Eve had to lengthen her stride to keep up with the other woman as they approached the room she had just left. "If you will wait for a moment." Shuang didn't even attempt to make the statement seem like a suggestion. "I will collect the weapons and walk downstairs with you. I would like to speak to your husband before the two of you leave for the day."

"Of course." Eve was all too happy to be left in the hallway as the other woman slipped into her room. There had been a small safe in the closet Eve had hidden in earlier. She wondered if the weapons had been hidden inside it. And whether she'd left behind any trace she'd been standing in the small space next to it.

She beat back the waves of paranoia fluttering inside her until Shuang rejoined her in the hall. Although Shuang had carried the weapons away from the third-floor room in a pile, this time she had a bag over her arm Eve didn't remember seeing when she'd been inside the office earlier.

Anxious to get away, Eve turned toward the elevator, unable to face a long walk down the stairway with the woman. Shuang looked at her oddly. "It seems you have lost more than the house you told me about earlier."

Her smile brittle, Eve said, "Pardon me?"

"Your earring." The woman tapped Eve's left lobe as she moved past her. "You have lost it since I saw you this morning."

CHAPTER SEVEN

IT WAS ONLY DAY ONE, but Malsovic could already see what Shuang apparently did not. This newest plan of hers to snatch the boy was going to get them all killed. Well, not her, of course. Somehow, she was never the one in danger.

He stood impassively, his arms folded across his chest as he listened to Harris explain the details Gallagher had revealed that day. According to the ex-agent, they wouldn't be mounting an assault on Raiker's heavily-secured facility. Their entry would rely on deception; a vendor making an expected delivery. And once inside, armed with false IDs and the necessary codes at every juncture, their access would be unlimited. Their prints and iris scans would be added to the computer on site by an ex-colleague still in Raiker's employ. The blueprints were detailed enough to show every nook and cranny of the property. Most importantly, they revealed the tunnels and spaces below ground where Raiker's family was reportedly staying.

Harris, Taufik and Amin took turns explaining what Gallagher had revealed that day. Malsovic said little. By the time he'd been forced to share his research with Shuang, the outline of the first kidnap attempt had been in place, if not the specifics. It should have worked. Logistically it had been much more precise than her latest idea. And decidedly less risky.

The woman was looking at him. Belatedly he realized he'd missed her question the first time she asked it. She repeated it now, her dark eyes snapping with temper. "Well? What are your thoughts, Lafka?"

It wouldn't do to tell her what he really was thinking. This latest plan of hers would likely not lead them to the boy at all, but to individual body bags. He chose his words carefully. "We need positive evidence the boy is there, on the property, in the underground shelter. Photo evidence."

"Of course." She sounded annoyed. "Were you not listening? Gallagher agreed to supply such proof. What other reservations do you have?"

"We would need to do a trial run prior to the actual attempt." He studied the long mural like paper tacked against the wall with notes and drawings of the details of the inner compound. "To test the accuracy of the information Gallagher gives us."

Shuang frowned. "A trial run means more expense and could tip off Raiker to what is coming. Why would we give him a forewarning? The element of surprise is always best."

"But according to Gallagher, no one would realize there had been a breach if all works as it should," he countered. He had a bad feeling about this idea of hers. Very bad. He did not trust the man Shuang had hired. But although he had continued his own research and pursued other leads in the months since they'd failed to abduct the boy, Malsovic currently had nothing better to suggest as an alternative.

And if he did happen upon a substitute plan, he wouldn't share it with Shuang.

"We will see." The words were dismissive and stoked the resentment inside him he normally took pains to hide. She turned back toward the other men. "I told Gallagher to bring proof tomorrow that the family is on site. You will continue with specifics on getting through every security level you will encounter on the property and begin to construct a list for what will be needed for your entry ruse. Malsovic will begin working on duplicating the necessary IDs from the one Gallagher left with you."

The other men nodded. Malsovic was a skilled forger. He had the necessary printing and digital equipment in his room. It was how he falsified the passports necessary to move the women out of their countries and into the United States. A man of his talents should be reaping far greater financial rewards than he was. The burn of the injustice was with him always.

His cell vibrated in his pocket, but he knew better than to check it here. Whoever was contacting him would be someone whom he still kept on the payroll in hopes his other leads would bear fruit. A feeling of urgency seized him even as he listened carefully to the rest of the men's report. Time was running out. If he did not come up with another idea very soon, he would be front and center in Shuang's next abduction attempt. Even if they were successful, he didn't trust her not to put a bullet in his brain the moment she no longer needed him.

"It's not just forced servitude." Eve's voice was adamant. "These women are sexual slaves. They aren't free to leave. I sent you the pictures I took of the bars on their bedroom windows. We have to arrange their rescue."

Declan had listened to part of her story on the way over to the bank. Hearing her share it with Raiker didn't lessen its impact. "You said the hotel had a history of that sort of thing up until seven years ago. Seems a bit coincidental it's back in the same business, even under different ownership."

The other man's expression was fierce. "Perhaps the issue isn't the ownership, but the players involved. How many women do you estimate are being held there in the hotel?"

"Brina said around thirty." There was a barely perceptible tremble to Eve's voice. "I should have taken a picture of the monitoring bracelet she wore on her ankle. It's more evidence. I could get it tomorrow."

"Hold off." Raiker was silent for a moment. Declan could almost see the wheels turning. "I don't want to put you or the girl in any more danger. Since your undercover assignment at the hotel is being conducted in conjunction with an FBI investigation into Royce's kidnapping, protocol says I notify them first. They'll bring in other agencies as they see fit."

"How soon?" she demanded. Declan slanted her a glance. She was visibly shaken. Of course, neither of them had expected their undercover mission would lead to discovering a human trafficking ring. "Every evening these women are being sexually abused. And Brina insisted one of them was murdered last night."

The news was another shocker. "You were busy today," he muttered. And her time spent out of the room had been nerve-wracking for both of them. Switching the camera angles for the floors in question hadn't been a problem. Finding reasons to get to his computer in a timely manner with the three men in the room had been. Once Harris had followed him to the laptop, and Declan had spent a couple minutes showing them the shot he had over the camera page depicting Raiker's compound. He hadn't been sure he'd get the cameras altered before Eve reached her destination, and the urgency he'd felt had been difficult to conceal.

"But she doesn't have direct knowledge of the death." Eve's expression went mutinous at Raiker's remark. "It's a tragedy, but the circumstances surrounding it will be investigated just as the women's plights will be. I can't tell you more until I've spoken to one of the feds."

"I want Brina offered a T Visa. She meets elements in all three categories: Process, Ways and Means, and Goal. She'll cooperate with the investigation. Maybe some of the others will, too, but she has nothing to return to in her home country."

Declan narrowed his gaze at her. It was almost as if another woman were sitting beside him. One he hadn't known for a handful of days. Hadn't lived with as long. He'd already suspected there was more to her than she let on. Now he was sure of it.

"She's smart and not afraid to speak up, despite the risks," Eve continued. "And she wants justice for her friend. She'll make a strong witness. The T Visa will give her an option to change her status in the country from temporary to permanent if she wants it. She deserves that much."

"And you'll make a strong advocate on her behalf," Raiker responded. "But we're getting ahead of ourselves. I'll let you know when there's a plan in place."

She looked as though she wanted to say more. But after a moment, she took a deep breath and nodded. Digging into her purse she brought out something wrapped in a white tissue. "This pen was on Shuang's desk. Maybe you'll be able to get prints from it."

Declan stilled. "You were in Shuang's room?" Fear

stabbed through him, cold and deadly as a blade. "You neglected to mention it." Her admission, he thought savagely, was purposeful. He should have guessed. The earphones Raiker had left for them were around her neck, and the MP3 player clipped to the collar of her coat rather than carrying both in her purse as she had this morning. He reached in his pocket, fingered the silver stud earring he'd found by his chair after she'd left for snacks. She could have lost it anywhere in her trips out of the room.

She could have lost it in Shuang's office. The knowledge had his gut twisting.

"I didn't have time to tell you everything on the way over. I used a master key Brina gave me. I was inside long enough to plant the listening device." Deliberately, she fixed her eyes on the computer screen where Raiker was listening silently. "I haven't heard anything of interest so far."

"Excellent." Satisfaction laced the other man's voice, an emotion Declan was unable to share. "The device is powerful enough to pick up even a whisper in even a much bigger space. All in all, the two of you accomplished quite a lot today. It gets riskier tomorrow. The closer you are to supplying them with all the information they need, the more danger you're in. Shuang doesn't strike me as one to leave loose ends." He seemed to consider for a moment. "What room were you working in today?"

"311," they said in unison.

He nodded decisively. "I'll get a few more people in a room as close by as I can manage. They'll be armed and can provide backup if necessary. I sent along a couple of location devices for the two of you to wear at all times. We'll be monitoring your whereabouts constantly. And Eve?" When he was certain he had her attention, he continued, "You did well today. But I want you to stick close to Declan tomorrow. Monitor the receiver on the bug. You'll raise too much suspicion if you're constantly roaming the hotel."

"She might raise suspicion if she doesn't at least occasionally go on a food run." Declan's tone was wry. "Her appetite today didn't go unnoticed."

"Just be careful. We already likely have the key players behind the abduction."

"But we're no closer to answers about the mystery of Royce's parentage," Declan reminded the man. The assignment didn't feel close to completion. Not by a long shot. "Even if you raid the place and pick everyone up, there's no guarantee you could get Shuang or Malsovic to talk. Just look at the two cop killers downtown. They haven't said a word yet, have they?"

"No." After a pause, Raiker continued. "And I'm not closing you down. Just reminding you of the threat level. It should be safe enough with the extra precautions we'll have in place for tomorrow. Oh, and I meant to tell you, there was no luck with prints off the gun. There were latents, but we didn't get a match in any of the databases."

"I worked with three of Shuang's men today," Declan told him. Eve pushed away from the table, and he watched her leave the transaction room as he told Raiker their names. "We haven't seen the driver of the car from when they tried to snatch us off the street. And Malsovic has made himself scarce."

"He's around." Eve's voice was muffled in the adjoining room as she stuck her head into the safe and withdrew with her fist closed around something. "I saw him today."

"You and I have a bit to catch up on, it would appear." It took effort to keep his voice mild. But there was nothing calm about the froth of emotion warring within him. Its intensity was alarming. Quite possibly chauvinistic, and he wasn't a chauvinist. He'd worked with partners before. It wasn't uncommon to divide up duties between them. There was no reason—none at all—for the danger Eve had put herself in today to fill him with this degree of apprehension.

"Don't forget the security measures I mentioned." The screen went black with Raiker's typical abruptness. Eve approached Declan to show him two objects cradled in her palm.

"This one must be yours." She held out a small silver circular tie clasp with an ornately worked G in the center. He eyed it doubtfully.

"Might seem sort of odd if I show up wearing a suit and tie tomorrow."

"No need." She hitched a hip on the table close to him and leaned forward, pushing aside his opened coat. "If you don't wear a shirt with a pocket tomorrow, you can just leave it in a jeans pocket, I suppose." Her fingers were nimble as she undid the first three buttons of his shirt, the backs of them brushing his skin. His flesh heated beneath her touch. He clenched his jaw at the involuntary reaction. With a few deft moves, she had the pin hidden inside the pocket, with the safety clasp on the inside of his shirt against his chest. She straightened, leaving him to re-button his shirt himself, for which he was grateful. His fingers felt thick. Clumsy. And he found himself wishing she'd move away from her perch on the table near him.

"Oh, cool." She held the remaining item out to show him. The embedded GPS device was attached to a hairpin. Eve lifted her hair and slipped it in above her nape, then dropped her arms to let the blond waves cascade to her shoulders again.

The room was getting warm. Or else he was. Declan bolted upright from his chair, slid the laptop further down the table, and shut it off. "Did you put the pen in the safety deposit box to be retrieved for prints?"

Her expression wary, she nodded.

"Good." He was aware her gaze didn't leave him as he rounded the table and replaced the computer in the safe, closing and locking it.

"You seem...tense."

"I get that way when my partner withholds information." He straightened from the crouched position in front of the box and turned toward the door.

"I didn't *withhold* anything." There was a tinge of temper in her tone he hadn't heard there before. "I just didn't have time to tell you everything on the way here. I haven't hatched a big conspiracy to keep you in the dark. We need to talk."

"We do indeed." There was something supremely annoying about knowing he was acting like an ass and still being unable to do anything to change it. "You can start by telling me about this." He dug the earring out of his pocket and held it up to show her.

"Oh, thank God." Her shoulders slumped in obvious relief. "Where did you find it?"

"By my chair," he said, a savage edge to his voice as she took it from him. "But the more important question is where *could* you have lost it? On a floor you had no business being on? Or worse, in Shuang's office? If it had been found in any of those places, it would have screwed us for the rest of this assignment." She'd taken the other earring out, he noted now, and was spending an inordinate amount of time placing the pair in a zippered pocket in her purse.

"You're right. It would have made our situation a bit... untenable." Her smile didn't make it to her eyes. "But on the bright side, this saves me a trip to Shuang's office tomorrow to look for it. As it is, I'll forgo jewelry from now on."

Just the thought of her making another foray into Shuang's space glazed his veins with ice. "Good idea. You can fill me in on the rest of your day on the way to the hospital."

"I never said..."

His smile was grim. "No, you didn't. Figured it out on my own. Not rocket science, of course, after last night. You've been in touch with your family today?" She trailed behind him out of the transaction room and across the bank lobby.

"I...yes. I spoke to my mother this morning and again this afternoon when I was out of the hotel room. My father had more tests and received good news. They were even considering releasing him today, except he started running a slight fever."

He held the front door of the bank open for her, then followed her through it. He almost welcomed the slap of cold air. Maybe it would clear his head of the unfamiliar turmoil filling it.

Jamming his hands in his pockets, he looked around for a cab. The street was snarled with traffic and would be until the rush hours—plural—were over. "We might need to take a bus." He glanced at Eve to find her staring fixedly across the street. Catching his gaze on her, she moved closer to his side.

"Under the striped awning over there. He just dodged into the doorway. Do you see him?"

Declan drew his phone out of his pocket and pretended to be texting. It took another minute for the shadow to unfold from its hiding place again, then duck back quickly. "Not well enough to recognize him."

"It's the one who held the gun on us when they tried to snatch us off the street." She tucked her arm in the crook of his elbow, and they began to move slowly down the walk. "I saw him talking to Malsovic today at the hotel."

It had already become readily apparent her day had been much more fruitful than his. And a helluva lot riskier. The knowledge did nothing to loosen the vise constricting his chest. "Shuang seems to have a relatively small group of men in her employ." And none were particularly well-versed in the art of a tail. "Smaller since they failed to abduct Royce. I wonder if we've seen all of them now."

"She knew where we were going. I told her." At his side-long glance, she muttered, "Long story. But she knew we were going to a bank, because I spun some long account of our house woes ..."

"It's no problem." With a surreptitious look across the street, he saw the man was staying several yards behind them, remaining close to the shelter of the buildings. "She's had someone tailing us ever since we met with her for the first time. And the bank cover holds."

"The problem," she said with inflection, "is what to do about him now. I'm not going to lead him to the hospital where my parents are."

"You won't have to." Outwitting the doofus who'd attempted to kidnap them might give him an outlet for the temper that had lodged in his gut earlier and showed no signs of dissipating. "Let's have a little fun with this." He steered her closer to the buildings, lingering before store-fronts adorned with Christmas finery. Their pace slowed, as if window shopping. After several minutes, she hunched further into her coat and blew out a breath. A cloud of condensation immediately formed on the plate glass in front of her.

"What part of this is supposed to be fun?"

"It is a little cold," he acknowledged. The man trailing them had to be just as chilled. And Declan had been on enough surveillance ops to know physical discomfort often led to sloppy mistakes. "I suppose it was too much to ask for a toy store to be located in the area. I'm actually in need of another gift for Sadie. What the hell is a Teeter Popper?"

She smiled. "I'm not sure, but I'm certain I can find it online for you."

"I'm going to take you up on that." He watched their tail's reflection in the window in front of them. "Let's go inside here."

He pulled open the door to a women's clothing store, ushered her in. She looked around unenthusiastically. "Are we supposed to be stalling? Because I'd prefer to wait in another bakery."

"Not surprising." He steered her to a rack of clothes on the wall out of view of the window. "Anyway...browsing. How painful can it be?"

"About equal to being beat repeatedly in the head with a golf club."

"You don't enjoy shopping?" If he backed up a few feet, Declan had an excellent view of the opposite sidewalk. But he was unable to see their tail. Wait. There was a flash of movement as the man darted a couple buildings closer.

"It's not innate to the gender." It might have been his imagination she sounded a bit defensive. "Just like every man doesn't necessarily have to like sports."

His tone was absent. "What's not to like about sports?" A sales clerk was bearing down on them, her smile as plastic and bright as the artificial tree in the corner. "Stay away from the window," he told Eve, and headed toward the back of the store to search for another exit. He was gratified when he found one. Slipping outside, he walked down the alley half a block where it opened to the street. He turned right and made note of the name and address of the first storefront there before heading back toward the women's clothing store where he'd left Eve.

The sales clerk he'd seen minutes ago had a stack of clothes over her arms and was herding her down a hallway toward dressing rooms. He ambled to the front counter, which spotlighted him for anyone with a view of the window. Pretending an interest in an arrangement of perfumes, Declan watched for their tail.

He almost thought the man had given up. But after a few minutes, he caught sight of him inside a cigar store directly across the street. He'd followed their lead in getting out of the bone-chilling cold and had found a warmer place to wait.

"Mr. Gallagher." It was the store clerk, smiling prettily. "Your wife has asked you to come back closer to the dressing rooms so you can see some of the outfits I put together for her."

"Really?" Intrigued, he pushed away from the counter. Maybe Eve had overcome her stated aversion to shopping. And since they had time to kill, Declan could think of worse ways to do it than to watch Eve Larrison waltz around in the newest fashions.

Pulling his cell out of his pocket, he found the number for the cab company they'd used last night and called it. He dropped down in one of the chairs discreetly placed near the curtained dressing rooms while he made arrangements for a taxi to pick them up at the address he'd selected around the corner in the alley, instructing them to call him when the cab had arrived.

He'd no sooner returned his cell to his pocket than Eve's

face popped out of the second dressing room down. "Declan!" she hissed. There was a measure of panic in her expression he'd never noticed there before. "She's making me try on clothes!"

"It's no problem," he responded in Scottish Gaelic. "We haven't lost our tail, but we'll give him the slip in a bit. Go ahead. We've got a bit of time."

"I don't want to go ahead, you dunce! Get me out of here!"

"Do you need help?" The dark-haired clerk sailed toward them. "Can I get you a different size in anything?"

"No!" Eve ducked back inside the dressing room. Her voice grew muffled. "No, thank you. I'm doing just fine."

Declan grinned. She hadn't been kidding earlier. She really did seem to despise shopping. It wasn't his favorite pastime, but he didn't approach it with the abject terror Eve seemed to. He settled more comfortably into his seat and hooked an ankle across one knee. Given her reaction, it'd be downright cruel to consider this payback for the bad moments she'd given him today. But there was no denying the next few minutes were likely to prove entertaining.

STEPPING INSIDE THE STRIP CLUB, he squinted in the shadowy interior. Spotting his contact, he made his way across the room. Rick Sorenson was seated near the stage, in almost the same spot he'd been the first time Malsovic had followed him from the nursing home six weeks earlier. Approaching the younger man, he pulled out a chair next to him. Sat.

"Your text said you something to report," he started without preamble.

"Hey, Sergei." Because of course Malsovic hadn't given him the name he was using currently. Sorenson raised his half full beer in a salute without taking his eyes off the gyrating woman on stage. "Yeah, I think I heard something today you're really going to be interested in." He tore his gaze away from the stripper longer enough to repeat, "*Really* interested."

"Hopefully it is of more interest than any of the other information you have shared." His patience with the man was nearing an end. He'd stumbled on Royce Benning's daughter by accident months ago, but every bit of information he'd gleaned since then had been due to his own diligence and hard work. Discovering Jaid Raiker had a mother had been a nugget of information he'd been massaging for months, hoping it would pay off and somehow lead him to the boy.

But the old lady had been stuck in a nursing home since he'd tracked her down, and despite his cultivation of Sorenson, knowing the location of Patricia Marlowe still hadn't borne fruit. "You want a beer?" The young man swiveled in his chair to summon a waitress. "You have to order something or you'll be asked to leave."

"Tell me your news."

But Malsovic had to wait for the scantily clad server to come and take his order before the man beside him finally responded. "I've been paying a lot of attention to the old bat. Patricia Marlowe. Been extra nice to her, which believe me isn't easy since the woman can be a real pain in the ass."

"I told you to give others there the same treatment," Malsovic reminded him. The security posted around the elderly woman would surely scrutinize everyone their client came in contact with. They would have run a background check on all the workers at the rest home, including Sorenson, one of the certified nursing assistants often assigned to the woman's care. Had they found anything in the check, the CNA would have been removed by now. But if he acted as though he were trying to curry favor with the woman, it would be a red flag to the people protecting her.

"Yeah, yeah, I've told you, I have been. But old lady Marlowe seems to like me, at least as much as she does most people. And today, she told me she's leaving soon."

Malsovic stilled. Here at last was something worthy of sharing. "When? And going where?"

The stripper's routine ended, and Sorenson applauded enthusiastically. "Soon. A day or two she said. And she said she was going to join her family." His pause then was meaningful. "I figure you might be interested, seeing's how she has only spoken to her daughter on video chat as long as she's been there."

"I am." Malsovic sat back in his chair as the waitress returned to set a beer in front of him. He dug in his pocket for his wallet and held out a ten. When she snatched it from him and turned away, he knew not to expect change. American women. There was a dangerous burn in his chest as he spent a moment watching her wend her way through the tables. All of them seemed to have a sense of entitlement far above their station in life.

"I spun this whole big story about how much I was going to miss her, and how I hoped she stayed in touch. Laid it on thicker than usual, because those guys usually hanging close to her room weren't around to hear." The young man's attention was snared then by the announcement of the next stripper coming on stage, but after a moment, he glanced back at his companion. "I was hoping to get her to tell me where she was going, you know, so I could pass it on. But instead she says to me, 'Maybe you can accompany me,

Richard. I won't require trained nursing care, but it would be nice to have a familiar face help me with my exercises.'" He sat back in his chair, reached for his beer.

Malsovic leaned closer. "What did you say?"

Sorenson took a gulp from the bottle and set it on the table again. "What I figured you'd want me to say. I'd love to. I'd get the time off if she wanted. Blah blah blah. Pure suck up time, right? I asked where she'd be going, and she said she couldn't tell anyone. But if I didn't mind going on a mystery trip with her, she was certain her daughter would arrange it if the old bat insisted. Then one of those bodyguards came in the room, and I dropped it. Didn't want him to get the idea I'd been pumping the old lady." He looked at Malsovic then and his tone faltered. "Thought you'd be happy about this."

Baring his teeth, Malsovic said, "This is me. Happy. You did well. Better than I had hoped." He reached for his wallet again and took out a hundred. Slid it across the table to the man. "There will be much more coming if you can find out for sure when she is leaving. How she will travel." It would require a stroke of luck for the CNA to be allowed to accompany the woman. Good fortune had largely been absent from Malsovic's life.

The performer began spinning the tassels dangling from her breasts in opposite directions. He was certain he'd lost Sorenson's attention for good. His chair scraped back as he stood. "Contact me immediately tomorrow with what you find out."

Mouth open slightly, the other man only nodded. Turning on his heel, Malsovic strode quickly away, scarcely able to control his exuberance. The Americans had a saying: to catch a break. He knew this was his. At the very least, Sorenson would be able to discover a release date for the old woman. Then her car could be followed. He could verify what Gallagher was telling them about the location of the boy.

Malsovic pushed through the door, ducking his head against the cutting wind as he walked into the darkness. Perhaps something could be hidden in the woman's luggage or the vehicle she would ride in. Something to facilitate his access to the area.

Ideas swirled in his mind. He'd have to think of something fast. This was his chance to beat Shuang. He let himself bask in the thrill of outwitting her. She'd make a powerful enemy.

But once the boy was his, Malsovic would have power. Far more than hers. Enough to finally win him the financial rewards he'd always dreamed of.

"You can stay in the waiting room. I'll only be about an hour."

Eve's tone was frigid. She hadn't yet forgiven him for the incident in the store. The salesclerk, scenting an imminent sale, had been unshakeable, even whisking back the curtain of Eve's dressing room numerous times to provide her with even more items "just perfect for her." She'd been coerced a couple times to walk out to show Declan what she was wearing. And he hadn't been able to fault the clerk's taste, especially in one particular instance.

It might be a while before he forgot the sight of Eve in the snug sparkly blue dress that had left her shoulders and half her thighs bare, clinging to...just about everywhere. The clerk had gushed about it being a fabulous holiday party dress. Declan had little experience with holiday parties, but the woman had been right about one thing. It'd been perfect.

"Raiker wants us to stick together." He sent a careful eye around the hospital lobby and turned so he could see anyone pulling up to the bay out front. They'd lost the tail. He was certain of it. The man hadn't been in position to see them leave the dress shop through the back entrance. Wouldn't have had time to summon a cab to follow even if he had sighted them.

But you didn't survive in deep cover by underestimating the enemy.

They passed the volunteer seated at the front desk and walked toward a bank of elevators, and all the while, she continued her objections in Scottish. "Your presence can't be as easily explained today as it was last night. I'd prefer not to have to lie to my parents about why you're here."

"No dishonesty will be required." They paused before the elevators, and he tapped the earbuds still dangling from her neck. "We're working tonight. Doing some time-sensitive translation."

Still, she made no move to press the button that would take them to her father's floor. "You can wait outside his room."

It was a concession, and because he could see what it cost her, Declan nodded. It would be close enough to ensure against the infinitesimal chance they'd been followed, while still giving her a modicum of privacy with her family. And though there was a curiosity blooming inside him regarding the people who had raised Eve, he wasn't the type to go barging through others' privacy barriers.

At least, he never had been before.

They stepped into the first elevator going up with a

handful of others, and she reached forward to press the fifth floor button. He was content to trail behind her when the doors slid silently open. She marched down to the room without a glance at the nurse's station and, easing the door open, went inside.

Declan took up a stance against the wall next to the door, arms folded across his chest. He could clearly hear the voices in the room as Eve greeted her mother and father.

"Such a fuss." The querulous masculine tone bore more than a slight resemblance to Vincent Larrison's. "I'm fine. Could have gone home today if not for this blasted temperature. But the doctor said tomorrow for certain."

"He said maybe." The cool brisk tone disputing the man was feminine. "But your fever has broken. If it doesn't return, I'm sure you'll browbeat the staff into releasing you. Hello, Savvy. With a proper regimen of medication, exercise and diet, your father may be able to avoid surgery. Isn't that wonderful news?"

Declan's interest was piqued. Her brother had called Eve Savvy a couple times last night. A nickname, perhaps. He found himself more than a little curious about it. He'd asked her about it last night, but she'd deflected.

With determined mental effort, he skirted the memory of the minutes he'd spent putting her to bed. This assignment was getting snarled up, and he was a man who liked things smooth. He needed some time and space to put things together, starting with every detail of what had gone down in the hotel today.

"There's really no use for Leslie and Vincent to come here later this evening," Eve's mother was saying. "Why don't you step out to the waiting room down the hall and call them to tell them? You can't use cells in this room because of your father's machine."

"They may already be on their way." He was just able to pick up Eve's reply.

"Then they can go back home. It's a needless trip, and they have the children to consider. Don't you agree, Ronald?"

"It's not necessary." Masculine tones sounded again. "I'm fine. I don't need to be fussed over."

"All right, I'll try to reach them." A moment later, Eve came through the door. Without more than a warning glance in his direction, she headed toward the waiting area they'd passed near the elevators.

"Oh, and Eve." The door pushed open again and a woman stepped out. When she saw him, she stopped in her tracks. "Who are you? And why are you lurking outside my husband's room?"

Pushing away from the wall, Declan said, "You must be Mrs. Larrison. I'm Declan Gallagher. I work with Eve. As a matter of fact, we're going to be working late tonight, but she wanted to stop by and see her father first."

Here at last was one family member who bore a bit of resemblance to Eve. They were a similar height, but the older woman's graying blond hair was worn in a no-nonsense short cut. Her features were sharper, more angular than her youngest daughter's. And Declan had never seen that sort of suspicion in Eve's expression.

"Gallagher." Her eyes were a couple shades lighter blue than Eve's. The expression in them shrewd. "Vincent mentioned you'd brought Eve here last night. How odd you're together again today."

Her inflection gave "odd" a very different definition altogether. Declan tried for a disarming smile. "The job we're currently tasked with is time sensitive, which is why we're putting in extra hours. Of course, if you need Eve here tonight, I'm sure I can manage by myself."

"Nonsense." She stared in the direction Eve had disappeared. "Ronald doesn't want a fuss, and we certainly understand the demands of a career. Even Savvy's."

He wondered about the qualifier, but her use of the nickname again interested him more. "I heard your son call Eve Savvy, too. Is it a family nickname?"

"Oh." The woman gave a flutter of a hand. "It's just a silly family joke. She has this talent for languages, you know. But she was always hopeless with upper level applied science or mathematics. For the longest time, Ronald and I thought she was being deliberately obtuse. She had tutors and the finest schools. Vincent once quipped she was an idiot-savant. Which is a gross exaggeration, of course. There's certainly nothing wrong with being average. Her savant-like ear for languages has found her a niche, hasn't it?"

Declan froze at her words, but she seemed not to notice. "I'm sorry, I really need to catch Eve so I can speak to her siblings if she hasn't already disconnected. Excuse me." She hurried off.

A slow burn of anger ignited in his chest as he stared after her. Idiot-savant? The remark was so carelessly offensive, he could hardly wrap his head around it. What sort of family would dismiss Eve's gift so callously?

I'm the mutant in the family—disappointingly average.

And Declan knew he'd just been handed one more piece to the puzzle that was Eve Larrison. And it was one he would have felt far better to have not learned at all.

CHAPTER EIGHT

"WHERE ARE YOU?"

At Raiker's question, Declan moved in the direction of the waiting room Eve had vacated a half hour earlier, his cell to his ear. "George Washington University Hospital. Eve's father was admitted last night. Apparently, he'll be released tomorrow."

"Perfect. You're less than twenty minutes from the Office of the Chief Medical Examiner. How soon can you leave?"

"Uh..." Declan glanced in the direction of the closed hospital door. Eve and her mother had gone back in Larrison's room, and neither had exited again. "As soon as we need to, I guess. Why?" The fifth floor waiting room was very nearly isolated at this time of the evening. He found a corner with no one nearby and dropped into a chair there.

"After your report earlier this evening, I made some calls. One was to Detective Ramos, who caught Hobart's case. I told him we'd received a tip that the same killer might have struck again. Or at least dumped another body. Thought it would be worthwhile for him to check the interagency crime databases and see if anything had shown up in the area around the C&O Canal."

Declan's gut knotted. "And something did."

"A woman's body was fished out of the Potomac early this afternoon near Great Falls. A park ranger spotted something caught on the rocks this morning. It took the rescue unit most of the day to retrieve the body. I called Cal Stillions, our case contact in the Bureau. He's handling your invitation to the OCME to facilitate a possible identification of the body."

Declan sent a sober glance toward Larrison's room. "Eve will need to communicate with Brina again tomorrow." He agreed with Raiker's earlier assessment. He'd feel a lot better to have Eve in his sight for the remainder of time they were in the hotel. Especially when he thought of how easily her lost earring could have shown up in a far more dangerous spot.

"If the housekeeper IDs this woman as her missing friend, it lends instant credibility to her story and fast tracks the eventual raid on the hotel to rescue those women. It's important to get as much information as we can out of your cover in the next twenty-four hours. Once the feds open a trafficking investigation, your assignment will be curtailed."

He'd had the same thought. "It was only supposed to take two or three days anyway. We'll have enough by then." They'd have to in order to ensure Royce Raiker's safety.

"Things are moving fast. I'll need more frequent updates tomorrow as they occur. Have Eve use the cell I provided to send emails as needed. It's secure. Tell her to ask the housekeeper about any identifying marks the missing woman might have." He broke off, and Declan heard him speaking in an undertone to someone else. Then he was back. "You know what to do. Stay safe." The call ended.

Declan walked back toward Larrison's room, his mood grim. Staying safe was the problem. How did he keep Eve secure when she was out of his sight tomorrow? He was going to have to rethink his strategy with the cameras. Today he'd focused on trying to make alterations slight enough to garner no attention before they were switched back. It might not be an option the next day, at least not without making Shuang's men suspicious. He sent her a text. *AR called. Need to leave.*

It was less than five minutes before she joined him outside the room, a quizzical expression on her face. "Something's come up since we last spoke to him?" she asked in a low voice as he guided her toward the elevators. "Whatever it is, we're stopping at the cafeteria first. We didn't have dinner. And those chips I brought in this afternoon aren't going to hold me for much longer."

"Suck it up," he advised, drilling the down button with a forefinger. "Something tells me you aren't going to want a full stomach for our visit to the morgue."

"Gallagher and Larrison?" FBI Agent Cal Stillions was tall and lean to the point of looking skeletal. An unfortunate descriptor, Eve thought, given the setting. The man unfolded himself from a chair just inside the OCME lobby and pushed open the doors to allow them entrance into the semi-darkened building. He flashed his shield then pulled out his phone and silently compared them to pictures Raiker must have sent of them. "All right," he said finally, turning on his heel and heading down a hallway. "Follow me."

In the daylight, the building wouldn't seem in the least spooky, Eve thought. It was fairly new, with light-colored walls and tiled floors. But the place was deserted and dimly lit. "Office hours close at four-thirty," the man said over his shoulder. "But they have a technician staffing the place around the clock. She'll give us a quick look at the body."

"We won't be able to ID it," Declan said. He drew abreast with the man as they walked, their footsteps echoing hollowly in the empty hallway. "But if we get photos, we can show them to someone tomorrow who possibly could."

The agent grunted. "Hopefully. I hear it got pretty banged up in the water. There's no ice on the river around the Great Falls. Current's too fast there." He said nothing more until they reached the morgue area, where they stopped in front of locked metal doors. Stillions pressed a button on the wall and waited.

It took a minute for a female in scrubs to approach and open the door. "These are the two I've been waiting for," the agent said.

Silently, she turned and headed down another hallway. "The autopsy won't be scheduled for another day or two." Her words trailed behind her as she walked. "You can view the body, but any information about it has to come from one of the MEs."

"We're just after a viewing for now," Stillions assured her. They followed the woman into another room she had to unlock. Eve had been bracing herself for the smells they would encounter, but the overwhelming scent in the room was one of antiseptic. One wall was lined with white metal doors, each two feet by three feet. The doors were stacked three high. Stopping at one midway down the row, the woman opened its heavy silver door and pulled out the long metal table. Declan stepped forward to the side of the covered body. Even being braced for the expected odor didn't prepare Eve for the reality of it. The overpowering smells of river water and decaying flesh had her swallowing hard a couple times before crossing to stand beside the technician.

Without ceremony, the woman lifted the sheet from the face of the corpse and folded it back. "Not badly bloated," Declan observed, his voice was neutral.

"I'm told the body got hung up on the boulders, which tells me it must have been dumped a ways upstream. If it had gone over the falls it would be in worse shape."

The agent's words had a wave of nausea rocking Eve. The corpse's face was covered with slices in the skin, faintly purpled. No doubt the damage had occurred when it had come in contact with the rocks and debris in the river. The lips were shriveled and pink. The fingers were similarly withered. "How far away was the body from the C&O Canal area?"

Stillions scratched his head. His haircut was so short his scalp was visible. "If this is the same guy who offed Hobart, he doesn't stray far from his favorite spot. Probably thought dumping the body in the water there meant it would travel miles in a couple days. The current is pretty powerful. The body probably would have been long gone by tomorrow if it hadn't gotten hung up on the boulder."

Eve forced herself to study the corpse. Was it Dajana, Brina's friend? The hair was dark, as were the wide staring eyes with pinpoints of red in them. She brought her coat sleeve up to her nose. Breathed through her mouth as she bent closer. There seemed to be bruising around the victim's throat, which had to have occurred before death.

The woman was thin. Brina was too, Eve recalled, as had been the other housekeepers she'd approached. Malsovic probably kept them half-starved as well as imprisoned.

The thought had her looking at the tech. "Can I see her ankles?"

The woman sent a look to the FBI agent and shrugged, silently lifting away the sheet covering the rest of the body. Eve moved further down the table. Brina's electronic bracelet had been on her right foot, she recalled, but there was no matching one on the victim. If this was Dajana, it would almost certainly have been removed before disposing of the body. She peered more closely before looking at the tech. "That looks like bruising around her right ankle."

The technician looked in the direction Eve was indicating. "Those would have occurred ante-mortem, before death."

Would Brina sport the same faint blue smudges on her skin from the constant friction of the heavy bracelet? Eve had to believe she would. "She was dumped nude?"

"Any clothes or covering used to wrap her in would have been torn away by the current." Declan's words had Stillions giving him a closer look. "It'll take the autopsy to tell us what kind of damage was sustained before death."

And if the victim was Dajana, only Brina could give voice to the emotional damage done to the woman. Only she could bring the victim justice.

With unsteady hands, Eve drew her cell out of her purse. "I need to take pictures to show my contact tomorrow for a possible ID," she told Stillions. The man nodded his permission. Eve took several shots of the body from different angles, including a few of the feet. The faint bruises there seemed telling, but she knew they wouldn't be enough for a positive identification. And there were no other identifying marks she could see on the body.

When she'd finished, she replaced the phone and stepped away. Her lungs felt strangled, and she was more than ready to exit the room. But Eve knew she wouldn't be leaving the image of the unidentified body behind.

She intercepted Declan's quizzical look and nodded. "I think we're done here," he said to the federal agent, and the three of them left the room. When they got to the hallway outside the area, Eve gulped in a deep breath.

"I'd like to be notified once you hear from your contact regarding the identification," Stillions said.

"Raiker will let you know immediately," Declan assured him.

"What if she can't make a positive ID from the pictures I took?" Eve thought of the damage to the face of the corpse, the forceful battering the body had taken in the river.

The agent shrugged as he drew on leather gloves that matched his drab brown winter jacket. "There are other methods of identification. Does she have access to items belonging to the missing woman we could get DNA from? Or know of a dentist she might have visited? Even a photo from when the victim was alive could be used by a forensic anthropologist to do a match to the unidentified victim in the morgue." His smile looked more like a grimace. "It just would be faster if she can make an identification from the pictures you took."

They separated in the parking lot outside the OCME building without saying anything more, Eve and Declan moving toward the cab they'd kept waiting while they were inside. "Where to next?" the driver asked once they'd gotten in.

Declan looked at Eve. "I assume our next stop is a

restaurant."

She turned her face to the window, a vivid mental image in her mind of the body they'd left behind. A woman who would never have another meal. Never see her family again. "Let's go back to the apartment. I'm not very hungry."

IN THE END, he called ahead for takeout from Luigi's Pizza, because it was on the way—sort of—and he didn't trust Eve's appetite not to return. It was clear the session in the morgue had rocked her. And while they still needed to talk over the details of the day, he could give her time to regain her equilibrium. Declan still remembered his first dead body. The experience had left marks. It should. Too often those who took death lightly were the ones who dealt it.

He followed her into the apartment, pretending not to notice their tail from earlier this evening had taken up position across the street in the doorway of a liquor store. Maybe he'd see the pizza box Declan carried and assume he'd lost them when they went to get something to eat. It didn't much matter either way.

In Scottish Gaelic he asked, "Are you picking up anything from the transmitter you planted?" He hunted down plates and napkins. He skipped silverware, because using a fork and knife to eat pizza was for sissies. Loading up two plates, he set both on the table before going to the refrigerator for a couple of beers. He'd never seen Eve drink one, but after the day she'd had, Declan figured some alcohol was probably in order.

"Shuang received two calls after we left today." Whereas before she'd affix the earbuds only if she heard sound emanating from it, once she'd entered the apartment, she put one bud into her ear and left the other to dangle free. "Both seemed to be handling problems from the hotel management. One sounded like an issue with the cleaning services, which didn't bode well for the housekeepers, because apparently, a guest complained about stained linens."

Despite her words earlier, she came over to the tiny table and sat down in front of one of the plates. When he twisted off the tops of the beers and set one in front of her, she didn't protest. "She must have blamed Lin, a Chinese housekeeper I spoke to this morning. She summoned the woman to her office and...disciplined her."

He could tell from her tone the punishment hadn't been only verbal. After a pause, Eve went on. "They spoke long enough for me to discern that Shuang likely came from Min Dong, in the eastern Min province, as she speaks with a Minhou dialect." Her mouth twisted. "The housekeeper was allowed to speak far less, but she's almost certainly from Tibet. The second phone call was from someone she called Khalid. And it was much more interesting. Shuang kept assuring him the 'issue' from last night had been taken care of." Eve stared at the pizza on her plate. "I have to wonder now if she was referring to Dajana."

Declan had had the same thought. "She didn't allude to anything more specific?"

"No." For the first time she reached for the pizza. "I can't help but believe she was being purposefully vague. She isn't stupid." She took a bite and swallowed before adding, "And she made a couple of calls while you were torturing me in the dress shop of horrors." He smiled at her descriptor, wistfully recalling the image of her in the blue dress. "No way to tell who she was calling, but it was obviously a male. She was quite upset when her calls went unanswered, and she made a couple of disparaging remarks about his questionable parentage."

She picked up the beer and took a sip. "I had to wonder if she was trying to reach Malsovic."

Declan started with the beer before setting it aside and reaching for the pizza. "Why?"

Her appetite had obviously returned. She took another bite and swallowed before answering. "Today when I entered her office to plant the listening device, I was just about to leave when Malsovic started pounding on the door. I didn't expect him to enter the room without her answering but slipped into the closet just in case. Which was a good thing as it turns out, because he let himself in."

The pizza he'd just consumed turned to lead in Declan's stomach. "He caught you in there?"

Shaking her head violently, she took another bite. Washed it down with a drink from her beer. "No. It sounded like he was trying to get into her computer. From the sound of his cursing, I don't think he was able to. I got the distinct impression he doesn't trust her. Why else would he be trying to access her computer files?"

He was still grappling with what she'd just revealed. Not only had she taken a chance on entering Shuang's private room, she'd very nearly been caught there. Declan felt a cold sweat breaking out on his forehead. "You took a helluva risk."

"The device had to be planted. It was a scary coincidence that Malsovic had a similar idea at the same time I did, but I'm just glad it was the computer he was after and not the safe in the closet."

Now he was the one who'd lost his appetite. Declan set his bottle down with a bit more force than was necessary.

"You don't leave the room without me tomorrow. We'll find a way to talk to Brina together before we leave the hotel."

She was eating in earnest now, not even bothering to set the pizza down to argue. She just waved a dismissive hand at him. Her gesture, coupled with the report she'd given to Raiker earlier tonight, had his temper igniting. "I'm serious. You're to stay put tomorrow where I can see you at all times. The assignment is far outside your qualifications. You don't take the dangers seriously enough. And your inexperience in situations like this puts us all at risk when you take chances you shouldn't. As evidenced by the lost earring today."

Her narrowed blue gaze shot sparks. He should have ignited beneath her glare. "Inexperience?" She set the pizza down on her plate. Wiped her fingers with brisk deliberate movements. "You know nothing about my experience. But I'd think you'd have a bit more faith in your employer's knowledge. After all, he paired the two of us."

He bared his teeth. "We may be partnered on this assignment, but you're stepping outside your realm of expertise here. I'm reining you back in. We'll get the job done without you taking foolish chances."

"Foolish?" It was a good thing they were speaking Scottish because both of their voices had risen. "How did you expect to get the device planted? By donning a cloak of invisibility? If you want assignments without risk, maybe you need to change careers."

"I accept the danger. I just don't accept *you* making the decisions putting us in jeopardy."

Later, he'd realize the exact moment he'd lost control of the conversation. But right now, the fear that had built in him with each new revelation today boiled over into a frothing mass of temper. "Your talent on this case is specific.

Languages. Period. From this moment on, you stick to translation and leave the rest of the case to me."

"You pig-headed, narrow-minded, douche nozzle." He had a moment's panic when he noticed her eyes were glassy with tears. But they didn't negate the heat in her voice. She rose out of her chair so fast it toppled to the floor behind her. "I don't know what burr you've got up your narrow Scottish ass, but you need to extricate it before we walk into the hotel tomorrow. We. Are. Partners. And maybe we each have individual areas of strength, but you don't have near the deductive powers you imagine if you believe my knowledge of languages is all I bring to the table." The rest of her remarks were muttered in a foreign tongue, which he imagined he was fortunate not to understand.

The slam of the bedroom door punctuated her words and brought back all too vivid memories of various female family members enacting similarly dramatic exits from a room. But Eve wasn't being dramatic. She was well and truly pissed. Which was fine, because Declan was pretty pissed himself.

When he was a kid, his gran had spent a few months teaching him to control what she'd called his roiling black fury. He'd been mad at the world back then, lashing out as his family was shredded by a bitter divorce and warring parents. But age and his grandparents' patience had taught him to harness his temper, tamp it down, tuck it in. A man didn't last long undercover if he couldn't keep his feelings in check. And a cop didn't climb through the ranks like he had if he became known as a hothead.

He grabbed the bottle of beer off the table, brooded over it. These days he was the one known in the family for his ability to stay calm and logical amidst theatrical fireworks.

Which didn't at all explain his lack of calm just

moments ago. Hell, hours ago. He couldn't deny something had ignited in his gut when Eve had relayed the details of her day. Even thinking of what might have happened if Malsovic had opened Shuang's closet door could still turn his blood cold.

The image surely was responsible for a bit of this uncustomary flare of anger. Coupled with a white knight mentality that ran wide and deep within him. Recognizing his weakness should have meant controlling it. But somehow control had gone out the window once Eve Larrison had walked into his life.

The thought brought a scowl, and he tipped the bottle to his lips, drained it. Because it was just setting there, he reached for the beer Eve had left behind. He didn't appreciate feeling like his normal restraint had slipped its leash. Just like he didn't enjoy experiencing shame for the things he'd said and how he'd said them. Or the way he'd made her feel.

Which maybe was awfully similar to the way she'd felt growing up in her family of neurotic geniuses.

Declan brought the beer to his lips. Drank. The alcohol didn't make him feel less lousy. A lot of what she'd told him —a lot of what she showed others—was a sham. Or at least only the outer shell of whom she was inside. But he didn't know why she bothered with the farce, and he was a man used to questioning rather than accepting the obvious. He hadn't done so with her—at least not enough—which made her shot about his lack of deductive skills painfully true.

He took out his secured cell and pulled up the Internet. Sipped at the beer as he started searching. And it only took a half an hour for some of the various details about Eve Larrison to click into place.

Sitting back in his chair, he finished the beer while he

considered the picture he'd come up with. The answers had been there. But she was damn good at handing out half-truths. So practiced at the art of deception he could be forgiven—maybe—for not seeing it at first. It was like being expected to put a jigsaw puzzle together when you didn't have the picture on the box to go by.

He had a feeling she'd counted on just that.

There was nothing quite as uncomfortable as knowing you owed someone an apology. Unless it was realizing you'd hurt someone who'd done nothing to deserve it. Because both were true, he got up from the table and went to her closed door and knocked.

He took her silence as permission and eased the door open. Eve was seated upright on the bed. There was nowhere else in the room to sit. Both earbuds were in. And she didn't look up when he entered.

"Eve." The quick glance she flicked his way was wary. He went to the side of the mattress. Nudged her over so he could sit. She took one earbud out. Still silent. She wasn't making it easy. But then he didn't deserve easy. "I was out of line out there. What I said earlier. I'm sorry. I was everything you said. Pig-headed. Narrow minded. And a...what else was it?"

"Douche nozzle."

His mouth quirked. "Although I'm unfamiliar with the term, I figure it's fitting, as well. I didn't give you the respect you deserve. As my partner. My protective instincts can get in the way of my good judgment sometimes, and right or wrong, you seem to set them all off. Which is my problem," he hastened to add when she looked ready to interject something. "Not yours. I made it yours, and I want to apologize."

"It can't happen again." Her tone was as chilly as a

wintry Atlantic breeze. "We have to be able to trust each other's instincts."

"I do. I will," he corrected. "You could have been upfront about your experience. I'm not going to blow your cover for the State Department."

She went still, her eyes huge in her face. "What are you talking about?"

"I mean you said more than once people see what they want when they look at you. I'm betting you've used it to your advantage. You work in IC at the Department of State, don't you? The intelligence community?"

"I have no idea what you're referring to. I've told you before, I translate documents..."

"See, that's part of the problem. The smokescreen you put up." Putting a fist on the mattress beside his hips, he hitched his weight around to more fully face her. "It's convincing. You make damn sure of it. But you're right. My deductive powers were shit for not seeing through it earlier. There were glimmers. Like today, when you were telling Raiker about Brina. I had to look up what a T Visa even is."

She'd gone very still, like an animal scenting danger. "So, it's my fault?" she finally said spiritedly. "You have an interesting way of apologizing. And an even more interesting imagination."

He didn't expect her to reveal details. Whatever she did for DOS, it would rely on secrecy and she didn't owe him a thing. Certainly not her cover. "No, it's not your fault. No one has a right to make you feel like *less*. And I'm sorry I did."

Her eyes held mingled wariness and surprise. And it was the surprise that did it. Whether she was unused to people apologizing to her or shocked to hear him do so, the expression caught something inside him. Something that would have been better off buried.

His hand rose without directive from his brain. With one finger, he traced her delicate jawline. Something about her derailed his usually trustworthy instincts, because they should have been screaming at him now.

Leaning forward, he brushed her lips softly with his. Once. Twice. If he'd stopped there, the gesture could have been construed as an extension of the apology. But, of course, he didn't stop there. Couldn't.

The first taste of her called to something inside him. Eve was a mixture of contradictions, so why would the taste of her be any different? There was softness there. A hint of vulnerability. But layered beneath both was a dark and sensual flavor to tease his senses. One hinting at more, much more than the expected.

His hand cupped her jaw now, fingers at her nape, to urge her closer as his mouth moved against hers. It was pure indulgence. The thought glimmered in the back of his mind before dissipating into bits of haze. A hammering in his pulse had him deepening the kiss. Pressing her lips apart so he could dive a little deeper. As if he could unlock all her secrets just by tasting her.

It was like chasing fire. With every taste he was tempted to delve further. And when her tongue came up to meet his, in one languorous glide, he felt the jolt of it through his system and went in search of the heat.

His mouth ate at hers, devoid of his usual finesse. He hadn't expected to find the contrasts of the woman went this deep. Hadn't expected one kiss could fire an irresistible compulsion to discover even more.

Faint voices could be heard close by. The sound took a moment to filter through the sensual haze. Another one to have his mouth lifting from hers. Awareness flashed across her expression, and she reached between their bodies for the second earbud. Fumbled with it a little as she put it in place. The slightly dazed expression in her eyes lifted abruptly. He had a moment to mourn the change before she whispered, "Shuang."

The name dashed the sensual fog like nothing else could. "On the phone?"

She shook her head. "Talking to someone in the office. Asking where the hell have you been? I called several times. This is unacceptable. You do not have my permission to—" She broke off, appeared to be listening intently. "It's Malsovic she's talking to. She's berating him. Seems enraged. He had to have been the one she was trying to call earlier. She demands to know what he's been doing."

Declan would give a good deal to know the same. If Shuang hadn't known the man's whereabouts, he hadn't been on an errand for her. What else would have taken him away from the hotel so long?

"Every time he tries to answer, she shuts him down. Wow. Says she should have killed him when she had the chance. He says..." Her gaze flew to his. "She wouldn't have known the boy was still alive if not for him. He did the research. He discovered who had him all these years. She owes him respect for bringing her the information."

"The boy. Royce?" The little Raiker had shared about his stepson's birth played across Declan's memory. They already knew Malsovic and Shuang were behind the attempted kidnapping. But could the two also have knowledge about the circumstances of his parentage?

"Shuang says she's the only one who can turn his information to cash. It's useless without her. And so is he. Now he's placating her. Says he's been out lining up resources they'll need for their next attempt." Eve went silent for a moment as she listened. "Shuang isn't buying it. Says she doesn't need him for the next try. He can't be trusted. He says she needs him every time there's a body to be gotten rid of."

A ball of fury knotted in Declan's gut. There hadn't been much doubt about who would have been charged with dumping Dajana. Malsovic's international reputation had preceded him. He was every bit as brutal as Raiker had warned. And the thought of how close the man had come to discovering Eve in Shuang's room today carved a furrow in Declan's chest.

"Shuang is calming down. Demanding to know if he has a place away from the hotel. Apparently, that's forbidden. He denies it. She calls him a liar. Now he's telling her they need more men for the next attempt on the boy. More weapons. She tells him it's not his job to think. Only to do what he's told. Warns him against being out of contact again. He apologizes." Eve listened a few more moments. "She dismissed him. Told him to check on the women. It sounds like he went."

"There's no doubt about who's in charge of the operation. I need to email Raiker the part about Royce." But Declan made no move to get off the bed, still turning over the information in his mind.

"I don't get it." Eve could have plucked the words from his head. "How did Malsovic know to start looking for Royce? Was he around at the time of his birth? Does he know the circumstances surrounding it?"

"Maybe Raiker can find out when the man was in the country under any of his known aliases." Still he wished the two had revealed more. "It would be nice to know how they think they can cash in on kidnapping Royce." The easiest way would be to ransom him to Raiker. But despite the woman's talk of the man at their first meeting, Declan had the feeling she had no real interest in Raiker at all, except as a means to get to the boy.

"Maybe his real parents would be expected to pay if Royce were delivered to them. Maybe they're even working for one of them," Eve said soberly.

"If there was someone who had a right to the child, there are legal channels to go through." He shook his head, trying to recall exactly what Raiker had said about the boy's birth. They still had more questions than answers.

He glanced at Eve. Promptly forgot what he'd been about to say. The overheard conversation might be a break through. It sure as hell had come at a convenient time. Because if there hadn't been an interruption, Declan wasn't at all sure he hadn't been about to make a mistake with Eve Larrison. His brain screamed at him to move. Now. Before he had another lapse of judgment. His body showed no signs of obeying.

Her lips were parted, as if she'd been about to speak before the thought drifted away. Much like his brain cells had. And her eyes...if he looked hard, he could see a remnant of the earlier dreaminess. A hint of the desire that had turned his best intentions to ashes. "I..." It was suddenly difficult to summon logic. "I should email Raiker."

"Yes."

"My cell is on the table."

"Okay."

He gave his head a quick shake to clear it. "So...yeah. Let me know if you hear anything more."

"I will."

Hauling in a breath, he lurched from his perch on the

mattress to go to the bedroom door. And wondered why it felt like he was fleeing.

~

"Mother is being difficult." Jaid grimaced after saying the words. It certainly wasn't the first time she'd uttered them. Nor the first time they'd been true. "The nursing home assures me she's ready for dismissal and needs no follow up care other than to maintain her exercises."

"She's allowed to be a bit out of sorts after what she's been through."

Jaid looked at Adam on the computer screen, wishing she hadn't pushed him to accept a job that would have him hundreds of miles away, for days at a time. Only he could cut through even the most challenging of Patricia Marlowe's moods. Jaid had always suspected her mother was more than a little intimidated by her husband. At least she argued with him much less than she did her daughter. And he was correct. After a serious car accident, two subsequent surgeries and two months of intensive follow-up rehab, the woman could be forgiven for making a few demands.

"I talked to Stephen Mulder this morning. They've dialed the threat level down. It should be safe enough for Patricia to join us. What is she being difficult about?"

Ironically there was a note of tolerance in his voice. Adam indulged Patricia. There was no other way to describe it. Jaid had often thought it was because of losing his own mother when he'd been a boy. "She's taken a liking to one of the CNAs and insists he come with her. A young man. She wants him along to help her with her exercises for the first days on her own."

"Not an outrageous request." Adam's tone was guarded.

"Which one?"

Consulting the notebook before her, she said, "A Rick Sorenson. I talked to Timmons and Garrett. They say he's been attentive to her, but no more than he is to other residents, at least as far as they could tell. I spoke to the head nurse, Becky Carson, and she didn't have any objections."

"I'll take another look at his background check. He'd be allowed no technology, and Timmons and Garrett know what to look for when they search his luggage. I'll get back to you on it."

"Has Gallagher come up with anything helpful on Royce?"

"He and Eve have learned much more than I was expecting, although not all of what they've discovered pertains to Royce." He gave her a quick rundown of the day's events.

"Maybe we should just go ahead and scoop the kidnappers up now." A feeling of urgency surged inside her. "If we think they're acting alone, we may as well take the players out of the equation. They might give us the rest of the details in custody."

"We can grab them at any time. There would be no problem tying Malsovic to Royce's kidnapping, but we have nothing to link Shuang to it, and she's a threat as long as she's free. I want to be sure she's wrapped up tight, even if it's from the trafficking ring they appear to be running."

Jaid heaved a sigh. He was right. She realized it, but sometimes emotion trumped logic. "God help me, once Mother arrives, dealing with her while keeping Royce amused might just turn me to drink."

His smile was wicked. "I'm told Mulder keeps an incredible wine cellar. You'll hold up. This thing is almost over."

"So you keep saying."

"Because it's true." He considered her for a moment, and she had a sudden impulse to smooth her hair. He could make her feel as fidgety as a schoolgirl when the high school football star walked by. "When this is over...you and I are due for a vacation."

"I'm going to hold you to that." She tried for a light tone.

"Use your spare time picking out where we're going to go." His expression, his tone, became more intimate. "Somewhere clothing is optional would be a good start."

Her heart stuttered for a moment, before picking up speed. "I've got a few ideas already."

"Mom! I don't have to go to bed yet, do I? It's not even nine o'clock!"

Her smile turned wry. There was nothing like a nine-year-old hollering in the background to shatter a mood. "Duty calls. Or in Royce's case, bellows. Let me know the moment you hear anything."

"Tell him I picked up some Orioles memorabilia for his collection."

They said their goodbyes, more hurriedly than she would have liked, and Jaid made her way out of the office to where Royce was in a heated discussion with his tutor about bedtime. Baseball was a topic Adam and Royce bonded on, although if Adam had been a baseball fan before her son came into his life, it had been news to her. Sometimes she thought he was the one making all the concessions in their marriage. Taking on a ready-made family with her son and her mother. He never seemed to mind.

Which meant despite the danger swirling around Royce right now, despite all the uncertainty, she'd gotten supremely lucky with the man she'd married.

CHAPTER NINE

"THERE." Declan sat back on his heels to study Eve critically. Twirled a finger. "Turn around. Slowly. Wait." She gritted her teeth as he put his hands on her again, pushing up her loose blouse and making a minute adjustment to her undercover holster tank. The task had the backs of his fingers much too close to the bare skin atop her breast. "The grip of the weapon is still protruding a bit beneath your shirt. Do you have something to wear over it? Like a sweater?"

Eager to escape, she backed away and went to the small dresser. Withdrew a gray cardigan with a tapered hemline and pulled it on. "I didn't need to load the weapon," she groused. "I'm going to sweat bullets."

His mouth quirked at the pun, and again, he gestured for her to turn around while he tipped his head to study her critically. "You'll pass. But only if they don't insist on a frisk."

"I avoided a pat down on the street the day they tried to abduct us. I think I can manage."

He was quiet for a moment, as if choosing his words

carefully. "This is just a precaution. We're not in grave danger. Just being prepared."

Her stomach did a neat flip. She was used to him sugar-coating things for her benefit, but Eve knew exactly why they were both armed to the teeth today. It was the last day of the op. Once Shuang had what she wanted from him— they were dispensable. She knew exactly what was at stake today. They were loose ends.

"Don't worry. I'll do what's required."

That earned her a cool look, but he didn't respond to her words, instead saying, "Is your access to the weapon hampered in any way?"

In answer, she pushed back the cardigan with one smooth move, reaching into the rounded neckline of the blouse and withdrew the gun. His gaze narrowed. "Something tells me you've done this before."

"Carried one. Never had to use it." That detail was critical, she knew. Understanding the mechanics of firing a weapon was not the same as holding it on another human being. Because she'd had enough training to be certain that one didn't point a gun at someone else without the express purpose of using it.

The thought made her pulse go jittery. Surely it was that and not the fact that her flesh still felt hypersensitive everywhere Declan had touched her bare skin. Eve liked to think she would have withstood his ministrations more stoically if not for that kiss last night.

She'd been poleaxed by his apology. It was far better than the half-hearted one he'd tendered when he'd thought she'd awakened him for sex. Men, in her experience, weren't prone to admitting mistakes, at least not without a caveat that shifted at least part of the blame onto another for taking offense to begin with. His apology had revealed another facet of him that she would have been more comfortable believing didn't exist.

The world made excuses for males who looked like Declan Gallagher. Eve couldn't be sure she wouldn't have done so herself. She was a peacemaker by nature and notoriously poor at holding a grudge. Her usual mode of operation would be to carry on the next day as if nothing had happened.

His kiss had made that damn difficult. Just the memory of his lips on hers had a flush heating her system from the inside out. She had no idea what had instigated it. Or why she'd allowed it. Not just allowed. Participated. Enjoyed. Lost just a little brain function.

Okay. Maybe a *lot* of brain function. There was no other explanation. She wanted to believe that she would have put a stop to it. Eventually. But the truth was if Shuang's voice hadn't sounded in her ears, she couldn't be certain exactly what would have happened.

For a woman who'd spent the past eight years fighting to be taken seriously in her workplace, that admission was more than a little appalling.

She trailed after Declan when he left the bedroom and watched him strap on one weapon then secure a second gun in an ankle holster. Eve would do well to follow his example and act as though nothing had changed between them last night.

Because nothing had. He'd made a guess about her work at DOS, one she'd neither corroborated nor refuted. She wouldn't. In mere days, she'd complete this assignment and return to her own work. She'd be finished with Declan Gallagher.

And she wouldn't allow herself to feel regret about that either.

~

"WHAT IS ALL THIS?"

They'd emptied the safe at the bank and carried the contents to the transaction room. Besides the laptop, there was a small electronic device in one case and a larger machine in another. Declan had the laptop powered up and was studying the hotel's bank of security cameras.

"Raiker had it delivered. They're fingerprint and iris scanners. I need them to make a convincing pretense of getting these dirtballs entered into his security system."

She peered at the screen and then at him. "You're not going to alter the hotel cameras now before we get there, are you?"

"I need to do something different from yesterday." He glanced at her and her pulse did a quick jitter, much as it had when he'd walked out of the bathroom that morning. He wore jeans and a white shirt and hadn't bothered shaving. Some men appeared scruffy with stubble. On Declan Gallagher, the effect was devastating. It heightened the sheen of danger that surrounded him and made his gray eyes even more piercing.

Deliberately she looked away. Last night had already proven she was a bit too susceptible to him, and she definitely didn't want to duplicate that error in judgment. "Won't it alert IT if all the floor cameras start acting up at the same time?"

Blessedly, her words had him switching his focus back to the monitor. "Yeah. But I'm going to be at the computer a lot today with the men standing around for scans, and I can't risk them noticing me adjusting the cameras one at a time whenever you alert me about which floor you're on."

"So, what are you going to do with them?"

"I've already changed the angles of the cameras on the guest floors to face the ceiling or a wall. And if you stop talking, I'm going to change the passwords again and write a quick code that will make them shut down completely if someone else starts messing with them."

Eve's brows rose. Clearly, computer work made him testy. But she was intrigued as he scowled at the screen and muttered under his breath, his fingers dancing over the keyboard as he typed what looked like hieroglyphics. She moved away, taking her cell out of her purse. She was adept at her own type of online magic, and she'd take the next little while to work it.

They labored in silence for fifteen minutes before he finally let out a sigh. "Okay. Done."

"As it happens, so am I." She held out her phone to show him the screen. "Your niece's Christmas gift? I found four sites that sell it, compared prices and eliminated the ones that don't offer free shipping. Plenty of time to get it before Christmas."

He took the phone from her and made the picture larger. "So that's a Teeter Popper." His smile was indulgent. "That does look like something Sadie would love. She sent me her gift request through video chat on her mom's iPad. She was quite specific. It must be pink." He handed the cell back to her. "Send me the link, will you? This will score me points with my stepsister Bella, too. She's still harboring a grudge about the guinea pig I bought Sadie for her birthday. Not sure how I was supposed to know it was pregnant."

Hiding a smile, Eve did as he requested. Lots of men were indulgent uncles. Even more loved children. It shouldn't make him more appealing. She told herself that and tried to believe it, because last night had already proven that he was all too irresistible already.

∽

THE VIDEO WAS CONVINCING. Declan had emailed the clip from his phone so Shuang's men could watch it on the laptop he'd brought from the bank. He had to wonder where Raiker had shot it. It showed him with Royce and Jaid in a large living area completely devoid of windows. Although it was well lit, the space had no natural light, lending credibility to the story Declan was spinning about the underground spaces on the property of Raiker Forensics.

The time stamp that appeared in the corner of the screen read "RaikerShelter#1," with a date from earlier in the week. "This would be the main room. There are three bedrooms, a dining area and a couple of bathrooms. Not cramped by any means, but small enough that Raiker wouldn't have many security operatives living there with him." He lifted a shoulder. "And why would he? He'd never believe that an unauthorized person could get on the property, much less access this area. Only a few of his employees even know this space exists."

He waited for the men to watch the entire video. Then stepped forward to tap the screen. "This door? It opens to a staircase that leads directly to Raiker's offices at headquarters. Today, we'll do iris scans and prints on each of you, which I'll relay to my contact still in Raiker's employ. He'll upload them into the computer for the highest security clearance level. No one will stop you. You'll be in the system."

He glanced at Eve who was sitting in a chair across the room, feet tucked beneath her, her cardigan pulled close to her body while she pretended to listen to music. She hadn't mentioned breakfast yet. He wondered if that was because the listening device had picked up something of interest, or if she was biding her time until the housekeeping staff was in place. He suspected the latter.

Returning his focus to the men surrounding him, he flipped to a clip that purported to be from Raiker's offices. Declan had been in the area numerous times and knew the space in the video bore no resemblance to the real rooms. This area was oversized, lined with bookcases and dominated by a desk the size of a small pond. The only similarity between the scene and Raiker's office was the leather furniture scattered about.

He did a close up of the bookcase directly behind the desk. "Between the fourth and fifth shelves," he touched the spot he was indicating on the screen, "you'll find a switch behind the books. That will move the shelf aside and reveal the staircase to the underground shelter. There's another door for you to enter at the bottom of the stairway, but again, it will require iris scans and prints. By the time you're that far, you'll have no problem getting in."

"We will need proof that our information is in the private network," Harris said.

Declan bared his teeth. "And you'll get that proof. As soon as Shuang wires the rest of the money we agreed upon to my account."

They didn't like that. One of them muttered something to the others in a foreign language. Declan turned to the machines he'd set on the table beside the computer. He disconnected his phone from the laptop and plugged in the small print scanner. It was a small slender box no more than two inches by three with a finger-sized groove in the center. Declan turned to the keyboard and brought up a dummy email account created for this purpose. He addressed the mail to his supposed colleague and then looked up to survey the three watching him warily.

"Let's start with Harris." He made a c'mon gesture, pretended to wait impatiently for him to move forward. "Put your finger here. Press down." A moment later a graphic display of the ridges and swirls of the man's prints appeared on the screen in front of them. "What's the name? Spell it for me." The man did so and, Declan typed it below the print. "Stay put for a minute." He switched the print scan for the large camera and rose. "Come closer."

Harris looked at his colleagues before doing as he was bid. Declan held it near the man's right eye. "Don't blink." He took the picture. Moved the instrument away. "The camera will not only capture the image of your iris, it'll do calculations to measure the exact pattern in it. That image will be fed into the scanner, which shoots near infra-red light into the eyeball to determine the unique structures of the iris from the light that returns." Harris stepped away. and Declan busied himself uploading the image to the body of the email with Harris's name and sending the message. He brought up another empty email document and looked expectantly at the two remaining men. "Who's next?"

It was with an odd sense of *déjà vu* that Eve escaped the room again under the guise of ordering breakfast from the dining room. Once she'd done so, she headed for the stair-case toward the upper floors. She had no idea where she'd find Brina but thought the best place to look would be the floor where she'd first found her yesterday morning.

When she peeked out the exit door into the hallway, the familiar housekeeping cart could be seen in front of one of the rooms. She looked in the door and saw Brina, but she wasn't alone. Eve didn't recognize the other woman wearing a maid's uniform. Her gaze went immediately to her ankle. Noted the bulge beneath the thick, white cotton sock.

She knocked loudly on the doorjamb. "I'm sorry to bother you, but I'm having trouble with the ice machine. Could one of you help me?"

The second housekeeper looked at Eve and shrugged helplessly. "No English."

"Please come." Eve gestured into the hallway. "I'll show you." Brina, she noted, was making a studied attempt to not look at her at all as she dusted a lamp. A pretense, she hoped, for the other woman's sake.

When neither of them moved, Eve slapped her hand against the doorjamb, as if peeved. "If I have to call management, believe me, I'll tell them how unhelpful you both have been."

Brina finally looked at the other woman. "We will be in trouble if she complains." Thai, Eve interpreted. Not grammatically correct, but understandable.

"You go. I will not tell Shuang." She flushed under the glare Brina leveled at her.

"You tell her all else. You go."

The second housekeeper shook her head. "Please. I cannot understand what this woman wants. You will keep us both out of trouble."

With a show of unwillingness, Brina stepped over the vacuum cleaner and came to the door. "How can I help you?" she asked in English.

"Thank you so much," Eve said as she turned to lead the way to the alcove that housed the soft drinks and ice machine. "I think the ice machine is stuck, and I can't get my hand up there far enough to unplug it. With your help,

I'm sure we can get it to work." She kept up the chatter until they reached the area in question before dropping the farce. Drawing out her cell phone, she spoke in Serbian, "I have something to show you." Positioning herself in front of the ice machine, she waited for the other woman to stand beside her. Bringing up the pictures she'd taken in the morgue, she murmured, "A body was found in the river."

Brina's gasp told her better than words that their victim had been ID'd. "Dajana." Her whisper was thick with unshed tears. "It is my friend."

"I'm sorry." The words were as inadequate as the rage Eve felt on both women's behalf. "I know this is a horrible shock."

The housekeeper handed back the phone. "How did you find her?"

"I just told others what you had shared with me. There will be help coming. But you can't tell any of the others."

Brina's expression was bitter. "There is no one else I would trust, now that Dajana is dead. They are too afraid. They think they might be next. And Buppha, the girl with me in the room, she tells all she knows to Shuang. She thinks to get favored treatment. Shuang paired us because I got behind yesterday. To make sure I am working my hardest."

"Do the owners of the hotel ever visit here? Do you think they know what is happening with you and the other women?" Maybe the trafficking ring went deeper than Malsovic and Shuang.

Brina shook her head uncomprehendingly. "There are no others. Shuang is the owner of the hotel. I know this because last year I overheard her and Malsovic talking. She said the place is hers, and if he did not do as she says, he could leave."

Shocked, Eve stared at her. Raiker had said the place was owned by a group of Pakistanis, but she knew it was possible to create a false front for a property to hide true ownership.

Belatedly aware of the passing moments, urgency began rapping at Eve's skull. "You must get back before Buppha gets suspicious. Can I find something that belonged to Dajana in your rooms? A toothbrush or hairbrush..." Her words tapered off at Brina's headshake.

"All has been collected and taken away, but no one has asked about the pass key. Maybe they have not thought of it yet." She took a deep breath, as if willing emotion away. "The police...they care that Dajana is dead?"

"Yes. And what is happening with all of you here at the hotel will be investigated," Eve assured her.

The woman looked unconvinced. "Sometimes they need evidence. Like you asked for Dajana's things. They are gone, but I can get you more proof of what they do with us."

"We'll take care of that."

But the woman's face was mutinous. "I can bring you something from Malsovic's room. He has cards. All of us have a picture on one. He hands them out, in a deck, you see? For the men to pick which of us they want. He has many decks. I could bring you one. You could show it to the police."

Nausea, a nasty tangle of it, twisted in Eve's belly. Somehow the information underscored the callousness with which Malsovic regarded the women. They weren't people. They were things. Possessions to be bought, sold and bartered.

And she tended to think the cards would be valuable indeed. Not just to provide a push if justice moved too slowly. But to supply a photo ID to law enforcement of all the women being held, so they'd know who needed rescuing when a raid was launched.

"It's too risky. If he caught you..." He might kill her. Eve left the words unsaid, but the fear she felt for the housekeeper was all too real. Lives were meaningless to the man. And he thought he owned these women.

Skirting her gaze, the housekeeper turned to leave. "I must get back to cleaning."

Eve stopped her with a hand on her arm. The vow came from her lips before it consciously formed in her brain. "I'll go to his room. I'll get a set of the cards to show to the authorities."

Brina fixed her with a look. "You promise this?"

Already Eve was regretting the words. In light of the argument she and Declan had had last night, she knew without asking that he'd disapprove of the plan. But she also recognized that Brina would endanger her life to get her hands on the evidence, and Eve couldn't have the woman putting herself in jeopardy.

She didn't want to make another trip to the morgue.

"Yes. I promise."

Brina nodded once and walked away, leaving Eve with no practical idea of how she was going to keep her word.

She thought about it as she descended the stairway and made her way to the dining room to place an order with a waitress there for room 311. It had taken a pretense to draw out Shuang yesterday, but Eve couldn't imagine what kind of farce would convince Malsovic to vacate his room, short of pulling a fire alarm. And that would have consequences beyond her intent.

Dropping down on a couch in the lobby, she considered the problem. She was no closer to a solution when she saw a familiar face at the far end of the lobby, walking swiftly, a bit hunched over. Eve thought he was headed for the back-lobby exit, but he disappeared around a corner. It was the man who had tailed them. The one who had attempted to force them into a car a few days ago.

He'd been speaking with Malsovic yesterday, she recalled, getting to her feet. She wished now she'd gotten close enough to overhear what they had been saying. Curious, she trailed after him, half expecting that by the time she reached the bend in the hallway where he'd disappeared that he'd be gone. He wasn't. She pulled out her cell, pretended to be engrossed in it as she stood where she could keep him in her peripheral vision. He lounged against a wall, across from the exit as if in wait for someone. Moments later, he was joined by Malsovic.

The two spoke for several minutes, their expressions furtive. Then to Eve's surprise, they both walked out the door together. Without thinking twice, she rounded the corner and, cell still in her hand, half jogged to the exit they'd disappeared through. Neither man was in the vicinity when she peered out.

She couldn't believe Malsovic would leave the property after the tongue-lashing he'd gotten from Shuang last night for having done so. Eve waited another minute but saw no sign of either man. Slowly, she walked back to the lobby. Last night, he'd claimed he'd been searching for things the group would need for their next kidnapping attempt. Shuang hadn't appeared to buy it. Clearly little trust existed between the two. And now, after being expressly forbidden to do so, he appeared to have left the premises again.

It was possible he was on an errand for Shuang this time. Or maybe the men had only walked outside to finish their conversation in private.

Either way, she'd just been handed an opportunity to

get into Malsovic's room without being detected. Slipping her cell back in her purse, Eve swiftly left the area, crossed the lobby and headed for the staircase again. At this rate, she should be pounds lighter before this assignment was over. She used the time walking upstairs to text Raiker that Brina had made a positive ID on photos from the morgue without mentioning what Eve meant to do next.

Sometimes it was easier to beg forgiveness than to ask permission.

On the surface, there was nothing about room 823 that stood out. She'd waited in the stairwell until the hallway was empty, and the housekeeper assigned to the floor was busy, before slipping inside the room. She tried the safe in the closet and found it locked. Then Eve moved to the drawer of the desk and found nothing of note inside.

Undeterred, she went to the dresser. Her fingers faltered when she unearthed two thick black metal bracelets beneath a pile of shirts. Ankle monitors, just like the one Brina had shown her. Eve didn't need to wonder if one of them had belonged to Dajana. Shoving the drawer in, she pulled open another. And discovered stacks of cards bound together with rubber bands.

Withdrawing one, she pulled the band off and fanned the cards out. Revulsion rippled down her spine. In each picture, a woman was pictured in skimpy lingerie and suggestive poses. It was exactly as Brina had claimed. The woman hadn't been wrong yet. She secured them again with the rubber band and dropped them in her purse.

A quick search of the rest of the drawers and the closet turned up extra ammunition for a gun that wasn't present, at least not anywhere she looked. Next, she checked under the mattress. Finding nothing, she looked beneath the bed. Pulled out the nearest item.

It was a bundle of some sort, wrapped in a man's flannel shirt. When Eve unrolled it she saw another handgun, a passport and a driver's license issued by the State of Virginia. The image on the license had her catching her breath. She used the edge of the shirt to flip open the passport. Both photos showed the same male. The one she'd seen a picture of on her first trip to Raiker's office. And again, of the decomposing corpse found at C&O Park. The kidnapper known as Marlin Hobart.

The names on the identification both read Steven Gosling. Drawing out her phone, she took a photo of the license. Flipping through the passport she saw the man listed Sydney, Australia as his native country. But he'd made frequent trips to Serbia and the US.

And somewhere along the line, he'd crossed paths with Malsovic. The fact that he had the dead man's belongings made it seem even likelier that he'd been Hobart's killer.

The only other things under the bed was a rifle and boxes of ammo. Carefully she replaced the bundle, straightened and smoothed the bedspread back in place.

Her gaze landed on the laptop sitting on top of the desk. Crossing to it, Eve lifted the lid, half expecting it to be turned off or password protected. To her shock, it was on, open to a search page. The browser language was set to Serbian. Perhaps Malsovic had been called away abruptly. Or maybe he thought the fact that the language was in his native tongue would be enough of a deterrent to anyone who came looking.

Eve checked the history, bringing up each of the last five searches. The subject of every one of them was Rizqi bin Osman. The man who had owned the property until seven years ago, she recalled. Raiker had said he'd operated a human trafficking ring much like the one in the hotel now. But why was Malsovic checking on the man?

She tucked the questions away for later and moved the search window down to look at his desktop. It was empty. Undeterred, she went to the hard drive and searched for stored documents. Found nothing.

Her pulse was pounding, her heart rapping in her chest. She'd been inside the room for nearly ten minutes, and there were few things she wanted to experience less than being here when Malsovic came back. She restored the laptop to its previous window, closed the lid and walked to the door. Checking the peephole, she saw no one nearby so eased the door open to look out. She wasn't worried about the couple coming down the hallway toward her. They wouldn't know the room she was departing wasn't hers. But the housekeeper just down the hall would.

The walls seemed to press in on her as she waited for the woman to roll her cart to the next room. To go inside it. If Eve had needed proof of what Lafka Malsovic was, she'd seen it here today. Justice couldn't be delivered soon enough.

The first chance she had, she darted out of the room and bee-lined for the stairwell. It was another one for the books. Despite the fact that breakfast would be sent to 311 in thirty minutes or so, once again Eve had lost her appetite.

"I took your men through a simulated breach on Raiker's property multiple times. They have an excellent grasp of the plan that will get them inside to access the family's area." Shuang had brought the weapons down again. Now she stood listening to Declan explain what he'd covered with her employees that day. "I sent their iris photos and fingerprints to my friend inside." Later in the afternoon, Malsovic had come to the room for the first time, and Declan had followed the same procedure for him. He'd left immediately afterwards, without exchanging more than a few words with the other men. Declan gave Shuang a thin smile. "There's a little matter of the second half of my payment to be discussed."

"First I need to see screenshots proving that my employees are in Raiker's security system. Show that to me now, and I will wire the payment immediately."

"I will send you the screenshots this evening. Then if the money doesn't appear in my account within an hour, their identification will disappear from the system." He watched the rage bank in her expression before it was masked. "You are a businesswoman. I'm sure you understand."

"Of course." The politeness in her tone matched his. "You have done us a great service. I am grateful for your assistance."

"It was a pleasure." He aimed a look in Eve's direction, and she lazily unbent her legs from where they were folded beneath her and rose. She wasn't wearing boots today and hadn't had a knife. She'd allowed Amin to search her purse, but no one had made a move to frisk either of them. Declan knew the action had less to do with trust and much more to do with the fact that the other men hid second weapons just as he did. Three against one—or even two—were comforting odds.

"I will look for the email no later than seven o'clock. You can deliver it by then?"

He inclined his head. "It will be there."

"Then you are free to go." Her smile looked forced

when she gazed at Eve as she came up to join them. "You go to the bank again today?"

"It's so tedious, but yes. We have a buyer for our house, and we need to get the liens lifted against it so we can..."

"Honey, Ms. Shuang doesn't want to hear about our financial situation." Declan collected his weapon from the pile on the table, nerves jumping. He could sense the readiness in the other three men. They were just waiting for a signal from Shuang. But he thought they were safe enough inside the hotel. She wasn't about to order a shootout here.

But once they were off the property and she had the proof she required, he knew she wouldn't hesitate to order their deaths.

"Can one of my men drop you off at your destination?"

"No, thank you." He stood, collected his coat from the chair it was draped over. Eve slipped into hers. "We'll take a cab." Declan turned to Shuang. Stuck out his hand. "If there's anything else I can do for you, please let me know."

The air in the room hummed with tension. Her smile was frigid as she placed her hand in his. "Who knows? I may do so."

Zupan tried not to tremble as he was beckoned into the third-floor room where the other men were going over the plans once more. "You have a chance to redeem yourself," Shuang told him. Her Slovenian was mixed with English. "Do not fail me again."

He shook his head violently. "I will not fail." Earlier that day, he'd entered into an agreement with Malsovic, and his allegiance had been bought. But Lafka wasn't here, and a man did what he must to stay alive.

She gestured for him to sit down in front of a computer. "Here is the email account that Gallagher will use to send me the evidence I have requested." She handed him a sheet of paper. "This has the email address I set up for this purpose and the login information. And here is the account number that I must use to make a deposit." She indicated it on the sheet. "I want you to fix it so the money rests there for a few hours before transferring to another account. Is that possible?"

Relief filled him. Zupan would have agreed to anything at that moment, but this was something he was able to do. "Yes, it can be done. I need the account number where you want the money to end up."

She handed him a second piece of paper to study. "I will take care of it." He would succeed, or he would not live to join Lafka in his new plan. And he trusted Malsovic slightly more than he did Xie Shuang.

"We could have overpowered him here." Amin dared to say what Harris and Taufik were thinking. "We could have forced him to give us the evidence you wanted. He would have done anything we asked if we put a gun to his woman's head."

"The man is not stupid. The woman, yes. Gallagher would have taken precautions." She gave them a satisfied smile. "I, too, took precautions. The result will be the same. And I will have the information, the money, while the two will still be dead. Malsovic will make certain of that."

~

"Are we still on the expense account?" Eve pushed away her empty plate. "The sushi here was phenomenal. But I'd have been happy with pizza."

"I'm sure you would have." It occurred to Declan that in all the times he'd had to feed her, she hadn't been difficult to please. "I think we've earned a decent meal after what we accomplished these past few days."

"I sent Raiker the information Brina gave me about Shuang owning the hotel."

He'd been as surprised as Eve by the news, and he was reserving judgment on its accuracy. Despite the questions that remained about how the woman would have managed to acquire the property, he almost hoped it was true. At least then it would be more likely that they had the mastermind responsible for Royce's attempted abduction.

The waiter tipped more wine in Eve's glass, and she sent him a smile that had the poor guy looking more than a little dazzled. She had a way of doing that. If Declan weren't careful, he'd be in danger of being dazzled himself. If he felt himself falling, even a little bit, all he had to do was remember his reaction when she'd told him how she'd acquired that deck of cards.

The familiar burn was back in his belly. He'd kept his reaction to himself this time. At least he'd learned that much from last night. Whatever Eve's previous experience, he had to trust it. And not dwell on what the hell might have happened if Malsovic had come back to his room while she'd been searching it.

Feeling in need of fortification, he sipped from his own glass. It really was damn fine wine. "How is your father?"

"I called a few hours ago, and he sounded cranky." Her smile was wry. "Which probably means he's feeling better. He's already talking about returning to work. Mother will make sure he follows doctor's orders in that regard, however. He's on medication to treat his condition and coupled with the lifestyle changes recommended by his doctor, hopefully he'll be fine."

"He should be feeling better by the holidays." He nodded at the waiter to bring the check.

"Hopefully. Christmas is a bit more festive since the grandchildren arrived." She sipped at her wine. "My parents are atheists, so our celebration of the day when I was growing up was nontraditional. Now, however, there's some limited gift giving when we all get together, although my siblings are insistent that their children receive only educational presents." Her smile was mischievous. "I take pleasure in skirting the rule to make the gifts more fun. Last year, I bought Cynthia an edible chemistry kit."

He had the same philosophy, although he knew most of his family were just waiting for him to have kids for a little payback. Declan wasn't opposed to the thought of children in his future. It was the idea of marriage that had him wary. His gran and grandda aside, his family wasn't noted for their success with long-term commitments. That didn't, however, seem to stop them from skipping into and out of relationships with abandon.

"If all this gets wrapped up soon, it'll be the best imaginable gift for the Raiker family."

Declan nodded. "Adam seemed satisfied with what we've accomplished so far. The cards with the women's likenesses on them will speed up the move on the hotel." He wasn't any closer to appreciating the chance Eve had taken to get the cards, but they verified Brina's story. "With one woman dead, I have to believe the raid on the Latifma is imminent. We're lucky we got what information we did. Likely we wouldn't have been given more time if we'd needed it."

"Twenty-nine women soon to be rescued?" Eve raised

her glass. "I'll drink to that." They were silent for a moment. He knew she felt a special kinship with the imprisoned females. She'd taken risks for them above and beyond what the op had called for. It was difficult to think about what they'd suffered at Malsovic's hands. Whatever they had awaiting them, even if they were sent back to their home countries, it had to be better than the life they'd been forced to live here.

"Why do you think Malsovic was looking up bin Osman?" Eve's fingers absently worried the fluted stem of her glass. "It already seemed as if they were taking a page out of his book. Running the same type of human trafficking ring in the exact hotel bin Osman had. Do you think he's running things from afar? No," she answered her own question before he could weigh in. "If they have a relationship with the man, Malsovic wouldn't need to look him up. Unless it's Shuang who knows him. Is it possible that Shuang and Malsovic were at the Latifma at the same time bin Osman was?"

Declan lifted a shoulder. "Anything's possible. Although neither of their names showed up in the accounts of the raid seven years ago." He stopped to pull out his card and place it on the tray the waiter had produced with the bill. "We're really no closer to figuring out the mystery surrounding Royce's birth." And their failure to do so burned. Circumstances dictated that their time at the hotel was over, but he didn't like leaving a job half done. "Answers to those questions will have to come from Shuang and Malsovic." And would likely require a promise of reduced sentencing to get one of them to flip on the other. That didn't sit well with him either, but he'd learned from his time in law enforcement that justice was often a series of tradeoffs. He knew without asking that Eve would vehemently oppose the sentiment.

"There's been nothing else picked up from the listening device in Shuang's office?"

"No, and that's odd, isn't it?" Pensively, she rubbed at the condensation on the glass with one index finger. The wire holding the earbuds was draped around her shoulders. The MP3 player was clipped to her cardigan. "No phone calls. No talking. The device is voice activated. Either the office has been vacant since we left, or Shuang is working uninterrupted."

He reached for his wine glass. He preferred beer, but his grandfather had a sophisticated palate and an extensive wine cellar. Declan would never be a connoisseur, but he'd developed an appreciation for a well-aged white Bordeaux. "There would have been conversations after we left. You can count on it. Maybe held in 311. Evaluating the information I shared." He paused to drink and then added, "Shuang would try to figure a way out of making the final payment."

"But you sent the last piece of evidence she requested."

"And the payment hit my account—or rather, the one Raiker set up for this purpose—minutes ago." Unless he'd underestimated the woman, she wouldn't give up that easy. There was no reason to alarm Eve. But the danger of their assignment hadn't ebbed since they'd walked out of the hotel alive. It had peaked.

"Raiker thinks she'll send Malsovic after us." Her words, coming on the heels of his resolve to remain silent about it, was enough to rock him a little. "It would be in character. It doesn't retrieve the payment—I can't figure that part out. But that's the reason he won't let us return to the apartment. Or to our homes."

She didn't want his protection. She'd made that clear enough. But it was his nature to calm. "Merely a precaution. We hole up in a secure location Raiker picked out for a day or two." Because surely it wouldn't take more than that for the whole group operating out of the Latifma to be caught up in the raid. "Then we go our separate ways." And if that thought brought a pang, he'd blame it on too much raw fish.

"Sure." She brought her glass to her lips and regarded him over the brim. Taking a sip, she set it down and reached out to pat his hand. "And I don't want you to worry about that armored car with special plates and the driver who looks like a trained operative that Adam sent to fetch us from the bank. The driver is probably really a preschool teacher. And the car likely a rental."

Amusement mingled with annoyance. "Have I told you that you're a smartass?"

She sipped again. "I believe you may have mentioned it."

The waiter returned with Declan's card, and he slipped it in his wallet before scribbling his name and the tip amount on the slip. "All right. Nothing wrong with taking proactive measures, is there?"

"Not at all. But let's call them what they are." Her gaze caught his, held it. "I don't require mollycoddling. I thought we settled that last night."

He was beginning to believe they had settled very little the previous evening. Had in fact started something that he was still grappling to come to terms with. "We did. We have more to settle on the way to our temporary home, however." Pulling out his cell, he texted the driver to bring the car to the back entrance of the restaurant. Then rose.

Eve followed suit. "And what's that?"

"The sleeping arrangements for this evening." Her

expression showed a gratifying flicker of shock, followed by another emotion too fleeting to be identified. His hand touching her elbow lightly, he walked them to where they'd left their coats. "If there's only one bedroom this time around, I'm telling you right now, you get the couch. My back is starting to feel like an accordion."

"The one and perhaps only benefit of being short is that I'll never suffer from the same problem." Her pause was deliberate. "So, I'll flip you for it."

The words lightened something in him. He helped her with her coat. Donned his own. "An offer that embodies the Christmas spirit. You're on." With his coin. And him doing the flipping. He liked his odds better that way.

When it came to Eve Larrison, he'd take any edge he could get.

The restaurant was flanked front and back by heavily trafficked streets, surrounded by parking on all sides. The back had been the least congested when they came in, but it was full of cars now. Their vehicle was idling fifteen feet from the door. The driver, Kellan Burke, was indeed one of Raiker's operatives. Like Declan, he'd started out in law enforcement, although Burke had been with the Baltimore Police Department prior to joining Raiker Forensics.

Icicle lights dangled from the overhang of the restaurant's roof, spilling more light into the lot and lending it a faintly festive air. Burke got out of the car. Began rounding the hood. A taxi pulled into the lot and stopped parallel to the vehicle. A heavily bundled driver exited to open the passenger door on his side. Took something from the back seat and whirled around.

"Gun!"

Declan would never know which of them shouted it first. He tackled Eve, taking them both to the ground with

Burke's car between them and the taxi. The crack of the first rifle shot was loud. The next two shots pinged off metal, kicked stone from the restaurant siding that was flung back at them like tiny razor-sharp missiles.

"Stay down!" He scrambled to their vehicle. Burke had taken up position behind the right front wheel, so Declan took the back. Kell fired twice before Declan got his gun wrestled from inside his coat and fired, ducking when the rifle sounded again.

Eve appeared at his side, weapon in her hand. He spared her a quick hard glance. "I told you—"

"To stay down. I am." She belly-crawled a foot from him and aimed her weapon beneath the armored car. Put three rounds in the taxi's front tire. The vehicle began to list to one side almost immediately.

The shooter fired twice more. Then he was running, darting for cover between the parked cars. Declan and Kellan rose as one to give chase. The man sprinted out into the traffic, barreling across the street, his escape accompanied by screeching tires and blaring horns as he dodged cars and bolted to the opposite curb and down the sidewalk.

Burke ran to the edge of the parking lot, but Declan already knew it was a lost cause. The shooter had disappeared from sight, swallowed up by the crowd on the opposite sidewalk, their fists clutching shopping bags.

Belatedly, he turned to look for Eve, found her getting to her feet, her weapon still in one hand while she brushed ineffectually at the dirt on her pants. When she turned to face him, his stomach did a quick vicious lurch. "Goddammit, Evie." He closed the distance between them with two quick steps. "You're *bleeding.*"

CHAPTER TEN

MALSOVIC KEPT his head low as he shouldered his way through the crowd and darted into an alley at the first opportunity. Despite the mobs of people, a man couldn't walk down a street in this neighborhood carrying a rifle and expect to go unnoticed.

He unloaded the weapon as he walked, slipping the ammo into his pocket with the ejected brass he'd scooped up before making his escape. He ditched the rifle in the first Dumpster he came to and continued moving fast. Not running. Police in this country associated running with guilt.

It had been a calculated risk to take out Gallagher behind the restaurant, and his failure to do was upsetting. The man wasn't dumb enough to go back to the apartment where they'd been staying. Even Malsovic gave him that much credit. So, the options had been to try for them when they'd stopped to eat, or to follow them to their new home. He'd liked the odds of the restaurant.

Èmó would be enraged. He couldn't go back to the hotel even if he wanted to. He didn't. After his final meeting with

Sorenson this morning, Malsovic had put his own plan in motion. He didn't need Shuang anymore. The boy would soon be his, and he wouldn't be sharing the proceeds with anyone.

Still, a man had his pride. And it was rare indeed for him to leave a target still standing.

He detoured into a store doorway and pulled out his phone. Texted Zupan an address. It was important that he meet with the man before Shuang knew of his failure with Gallagher and the blonde. When she learned of it, she would send people for him. He wasn't worried. She had no one in her employ who could match him in skills or cunning.

And soon—very soon now—that cunning would make him rich beyond his wildest dreams.

"I'm FINE." Her tone reflected her rapidly deteriorating patience, both for the agents flanking her and the hours-long process after the shooting. "I don't need the bandage changed. Dammit, Declan." Just as he'd been doing for most of the evening, he ignored her objection, merely brushing away the hand she brought up to protect her cheek and gently loosening the tape around the gauze there.

"Just let him baby you some." Kellan Burke's green eyes twinkled behind his trendy, dark-rimmed glasses. "You're not going to stop him anyhow. The way he's fussed over your wound, I thought maybe you'd been gut shot. Bet that shaved a couple years off his life."

"Remember, I saw you moments after Macy went into labor," Declan said mildly, peeling down the blood-soaked gauze and reaching for the antiseptic cream. "I figured they were going to have to get a gurney for you."

Burke winked at Eve. "Sympathy pains. I'm a very empathetic guy. Surrender to the inevitable. It'll make him feel better."

Inevitable was an apt word for what they'd been through since the shooting. They were still in the police conference room. Their statements had been held up while FBI agent Cal Stillions had been summoned, and she'd been diverted for a totally unnecessary trip to the ER to remove the small slivers of stone and debris that had lodged in her cheek and forehead. Her protests that she could clean the damage herself with tweezers had been overruled. Mostly because of Declan's insistence that she get expert medical care.

She blew out a sigh and did as Kellan advised. Slumping in her chair, she withstood Declan's ministrations with the last remnant of patience she could summon. The wounds would continue to sting for a while, but they didn't require this level of solicitude. Her nerves were still hyper alert after the shoot-out. Surely that was the reason the merest brush of his fingers left a trail of heat in its wake.

Looking at the man from beneath her lashes, she wondered where all his concern stemmed from. Or maybe she already knew. He had a protective streak a mile wide. She could live with that. But she couldn't—wouldn't—stand for any misplaced guilt he might be feeling about her minor injury.

The door to the conference room opened, and Stillions walked in again, without the police detective this time. His gaze went from the bag of first aid supplies the hospital had sent with her, and then to her wound. "Damn, Gallagher, you could moonlight as a medic."

Eve silently agreed. Certainly, his touch was as gentle as the nurse's had been when her wound was cleaned and dressed earlier. The actual extraction of the tiny splinters of stone had been a little less pleasant. "I hope you're going to tell us we can go home. Finally." Not home, actually, but to yet another unfamiliar location. She didn't even care about that as long as it had food and a warm bed.

"Eventually." The man draped his painfully thin body over the back of a chair across the table and surveyed them. His suit was navy today. Just as ill-fitting as the brown one she'd seen him in at the morgue. Eve wondered if the man were recovering from a long illness.

"I just got off the phone with Raiker." He paused a moment while Declan placed new tape on the bandage to keep it in place. "Since he last spoke to you two, he got a hit off the prints from the pen you gave him." His inflection made it a question. At Eve's nod, he went on. "The woman you've been dealing with isn't Xie Shuang. Her real name is Sun Yanyu. She was scooped up in an ICE raid here in DC seven years ago and returned to China."

A niggling sense of intuition made Eve ask, "Do you know the location of the raid?"

The man rubbed his narrow jaw. "Now that you mention it. It was a hotel called the Kaula. I believe you know it as the Latifma."

Eve and Declan exchanged a glance. "There's coincidence, and then there's exact duplication," she murmured.

"Raiker said he had pictures taken of her that first meeting. They aren't an exact match for the photos immediately after the raid, although the resemblance is there. I'm guessing she's had surgery to alter her appearance. Changed her nose. Narrowed the jawline."

"And how would a woman who was ostensibly held as a

sexual slave find the money for those sorts of procedures?" Eve wondered aloud. Her imagination was filling in answers to the mental questions that rose, and she needed to sort through them before reaching any conclusions. She was tired, more than a little grumpy and not at all inclined to give Xie Shuang—or Sun Yanyu—the benefit of the doubt.

Whatever she might have experienced in her past, it was what Shuang was now that mattered. And everything they'd discovered about the woman said she was nothing short of a monster.

Declan wadded up the wrappings and old bandages and got up to drop both in the metal trashcan in the corner of the room. Then he started putting the supplies they'd used in the sack. "Raiker say anything else?"

"Just that everything you need would be found in the safe house Burke is taking you to. Your weapons will be returned after the investigation into the shooting. Since you named Lafka Malsovic as the probable suspect, the DCPD and FBI are currently planning a joint sweep of the hotel. I'll be on location."

Relief spread inside her. A rescue would be mounted. Brina and the other women would soon be safe. Hopefully before Shuang discovered that Malsovic had failed his mission tonight. She didn't trust what the other woman might do in a fit of temper.

"Did they find any brass on scene?"

The agent shook his head woefully at Declan's question. "But officers are canvassing the area. Maybe they'll get lucky and find the weapon. He would have had to dump it unless he had a vehicle pick him up nearby."

There would have been time to arrange for that, Eve thought, with a sidelong look at Declan. If Malsovic had followed them to the restaurant, he would have known he had at least an hour in which to make arrangements.

"What'd you find when you traced the cab?" Kellan Burke spread his hands when Stillions stared at him. "C'mon, it'd be the first thing you'd look at and the easiest to follow up on."

"They're still sweating the cabbie in one of the other rooms. He claims he was carjacked on Fifth and Central, but all the cabs are equipped with GPS tracking. His last reported stop before that was the Latifma Hotel."

"Damn canny move," Burke muttered, his chagrin apparent. "Easy enough to spot a tail, especially on streets as congested as we were traveling. But the ratio of cabs to cars is about two to one downtown. He didn't make the mistake of following us into the parking lot too soon. He was waiting somewhere nearby, ready when you two came out."

"Well, he got a bit more than he bargained for there." Declan's smile was grim. "I would have liked to think one of us hit him, but I didn't see any blood on the pavement. Probably just wishful thinking."

"With luck, we'll pick him up tonight."

Eve's head jerked up to stare at Stillions. "The raid is tonight?"

"Did I say that?" The man looked bemused. "Surely not. It's not like me to give away classified information. But the matter has taken on more urgency with DCPD's need to bring in Malsovic for questioning. And the Bureau isn't about to let them into that hotel without us, so..."

Eve reached over to squeeze Declan's hand impulsively. The women had hours rather than days longer to suffer. Relief flooded through her. When he turned to look at her, she almost snatched her hand back, conscious of her action. But before she could do so, his fingers shifted so he could skate his thumb across the back of her hand. The action left a trail of heat in its wake. She eased her hand away. The culmination of events in the past few hours were definitely affecting her if she was susceptible to his slightest touch.

Eve caught Burke's eyes on them and read his thoughts in his slow wicked smile. Her glare had him wiping the grin from his face, but she knew it lurked beneath his purposefully sober demeanor. His mind was all too easy to read, but he was wrong. She'd make sure of it.

Vulnerability wasn't a trait she'd cultivated over the years. It would never have been tolerated in her family. Nor would it have furthered her career at the State Department. Weakness wasn't in Eve's vocabulary.

And she wasn't about to change that by being weak with Declan Gallagher.

"You know, Eve and I could be valuable assets when it comes to tonight's raid."

Declan's words startled her, but they didn't have any noticeable effect on the federal agent. He just raised a brow. "How do you figure?"

"How many languages would you estimate are represented by the women held at the hotel, Eve?"

"Chinese, Thai, Serbian, Slovenian...no telling how many others."

Declan gave a slow nod. "She can save you a ton of time with translation when the women are brought in."

Stillions seemed to give the words consideration. "That could be helpful after the raid. Doesn't explain a need for you having a part, though."

"I know the inside of the hotel." His smile was complacent. "I assume your warrant will include access to its security system, and I rewrote the code for the cameras." He had, Eve recalled, just that morning, although he'd returned them to working order this afternoon. "Not to be immodest, but it'll take hours for Cybercrimes to crack it. I'm guessing that's energy your team would rather focus elsewhere. I can switch the cameras on and off, alter their views to your split-second recommendations, watch for civilians... I'm a useful guy."

Silence stretched long enough for Eve to grow uncomfortable. Stillions fixed Declan with a gimlet stare. "And you did all this without a warrant."

"I sort of stumbled into the online security by accident."

"Uh-huh." The agent's sarcasm was unmistakable. But after a long moment, he lifted a shoulder. "All right. You can have a *limited* role."

From the look on Declan's face, Eve knew he'd gotten exactly what he wanted. Her stomach did a slow roll as she considered the ramifications. They'd already been shot at once tonight. She hoped Declan's part in the raid wouldn't put him in the line of fire again.

"How LONG HAVE you had this place, Lafka?" Zupan wandered around the small space, poking into all the cabinets and the refrigerator. He made a pleased sound when he saw a six-pack inside but had the good manners to close the door without taking a beer.

"A while." They spoke in English because Malsovic was too damn tired to try to recall the smattering of Slovenian he'd picked up over the years. Zupan had told him about Shuang's account that he'd just bounced money to. If he had managed to move it once, surely he could again—into one of Malsovic's. The money would go a long way toward paying for the abduction operation he was putting together.

What he'd spent on it so far that day had all but bankrupted him.

"There is no need for you to go back to the hotel. Shuang grows more unpredictable all the time." The other man bobbed his head in agreement. "I fear this plan of hers will get us all killed. I have a better idea. We will get the boy before her. We'll share the riches from that equally."

Zupan was a simple man. He had to be to believe that Malsovic would cut him in for half when the other man brought nothing of note to the table. However, if he could really move Shuang's money...that might be worth a bonus.

Cash was the best way he knew to buy loyalty. Èmó hadn't realized that. She'd ruled through fear and brutality. Violence had its place, but the way the woman operated, she wouldn't have the manpower to make another attempt for the boy. Once she discovered Malsovic had failed to kill Gallagher, her rage would have no bounds. That did not bode well for the men still in her employ.

"I have not heard much of her plan," the other man was saying. "Taufik, Harris and Amin have been avoiding me."

"So let them be the ones to suffer Shuang's wrath. And take all the risks for her."

The other man nodded, a slow smile spreading across his face. "Yes, let them feel her whip when they..." His gaze traveled across the small space to the laptop open on the sagging couch. "What is that on your computer? That blinking light?"

Malsovic followed his gaze. "That...that is what hundreds of thousands of dollars look like." The less the other man knew, the better. So he didn't tell him about Rick Sorenson, or the man's relationship with Jaid Raiker's mother. The young man had performed well so far, as the location mark on the computer screen showed. Sorenson surely would have been searched before being allowed in the car with the old woman, so Malsovic had told him to find a way to slip the GPS device into the lining of the old lady's bag.

He walked over to the computer now, sank down on the stained couch. Frowned as he looked at the screen. GPS would provide him with a foolproof way to be certain of the boy's location before he put himself into danger by going after him.

But something was wrong. The map surrounding the blinking light didn't show the area where Raiker's compound was located. It was two hundred miles to the south and east.

A jolt of rage seized him. Had Sorenson double-crossed him? Tossed the device into a passing car?

"Lafka, what is the matter?"

He couldn't answer. Could barely see through the fog of fear and fury that was consuming him. He zoomed in on the map. Looked closely at the surrounding area. It was on the ocean, or close enough to it that it made no difference. Why would the old lady's suitcase be... Comprehension swept through him then. Gallagher had lied to Shuang. To the other men. The boy wasn't on Raiker's compound at all.

He was a couple hundred miles away. Safe. Or so Raiker believed.

Malsovic began to laugh, and Zupan took a careful step away at the ugly sound. This was too good. Much too good. He had been afraid that Shuang's plan would get them killed, and all this time, he'd been right. Gallagher must have deliberately attempted to set them up. The video that showed the boy on Raiker's compound had been a fake.

And Shuang was prepared to send her men into a trap.

"Come." He closed the computer and unplugged the

power cord, leaving the small MiFi device attached. It would allow him to access the Internet even in the truck, and they would be taking a trip now.

"Where are we going?"

He glanced at the other man. "Bring the beer you saw in the refrigerator. We have a journey ahead of us." First, they needed to walk to where they'd parked the panel truck he'd rented today, which Zupan had used to pick him up earlier. The lot they'd left it in was at least at a mile away. "I will drive you to the hotel. You must go to my room, bring me all the digital equipment I have there and my passport from the safe."

Zupan had looked much more enthusiastic about the beer than he was about returning to the hotel. "I thought you said I didn't have to go back there?"

"You don't. Not to stay."

The man set the six-pack on the table as he picked up his coat. "I should get my passport, as well. I will go in the back entrance. Take the cargo elevator. No one will see me."

There was no reason for the man to get his passport, because Malsovic had no intention of leaving the country with him. But that news was not for now.

"Yes, you should have your ID. Then we go for a drive."

Once he made certain he'd found the right property where the kid was being kept, there was still much work to be done, and quickly.

Urgency pressed at his skull as he donned his coat, picked up the computer and headed out the door. Zupan carried the six pack inside his jacket. Malsovic had everything in place. He just needed to adjust the location.

Success was so close he could all but taste it.

~

"No NEED TO flip for the bed."

"Honesty compels me to admit I was planning on cheating anyway." Declan prowled through the space after he'd unloaded their weapons and put them away. Checking the security, Eve thought, but also mapping the condo where they'd be spending at least the next several hours.

"Really." She smirked. "I was going to use my own coin. And flip it myself."

"You..." In the act of poking his head into one of the bedrooms, he glanced at her over his shoulder. "I would never have suspected it. And you look so innocent, too."

"Sometimes that comes in handy." Eve walked over to the other bedroom and was surprised to discover that her bag was already sitting on the bed. Someone had packed their things and delivered them here. She wondered if Burke had drawn that duty, too. "Maybe you'd like to play a game of Blackjack later."

"Why do I have the feeling I'm being sandbagged?" There was a tinge of amusement in his tone. She was pretty sure that she'd rob him of that after four hands of cards. As well as most of what he had in his wallet.

"Dibs on the bathroom first."

She went in to take out her toiletries and fresh clothes. It gave her an odd feeling to know that a stranger had packed her things. But that feeling was the last of her worries when she got to the nicely appointed bathroom and stripped off the blouse and sweater before taking a look in the mirror for the first time in hours.

"Oh. My. God." Aghast, Eve leaned closer to her reflection to assess the damage.

"What?" He was across the apartment and by her side so quickly, she jumped a little. Clearly she'd neglected to lock the door.

"This." She gestured to herself. "I look like the wrath of God. If God gets as irritated as I do by frizzy hair and a banged-up face."

He leaned a shoulder against the doorjamb. When had he unbuttoned his shirt? Because her gaze wanted to linger on that wall of muscled chest with its neat pattern of hair, she forced her eyes back to the mirror again. Winced.

"I think God might cut you a little slack given the day you've had." His eyes met hers in the mirror. "The cuts will heal. And the curls..." His mouth quirked. "They're actually sort of cute when they do that spiral thing."

Cute. She couldn't prevent an eye roll. All that was missing was a pat on the head and a lollypop.

"Great. What's next, the inevitable Shirley Temple joke?" She'd heard it ever since she could remember.

His brow furrowed. "Who? You mean that little kid in the old movies? You look young, but not that young. No one would mistake you for a kid, Evie."

There was heat in his eyes, a sudden flare of it. And that quickly, her ire dissipated. She was tired. Surely she was misinterpreting the look in his eyes. The note in his voice when he called her "Evie."

"The cut on your forehead bled the worst." His jaw went tight. "Seems like they always do. You had blood in your hair. Pouring down your face. I thought you'd been grazed by a bullet. Or worse." She watched, frozen, as he reached out to touch the shoulder of her tank. There was a quarter-sized bloodstain there, which meant that the blood had soaked through her sweaters. She hadn't noticed. Just like she hadn't noticed until now that the holster tank was body-hugging tight.

Eve swallowed. "I think there were a few spots where my scalp got nicked. They cleaned them out with antiseptic. They probably bled the most." The intensity in his gaze made it difficult to think. She had the oddest urge to raise her hand, to stroke his shadowed jaw. To press her mouth to its hair-roughened surface before moving her lips to his.

There were reasons—good ones—why the idea was unwise. But they seemed difficult to summon. Her thoughts had scattered. His face lowered to hers. Without conscious volition, she took a step closer.

The distant sound of a voice had her jumping as though she'd been scalded. Uncomprehendingly, her gaze met his. The desire she saw there made everything inside her going molten.

Then he looked past her, to where the receiver sat on the counter. "We've got audio."

She turned to grab the earbuds, fumbling to put them in place. It took a moment for her to make sense of what she was hearing. "Shuang is on the phone. Speaking Malay." She listened intently for a minute. "She's trying to convince someone named Umar to help arrange contact with Rizqi bin Osman." Eve broke off, focused on the conversation a while longer. "He must have refused, because she's hung up, and she's furious. Throwing things, from the sound of it and muttering some very imaginative curses in Chinese."

Declan looked as mystified as she felt. "Why would she be so desperate to speak to the man who had enslaved her up until seven years ago?"

"Maybe Brina was wrong. Maybe Shuang isn't the owner of the hotel."

She didn't even complete the thought before he was shaking his head. "You think she's working for him? Again, why would she? And if she were, why would she have to arrange contact through a third party?"

Shuang's tantrum seemed to have subsided. It sounded

as if she was typing at her keyboard. "We might discover those answers tonight."

He cleared his throat. Didn't meet her gaze. "No telling how soon Stillions will call. I'll take the shower after you."

"Right." She could be as studiedly nonchalant as he was. More so. She turned to rummage in the cupboard for a towel. Clutched it tightly as she gestured to the door. "I'll just, um, get started."

"Yeah." He still wasn't looking at her. "Okay."

It helped, a smidgeon, that he appeared as discomfited as her. "If you could?" She made a shooing motion. "Go."

The word seemed to jolt him into action. Silently, he turned and went through the door, easing it shut behind him. She propped her free hand on the counter, the strength streaming from her limbs. That was twice the listening device had interrupted them, and the irony wasn't lost on her. Hopefully, Shuang would be in custody in a matter of hours. And when she was, Eve would have to figure out a way to resist Declan Gallagher on her own.

It would help, she thought as she moved to turn on the shower, if she could recall why it seemed so important that she continue to do so.

"THE CAMERAS WERE RETURNED to their normal position around noon today, so if anyone suspected that they weren't working properly, they'd believe the problem had taken care of itself hours ago." Declan covered his whisper mic with his hand when he spoke, to avoid having his words broadcasted to the tactical team in place outside the hotel.

Eve, Cal Stillions and ICE Agent Fred Turpen huddled in the backseat of Stillion's vehicle, peering at the screen of

Declan's laptop which showed all eighteen cameras. The men were clad in flak jackets emblazoned with their agency name, worn over Kevlar vests. They were equipped with mics, as well. It had been made very clear to Declan that Stillions hadn't been kidding about his limited role. Despite the fact that he wore a mobile laptop harness so he could easily carry the open computer, he had strict orders to remain in the vehicle with Eve, providing the team members with intelligence regarding any activity shown on the cameras. If Declan chafed under the restrictions, he consoled himself that any role at all was better than sitting in the apartment wondering what the hell was happening.

Declan tapped on the camera for floor fifteen, bringing it to a full screen view. It showed an empty hallway for several moments. Then the elevator doors opened, and Harris stepped out with a slight, dark-haired woman wearing a very short, tight red dress with stilt-like heels. He gave her a small push, and they headed toward the end of the hallway.

"Brina told Eve that one of the men guarded them all night, so there may be another in room 1501 or 1502." He checked the time on the computer. Just after one AM. "No way to know whether some of them may still be in a customer's room, but with the electronic bracelets they wear, I'm guessing the prostitution activity takes place on the premises."

"We've got the cards." Turpen spoke for the first time, his palm covering his mic. "If they aren't all accounted for in the two rooms, we'll go looking for them."

"But what if the guard is armed?" Worry sounded in Eve's voice. "It could easily turn into a hostage situation."

"We've done this before, Ms. Larrison," Stillions reassured her. "We have precautions in place."

Declan sent her a quick glance in the shadowy interior of the car. She was astute enough to realize that as well planned as these operations were, something unexpected could always crop up, sending the op haywire.

It was a multi-agency operation. DCPD was providing the tactical team, and both FBI and ICE were on scene. But from what he could tell, it was Stillions at the controls.

"Breach in five." The disembodied voice from the sergeant in the command unit down the street sounded. Without another word, the two agents got out of the car and disappeared into the night.

Declan brought up the image for the front desk. There was only one attendant working, and he was staring intently at something on his phone. The lobby was deserted. He knew from what he'd seen minutes earlier on the images that officers were already in place outside the other exits. Declan had run off the blueprints of the property that Raiker had provided them when they started this assignment. No one would be escaping the hotel.

Eve angled closer for a better view of the computer. "You'd have to have nerves of steel to do this for a living," she muttered. He zoomed in on the image of floor fifteen again. "Adult male seen exiting room 1501," he said quietly into the mic. "Probably leaving at least one guard inside the room." Harris was walking quickly down the hall and disappeared into an open elevator. Declan reverted to the screen showing the multiple camera views. The other images for the guest floors showed empty hallways.

Eve's slight gasp alerted Declan. He glanced up and saw a long stream of officers in riot gear running up to the front entrance. He could make out Stillions' lanky form at the rear as the men entered the facility. Returning his gaze to the laptop, he saw that several men splintered off and ran toward the front desk, surrounding the clerk on duty. "You have an elderly gentleman on floor six with an ice bucket in his hand heading east down the hallway," he said quietly into the mic.

"Entrance secured," came a voice.

"Adult male seen leaving fifteenth floor has entered a room on floor eight, south side of the hall," Declan reported. Malsovic's room was on the eighth floor, and he wondered now if all of Shuang's men had rooms close together. "Likelihood of at least four armed accomplices on floor eight."

"Floor eight, 821, 822, 823. Floor seven, 701. Floor fifteen, 1501, 1502," came a voice. Declan figured they'd gotten the needed information from the attendant at the front desk.

"Floor one clear," another voice sounded.

There wasn't a camera on the main floor that wasn't near an exit, so Declan had no way of monitoring the team's movements except for the snippets that came through the mic. Time seemed to slow. Stretch interminably. "Floor six is clear again," he said as the older man returned to his room with the ice bucket. Another minute passed.

A door opened on floor seven. And Declan knew who he'd see coming out of the room. "Armed woman in the hallway of seventh floor. Heading to the elevator."

"Shuang," Eve breathed.

Adrenaline was spiking, but he kept his voice calm as he marked the woman's progress on the camera. "Entering elevator on floor seven." An officer was supposed to have dismantled the elevator operation, Declan knew. If he'd been successful, Shuang wouldn't get far.

A moment later she reentered the hallway. "Armed woman left elevator and is back in floor seven hallway," he said. He watched her progress for another second before her intentions became clear. "She's heading toward stairway."

Simultaneously he heard, "Prepare for entry."

"Do not enter floor seven." It took effort to keep his voice calm as he tracked Shuang's movements. "Shooter on floor seven."

There was a burst of activity on some of the cameras. SWAT officers poured out of the stairwell onto the eighth and fifteenth floors and swarmed toward the predetermined rooms, parting for the two tactical officers holding a battering ram. Once one door was breached, the duo would take on another, while other officers raced into the room, weapons ready.

"Shooter on floor seven nearing the stairwell." Team members in riot gear were coming out of one of the rooms on the eighth floor to join their teammates who had breached the other two rooms. He could hear screams through his mic, and Declan knew they came from the awakened women in rooms 1501 and 1502.

"Armed woman on seventh floor four, steps from stairwell door." Declan monitored Shuang's movements closely. "Weapon in right hand. Reaching for doorknob with left in three...two...one." The scene exploded a moment later, and a tactical officer carrying an armored shield burst through the door, slamming into the woman, knocking her off balance. He was joined by several other officers. One of them tackled Shuang, dislodging the weapon from her hand and restraining her while another performed a body search.

The eighth-floor camera showed the policemen herding a couple of handcuffed men from two rooms next to each other. Harris and Amin. The one on the fifteenth showed a subdued and restrained Taufik flanked by two tactical team members, while others tried to contain the stream of women coming from the two rooms. All wore shapeless cotton gowns and were barefoot. Each had a thick black bracelet encircling one ankle. In the milling crowd, it was impossible to count to see if twenty-nine women were accounted for.

"They won't have coats," Eve whispered.

Without switching his focus from the laptop, Declan reached out to link his fingers with Eve's. With all the activity in the past few minutes, her concern remained with the women. He knew without looking that her gaze would be searching the image shown on the fifteenth-floor camera, searching for Brina.

It was with no small measure of satisfaction that he watched Shuang hauled to her feet, arms bound behind her, and hustled through the stairwell she'd been attempting to access. Since English wasn't the woman's first language, there was a good chance Eve would be involved in the woman's interrogation. And that, he thought grimly, was a scene he was going to insist on watching. He couldn't wait to see her face when she realized that they were still alive, and that she'd been duped by the two of them. Given the tantrum they'd heard on the receiver earlier this evening, she wouldn't take the news calmly.

"Do you have a visual on Malsovic or Zupan?" Stillions' voice sounded on the mic.

Declan felt Eve's hand squeeze his. "Negative. No image since we've been stationed here."

"We'll start clearing the floors one at a time. But chances are, they aren't on the premises."

"Eve spotted the two of them leave the hotel this morning, but I saw Malsovic this afternoon."

"We'll keep looking."

"If they don't find him..." Eve murmured.

"I know." Declan's voice was grim. As long as one of the

players in Royce Raiker's abduction attempt was on the loose, the boy was still in danger.

In contrast to the quick eruption of activity when the raid had been in progress, the next hour crawled by. He relayed the details that came from the whisper mic to Eve. They watched Shuang, Amin, Taufik and Harris get hustled away in police cars that had arrived on scene. Shortly afterwards, a chartered bus pulled up close to the front entrance. "The women are being brought to the elevators on the fifteenth floor," Declan told her. Before he knew what she was up to, she pulled her hand from his and opened the door. "Stay here."

But she was already gone. And he realized exactly where she was headed. Swearing, he opened the opposite door, balancing the harnessed laptop with his free hand, and jogged after her. He caught up with her as he rounded the bus, in time to see her get corralled by an officer charged with securing the perimeter.

"Translator at entrance," he said into the mic. "Needs clearance."

"Clear Eve Larrison," Stillions' voice sounded. As Declan neared, he saw her show the officer ID. The man nodded and handed it back before moving away.

The temperature was in the single digits, and a sharp wind cut through the coats that had seemed too warm while they waited inside the vehicle. Pretty soon, the women began filing out of the hotel, wearing thick white socks on their feet, but still clad in the nightdresses they'd worn earlier. Some were weeping, while a few wore an expression of shock. Others clutched each other, speaking rapidly in a foreign tongue.

Declan followed when Eve broke away to approach the cluster of women coming out the hotel doors. "Brina!"

One of the females detached herself from the group and walked rapidly toward Eve who hugged her. "You will be all right. I promise."

Brina gave her a quick squeeze and then stepped back. "I did not believe." She paid Declan no mind. Her attention was on Eve. "You said there would be help, but I could not let myself hope. Thank you. For all of us, but most of all for Dajana."

Eve's expression softened. "You were the one who helped your friend, by being brave enough to speak with me. You stood up for her, when no one else would." As two officers walked toward them, she said quickly, "I will see you soon. Now you must go." She stepped back, and the woman continued to the bus.

Declan went to her side, slipping an arm around her waist. He could feel her shivering, but he couldn't coax her back into their vehicle until the last of the twenty-nine women had climbed into the bus and, it had lumbered away in the first few miles toward freedom.

"I SHOULD BE EXHAUSTED. And I am, physically. But mentally..."

Declan helped Eve slip her coat off and draped it carelessly over the back of a chair. He followed it with his own. "Tough to turn your mind off after a scene like that."

"So many sad stories." And it was the tales the women had told, rather than the rescue operation preceding the interviews, that would keep her awake. "Three of them had been sold to Malsovic by family members and were terrified that if they returned home, the same thing would reoccur."

Those had perhaps been the most heartbreaking interviews to conduct.

With one hand balancing herself on the couch, Eve pulled her boots off. "Several were afraid of their families finding out how they had been victimized, and the shame that revelation would cause. Like Brina, many are reluctant to return to their families without the wages promised them by Malsovic to offset the money paid for the 'opportunity' he promised in America." And one, Buppha, had vehemently denied she'd been victimized at all. The trauma of prolonged psychological, sexual and physical abuse the women had suffered would take years to overcome.

He sat on the couch and toed off his shoes. "You're the reason those women won't spend the rest of their lives enslaved. Try to concentrate on that."

Eve shook her head, propping a hip on the arm of the couch next to him. "They owe their thanks to Brina. And when I find myself overwhelmed with their heartrending stories, remembering the interview with Xie Shuang will cheer me."

His face lightened. "I watched the live feed on a TV in the next room. The look on her face when you walked into the interview room was worth paying money to see."

The memory had a ribbon of satisfaction curling through her. "I prefer her expression when I started repeating Stillions' questions for her in her native language." Twice the woman had lunged across the table at her, venomous curses spewing from her lips. Each time, she'd been restrained by a second agent in the room. "Unfortunately, she didn't reveal much of interest before she stopped talking altogether." And no amount of probing from the federal agents had changed that.

"Stillions said the information you got from Khalid, the

attendant at the desk, and Shuang's men, Amin, Taufik and Harris, is more than enough to build a solid case against the woman."

She nodded. The men at least had been all too willing to talk, even though they'd painted themselves as victims. "But none of them can shed any light on what Shuang was planning for Royce Raiker. And our inability to discover that, along with the disappearance of Malsovic and Zupan, feels like a failure."

He took her hand and gave a tug, tumbling her off her perch and into his lap. Then he looked entirely too pleased with himself for her to believe he hadn't had success with the move. "We still have their computers to look at. Stillions said the evidence was all being expedited by Raiker's labs. We didn't fail. We just haven't finished yet."

Somehow her position on Declan's lap, the subtle pressure from the arm he'd looped around her waist, seemed far more dangerous than any of the activities they'd been engaged in for the past twenty-four hours. And still, she couldn't find the will to move. Her body melted, just a fraction, against his. "I don't want to be finished until Royce is safe. And I want to see the case of the women through to its conclusion. I don't get to do that enough. My job—" She stopped then, years of reticence about her career ingrained in her. Then she shocked herself by going on. "You were wrong about what I do. I'm not a member of the Intelligence Community at DOS. As a language specialist, I do provide translation and interpretation for high ranking members of the government."

She was discreet enough not to reveal how closely she worked with the White House and the Secretary of State. "But because of my expertise in languages, I'm sometimes loaned out for special assignments, by the request of a number of agencies." CIA, NSA, FBI and DEA had all made such requests in the past couple of years. And the covert assignments she'd taken part in had been far more exhilarating than interpreting for a sensitive trade agreement or translating during the brokering of a ceasefire between war-torn countries. "I blame my staid upbringing for my taste for excitement." Her gaze met his, and her heart stuttered a bit in her chest. Something she couldn't identify held her there, much too close to him, when every shred of logic urged her to move away.

His fingers brushed a strand of hair back from her face. A slight smile curved his lips. "I knew there was more to you than met the eye, Evie. You're freaking brilliant. Surely you realize that."

Her heart did a slow lazy spin in her chest. Brilliant. It wasn't true—not even close—but he could make her feel that way when he looked at her like this. He could make her feel...too much.

"My parents never used pet names or nicknames," she murmured. There was something about the glint in his eye that made it difficult to look away. "Which made the tag I got stuck with even more incongruous. I can't tell you how much better I like your name for me."

His eyes went to smoke. "I thought of it when I saw you first thing in the morning. Before you showered and tamed your hair, when it's a mass of wild ringlets around your face. The rest of the world sees Eve, the mask you don, but Evie... that's the part you try to hide from the world."

She tried to catch her breath. He looked too deeply. Saw too much. And that was just a fraction of the danger the man represented. Declan Gallagher had heartbreak written all over him. And that was one risk she'd always scrupulously managed to avoid. But there was temptation here, in the intensity of his expression. The firm wall of his chest, and the way his hand moved to rest possessively on her hip. She looked at his mouth, remembering the feel of it on hers. Hot. Devastating. Just a bit wicked. And Eve was reminded that some risks were worth taking.

She closed the distance between them, brushed his lips gently with hers. The softness there always surprised her; it was at odds with the innate toughness that was so much a part of him. His eyes went to slits, and she saw the desire in his expression. But although his lips moved beneath hers, he appeared content to allow her to set the pace. The freedom was more than a little heady.

Hooking her arm behind his neck Eve closed her eyes and gave herself over to the moment. There was so much to learn about a man from his kiss, she thought a little dreamily. The nuances of touch and taste. The gradual shift of pressure and increasing hunger until the kiss became a prelude to something more.

She'd dated her share of men, had slept with a few. None of them had elicited this rollicking in her pulse, this instant, steamy rise of emotion. The danger that Declan Gallagher exuded drew her as the moon drew the tide. But it was what she'd learned about the man himself that made him irresistible.

She shifted in his lap. Found him hard and ready against her hip. His arms looped loosely around her waist, but she could feel the steely hardness of bunched muscles. The tight rein of control. And she wondered what it would take to make him lose that leash of restraint. To make him want and shake and need.

Deliberately, without breaking contact, she moved to straddle him, her hands going to thread through his hair as she slicked her tongue over the seam of his mouth. For a moment he was still. Then that leash slipped.

One arm banded around her, and he pulled her closer, his mouth eating at hers, pressing her lips apart so his tongue could sweep in, stake a claim. And she couldn't resist reveling in the torrent she'd unharnessed.

There was a basic, carnal pleasure to be had in the mingling of breath, the clash of lips and teeth. But the ease with which sensation kick-started need caused a belated flicker of alarm. It would be a mistake to feel too much. Want too much. Eve recognized that. Just as she realized it was much too late to back pedal now. Thought fragmented as he nipped at her lip. Re-formed as he soothed it with the tip of his tongue. She had a sense of adventure that she kept hidden from the world. But she wondered now if Declan represented the biggest gamble she'd ever undertaken.

His hand slid beneath her sweater, and she jerked a little at the contact. His fingers spread against her skin, each digit an individual brand. Her palms itched with the need to reciprocate.

She unfastened the buttons on his shirt with fingers that had gone just a little unsteady. Then let her hand glide over his skin, one smooth stroke, and smiled against his lips when she felt his stomach jump and clench beneath her touch. There didn't seem to be an ounce of spare flesh on him. Just smooth, padded muscle, punctuated by intriguing peaks and hollows where bone met sinew.

His palm crept upward to cup her breast encased in the fabric of her bra, and Eve's nipple tightened as he brushed it deliberately with his thumb. Senses heightened unbearably. Every nerve ending quivered in anticipation of a deeper contact. He drew her bottom lip into his mouth and nipped not quite gently. The dual assault sent little pinwheels of desire swirling through her veins.

Their mouths twisted together, and conscious thought receded. There was only the taste of him, dark and faintly primitive. His clever fingers knew just how to tease and tantalize until she strained against him, desperate for more. And then his hand slipped inside her bra to cover her breast, and excitement thrummed through her system.

Her movements lacked finesse as she spread his shirt wide to skate both hands over his chest. Pent up need was pumping through her, lending a sense of urgency.

She wasn't aware that he'd unhooked her bra until it was loose. And then it was swept away with her sweater and he brought her closer, the breath hissing from between his teeth at the sensation. There was an intoxicating pleasure to be had pressed against him like this. Breasts against his chest. Flesh to flesh. To feel the leap of his heart when she scraped his nipple lightly with her nail. To hear his breathing lose its steady rhythm and go just a bit choppy. And to feel. God, to *feel*. His fingers rolled her nipples to taut knots of nerves that sent shocks of desire straight to her womb.

She'd known passion before, but not this longing that was like a fever in her blood. A yearning that could only be quenched by one man. Desperation sizzled, a lit match to a fuse. The strength of it had her squirming on his lap, eliciting a groan in response.

There was a ferocious hunger evident now as his mouth ate at hers. His arms wrapped around her, fitting her more tightly against him. She felt him rise, cradling her in his arms as he strode from the room. By the time her eyes had opened to half-mast, she already felt the mattress beneath her shoulders. Then he was following her down onto it.

There was no teasing in his touch now. Just unvarnished need sheened with desperation. And that fanned the flames of her own desire to a scorching level. Their mouths twisted together as their kiss became deeper. Wet. Frankly carnal. Hands battled to undo buttons and zippers.

She wasn't used to this fierce compulsion to strip a man bare, to press so close that there wouldn't even be a whisper of air between them. To explore every hard inch of his body and lose herself in a journey of discovery that she didn't want to end.

He released her mouth to drag her jeans down her thighs and stripped off his own clothes before stretching out beside her on the bed. She arched her back, moaning a little at the kiss of flesh wherever they touched. Heat, a quick stabbing spear of it, arrowed down her spine. She pressed her lips to his chest, running her palms from his strong shoulders to his belly where the muscles quivered beneath her touch. And lost her breath in the next moment when his hands cupped her breasts, stroking and squeezing them lightly in turn.

She nipped at his bicep in a savage need for flesh. Her fingers closed around his heavy cock, and it pulsed in her grasp, hard and ready. Straining for release. Her fingers glided down the shaft and back once, twice and again. Then faltered in their rhythm when he bent to reclaim her nipples.

Colors fragmented behind her eyelids. And when his teeth scraped flesh, an edgy blade of need nicked over nerve endings already unbearably sensitized. His fingers, those clever wicked fingers, traced the seam of her leg teasingly before delving inside her panties, cupping her where she was damp and heated.

Her head lolled, her breath coming in short ragged

pants. He took advantage of the position to raise his head and cruise his mouth along her throat, nipping at the sensitive cord there. And when his hand slipped inside her panties to part her folds, dipping one finger inside, Eve's limbs went to water.

Sensation after sensation battered at her. Even as he explored her, his thumb pressed and released against her clitoris in a manner designed to drive her to madness. It was a journey she was determined not to take alone.

She stroked him, alternating between a lighter touch and the firmer one his hunger would demand. He thrust against her hand demandingly, and her lips curved in a moment of pure feminine satisfaction. Her back bowed as sensation after sensation battered at her. A moment later, her climax ripped through her, graying her vision and startling a cry from her.

"Evie." She shivered at the sound of the nickname on his lips, his guttural tone. "More. Again."

She shook her head weakly. It was too much. Too soon. She couldn't think. Couldn't claw through the fog of release to climb the slippery slope of desire once again. But he proved her a liar in the next instant. His touch deft and insistent, he had pleasure building again in long lush waves. Helplessly, her hands climbed to his shoulders. Clutched there as her body quaked and followed him up and up to a peak he was relentlessly driving her toward.

Then he pushed her over it. Ruthlessly using hands and lips and teeth to intensify sensation from a thousand individual pulse points so the implosion went on and on until she was a weak shuddering mass.

Eve felt him move away, reached out a protesting hand. Her body still shook with the eddies of her release, but called for the feel of him, hot and hard pressed against her.

And then she heard the rustle of his clothes, knew he was digging in the pocket of his jeans. It was long moments before she felt the mattress dip beneath the weight of his knee. She curled her arm around his neck to draw him down to her. His heart was hammering against hers, his muscles quivering and jumping wherever she touched him. Anticipation pooled in the pit of her stomach. Because she was going to do her level best to fray his last thread of control.

Releasing him after a brief kiss, she hooked her thumbs in the sides of her panties and shimmied out of them, taking far longer than the act would usually require. Then caught his gaze on hers. Heavy lidded and intent. And impossibly, the blood in her veins went molten again.

He stretched out on top of her, his weight on his elbows. And when he entered her in one smooth stroke, she lost her breath. Both of them stilled, bodies quivering. Eve was a little stunned. A bit panicked. He filled her with a completeness that bordered on discomfort. She shifted slightly, feeling surrounded by the breadth of him. Then stopped as she felt the delicate throb of his penis. Softened as a fist of need clutched in her belly.

She opened her eyes. Found him watching. And her breath strangled in her lungs. His eyes were the color of night fog. And in that moment, she knew he saw nothing but her.

Eve arched her hips, a silent invitation that he met with a long slow thrust. His hand crept between their bodies to cup her breast, while the other slipped under her hips. She could read his urgency in the way the skin pulled tightly across his cheekbones. In his clenched jaw. But still he held back, keeping his movements controlled.

In the face of her earlier mind-shattering pleasure, it

seemed only fair to torch his effort at control. She smiled into his eyes. Reached down to touch him where their bodies were joined. And felt his body quake as his restraint abruptly snapped.

Declan surged against her over and over, and this time, Eve met him stroke for stroke. Tiny balls of heat were firing through her veins. Her senses scattered. The night rushed in, crowding their bodies on the bed. She could see nothing but him. Hear only the rasp of their breathing. The slap of flesh against flesh. The beat of her blood roaring through her veins. Hammering in her ears.

Her legs climbed his. She was wrapped around him, and still it wasn't close enough. His hips pounded against hers in a primal, frantic pace until he surged wildly, and she felt the last little bit of sanity wing away as the climax flung her over the precipice.

And when he followed her into madness, it was with her name on his lips.

CHAPTER ELEVEN

EVE FELT as though she was swimming to the top of a deep pool, an anchor on each ankle. Each time she nearly broke the surface, she was weighted down again to be pulled into a deep, slumberous warmth. One that tempted her to burrow deeper into it.

Then the weights were removed. The warmth disappeared. Her eyelids fluttered as she struggled to wake. A light slap on her bottom accomplished the task for her. She rolled and bolted upright in bed. Glared at the offender.

Then blinked. Declan was next to her. Not on her bed, but *in* it. He was leaning over her, reaching for something on the nightstand. The blankets were trapped beneath his hips, and she yanked at the sheet to have at least a modicum of cover. Memories from this morning came flooding back and suffused her with heat. They'd fallen asleep wrapped around each other, his leg pinning both of hers. Eve tiptoed through her feelings about that like searching through an emotional minefield. She couldn't find a single ounce of regret.

"Raiker." He mouthed the word at her. She straightened abruptly as he thumbed on the speakerphone.

"I'm told you were involved in the raid last night," the man began without preamble.

"We had a small part. Just returned from the interviews a few hours ago."

"Which is why I let you sleep in." Raiker actually sounded serious. But then, he always did. "I have your next assignment. Get back to me on video chat." The call ended with the abruptness Eve was beginning to associate with him.

Declan disconnected and sent her a slow smile. "Lucky he didn't have video on now."

"Video." Her eyes went wide, and she pushed at his bare chest. "We have to get dressed!"

"He'd probably appreciate it." Declan scratched his cheek. He'd shaved before they'd left to meet Stillions last night, but his jaw was again shadowed with whiskers. She just might get addicted to the look of him unshaven. "And he couldn't know that although we got home at nine AM, we didn't spend all the intervening time sleeping."

The flush his words elicited seemed to spread from the inside out. Eve didn't have vast experience in morning afters, and certainly none recently. But she knew it was ridiculous to feel embarrassed to slip from the bed nude after the hours he'd spent mapping every inch of her body with his hands. And mouth.

Warmth bloomed inside her, slow and insidious. "So." She tried for a matter-of-fact tone. "Your clothes are in the other room."

"They are, aren't they?" His smoke-colored eyes were laughing at her. And he didn't make a move from the bed.

She gave him a nudge with her shoulder. "Go put them on."

"Trying to get rid of me so I won't see you naked?" He leaned forward then to brush his mouth over hers. "An odd response for a woman who spent a few spectacular hours under me. Over me, too, in a few instances."

"Declan." Her mind went blank for an instant when her lips—completely devoid of logic or good judgment—kissed him back. "Raiker's waiting."

"Those are the only words that would get me out of your bed right now." With a lithe movement he rolled away from her and off the mattress. Then walked to the door, blissfully, unselfconsciously nude. She was female enough to enjoy watching the play of muscle across his shoulders and narrow hips before leaping from the bed and pulling on clothes. She met him at the desk in the corner of the front room, where he already had the laptop open and powering on.

"How long until you have the video chat going?"

He gave her an understanding look. "You've got a minute. No more."

Dashing into the bathroom, she grabbed a brush and dragged it urgently through her hair. There was nothing to be done with it short of washing and styling, and she didn't have time for that. Dragging the length into a ponytail, she secured it at her nape and hurried back to the computer. Seconds later, Adam Raiker's likeness filled the screen.

He appeared freshly shaven, dressed in a suit and far more awake than she felt. It was a bit of a jolt to look at the time on the computer and see it was already early afternoon.

"Sun Yanyu, the woman you knew as Xie Shuang, still isn't talking. And Malsovic hasn't been found yet." Adam's voice was carefully expressionless. "He must have left in a hurry. The safe in his room was open, and it was filled with identification papers on the women. Phony passports in their names. I'm told high-quality ones. But no ID was found for Malsovic. And nothing for the other man, Marko Zupan. They did find Hobart's ID where you discovered it under the bed in Malsovic's room."

"He had a lot of equipment in there," Eve recalled. "A laptop and several other machines that looked like printers."

"None were recovered."

"He's on the run," Declan said surely. "And when he leaves the country, you can bet it will be with a new name and a falsified passport."

"That would be the best-case scenario. We've got his likeness out to every airport in the country, as well as to Customs and Border Protection. He won't get far."

"If Zupan has disappeared, they're likely to be together, especially if the man's ID is missing, while the other three men's were not."

"Conjecture," Raiker said impatiently. "What we need are answers."

"Conjecture might lead to answers," Eve said, imperturbable. "For instance, all the spokes in this wheel seem to lead back to bin Osman at the center. Until seven years ago, he was running a similar illegal operation in the exact same hotel. You've placed Shuang there at the time it was raided. Malsovic shot Hobart with the same gun that killed your father-in-law nine years earlier. You've been looking for the link to your son. It seems to me that those three people are the connection. We don't know why yet," she admitted. "But if Shuang could be convinced to talk, I'm guessing she can tell us." The woman's real name was unimportant. Her relationship to Royce was.

"Perhaps. But she's buttoned up now. And with the other agencies involved, I don't have a great deal to bargain with."

"Shuang berated Malsovic for not being there a couple nights ago." Declan had pulled on jeans but hadn't bothered with a shirt. Next to him, Eve felt positively nun-like in jeans and a turtleneck. "Maybe he has a girlfriend stashed somewhere. An apartment."

"That's the working assumption. Burke has already started looking at apartment complexes within a ten-mile radius of the hotel. We'll assume for the moment that the man would want to stay fairly close. Perhaps within walking distance. You'll join him. He started with those in ethnic neighborhoods."

"Did anyone find the rifle last night?" Eve asked.

"It was discovered blocks from the hotel in a Dumpster. I've offered the services of my lab *pro bono*, so all physical evidence has been transported there. Including the computers taken from Shuang and the meeting room."

"I'm not so sure the attendant at the front desk didn't tip her off when SWAT entered the hotel," Declan said. "I can't figure any other way she would have known to try and escape. I blocked internal access to the cameras minutes before the raid began."

Raiker's smile was fierce. "She definitely knew what was happening. She'd started a multi-pass erase on her computer before she tried to escape. Doesn't matter. My people will recover what's there. They're working on her encrypted emails now. Few of them are in English. Eve." She started a little at the use of her name. "I'm sending a driver to bring you to my labs. It would be easiest to have you on site to translate whatever personal correspondence we're able to recover."

Adrenaline was already humming in her veins. "All right, I'll be ready. I'd appreciate it if you talked to the federal agents about a T Visa for Brina."

"I did. Stillions said you'd already brought it up." She had, several times, but she thought the request would carry more weight if it were repeated by Raiker. "I'll keep tabs on the issue," he added.

Because she doubted very much that the man made promises he didn't keep, she was satisfied with that.

"What are the orders for whoever finds Malsovic?"

Declan's question had a quick shudder working down Eve's spine. For the first time, it occurred to her to be concerned about the assignment Declan had been given. Malsovic was always dangerous. Cornered he'd be deadly.

"Of course, we want him alive if possible. But be prepared to use force to defend yourselves. No heroes, Gallagher." Raiker's tone brooked no argument. "The man has already ruined enough lives. I don't want you or Burke to be next on the list."

She barely noticed when the screen went black. Her attention was fixed on Declan. One corner of his mouth kicked up as he returned her gaze. He reached out a hand and slid the ponytail holder away. Gave her hair a shake.

"Declan." Caught between concern for him and exasperation, she pushed back the curls with one hand.

"Eve." He cocked his head, considering her. "I think I could get used to this. Why don't you just wear it like that?"

She gave him a pitying look, brushed his hand away when he reached up to stretch out a curl. "Spoken like someone with straight hair. Be serious. What Raiker said earlier? About staying safe?" She had his attention now. His smoke-colored eyes sobered. "He wasn't disparaging your abilities. Wasn't being overprotective."

"Where exactly is this going?"

"It's going right here." She reached up to cup his jaw, was momentarily distracted by the rasp of his whiskers against her fingertips. "I trust you as an agent." And she'd shown far more trust of him as a man hours earlier. "So, I know you'll make smart decisions. I will be seriously pissed off if you get yourself shot today."

His smile was slow and wide and devastating. "I think I've already learned the dangers of pissing you off." The kiss he pressed to her lips would have to last her all day. And maybe, just maybe, the memory of it would keep worry about his safety at bay.

"Shuang has a dozen communications here, all written in the past three months, that mention bin Osman. On all, she signed her name as Sun Yanyu." Eve was sitting in a conference room in the computer forensics wing of Raiker's lab building. The structure was huge, with eight different laboratories and countless other examination and conference rooms. She was certain that if Macy Burke hadn't been guiding her, she could be hopelessly lost for days before ever finding her way out of the structure again.

Macy, who was Raiker's top forensic linguist as well as Kellan Burke's wife, had printed off the emails. Eve had them spread across the table in chronological order. "All are written in Malay."

"So Yanyu is bilingual," the other woman observed.

Eve was scanning the first of the emails. "Many Chinese are able to converse in Malay and English. It is also common for Malaysian youth to be multi-lingual. These emails are to five different people." Eve picked up the documents, scanning each before setting it down to go on to the next. "A couple appear to be lining up a new supplier for more women." The news was surprising. Malsovic had still been on site, yet these communications were dated several weeks ago. Had the two had a falling out, perhaps after the attempted kidnapping? Or had Shuang been planning to get rid of the man?

Studying the remaining correspondences, she said, "There are three recipients for the rest of these, all with the same subject. She was looking for bin Osman and was apparently unable to contact him directly." Eve went silent for a moment as she mentally translated the rest of the text. "She was asking for contact information. And was being stonewalled." She'd had a similar reason for the last call they'd picked up on the transmitter, Eve recalled.

"But there's no indication of why she was looking for the man."

"Not yet." And that was really the question burning inside Eve. She set down the document and moved on to the next. "I'll type up the translation for each of these before I go. We know they were both in the US up to seven years ago, at the same hotel where she now resides. If bin Osman was the head of the same human trafficking operation that she was a victim of, why would she want anything to do with him now? The story she told the police at the time is that he brought her to the country under false pretenses and forced her into prostitution." It was hard to feel sympathy for the woman since a few years later, she'd done the same to other females. And according to Brina, Shuang had been brutal. "But enduring a trauma like that can affect people differently."

Perhaps it had stripped the woman of empathy for others. And had given her the idea for how she could wield power, by transforming herself from victim to predator. "It might give her a peculiar sense of satisfaction in running the operation in the same hotel where she'd been held prisoner."

Eve read silently for several minutes, working through most of the pages quickly before she slowed, shock working through her. "This one is from Ahmed Pascal, and the tone is quite combative." She began to translate aloud. *"I have mentioned your interest to Rizqi bin Osman, and he has instructed me to tell you that he wishes you die a thousand deaths. If you attempt to come here and see him yourself, be assured I will personally see that you meet with the end he wishes for you."*

"Harsh words," observed Macy. She was far quieter and more serious than her husband. Eve found herself wondering how the two had gotten together. "But bin Osman escaped the country and any punishment when his hotel was raided, correct?"

"That's what Raiker said." Eve sat back. Considered. "Of course, he would have lost the hotel. His..." she made a moue of distaste, "inventory, to use a word. His livelihood. That would have been a substantial financial loss. But why would he blame Shuang for that?" She couldn't get used to using the woman's real name.

Her gaze returned to the sheets in front of her. "In the next one she begs Pascal to carry a message to bin Osman about a business proposition that she knows the man will want to hear." She set the note down and slid the final sheet forward so she could read it. Felt herself go a bit lightheaded when she did.

"Are you all right?" Alarm showed in Macy's expression. "You look like you've seen a ghost. What does it say?"

Swallowing, Eve reread the missive. The translation

remained the same. "Apparently Pascal didn't respond, because she contacted him again yesterday. '*Tell Rizqi I found his missing son. For half a million dollars, I will deliver him, with DNA proof of their relationship.*'" Feeling slightly frantic, she shuffled through the papers again, although she knew she'd seen everything that was there. "There were two attachments to that one." Shoving away from the table, she turned toward the door. "We have to alert them in the technology lab. Those attachments must be recovered."

"All right." A flush of excitement flagged the other woman's cheeks as she led Eve down the maze of hallways to the lab. "But something tells me you already have an idea of what might be in them."

"I'm hoping I'm wrong." But even as she uttered the words, she knew she wasn't. Because Eve was already positive that at least one attachment would be a photo of Royce Raiker.

"It'd be easier to find a dime at the bottom of a mineshaft. A twig in a forest. A proverbial needle in a haystack."

Kellan Burke's analogies weren't far off from the reality, Declan admitted silently. The man had been at this task longer than he had, going to apartment buildings all day, working a circular grid outward from the Latifma Hotel. Every hour, they conferred with the liaison for the DCPD canvas charged with the same job. The liaison had switched two hours ago, at shift change. For Declan and Kell, there seemed no end in sight.

"I've been keeping track." They trudged up the steps of an apartment building that could have been a twin for the one Declan and Eve had stayed in, down to the non-existent security and broken lock on the front door. The faded, red brick façade was in dire need of tuck-pointing repair, and the cement stoop had a decided list to one side. "Wanna know how many of these shitholes I've visited today?"

"Not really." Because there was nothing keeping them out, Declan pulled open the front door to walk into the dingy foyer.

"Forty-seven." Burke crowded in behind him. The temperatures that day had warmed just enough for a miserable icy drizzle that showed no signs of dissipating.

"What part of 'not really' did you not understand?" There was no sign to point them in the direction of the landlord. The place had to have one. Somehow all these apartments got rented, proving there was never any shortage of desperate people. He went to the first door on the right, just inside the hall, figuring it was as good a place as any to start as any.

"We're three miles out from the hotel. Almost exactly. That's a ways to walk. He could take a bus." Burke countered his own statement. "Probably does. But he'd catch one a few blocks from the hotel. He wouldn't want anyone to wonder where he was going and follow him."

Finally seeing a small doorbell that had been painted the same color as the door and jamb, Declan tried ringing it. Heard someone moving around inside. Still, it was several moments before the door pulled open a crack, with one bifocaled eye pressed against the opening. "Come back during day."

"We'll just take a moment, ma'am," Declan said smoothly, reaching into his pocket for the photo of Malsovic they'd been showing all day. He unfolded it, held it up. "Are you the landlord? We're looking for this man."

He saw the fear that flashed in her gaze. "No. Do not know him." The door shut quickly.

The two men looked at each other. In silent agreement, Declan pounded on the door again. "Ma'am, we'd like to ask you a couple of questions."

"Go away!" The woman's voice was fierce. "I will call police!"

"*We* will call the police," Kellan put in. "And you can answer their questions instead. But we're not leaving until you open that door."

"What are you doing harassing my mother?" A middle-aged, stocky man pushed through the entrance, a scowl on his face, which was reddened from the cold. "Get the hell out of here before I kick both your asses."

"You're welcome to try," Declan invited politely. A serious brawl might be just the thing to wear off this edge of irritation that had increased with each place they'd failed to find Malsovic. "But if your mother is the landlord, we need to talk to her about someone. She said she didn't know this man." He held out the picture again. "I think she's lying."

The truculence fading from his expression, the newcomer reached out and took the photo. "Yeah, she knows him. Sergei Peterol. Son of a bitch. He's been here years, since before we ever took this job. I'm the landlord," he admitted. "She takes the calls all day. Collects the rent. I take care of the repairs after work." From the looks of the place, the repairs were few and far between. Coolly, he looked them both up and down. "You cops?"

"Working with them." Kellan had already turned half away to text the DCPD liaison. "Do you know if Peterol is here now?"

In answer, the newcomer reached out and hammered on his mother's door. "*Nene!*" He released a spate of words in a foreign tongue that had Declan wishing Eve were here for translation. The older woman opened the door again, shouted back at him in the same language. Whatever the woman was saying, she was quite emphatic. After several moments of squabbling, the man threw up his hands and turned to them as his mother slammed the door again. "She is frightened of Peterol. I am not. He is a common thug. A criminal probably. But she worries if we talk about him, he will take vengeance."

"The cops will be here within the hour with a warrant," Kell put in. Declan hoped like hell the man was right. "Peterol is wanted for questioning in two attempted murder charges. You don't want to get in the middle of that."

The landlord gave in. "Room 406. He isn't here often. Sometimes we don't see him for weeks at a time. But he was here last night, with a friend. I don't know if he is at home now. You can go see. If not, when you have a warrant, I am across the hall. Michael Vrioni." He brushed past them to go to his apartment. Unlocked it and went inside.

Declan and Kell looked at each other wordlessly before heading for the stairs. The building seemed to grow shabbier with each floor they passed. When they reached 406, Declan pressed an ear against the door. Heard nothing. He banged on it, already knowing the place was empty. Without a word, they fanned out to the doors flanking Malsovic's and knocked. It was Kell who hit pay dirt.

The boy who pulled the door open was no more than five. He stood there surveying them silently with solemn brown eyes. "Is your mother home?"

At Kell's question, he screeched, "Mama!" without turning his head.

A young woman hurried into the room. "Jaden, how

many times do I have to tell you not to open the door to strangers?"

"How do I know they're strangers if I don't open the door?" the boy asked reasonably. The woman was holding another child, not more than two, who looked like he'd be a carbon copy of his brother who was still staring at them.

"Ma'am, do you recognize this man?"

She peered at the photo Declan held out, made a grimace of recognition. "He lives in the next apartment. He's a pig. The kind of pig who thinks women are nothing, you know? But he is not here much. And when he is, at least he's quiet. I never hear a TV or music coming from there."

"We understand he was here last night."

She nodded with enough enthusiasm to have the topknot she'd pulled her hair into shifting precariously. "Him. And another man, too. Taller with a dark beard. They came, left for a while and then returned very late last night. I heard them talking when I was up with this one." She jerked her head toward the child she held. "Then this afternoon, they left again. He has not come back."

Declan felt his earlier adrenaline fading. "You've been here all day?"

"Where am I going to go hauling two kids around? Yeah, I'm here most days. It's my own little piece of paradise."

Kellan asked other questions, but it was plain the woman had told them all she knew. As they went to the door, Declan found himself hoping the search warrant would arrive with record speed. Whatever else they found inside 406, it was a sure bet they weren't going to find Malsovic. But they might discover a clue about where he'd gone next.

~

"TIME FOR BED."

"Ten more minutes," Royce wheedled his mother, never taking his eyes off the video game. "We're only in the fifth of our seven-game series. If I win now, I beat Rick."

"That's what you think, oh short one." Rick Sorenson was bent over the controllers, his gaze as avid as the boy's. "I have my best batters in the lineup next round, and you're not doing so hot against Valenzuela's curve...oh!"

"Eat your words, Sorenson," the boy chortled as his onscreen player got two RBIs on a double. "Your pitcher's so tired, he's throwing meat. I knew his arm would never last—No , Mom! don't turn it off!" Royce paused the game. Looked at his mother's face and sighed. "At least give me a chance to save it so we can continue tomorrow."

Rick Sorenson straightened and picked up his water bottle, tapped it against Royce's in a light toast before downing the rest of it. "You're a good strategist. I'm going to spend the rest of the night figuring out how to outwit you."

Much to his satisfaction, the boy guzzled the rest of his water, too. "You can try. But I'm a master at this game."

"Yeah, yeah."

Royce rose reluctantly. "It's not even nine o'clock."

"Not yet, but it will be by the time you're done dragging your feet and get in bed." He and his mom started from the room.

"Look at it this way," Sorenson called out as he picked up the controllers and put them in the basket beneath the game system. "You stayed up a half hour later than your grandma." The old lady had turned in early, citing exhaustion. He was the one who should be complaining about exhaustion. Ten hours of Patricia Marlowe ordering him around had had him reconsidering his agreement for this job.

But yeah, when she was asleep, the thought of the five thousand Sergei had paid him was more than enough to convince him the next couple of days would be worth it.

He picked up the TV remote and dropped into a leather chair. Clicked the TV on. This place was sweet. Like a mansion on a movie set. He hadn't been through the whole thing. Likely wouldn't get the chance. During the day, he'd stayed close to the old lady's side. But his stint here would be short. When it was over, he'd go home only long enough to pack before buying a plane ticket to San Diego. Settling on a Bulls game, he kicked back in the recliner and prepared to relax.

This gig wasn't so tough. Slipping that device into the lining of one of the old lady's bags had been a piece of cake. Dropping the tablet Sergei had given him into the kid's water bottle had required a bit more sleight of hand. The place was brimming with security. Every time he turned around, it seemed like a guard was standing there. Or the mother.

"I thought I'd find Jaid in here."

Rick looked up, then brought the recliner upright in a single rapid motion. "No, sir. She's putting Royce to bed."

"Ah." The guy looked at his watch. "I lost track of time." He nodded toward the TV, which had cut to a commercial break. "Is that the Bulls game? What's the score?"

"Heat's up by six, thirty-five to twenty-nine. But it's not even midway through the first half."

The man gave him something that might pass for a smile. "Maybe I'll be able to catch the end of it." He withdrew from the room, probably going after his wife and kid, and Sorenson breathed a little easier. The guards were bad enough, but this guy was spooky, with the eye patch and those scars and that voice. He looked like he'd been through a war. The truth was, he creeped him out even more than Sergei did, and Sergei put out some seriously dangerous vibes of his own.

The game came back on, but Rick was too distracted to pay much attention to it. Just a couple more things to do, and he'd be free and clear. Taking that device out of the old woman's luggage and getting rid of it would be first on the list. Rick didn't know a reason in the world why he couldn't just flush the thing. It was small enough.

He was in and out of the old lady's room all the time, so that wouldn't be a problem. He'd filched the pill bottle he'd stuck with her things while she was getting ready for bed. Took out the two capsules he'd carefully buried in her medication. If this thing wasn't going down tonight, he'd need to get his hands on the woman's cell phone, so he could send Sergei a message.

His nerves jittered, and he longed for a joint to settle them. Just another day or two, he promised himself, focusing on the TV screen. This would all be over, and he'd be on a beach. Was it warm enough in California to go to the beach in the winter? If it wasn't, maybe he'd head to Mexico. Plenty of opportunities there for an enterprising guy.

The Bulls had pulled within two when he heard a shout from several rooms away. "Royce!"

Rick came upright in his chair, adrenaline spiking as he ran in the direction of the voice. No need to sneak into the old lady's room for that phone call.

It was happening tonight.

Rick came to the fringe of the circle of people surrounding the kid on the floor. Shit, it looked like the real thing. The boy was shaking violently, his eyes rolling in the back of his head, drool coming from his mouth. Whatever Sergei had given him to slip in the kid's water had either really given him a seizure or stimulated a damn good imitation.

Belatedly remembering the pretense he was engaged in, he shouldered through the security guards to where Raiker and his wife were kneeling on the floor next to the boy. "Roll him to his side," Rick said, but the woman was already doing so. "Lift his chin." He squatted and raised the boy's chin slightly. "It will help his breathing." He looked at Raiker. Almost quelled under the ferocious expression on the man's face. "How long has this been going on?"

"Two minutes?" He glanced at his wife for corroboration.

"About that." She threw a wild glance at Rick. "What else should we do?"

He reached for the reassuring tone that was so useful at the nursing home. "You're doing it. He's not going to swallow his tongue, that's a myth. We just have to wait this out. Did he have a fall today?"

"I..." Her gaze never left her son's face. "No, not that I know of."

"Has he run a high fever recently?"

"No. He's been fine. Perfectly healthy. Should I call 911?"

"Only if the seizure lasts longer than five minutes." He knew that because Sergei had told him. It had seemed imperative to him that the kid be out longer than that. But shit, the seizure showed no signs of stopping, and Rick was getting a bit queasy. What the hell had been in that capsule he'd opened and dumped in the kid's water? Whatever it was, it had triggered one hell of a reaction, and he was worried now that Sergei had lied his ass off about it not harming the boy. What if he died?

Mentally scrambling to remember his part, he asked, "Does he have a history of epilepsy?"

"No." It was Raiker who answered. "This is his first seizure, isn't it, Jaid?"

She nodded her head. "But he was confused before he went down. I thought he was just messing with me. To draw out bedtime, you know? He put hand soap on his toothbrush and looked at me so oddly when I asked him what he was doing. Then he just...he dropped the toothbrush. Tried to talk, but he wasn't making sense." She stared at him, fright visible in her expression. "What is wrong with him? God, hasn't he been through enough?"

"Four minutes." Adam's tone was quiet. "I'm calling 911."

Rick didn't argue with him. What the parents did at this point wasn't part of his deal. He'd done what he'd been paid for. His gaze went to the kid again. Was the shaking letting up a little? The boy didn't seem to be conscious, and Rick knew that wasn't a good thing, especially if he didn't come to after the seizure was over. "You may not require an ambulance, but you should definitely get him to an emergency room when he comes to," he told Jaid. "I don't want you to worry too much. Ten percent of kids have one seizure and never have another one." That would be a lot easier to believe if Royce's showed any signs of stopping. "But you'll want to get him checked out. They'll do an EEG."

She nodded jerkily, and he heard Raiker say, "It's been over five minutes now. Yes, we've timed it. You're sending an ambulance?" He had the kind of voice that people listened to, even though it was low and gravelly. He sounded like a man used to giving commands and having them obeyed.

"His eyelids are fluttering. He might be coming to." Rick wished he would. Five thousand dollars wasn't going to be enough money if he ended up killing the kid. He swallowed hard, watching the boy he'd just played video games with, shaking and shuddering involuntarily. No amount of cash was worth being responsible for the kid's death.

THE AMBULANCE'S siren was off, but the strobe was still flashing as it rumbled down the road away from the estate. It was closely followed by another vehicle, a dark SUV. More than that, Malsovic could not make out. "One vehicle following the ambulance," he whispered into his radio. "Get in position."

"We know what to do" came the disembodied response, and he grimaced. Hiring near strangers for such a job carried a risk. He could not be certain of their competency once it started. But he also wouldn't need to worry about them when the operation was over.

He was positioned at the end of a private road that ran in front of the property. It was heavily wooded, but the trees and bushes were winter bare. His men's vehicles were pulled deeper in the woods, motors running. Had it been daylight, they would have been visible. As it was, they would not be seen until it was too late.

The ambulance rolled by, blocking Malsovic's view. He couldn't see the first of his men's vehicles pull out to stop crossways in the road, but the ambulance slowed, so it must have. Before the SUV behind it could respond, the men crouched behind the second vehicle and opened fire on it.

The barrage of gunfire was deafening in the night. Zupan would be waiting with the panel truck a mile west of here. Malsovic ran through the woods, in front of the car that protected the gunmen. Beyond, toward the ambulance, which was now stopped with both front doors hanging open.

The SUV slowed to a halt to avoid running into the emergency vehicle. A moment later, those inside it began to return fire. They would be no match for the machine guns his people were armed with. Malsovic knew weapons. And those he'd purchased—like the hired men—were killers.

The pumping of his heart filled his ears. He ran faster, until he was past the shooting. Only then did he dare cross out of the woods toward the ambulance. Shouting filled the air. And a sound that shouldn't be there. Gunfire from inside the vehicle.

"Don't harm the boy!" He shouted it in Serbian and again in English.

"The woman's armed!" One of the men yelled. "Filip is shot."

He changed course and ran around to the back of the vehicle, jumping over the body of one of the medics. He drew his gun to shoot repeatedly at the handle of the locked, double back doors. He pulled one open and dove inside, bullets pinging as they lodged in the door. There was a body on the floor. The woman was on the gurney covering the boy, spraying bullets. Her attention was now diverted. She swung her weapon from the sliding window separating the cab of the vehicle from the back. Malsovic fired. Saw her body jerk. Then jerk again when his man from the front shot, too.

"Mom!" The boy was trying to rise, but his movements were slow. Clumsy. "Mom!"

"Drive!" Malsovic bellowed. He caught the kid around the neck and brought the gun down on his head in a quick, vicious move. When his body went limp, he dumped him on the gurney and went to the woman bleeding out on the floor. Dragging her to the rear of the vehicle, he heaved her body out of the ambulance as it lurched forward. His men would soon leave in the other car. For the next couple of minutes, he was tossed about the back area before the vehicle slowed. Malsovic raised his weapon when the rear door opened.

Seeing it was Zupan, he lowered the gun. "Take the boy." He lifted the kid and passed him to the other man who ran with him to the vehicle. Placed him in the panel truck. Malsovic got in after him. He hadn't forgotten what the boy was capable of. The little fuck had ruined everything in the last abduction attempt. He reached immediately for the roll of duct tape and went to work securing him while Zupan got in the driver's seat and took off.

Once the kid was bound, Malsovic made his way to the front and climbed into the passenger seat. He looked in the rearview mirror. No one was following. The man who'd driven the ambulance had run in the opposite direction, where he'd join the others as they made their escape. And the people in the SUV would waste valuable time checking on the woman.

A feeling of euphoria filled him, and he smiled broadly, settling back into his seat. Pulled on his seatbelt. "Obey the speed limit. No sharp turns. I don't want him bruised from rolling around." It wouldn't do to handle the kid carelessly at this point.

The boy was going to make him rich.

CHAPTER TWELVE

"JAID RAIKER IS undergoing emergency surgery at this moment." Paulie Samuels' expression on the video call held an uncustomary grimness. He was Raiker's right hand man and closest friend, his normal ebullience frequently at odds with his employer's fiercer attitude. He loved gambling, fast horses and cards. But today, he was as solemn as Declan had ever seen him.

"Adam is, of course, at the hospital. The SUV he and the security detail were in was fully armored with bullet-proof glass and run-flat tires. Two of the men were winged, because they had the windows down to return fire. Three of the gunmen were captured but haven't revealed any further details about who hired them." Paulie cleared his throat, seemed to struggle to push aside emotion before going on. "Jaid took out one of the guys who ambushed the ambulance. We think she wounded at least one more. Since she has gunshot wounds in the front and back, it appears she was hit by two different gunmen."

"Bastards." Declan's voice was bitter. Eve's hand reached for his. Clutched it.

"Her condition is critical. And so is the situation with Royce. While Jaid fights for her life, we're going to bring him back to her. Because I don't want to have to be the one to tell her when she wakes up that she's lost her son."

"You won't have to," he said fiercely. There was a fire in his gut, one burning for retribution. "It was Malsovic. Had to be. Adam has a file on him, if you haven't seen it. He was already gone when the hotel raid went down. But for something of this size...he had assistance."

"Two vehicles filled with gunmen worth of help." Paulie's gaze was steely. "And maybe someone on the inside, as well. We're running tests on everything Royce ate and drank in the past twenty-four hours, and right now, no one in the compound has been cleared, with the exception of family. We're looking hard at the CNA who accompanied Jaid's mother to where they were staying. We've got a warrant to check his bank records first thing in the morning. If he was paid off, we'll find out. And then we'll discover the rest. I'm taking care of that myself. Adam said you'd be the one with the best prediction of where the kidnapper would take Royce. That's why I'm talking to you first before I do a conference call with the other agents."

Declan slanted a gaze at Eve in the seat next to his. She was pale but stoic, with no sign of the tears she'd wept when they'd heard the news hours earlier. "One of the masterminds behind the first attempt to kidnap Royce was scooped up in a raid last night. With twenty-nine counts of human trafficking against her, it's doubtful she'll see the light of day any time soon. Our translator on this case, Eve Larrison," he nodded in her direction, "has gone over all the communications retrieved from computers seized last night." He gave her a gentle nudge. She'd discovered the rest. The news was hers to share.

Her voice husky, she said, "What we've found on her computer leads us to believe that Royce was kidnapped because Malsovic, and Sun Yanyu, who was arrested last night, think he's the son of Rizqi bin Osman. The man escaped the city seven years ago after running a very similar human trafficking operation that was operating in the hotel recently. Adam had shared the fact that Jaid Raiker's father somehow ended up with the infant and took him to Jaid for safekeeping."

"When Burke and I located Malsovic's apartment last night, we found a cardboard box behind the couch filled with information on Royce Benning."

"Jaid's father." Paulie nodded. Declan had the distinct impression that the details about how the boy had come to live with Jaid weren't news to the other man. "He left when she was eleven."

"That might coincide with the timing of when he started working for bin Osman." He'd managed to surprise Samuels. "According to the documentation we found, Benning owed the man for drugs and began dealing for him to pay off his debt. Then there isn't much information until nine years ago. Details of Benning's friends. Places he'd been seen. People he'd been seen with."

"Which correlates to the time Jaid's father was killed. So where will Malsovic go?"

"Bin Osman is in Malaysia," Declan told him. "In Johor Bahru, specifically. It's located in the southern portion of the country, with over a million residents and a substantial tourism industry, thanks in large part to its proximity to Singapore. FBI Agent Stillions has been involved in this case and has learned that bin Osman has a sprawling criminal network operating in the city and beyond. The man has nine daughters, but no other sons."

"And this Malsovic is working for bin Osman?" demanded Samuels. "Is that what this is about?"

"I don't think so, although he appears to be familiar with Royce's parentage. He hopes to sell Royce to him," Eve put in quietly. Paulie's face went fierce. "Yanyu put out an offer for a million dollars to deliver the boy to bin Osman. It's still unclear, but there may have been bad blood between her and Malsovic. Or maybe he decided to cut her out of the operation and strike out on his own. But there's no doubt that finding Royce means going to Malaysia. To bin Osman."

"Yesterday Adam got started on getting Malsovic's name and face to all the airports and border security."

The rage that threatened to well when Declan thought of the boy at the mercy of the ruthless Malsovic had to be tucked away. Declan concentrated on doing just that before going on. "Catching the bastard at a border, an airline, a port—that would make things a whole lot easier. And safer for Royce. But Malsovic's an expert forger. I figure he created all the IDs for the women he trafficked here. He'll manufacture one for the boy. He likely had the equipment in his room at the hotel, but it was missing when it was raided last night. Nor did we find it at his apartment."

Eve spoke again. "The IT people in Raiker's lab were able to recover two attachments from the last encrypted email Yanyu sent bin Osman's contact. One was what looks like a telephoto picture of Royce. The other was a copy of prenatal DNA paternity testing done nine years ago. The female's name was Lexie Walker, possibly American. The male was bin Osman. The fetus was a boy. The results showed ninety-nine percent certainty that bin Osman was the father."

"I'll have an agent dig up everything they can find on

her. Have another couple keep up the pressure on the airlines, ports and border customs. I'm sending Kellan Burke and Finn Carstens with you." For a man unused to being in charge, Paulie fell seamlessly into the role. "Royce will probably be safe enough until he's delivered to bin Osman, but we don't want to take any chances. He's now been missing four hours and thirty-six minutes. Adam wants to keep his jet on hand until he's sure Jaid's out of danger, so you'll have to line up a charter. The clock is ticking."

His sign off was every bit as abrupt as Raiker's. Declan looked at Eve. "How soon can you be ready for a twenty-four-hour flight to Malaysia?"

All signs of the shock and regret she'd expressed when she heard the news hours earlier had vanished. Her expression was as determined as he'd ever seen it. "I'm ready when you are."

~

NATURE CONSPIRED AGAINST THEM. The day's rain had turned to ice as the temperature dropped, closing runways and delaying flights. Forty hours had passed by the time their chartered plane reached their destination. Four hours to clear customs and collect their luggage in Kuala Lumpur. Another four to rent a car and drive to Johor Bahru. Find a hotel. All in the middle of the night in a blinding rain storm. They could look forward to more of the same weather since it was monsoon season. "He couldn't travel to the South Pacific. A nice beach some-where," Eve muttered as they were led to their rooms, rain running off them in rivulets as they took an elevator to the twelfth floor with their bags. "No. We have to have eighty-degree temperatures and one hundred percent humidity."

"I'll take eighty degrees over the temps we've been having in DC, rain or not," Kellan declared.

Finn Carstens just gave her one of his quick smiles. With the man's slightly dreamy hazel eyes and dark wavy hair, he looked more like a poet than a doctor. And that's just what the man was, Declan had told her. She still hadn't figured out his role in Raiker's agency.

"Two doubles in each." Burke pushed open the first door and did a quick visual check. "The guys can take one room and leave you to hog the other yourself, Eve."

"I don't want her alone. Not even with us next door," Declan put in before she could say anything. "One of us needs to stay with her. Like you say, there are two beds."

The other man's smile was wide. "I'm guessing you're volunteering for the duty. What the hell. You guys *are* married."

"What?" Finn looked a bit confused. "Really?"

"For the assignment," Declan clarified.

"Ah."

"We'll drop off our luggage and be back in a few minutes." Already he was steering Eve to the next room. "And then we need to go over the intelligence the team has on bin Osman and Lexie Walker." Updates had come frequently during the trip, but they needed to put them all together for a clearer picture of the man Malsovic would likely be dealing with.

And plan their next move. He closed the door behind him and eyed Eve knowingly as she dropped her bag next to one of the beds. "How jet-lagged are you?"

"No more than you three are, I imagine." But there was exhaustion stamped on her face despite her words. They'd spent a full day in the air and there was an eleven-hour time difference. Where it would have been ten in the morning in DC, it was about nine PM here. "I've never been to Malaysia before. I was shocked by the high rises and traffic."

"And the rain."

"I was prepared for that. But not happy about it. And the umbrellas I brought were in my bag, so a lot of good they did me." She was studying him with a slight smile on her face. "You know your insistence of sharing my room did not go unnoticed by the other two."

He tossed his bag near enough to the other bed to satisfy him. "What I said was true. This area of the country isn't particularly safe to begin with. A woman alone would be asking for trouble."

"So is a woman in a motel room with Declan Gallagher."

Something lightened inside him at the amusement lacing her words. "You'll be in as much trouble as you want to be," he assured her. He wasn't going to let her out of his sight. Nor suffer through an inevitable argument by bringing that up. This situation was too urgent for either of them to focus on anything but the job at hand. There were things they had to talk about—but not with the other two agents with them every minute, and not with their most important task still ahead of them.

Finding Royce and taking him home to his parents.

He slipped their computer bags off his shoulder and crossed to set them both on the desk tucked into the corner of the room. He opened one to take out the laptops before stopping to aim another glance at her as a thought struck. "You know, your blond hair is going to make you stand out like a sore thumb here."

"I've thought of that." She gave a quick grimace as she

dug in her purse and came up with a hairbrush. "I'll be too memorable. Later today...it is the next day here, right?" At his affirmation, she went on. "I packed a scarf to wear on my head. As much as this pains me to say, we're going to have to go shopping. I think it would be best if I bought a hijab to wear. It wouldn't look out of place with the Muslim population here, and it would keep my head covered."

He nodded, a feeling of relief filling him as he picked up their laptops and headed to the door. A hijab would cover her head almost completely, leaving only her face bare. It would be an effective disguise. But no one looking at her light skin and blue eyes would take her for a native. And the bandages she still wore would make her even more memorable. "You've given this some thought," he murmured, as she trailed behind him out the door.

"I'm full of ideas," she said cryptically.

The words didn't exactly ease the band of tension in his chest. There was only one thing that would—to make sure they kept a tight lid on any ideas that put her front and center of this operation.

ZUPAN WAS SNORING LOUDLY. Malsovic shot the man a murderous glance from his spot two seats over. The boy was between them, whether asleep or still barely conscious from the latest injection, it was hard to tell. Nor did it matter.

The kid was a troublemaker. Just as he had been in the Suburban during that first plan to take him. Hobart had fucked up, of course. But all would have been well had the boy not made hassles.

The flight to Malaysia was a long one, but Malsovic had always had a problem sleeping on a plane. And now there was too much to worry about. He had many contacts in Malaysia, as in all of Southeast Asia. Contacts that could get a message to bin Osman. And to others, who might be compelled to pay for the boy if bin Osman could not be persuaded.

But despite the plans he'd put into motion, he was aware of the many ways they could go awry.

He hadn't expected to keep Zupan alive this long, but the man had come in handy dealing with the boy. So Malsovic had grudgingly paid for his cruise fare to the Bahamas along with the two tickets he'd already purchased. And the flight from Nassau to Johor Bahru. It was more expensive to fly there than to Kuala Lumpur. But Zupan had plumped up Malsovic's bankroll when he'd managed to divert Gallagher's payment from Shuang's account to his own.

Smiling as he thought of the extra cash, he gave a nod. Yes, Zupan came in handy. He had shaved his beard and then dyed his own and the boy's hair to a similar mud brown for the passport photos. The two could pass for father and son even if one looked closely at the passports and birth certificate that Malsovic had produced. Malsovic had let his own beard grow, so his photo with the Band-Aid below his eye and the shadowed jaw looked a bit different than the picture on his last passport. There was also the fact that authorities would be looking for two people traveling together and not three.

A man who made himself useful deserved to live a bit longer. So Zupan would survive for a time.

Exactly as long as it took Malsovic to trade the boy for a lifetime of riches.

∾

"Our intelligence tells us that bin Osman has three homes. The one here is only a few miles away." Finn was reading from a missive they'd received from Paulie. "He has another on Danga Bay, but we can probably figure he isn't using it during monsoon season."

"Where's the third?" Kell asked around a gigantic yawn.

"Chiang Mai, Thailand."

"He could be there," Eve put in. She was sitting cross-legged in a chair, accessing the Internet on her laptop. "Dry winters, unlike in Malaysia."

"Let's hope it's just an occasional getaway. His business interests are here. How old a guy is he?"

Finn checked through the reports he'd brought up on his computer. "Sixty-two."

"Shuang seemed to have trouble getting to the man, even through email," Eve said without looking up from her screen. "That could have been because of the bad blood between them, or because he insulates himself. Possibly both. We have the advantage of knowing who she communicated with in her attempt to get a message to bin Osman, though."

Something in her tone alerted Declan. "You think we need to try and go through the same channels?"

Their gazes met over the top of her computer. She was going to have to broach this carefully. She already knew Declan well enough to realize he was conditioned to object to any plan that increased her visibility. "I think we can skip right to Ahmed Pascal. From Shuang's recovered communications, he seemed to be the closest to bin Osman. We should send him an email. Today. Ask for a meeting."

The three men looked at each other warily. "For what purpose?"

"We know Malsovic will be contacting bin Osman some

way. Chances are, his request for a meeting will be channeled through Pascal, or someone close to him. We find Royce by finding his captor. We don't know where he is, but we know where bin Osman is. Hence, we use bin Osman—or his emissary—to find Malsovic."

"We can do that by putting the residence under surveillance," Kell pointed out.

"We'll do that, too. But what's wrong with a direct approach?" Eve gathered steam as she presented her argument. "It gives us a chance to see Pascal for ourselves. We don't mention Malsovic's intent for contacting them. We make it clear that it's Malsovic we want. We pay cash for Pascal to let us know if the man gets in touch with him. And more for his location."

Declan shook his head. "That seems like an unnecessary risk. We'll do surveillance tomorrow. Today," he corrected. "We may find a rental close to bin Osman that will give us a good view of his exits. If not, there are enough of us to cover the whole place."

Finn had looked up from his laptop and was considering them. "I'm not sure there's much of a downside to what Eve is suggesting. Why not try it in addition to the surveillance? Yes, Pascal might try to tail her after a meeting. Probably will. But that should be easy enough to circumvent. And if there's even a slight chance he'll tip us off when Malsovic contacts him, it seems a risk worth taking."

"We find an Internet café later and send the communication from a computer there," Kell suggested. "That way if Pascal responds and we've thought of another way, he can't trace the email back to the server at this hotel."

Declan didn't like it. Eve could see that. And she had no doubt she'd be hearing about that later. Deliberately, she changed the subject. "What's the intel say about Lexie Walker? Was she American?"

"A seventeen-year-old runaway from Round Hill, Virginia," Kell told her. "Hard to say how she crossed paths with bin Osman. There's no death certificate on file for her, and her case is still open. Only family is a father doing a thirty-year stretch for raping an eleven-year-old girl, and a brother on death row for killing two police officers."

Little wonder that the girl had run away, Eve thought, with a flash of empathy. But she hadn't found a better life in DC. "What's the latest on Jaid's prognosis?"

Finn hesitated. "She was in surgery for twelve hours. They took her back in a while ago. There was another internal bleed."

His words cast a pall on the group and effectively voided Declan's earlier objection. She'd make sure of that. It was his nature to want Eve out of the line of danger. Raiker had probably felt the same about his wife. They could mitigate the risk she was suggesting. She already knew he'd insist on going with her.

With Jaid Raiker's life in the balance...with her son missing...they could really do no less.

THEY'D AGREED to get a few hours' sleep. All four of them resembled the walking dead after their long flight. Declan was stretched out beside her, his arms folded behind his head. But he wasn't sleeping. She wasn't either. As exhausted as they both were, too much was running through her mind. It would be the same for him. Worry about Jaid. Her son. And what the boy might be going through at Malsovic's hands.

"How old were you when the State Department recruited you?" he asked suddenly.

Of all the things she might have guessed he was thinking about, she wouldn't have predicted this. "I was a sophomore at Harvard. Majored in multiple languages and international studies." She'd been taken aback when she'd been approached by two DOS personnel. Intrigued by the later rigorous testing and the final offer.

He shifted on the bed, and she felt him curve against her back, tucking her in against his warmth. And immediately, she felt a bit lighter in the telling. "I really did start out translating documents and interpreting diplomatic conversations." It all seemed so long ago now, although it'd been only eight years. "But then I started being sent to various trainings. Weapons. Self-defense. Communications. And I knew I wasn't going to spend all of my career stuck at a desk all day."

"I already know how disappointed you were by that."

She smiled at the low rumble in her ear. "Since I have a feeling you have a similar taste for adventure, you're hardly one to talk."

"Raiker called you a secret weapon. I'm guessing that isn't far from the truth."

Her shrug was impatient. "Hardly that. But the element of surprise is an advantage, especially in delicate situations."

"But you've shared none of that with your family."

"This sounds like a cop out, but they're better off not knowing. They wouldn't understand the value in what I do. They would concentrate on the risk that sometimes accompanies my work, without giving any consideration for the reward." And the satisfaction she received from some of the covert assignments she'd been given far exceeded that elicited from simple interpretation and translation services. "They understand the tangible. Progress made in research. Advancements in science and technology that will help humanity. They would grapple to comprehend the intrinsic rewards of helping individuals."

"Like being the one responsible for the rescue of twenty-nine women."

"Not solely responsible, but having a hand in it, yes." It was easy to talk to him like this, wrapped in a lazy cocoon of intimacy. Easy to share things she'd spent a lifetime tucking away. "It makes them sound like bad people. They aren't. They're just very focused, and that focus doesn't leave much room for things outside their careers."

"You cut them a bit more slack than I would. But it's hard not to be able to share your work with those closest to you."

She thought about that and wondered if he found it true. "Maybe it's a tradeoff. My parents and siblings gravitated toward spouses who shared the same interests, similar jobs, and opinions on just about everything. Which is fine, for them, but I always wondered, where's..."

"The chemistry?" he supplied.

"Exactly." She turned in his arms and tipped her face up to his. "There has to be more to a relationship than seeking a carbon copy of myself." Like passion. Romance. Adventure. Her mind skirted the fact that this man embodied all three.

"People think of risk as physical danger." His tone was contemplative. One hand stroked absently down her spine. Up again. "In my family, the gamble is all emotional. Most of them leapfrog in and out of relationships so fast I can't keep track of them. None seem to have the staying power that gran and grandda have, and that's a bit daunting.

Maybe finding someone similar to yourself is a way to minimize the chance you'll tire of them."

"Maybe." But it sounded boring, and perhaps that was the reason she'd been more than a little selective with the men she dated. She'd spent her life in a state of suspended animation, waiting to break free of the family expectations that had just never fit her. Adulthood had brought with it the freedom to discover the things that did fit. Her stomach did a little flip as she realized that this man was one of them.

His hand settled on her hip, suffusing her with heat. "Knowing that you have experience with covert work doesn't make a bit of difference in one regard. It's not going to make me worry about you less during this thing, any more than you knowing my background will negate yours. You're under my skin, Evie. Don't know how it happened. Just that it did. I'm going to reserve the right to mitigate the risk where you're concerned. And I damn well won't apologize for that."

A curl of warmth spread through her belly. So, she was under his skin. She could appreciate the sentiment. Declan Gallagher had lodged himself firmly in her mind from the first time she'd laid eyes on him. "No apology necessary."

"Good." His teeth raked lightly at her shoulder. "Because I've used up my ratio with you."

There was nothing apologetic in the pressure of his mouth when it settled against hers. Nothing tentative in the way she returned his kiss. When they'd first made love, he'd ignited something inside her she'd never realized was banked and simmering. Now that she knew the feel of his flesh against hers, the glide of his hands on her skin, that fire inside could be summoned more easily. Hooking her leg over his thigh, she scored his bottom lip with her teeth and let herself sink into the flames.

His hand swept under her satin nightshirt and had it up and over her head in a rushed movement that spoke of need. She welcomed it. Returned it. Her fingers flexed on his biceps as her tongue did battle with his. One touch from him torched her control. The recognition would have alarmed her if she hadn't felt the way his heart thudded in his chest. Heard his ragged breathing. And knew he felt the same wild coursing in his blood she did.

Without releasing her lips, he cupped her breasts, brushing his thumbs along the sides before taking her nipples between his fingers to roll them gently. They peaked beneath his touch, and Eve reached down to push his boxer briefs over his hips and drag them down his thighs. He kicked them away. She didn't want slow, and she didn't want gentle. It may have taken her a while to be certain of just what she was looking for, but she knew she'd found it. This man. This moment. It was more. *He* was more than she'd ever thought to find.

She reached for him, felt his shaft leap and pulse in her hand. Her fingers closed around his cock, and she stroked him with a rhythm designed to drive them both a bit mad.

His touch was incinerating any thought of restraint. One moment caressing, the next just a few degrees shy of rough. His hand slipped between her thighs, rubbing lightly at the dampness there. Last time he'd reduced her to a shuddering heap. Tonight, she was determined to return the favor. But first, she had to evade those clever knowing hands. That expert seeking mouth.

When she released him and pulled away, he made a move to stop her. But his movements halted when she embarked on a sensual journey of discovery.

With her lips, she traced the angles on his chest, the dips and rises of his muscles and ribs. Moving lower, she swirled her tongue in the slight indentation of his navel. Trailed her finger along the ribbon of hair to where it arrowed to his sex.

The muscles in his belly clenched and jumped beneath her touch, the evidence of his reaction firing sparks of desire through her system. His penis was engorged, quivering. And when she took him in her mouth, his hips jerked helplessly.

She wrapped her fingers around him to stroke as she used the tip of her tongue to lash at the sensitive tip. And let the dark flavor of him work through her until it joined the fever in her blood.

He withstood the sensual torment for long moments. But when her intent changed, when the soft suction grew stronger, his fingers tightened on her shoulders. Urged her higher.

"Not this time. Not without you." It pleased her that his voice was ragged. And she was more than willing to comply with his request. The desperation had returned. Intensified. And when he reached for the foil wrapper he'd placed on the bedside table, she took it from him with fingers more than a little unsteady. Opened it. And rolled it over his length while everything inside her turned to steamy, molten heat.

She'd never wanted safe and comfortable and had found neither with this man. What she'd discovered was more, far more than she'd ever thought to discover. She didn't recognize herself with him, and although she knew the fact should frighten her, Eve found it exhilarating.

Positioning herself over him, she took him in, a fraction of an inch at a time. Her slowness had beads of perspiration sheening Declan's forehead. But although his fingers clenched on her hips, he allowed her to set the pace.

Groaned when she'd finally seated him completely inside her.

Her head fell back as she began to move, her eyes sliding closed in pleasure at the delicious friction. She'd meant to go slow and easy, but need streaked through her, unexpected and debilitating, dictating a more frenetic pace. His control snapped, and his hips surged powerfully under hers. The frantic rhythm brought a rush of pleasure. It threatened to pull her in, push her over. She forced her eyelids open, determined that she wouldn't fall alone.

And seeing him, eyes silvered in the shadows, fixed intently on her, had her heart stuttering. Then filling. And when she shattered, riding the spiral of release and the eddies of aftershock. She felt him come a moment later, their bodies shuddering and quaking together. With her last shred of conscious thought she recognized that she'd found what she'd never known she'd been seeking.

THEY WERE able to take a bus to the Johor Bahru City Square, which boasted a four-story mall rivaling anything DC had to offer. If Eve enjoyed shopping, she would have been in seventh heaven. As it was, the multitude of stores were both daunting and frustrating. She longed for the ease of purchasing online.

They'd split up. While she and Declan went to the mall, Kellan and Finn checked out bin Osman's residence in town. Putting off the inevitable as long as possible, she slowed as they passed an Internet café tucked into the first floor. Glanced at Declan.

His expression was resigned. He'd voiced no objection this morning when they'd resumed discussing their next steps, but Eve wasn't fooled. He'd do whatever he could to protect her in their time here. She could hardly fault him for that when she felt the same way about him.

"As long as we're doing this, I have an idea for some intelligence gathering."

He spoke in Scottish Gaelic, which told her that his idea had something to do with Royce's kidnapping. "Why don't you buy thirty minutes of computer time and a couple of coffees." He pulled out his wallet and handed her a bill.

"It's not going to take more than a couple minutes to send the message."

His smile was cocky. "It will if we send more than an email." He didn't say more, just sauntered over to the furthest computer and pulled up an extra seat. She went to the register and bought them each a kopi, Malaysian coffees, and paid for computer time. The cups she had to set on a nearby empty table, as numerous signs printed in Malay and Chinese warned users from having beverages near the computers.

She took a sip from hers before asking, "So what's your idea?"

He patted the chair next to him, and she left her cup to join him before the screen. "We know Pascal is close to bin Osman. I did a little research on him, but didn't find out much. Stillions would be able to get the dirt on him, if there is any. But I'm guessing I can learn a lot more if I can get into his computer, take a look around at the files he keeps."

Eve sent him a careful glance. "Did you learn how to do that in Cybercrimes?"

"My ability with all things digital was the reason I got into the cyber unit." He reached to snatch the coffee off the table and took a quick drink, keeping a careful eye on the teen at the register. "Go ahead. Access the phony email account I set up for you earlier."

Still unsure what he was about, she did as he requested and quickly composed the email they'd decided on, telling the man that she believed someone she knew would be trying to contact bin Osman about a delivery from the States, and that she was willing to pay well for any information regarding the individual's whereabouts. When she was about to sign off, he said, "Add a line that you aren't sure what name he'll be using, so you're enclosing a photo."

Her fingers poised over the keys, she pointed out, "I don't have a picture of Malsovic."

"I'll email you one."

She quickly typed the sentence, signed the email and then waited.

"Okay." He saved the email as a draft and then pulled out his phone, brought up a photo of Malsovic and sent it to her new email address. They waited a moment for it to arrive, and when it did, Declan bent over the computer and started typing furiously.

"You're writing more code. But what's it for?"

"I'm constructing a Trojan Horse that will infect his computer when he clicks on the photo." He didn't look up from his task. "I'll shrink the picture down too small to be seen clearly, and the normal reaction will be to click on it, make it larger. When he does so, the code will open a portal into his computer that will allow me to go on a virtual tour, looking at whatever I like."

She'd heard of such things. It was often the way malware got into a computer, but she couldn't imagine him knowing how to construct it. Computer code was a foreign language all its own, Eve decided. One she had no interest in ever learning.

"What if he doesn't click on it?"

"Then we're screwed. The Trojan Horse only works if he activates the code, in this case hidden in the picture itself. Give me a sec."

Because he seemed to need silence, Eve got up and went to the table, drinking her coffee as she watched the other patrons of the store. She intercepted more than a few open stares and knew it was her hair that garnered attention. And maybe the bandages that still adorned her face. The interest was a reminder of the need for the shopping she'd have to do after Declan was finished.

Twenty minutes later, his chair scraped as he closed out of the computer and rose. "All right. I got the photo attached to the email draft, signed it with the name you'll be using and sent. Even if he doesn't agree to meet with you, he still might be curious enough to look at the picture. It's worth a shot." He reached for the coffee, made a face when he drank and discovered it lukewarm. But he carried it with him out of the store.

He sipped from the coffee as she swiftly crossed the tiled area, heading to the stairs. "You move faster when you're shopping," he observed.

"So I can leave quicker," she muttered. She slowed to take a drink. Eve had a feeling she was going to require the fortification.

"You know the most interesting thing about this place?" he asked in Scottish as they climbed the stairs, and Eve surveyed the stores on the first floor. "Other than the writing on the shops, we could almost be in a mall in the States."

It was true enough. Even the range in the style of dress, from shorts and tee shirts to more traditional Muslim garb, could be seen in DC. Some places even had names spelled in English.

She slowed in front of one of them. "One store. Ten minutes."

He grinned, a quick flash of teeth. "I'll time you."

It was more like eighteen minutes and that had been long enough. But Declan's expression when Eve walked out of the boutique carrying two bags was shocked enough to make her feel like her time had been well-spent. "They allowed me to wear one of the outfits out," she explained. Had been more than happy to cut off the tags so she could do so.

The black slacks and simple white cotton blouse with three quarter sleeves was modest, but not out of place in any culture. The hijab she wore was gray, and covered her head and neck, leaving only her face bare. She had the dark thought that the garment would negate any worry about what the humidity did to her hair. Maybe she should consider wearing one back home whenever it rained.

Declan pulled out his phone and read a text. "Kell says they've got bin Osman's place in sight. It's heavily secured. No way Malsovic is getting to the man without an invite." He broke off to halt in front of a store window and, cupping her elbow, ushered her inside. When they'd exited, he was carrying more bags than she was and looking exceedingly pleased with himself.

"Christmas gifts?" It was a rare experience for her to shop, and she couldn't recall ever doing it before with a man. And especially not one who seemed to take such pleasure in selecting items.

"Gran will make something creative out of the fabric. What's the clerk call it? Batik? And Grandda collects miniatures. My grandfather is the most difficult to buy for since he owns half of the East Coast." She shot him a glance. Wasn't sure from his expression if he was joking. "But other than being a wine connoisseur, he's something of a tea aficionado. It's a sure bet he has no Malaysian teas in his cupboard."

"So...you just buy them things you think they'll like? And they're okay with that?" The idea was foreign to her. Even once her family had started exchanging gifts, they were quite specific about what to select, even going so far as to send along links for the suggested item. She'd learned to do the same, after she'd ended up with a replica of the Hubble telescope and tickets to an engineering festival. Anything Declan had bought minutes earlier would be infinitely preferable.

"Sometimes you strike out." They descended the stairs and headed across the ground floor of the mall. "But if you know someone well enough, you should be able to select something that suits them. And before you ask," he added with a sidelong glance, "if I were to select something for you, I already know what it would be."

It was a declaration meant to provoke. And not for the life of her would she inquire further, although he clearly wanted her to.

"Lucky for you that won't be necessary," she said airily. But couldn't banish the thought.

"The blue dress," he informed her as they strolled out of the mall into the garden that fronted one side. "The one you tried on in that shop in DC when we were trying to lose our tail." His smile was slow and wicked and completely devastating. "Although given the way you looked in it, it would really be a gift for both of us."

His gaze had liquid fire spreading through her veins. And the fact that it took just a look from him to summon an instant heated response was enough to tell Eve that she was in way too deep where Declan Gallagher was concerned. And she wasn't quite sure what she was going to do about that.

A cell alert sounded. Both of them searched for their phones in a move that could have been choreographed. "Mine." He shifted packages to one hand, so he could bring up the message. She halted beside him when he stopped to read it. There was no precipitation, but the clouds forming overhead heralded its imminent arrival. Declan's darkening expression was a reflection of the skyline.

"Stillions sent along some intel," he said in Scottish, and the two of them started moving again. "I'd been wondering how bin Osman recovered so quickly after fleeing the US seven years ago. Apparently, he made his fortune by murdering one of the most notorious criminals in the city and taking over the man's empire."

"And that's who Royce would be sold to." Eve shuddered, although the temperatures were already in the low eighties. She'd held onto the fact that the boy was likely to be physically unharmed if Malsovic meant to sell him to the man believed to be his father.

But there were different types of injury. And the thought of Royce being turned over to someone who valued human life so cheaply was chilling indeed.

THEY'D BEEN BACK in the hotel less than an hour, and Declan was poring over his laptop as they waited for Finn and Kell to return. "There's news here from Paulie," he reported, his gaze fixed on the screen. "They've finally figured out who spilled the information about Royce's pick-up procedure at school."

Intrigued, Eve asked, "One of the school employees?"

He shook his head. "A parent. Apparently, she was approached by Hobart and paid to change her daughter's pick-up procedure so she could report back on the details of Royce's. She's claiming duress, and who knows, he may have threatened her if she refused. It's a police matter now."

"Did he mention how Jaid is doing?"

"Not conscious, but holding her own, Paulie says."

Trepidation filled her. Bullets inflicted a tremendous amount of damage on the human body. "What's her condition?"

Declan's mouth flattened. "It remains critical."

As did the task they were engaged in here. Frustrated urgency filled her. There hadn't been enough progress on the case in the time since the shooting and Royce's kidnapping. Something had to come to a head soon.

"Maybe we should have rented a second car and monitored the country's airports." Although they had no way of knowing if that was how Malsovic would move the boy into the country. There'd been no hits on their identification. She knew someone would still be monitoring that end of things back in DC.

"I did discover something interesting. The second half of the payment Shuang deposited in the account Raiker set up for me? It's gone."

Eve frowned. "How is that possible? Money can't just change accounts."

"It does if the hacker is determined enough and highly skilled. Even more intriguing, it bounced back to an account for Shuang, but yesterday it moved to one in Sergei Peterol's name."

"So Malsovic is responsible?" Peterol was one of his aliases.

"Either he or Zupan."

"What do you do now?" Her online skills didn't run much beyond social media, email and shopping. But from the little she'd seen of Declan's expertise, there wasn't much online he couldn't do.

"Not sure." He clasped his hands, stretched. "I transferred the first half of the money right away. I could move this half myself, but I'm not certain we want to interfere with whatever Malsovic has planned. I alerted Paulie. He's got the necessary equipment and the expertise in digital forensics when it comes to retrieving it."

Her cell pinged, and there was a quick lurch in her stomach. "Email." Declan was across the room and at her side in the time it took her to open it. A quick spurt of dizzying relief hit her when she saw the sender. Ahmed Pascal.

"What's it say?"

Eve took a moment to scan the message. It was written in Malay to the persona she'd created, as her initial email had been.

Miss Coughlin,

I am intrigued by your proposition. While I cannot reveal any business matters concerning my employer, I am willing to listen to your request. I am available to meet today at three PM at Maco Vintage. Please let me know if this time is inconvenient for you.

Ahmed Pascal

"The tone's a bit more polite than the last communication he sent to Shuang," she murmured, her heart tripping fast and hard in her chest.

"It should be." Declan pulled out his own cell. Began to

tap a text message. "What did you offer for the information?"

"Five thousand."

His gaze rose to meet hers for a moment. "Money well spent if this pans out the way we hope. Otherwise..."

Eve could finish that sentence for him. Otherwise they'd have to come up with another way to find Royce Raiker. And she knew it wasn't her imagination that time was running out.

⌒

"How LONG HAVE you been in our country, Miss Coughlin?"

Eve sipped the shop's signature iced coffee from a porcelain cup before returning it to the matching saucer. "Not long." Ahmed Pascal was no more than five eight, slender with styled, dark hair swept back from his forehead and a neatly trimmed goatee. His suit was impeccably cut and his shoes, Italian leather. She didn't know how high up the man was in bin Osman's organization, but evidently his station paid well.

"I sent you a photo of a man as an email attachment. I followed his trail and know he is headed here. I also know he hopes to have some sort of deal with Rizqi bin Osman. That isn't my concern. But this man and I have unfinished business. Since I believe he might be in contact, I would be grateful if you share when he does. And where he might be staying."

Pascal brought his cup to his lips, his gaze never leaving hers as he drank. Lowering the cup, he murmured, "Grateful to the tune of five thousand US dollars, your email said."

"Yes." Eve strove to keep the nerves that were stuttering and thrumming inside her from showing in her expression. "I believe this man knows where my sister is. She's been missing for months, and he promised to give me the details regarding her whereabouts. Instead, he left the country, taking with him the money I had paid for the information."

"This isn't the States, Miss Coughlin." There was a hint of disdain in his words. "It is not safe for a woman alone to go on such a journey."

Wrapping both hands around her cup, she raised it for another drink. "I'm not alone." She watched his gaze dart around the small coffee and dessert shop. Knew he was gauging the other occupants for the possibility of who might be assisting her. "And I'm not helpless. As our soon-to-be mutual acquaintance will learn. This request will take little of your time but pay handsomely. I hope you will consider it."

He sat back in his seat. Studied her. "There are many variables to consider. It will depend, of course, on the importance this man holds for my employer. Right now, I can promise nothing. But if I am able to be of assistance, I will of course be willing."

"That is all I ask." Collecting her purse, she rose. "Thank you for your time. I hope to hear from you soon."

"The pleasure was mine." But the polite words weren't reflected in his watchful gaze. And Eve felt his eyes boring into her back as she wound through the tables and out to the front patio where a light drizzle had begun to fall.

She purposefully meandered, fully expecting to be followed. The street vendors wouldn't be out in full force until dark when the night market got underway. But the open-air shops she passed were full of wares, and she frequently stopped and browsed when an owner called out to her.

The next shop was full of women's clothing. Eve intended to pass it, this morning's ordeal still fresh in her mind. She didn't get the chance. As she neared the doorway, a hard hand grasped her arm, yanked her inside and off the street.

CHAPTER THIRTEEN

FIRST HER HAND flew to her heart. Then it fisted to slug the man at her side. "Declan! Are you trying to give me a heart attack?" She'd kept him in sight as she made her way along the street, but he'd stayed half a block ahead of her before disappearing completely. Now she knew why.

He tugged at the hijab she wore, and she helped him unwrap it before he dropped it into a shopping bag he held. From the depths of it, he pulled out a maxi skirt and a colorful scarf. "Put these on."

Swiftly she stepped into the skirt and pulled it over her trousers. Then arranged the scarf in a decorative style around her neck. After a moment, she reached up to loosen the bandages carefully before removing them, too. He gave her an approving nod, and they walked out of the shop arm in arm. Anyone following her would be looking for a woman alone, not a blonde in bright clothes with a man at her side. Hopefully, it would be enough to throw any interested parties off her trail.

They walked to the nearest bus stop and eventually made their way via public transportation back to the hotel.

The drizzle showed no signs of lifting, so by the time they reached their room, Eve could be fairly certain that her hair would provide the most effective disguise she could muster. Since dignity was beyond her at this point, she just raked her fingers through the curly mass and shook the moisture from it.

"What have Finn and Kellan come up with?"

In answer, he showed her a series of pictures they'd been sent since arriving at the compound this morning. The bin Osman residence was a mostly whitewashed, sprawling two-story that looked as though square boxes had been stacked haphazardly. The upper story section closest to the gate was red. It was all angles and thrusting flat roofs that extended over portions of the house. It was set well back from the street, an effort, perhaps, to deter anyone with explosives.

"Six thousand square feet, Finn figures, with a guard-house and a guesthouse out back. His oldest daughters and their families live in the guesthouse. Not palatial but definitely a luxury home in this area." The gate connected to stone pillars, which continued around the property in a ten-foot solid fence.

"There's no gate in back." One of the pictures showed a sparkling pool in the well-tended yard, but the wall around the property was complete.

"No. Makes me think there's an underground garage that leads to the street somewhere. I imagine there has to be another exit for an emergency escape." Declan flipped to another set of pictures. Of a slender man in a suit getting into a BMW sedan and driving out the gates. Ahmed Pascal.

"Pascal hasn't returned to bin Osman's residence since

your meet with him. And he hasn't clicked on the attachment you included in your email. At least not yet."

Maybe he'd yet do so, Eve thought. Now that he knew what he stood to gain by passing along a bit of information to her. "Does bin Osman conduct all his business from inside his residence?"

"According to the intelligence Stillions was able to get—maybe from one of your State Department colleagues stationed inside the country—the man rarely leaves the property. And then only under heavy security." His mouth twisted. "I guess if you live by the sword, you're afraid you're going to die the same way."

"Which explains the difficulty getting close to him."

"From the pictures they took, no one is arriving through the gate who bears the slightest resemblance to Malsovic." He flipped quickly through photos of cars coming and going. One showed a woman in her late twenties or early thirties who got out of the chauffeured sedan and walked confidently into the home. Another was of a stout man with salt and pepper hair who was welcomed into the house after being passed through the gate. And in another, a striking woman in her forties entered a car waiting in the drive and was driven away. "This guy," Declan tapped the picture of the man, "has been identified as bin Osman's top lawyer. Probably up to his neck in the man's dirty dealings."

"How high is Pascal in bin Osman's empire?" Eve wondered aloud. The man certainly hadn't lacked confidence. And his loyalty to his employer had seemed sincere.

"Definitely one of his lieutenants, based on the intel from the Feds. He has the power to grant access to bin Osman. It remains to be seen if he'll offer it to Malsovic."

"If he doesn't," Eve said, her gaze lifting to his, "our only chance is that he'll follow through and alert me when the contact is made." It wasn't just that they had no other viable plan for finding Malsovic in the country. It was that currently, this *was* the only viable plan.

AFTER GETTING SOMETHING TO EAT, Declan and Eve had switched places with Finn and Kellan for surveillance duty near bin Osman's. Given the report from the other two, Declan was beginning to believe it was a wasted chore. There was little likelihood that Malsovic would be allowed anywhere near that compound. It would probably be wiser to follow anyone who left. Surely someone would meet with Malsovic away from the residence, much as Pascal had with Eve. Tomorrow, they needed to rent a second car, so they could split up if they needed to.

It was after midnight when they returned to the hotel to find the two other men still up and huddled around a laptop in their room. The excitement in their expressions when they looked up was enough to divert Eve from the exhaustion that had overtaken her in the car. "Paulie thinks they've got a hit on photos of Malsovic and Royce from Interpol's network. Malsovic has a scruff of a beard." She and Declan went to look at the screen.

"He's covered the tattoo under his eye with something for the photo. Makeup, maybe," she observed. Royce's hair has been lightened. Eve swallowed hard looking at the picture of the boy. He appeared unwell. Unhappy. And she was reminded once again of the tremendous stress he was under.

He'd been medicated to simulate a seizure. Declan had gotten that information this evening from Raiker's labs. Which proved that Malsovic wasn't above using drugs to keep the boy under control as he moved him across borders. Royce would be in agony wondering whether his mom was dead. Which was worse than the truth. That she was alive. Barely. That she hadn't regained consciousness yet for more than a minute at a time.

"So, they flew into the city this evening from Nassau, Bahamas." Declan frowned. "Why didn't their passports show up in the States?"

"If they went by water rather than air, there are lots of foreign cruise ships that stop in Florida. Maybe he paid someone off," Finn suggested. "And the US Embassy in Kuala Lumpur has been alerted to Malsovic's and Royce's presence here. Their photos are being distributed to every law enforcement agency in the country."

The news didn't seem to provide as much comfort as it should, and Eve thought she knew why. Malaysia wasn't a partner country in The Hague Convention, an international agreement dealing with parental abductions. They couldn't count on much help from the police regarding Royce's situation. Once they found the boy, the US embassy would be needed to get him out of the country.

But first they had to find him.

"Can I use the laptop for a minute?" Kell and Finn parted so Declan could open another window and type in a URL. It took a moment for Eve to realize he was accessing her fake email account. Another to remember why. After a minute, Declan looked up, an expression of grim satisfaction on his face. "We may have caught out first break. Ahmed Pascal opened the attached photo of Malsovic that we sent him."

"And that means...what, exactly?" Kell asked.

"It means," Declan said, typing rapidly, "that he just invited us to take a look inside his computer."

⁓

UMAR MEGAT LIFTED his gaze from the documents and photos spread in front of him and stared at the man seated across the table. "This is very compelling evidence." He spoke in English because his guest spoke neither Malay nor Chinese. "But not definitive proof of the boy's lineage."

Malsovic threw a glance over his shoulder to make sure no one in the restaurant was paying them close attention. It was lunchtime, and the place was crowded. Then he returned his focus to his host. Two of his contacts had mentioned Megat as someone close to bin Osman. A cousin who would surely wish to curry favor with his powerful relative in order to move higher in his organization. Malsovic reached into his shirt pocket and took out a folded-up envelope. Opening it, he withdrew a vial of blood. Set it in front of the other man.

"This document is a copy of the bloodwork done on the infant nine years ago." He tapped the paper in question. "You have only to run lab tests on this blood for all the proof you need. You will be a hero. Your cousin will surely be grateful to the man who brought him his only son."

Megat pursed his lips. He was a fussy little man, Malsovic thought, better suited to accounting than being an integral part of bin Osman's network. But that was exactly what he was, proving again the injustice of the world.

When Megat reached out to scoop up the vial, Malsovic breathed a bit easier. "The lab work cannot be completed until tomorrow," Umar warned, slipping the glass tube into the briefcase he'd set on the floor next to him. "Even that fast will require some significant cost."

"It will be worth it." Now that success was so close, Malsovic could afford to be confident. It suited him to deal with an underling rather than bin Osman himself. Their last meeting had been acrimonious. The man had been furious that Royce Benning had died without giving up the infant's whereabouts. Better perhaps that he never learn exactly who returned his son to him.

Sweeping up the documents he'd set out for the man's consideration, Malsovic was stopped in the act when Megat put a hand over his. "I will keep these."

Malsovic sat back. "I have the originals in a safe place."

"As well you should." Collecting them, the Megat stuffed them in the briefcase. "If the lab tests come back with the results you say, these documents will help acquire the funds needed to complete our transaction."

"Half a million dollars." Malsovic barely dared to say the amount out loud.

The other man didn't blink. "If you are right about this, his father would pay much, much more to finally have the son who has been lost to him all this time."

The words left Malsovic with the distinct feeling that he had sold the boy too cheaply. But it would be enough money for him to move to another country, start another business. Begin a new life. And maybe there would be a way to up the price, to cover the expenses he'd incurred. Yes, he'd ask for more tomorrow. "You can call when you get the test results back."

"I will."

Megat rose and stuck out his hand. Malsovic shook it. "I thank you for coming to me with this important news. Until tomorrow."

Malsovic turned and made his way out of the crowded restaurant. He was canny enough to realize the man might have him followed, so he would take pains to lose any tail before he headed back to where he'd left Zupan and the boy. He could hardly hide his euphoria as he strode out to the sidewalk.

By this time tomorrow, he would be richer than he'd ever dreamed.

~

THE SUCCESS of the Trojan horse code that Declan had encrypted in the email attachment meant rearranging the duties of the day. He and Eve would stay at the hotel, where he'd sift through the man's stored documents and correspondence, and she'd translate them to see if there was any information they could use. Kell and Finn took surveillance duties again, this time with the intention of following the vehicles leaving bin Osman's compound, at least those holding men.

"What exactly are we looking for?" she asked after a few hours of reading documents aloud to him.

Declan worked his shoulders tiredly. He was growing as frustrated as she was. "I'm not sure. Maybe some information that would give us leverage over bin Osman. Or evidence of his criminal acts that we could then turn over to law enforcement."

Her voice sounded doubtful. "I don't think we could arrange that in time to prevent Malsovic handing over Royce. "And once he's on the property, we'd have a heck of a time getting him off from the looks of the security."

She was right. And they hadn't run across anything yet that provided them with compelling information they didn't already have. "Let's switch to email." He took a moment to access the man's email account and bypass the simple encryption code on the messages. Time crawled as Eve translated them, one after another for over an hour. He stopped her finally with a hand on her arm.

"Do you realize that so far he has daily emails to Nadia and Celine, bin Osman's eldest daughters, and only a couple a week to bin Osman himself?"

"I noticed that, too." She sat back and reached for a water bottle on the desk. Drank. "And they're almost nauseatingly ingratiating. Constant assurances of his loyalty and devotion to them. And the ones he writes and receives to and from Umar Megat seem filled with concern for keeping the women happy, as well. Maybe Pascal is more of an underling than we thought. Perhaps he reports mainly to the daughters."

He drank from his own water bottle. Drained it. "Stillions seems to think that the two women are integral parts of bin Osman's criminal enterprises."

"How does that help us?"

He didn't have the answer to that yet. But he had a feeling it existed in the rest of Pascal's correspondence. "I don't know. Let's keep reading."

"Do you have your people on him?"

"Yes. A half-dozen men on the street armed with his picture. He will try to cover his trail, but he cannot evade all of them." Ahmed Pascal sat down in the chair the man calling himself Goran Simic had vacated and looked at Umar Megat. "Do you believe it is true? Does he really have the son of bin Osman?"

"It might be true." The other man pulled the documents out that Simic had left with him and gave Pascal time to study them. "He also left me with a vial of the boy's blood, which I said I would have tested tomorrow."

Several minutes later, Pascal looked up. "This is very interesting, and there is clearly more here that this man is not telling you. My meeting was with a young woman. An American who knew he would contact one of us, and she's willing to pay for information about where to find him."

"We do not need this kind of trouble."

"No," Pascal said. "Whether the child is bin Osman's or not, our path forward is clear." Megat nodded. Both of them were employed by bin Osman, but their loyalty was with the man's oldest daughters who would one day run his network. Those in bin Osman's line of work did not live to an old age. They had started ensuring their continued employment years ago.

"So, we are agreed. We will find where Simic is staying. We will kill the boy." The daughters would not want a male heir to their father's empire. That much was clear.

"What about Simic? And the woman you met with."

Leaning forward, Pascal lowered his voice. "I have already constructed a plan for them, too."

Privacy had been Malsovic's first thought when he'd looked for a place to stay. The boy needed to be drugged or bound and gagged to keep him from shouting and trying to get away. He would attract too much attention in a hotel. A cheap place in a neighborhood where people took money and didn't ask questions suited their needs. There were many such places in Johor Bahru.

The woman rented the spaces by the week or the month.

She called them furnished condos, which was the worst kind of joke. They were a strip of one-story dwellings, each consisting of little more than a bedroom, front room and tiny kitchen with a bathroom by the back door. The backyard had wire fencing and a large metal doghouse left by the previous renters. The furniture looked a lot like the crap he'd had in his apartment in DC. It didn't matter. He wouldn't be there long.

After bringing them food, Malsovic had left Zupan with the boy before going to the next meeting he had arranged. Something he had learned from Shuang was not to place all his bets on one plan. If things did not work out with bin Osman, he would have something else lined up.

But when he returned late from that meeting, he resolved that the second plan would be a last resort. The payout would be less, as there would be many fees to negotiate out of his take. Zupan was asleep on the couch when he got in, the boy on the mattress in the bedroom. Malsovic changed out of his wet clothes and lay down beside him, exhaustion overpowering him. It had been an arduous few days. But before many more hours, his reward would be in hand.

"I have to go to the bathroom."

He groaned. He considered calling for Zupan but knew he wouldn't be heard over his snores. Rising, he grabbed the kid and pulled him to his feet. His arms and ankles were bound but Zupan must have taken the tape off his mouth to feed him and not replaced it. The man was soft where the boy was concerned.

Ungently, he supported the kid as he half hopped, half waddled to the tiny stall in the back of the house. As he waited, he looked through the house, out the front window. The rain pounded a steady beat on the metal roof. Against a window. In the darkness outside, he saw a light close to the house flick off.

"I'm done."

He didn't stop to think. Just grabbed some paper towels and shoved them in the kid's mouth before hoisting him up over a shoulder while he sidled to the back door. Unlocked it and eased it open. Resecured it before closing it behind him.

Lafka Malsovic had not survived this long by ignoring his instincts.

The rain came down in sheets. The back yard was slippery as he stepped into it. Once he almost landed on his ass as he picked his way across the grass. It was harder than he thought it would be to shove the boy inside the doghouse. He filled the space. "Stay here or I will kill you. Do you understand?" Without waiting for an answer, he started back toward the house.

He stopped when he heard the shots.

"WE NEED A NEW STRATEGY," Kellan Burke groused as he and Finn entered the hotel room. Water dripped off the men's clothes to soak into the carpet. It had been raining for hours. Eve was inclined to agree with the man's assessment. Her eyes burned from the hours spent poring over the documents and correspondence on Ahmed Pascal's computer. She'd long ago ceased to marvel at the ease with which Declan was able to copy the man's materials. If he had constructed a plan in which he would be using the information gleaned, he hadn't shared it with her yet.

"I looked it up today." Finn shook the moisture from his

clothes. "Johor Bahru averages rain half the days in December. Hopefully before we leave, we'll hit a dry spell."

"Maybe we could get a list of rental properties in the area and go around showing Malsovic's picture."

"That'd take Eve's assistance since she speaks the language."

As the men began to discuss the idea, her cell pinged, signaling an incoming email. Stifling a yawn, she opened it to scan it. Then slowed to reread it more carefully. "It's Pascal," she said excitedly, interrupting the men's discussion. "He has the address where Malsovic is staying." Disbelieving, her gaze met Declan's. "He left an account number for me to wire the money I promised if I find the man at this place."

"He gave you the information before he was paid for it?" Burke's voice was skeptical. "That sounds sketchy."

"He says he has contacts everywhere in the city. He can easily find me if I don't pay by morning."

"Map the address on your phone." Declan stood so suddenly his chair teetered behind him. "We have some shopping to do first."

"Flashlights." Finn was already heading to the door. "And rain gear."

Declan was right behind him. "I was thinking more in terms of weapons."

THE GUNFIRE HADN'T LASTED LONG. Afterwards, an eerie silence ensued. Malsovic crouched behind the aluminum doghouse. Even if Zupan had managed to draw one of the guns Malsovic had bought on the black market today, the man was a sound sleeper. He wouldn't have had a chance before the intruder put a bullet in him.

The stranger had saved Malsovic the trouble of getting rid of the man, but he felt no gratitude. Zupan would have been useful a while longer. He watched the small house carefully. Saw the flicker of a light inside a moment before he heard the back door open.

The rain covered the sound, but he could make out a shadowy figure walk into the yard. Slip in almost the same place Malsovic had. A flashlight turned on. Its beam was dim in the pouring rain. It played around the yard. Along the back of the house. After long moments, it headed toward the rear of the lot. Toward the doghouse.

Crouched on all fours, Malsovic waited for the man to come close. Squat to play his beam over the opening of the small hut. Then he shot the stranger, two quick bullets to the head. The constant drumming rain was better than a silencer. The man dropped to the ground, and Malsovic shoved his weapon into his waistband. Then he crept forward to drag the man to the fence at the rear of the property. He emptied his pockets before heaving the body over into the next yard. Collected the man's weapon and turned off the flashlight. And ran gingerly to the side of the house.

He only had to wait a minute. The door opened. "Ilic?" A second stranger stepped out, took a few steps. "Ilic?"

Malsovic shot him twice in the back. Again, he disarmed the man and went through his pockets, then shoved him over the fence. This time he waited ten minutes. Fifteen.

Twenty minutes later, he was certain there were no other gunmen in the house.

~

"Are we clear?"

Even though it was difficult to see him in the driving rain, Eve knew Declan's gaze would be fixed on her when he asked the question. "Perfectly."

"I'm with Finn through the front. Kellan will breach the back. Eve will stay here, just outside the back door. If an adult comes running out of it, use your knife."

She swallowed the protest she wanted to make. They'd agreed on most of the details. There were likely not more than two adults, Zupan and Malsovic, inside. And then there was the boy. If the kidnappers had obtained guns and opened fire, Royce could be harmed. She was almost glad that they didn't have guns to create the kind of firefight that would make injuries certain.

But knives against bullets made for scary odds. So, they'd go with the element of surprise.

And Eve would be stationed outside the back door in case one of them tried to escape that way. She hefted the knife in her hand. They'd gotten their supplies at the night market downtown. Weapons had been the first priority.

Her heart was knocking loud enough that she was afraid Kell would hear it from where he was positioned at the back door. She saw him reach a hand out. Felt a leap of fear when the door handle twisted under his palm. No locks? That didn't seem right. Before she could whisper a warning, he disappeared inside the dark home.

Malsovic gathered what he needed from the house, taking the weapon from near Zupan's body on the floor next to the couch.

It wasn't safe to linger, even with the gunmen dead. But

first he'd collected the guns that he'd paid dearly for. All their IDs. And the research he'd done about the boy's birth. He couldn't leave without it. He put everything he needed in a bag and slipped away. Went for the car where he'd left it parked three blocks over. And while he did, he wondered which of the two meetings about the boy that he'd had today had resulted in this betrayal. He'd have to be clear about that before going forward tomorrow.

He drove with lights off across the yards, halting behind the house two doors down, and crept back to the property. The rain hadn't let up. Stepping carefully over the fence, he headed for the doghouse. The boy had still been in the small shelter, chilled, but not so wet. Where would he go? Malsovic was about to pull him out when he saw movement on the street in front of the house. He dropped to all fours. Crawled behind the doghouse again.

Five minutes crept by, as slow as a dirge. His eyes strained to see in the darkness. Now he could make out only one figure near the back of the house. This one he'd take alive. It would be easy to discover with whom he was working before he killed him.

He crept to the entrance of the doghouse, pulled the boy out by the feet, keeping a careful eye on the figure near the back door. "It is time for you to go," he breathed the words into the boy's ear. "There is assistance by the fence." He reached in the boy's mouth to dislodge the paper towels and tossed them aside. "Call for help. As loud as you can."

The kid croaked, "Help. Help me."

"Louder!"

He hopped forward, his voice a bit stronger this time. "Help! Someone help me!"

Malsovic dropped to all fours, ducking behind the shelter. The figure was heading this way, sliding a bit in the slick mud and grass.

"Help me!"

"Royce. Royce Raiker, is that you?"

Malsovic nearly froze when he heard a female voice, but there was no time to waste. He waited for her to draw nearer before rushing out of his hiding place to tackle the woman. Rolled. Something went flying from her grasp. He pulled his weapon and brought it down over her head. She went limp.

Shoving the gun in his waistband, he easily caught the boy as he attempted to hop away and clamped one hand over his mouth. He carried the kid under one arm, hoisted the woman up with his free hand and half dragged her to the fence. He dumped the boy over and heaved the woman's still body on top of him. Then he jumped over the fence and hauled them to the car nearby, while the boy struggled and shouted.

There was room for both of them in the trunk.

AHMED PASCAL CHECKED the time again. Late. Things should have been over by now. The fact that the expected call hadn't come with the reassuring message was not good at all.

The two he'd sent to take care of the man, who called himself Simic, and the boy had failed. There was no other explanation. He would have been contacted if there was an unexpected issue, or if the house had been empty.

He unlocked his desk and drew out an unregistered drop phone. Called 999. "I heard shots at this address." He read off the house and street number Simic had been trailed to. "Please hurry." Disconnecting, he put the phone back in the desk. Relocked it. The best scenario was that Simic might have stayed around after killing his men, but Pascal doubted that. It was still likely, however, that the woman, Coughlin and her escort had gone to the address after he'd emailed her. Perhaps the police would find her there. Take her in for questioning.

If she mentioned Simic, the police still might look for the man. But they couldn't count on that. He took out his cell. Called Megat. Waited several rings for the man to answer. "We have a problem."

He'd known as soon as they entered the front door that they were too late. The man on the floor had lighter hair, and he was minus a beard, but Declan recognized him as the guy who'd tried to force them into the car to meet with Shuang that first day.

Likely, Malsovic had shot the man when he'd had no further need for him. Except...Declan noted the snarled pattern of muddy tracks on the floor. Leading from the front door and the back. Crisscrossing in the room where Zupan's body lay.

"The place is empty. No basement," Finn reported.

Declan noted the dead man's stocking feet. "At least three adults were here." He pointed to the tracks. The footprints were different sizes.

"You're thinking execution?"

"Maybe it was Malsovic and the boy they wanted." Declan felt his chest go tight. How much could a kid go through?

"So, someone kidnapped the kidnapper?" Finn sent a

careful look around. "Has anyone checked outside?"

Declan headed to where they'd stationed Eve. But when he got outside, she was nowhere in sight. "Eve," he called in a low voice. Maybe she was scouting the area. He should just wait for her to come back.

But a surge of urgency wouldn't let Declan stay put. "Split up and go the other way," he told Kell when the man followed him out. They circled the home. Met at the front door. Declan walked through the house again, desperation rapping at his skull.

"I think you better come out here."

He ran to the back when he heard Finn's voice. "Where'd you get that?" The man was holding the knife he'd given to Eve before they'd gotten out of the car.

"In the yard. And there's more." Kell and Declan followed him to the fence line separating the small yard from the ones on either side. Finn turned on the flashlight app on his cell and pointed it first at one side and then the other. "We've got bodies."

The words struck a frigid chord that vibrated through his system. Declan shot across the yard, nearly falling in the wet grass. But when he drew near, he could tell that the still figure in the grass wasn't Eve. Too tall. Too wide. He stopped in midstride and turned around. "I think they're the gunmen."

Kell continued to the unmoving figure. Jumped the fence to search it. "No ID."

Zupan dead in the living room. Two strangers dead in the neighboring yards. And Malsovic, Royce and Eve gone. The siren that sounded in the distance could have been coming from the alarm sprinting up his spine. Seizing his heart. "He got to her." The certainty was like a blade in Declan's chest. "Malsovic. He's got them both."

MALSOVIC WENT through the wallets and items he'd taken from the gunmen as he drove. The money, what there was of it, he shoved into his own pocket. The names on the IDs meant nothing to him. He tossed them in a pile with a set of car keys. The only other thing of interest was a scrap of paper with two numbers. He turned on the dash light to look at them. Frowned and wondered why one of them seemed familiar. Easing the car to the curb, he pulled his own cell from his pocket and brought up his recent calls.

The same number showed on his screen. He sat and contemplated for a full minute why Umar Megat's phone number would be carried by a man who'd broken in and killed Zupan.

The most likely explanation was that Megat had thought to acquire the boy without making payment.

Malsovic started the car again. His rage threatened to swallow him whole. Half a million dollars. Gone. His dreams of riches. Vanished.

But all was not lost. He turned around and pointed the car north, in the direction he'd traveled earlier tonight. This was why he'd had an alternate plan.

He drove for thirty minutes. In the darkness it was more difficult to find the rundown rural address he'd visited earlier that day, despite the fact that the rain had begun to let up. As helpful as the women had been, they wouldn't be happy to be awakened at this hour. Malsovic didn't care about that. He cared only about finishing this thing.

And now there was revenge to consider. Because after tonight, he was going to make damn sure bin Osman never got his son. He should have paid the money. Malsovic's hands clenched and unclenched on the steering wheel. He should have realized a powerful man had enemies who would be happy to gain leverage against the people they hated.

Rizqi bin Osman's son would be sold for that leverage. And the money, although likely not as great as what Malsovic had hoped for, would be no small sum.

He had to backtrack several times but finally found the place he'd visited earlier. He remembered the roof and door that had been painted a vivid pink. As he'd expected, the women inside were not glad to see him, but they opened the door for him all the same when he offered them the money he'd taken from the gunmen.

Then he went back to the car. Drew his gun and raised the trunk lid. He pulled his head back just in time to avoid the fist the woman swung as she sprang to a sitting position. "Get out, or I shoot the boy." Because he'd said it in Serbian, he repeated it in English. Then yanked the woman out of the trunk by a fist wrapped in her hijab.

He left the kid for the two Malay women to tend to and shoved the female inside the small home. In the darkness, one couldn't see the scruffy patch of land around the place with its fence and chickens and goats. And no close neighbors, which would come in handy.

There was a lamp on in the house. He shoved the female to her knees, and she turned a defiant face up to his. Malsovic stilled. That face. So familiar, despite the cuts and bruises. But surely not. He yanked at the hijab, pulling it from her head and stared, dumbfounded at the blond curls he'd uncovered.

It seemed impossible, but there was no denying it. The woman on the floor was the same one he'd failed to kill in DC. The one Shuang had called Eve Gallagher.

CHAPTER FOURTEEN

EVEN AS THE sirens drew closer, Declan refused to leave before searching the neighboring yards. A hot ball of despair had lodged in his gut at the thought of Eve in Malsovic's hands. But then it had occurred to him that as bad as the possibility was, there was a worse fate. The two dead bodies in the neighboring yards were silent testament to that.

Kellan went for the car while Declan and Finn split up, jumping the fence on either side of the small condo, the beams of their flashlights cutting arcs through the driving rain. He had to satisfy the hammering in his skull. She couldn't be dead. He wouldn't believe it.

It was difficult to see much of anything in the darkness, but if there were another body—not Eve's, it couldn't be Eve's—it would be near where they'd found the gunmen.

Tires screeched out front. Two police cars, their strobes washing the street in a kaleidoscope of light. Finn jogged to his side. "She's gone. We have to get away, too, man, before we're locked up. Then she'd be on her own."

He didn't need any more urging. It didn't take imagination to consider how the scene would look to the Johor Bahru police; three foreigners on a site littered with bodies. They'd be tied up for days, or longer, getting the situation sorted out, and Eve didn't have days. Neither did Royce Raiker.

So they ran. Fleet-footed through the night, slipping through the slick grass and mud as they traveled a roundabout path to where they'd left the vehicle a block away. Kell had the car running. They barely got in before he took off, heading in the opposite direction of the house they'd just left.

The sick cloud of dread spreading through him could fog his mind until only the urgency remained. Declan fought to batten it down, shove it aside. The thing Eve needed most from them right now was clear thinking.

It was the only thing that would save her.

He pulled out his smartphone and turned on the app they'd all downloaded. "She's wearing her GPS device, right?" Finn hung over the front seat with his phone in his hand. "We can track her. We can't be that far behind them."

"Twenty-five minutes, I figure."

"No more than twenty," Declan disputed Kell's estimate without looking up from his phone. "Here she is." The fist clutching his heart loosened a fraction. He and Eve had worn the devices since the second day at the Latifma. The other two men had added them before leaving on this assignment. Each showed up on the map in a different color. Eve's was a green dot that was moving steadily. "Heading northwest. About...twenty-two miles from here." Motion was good. He told himself that. Tried to believe it. If Malsovic was driving—and Declan could figure no other way the man had gotten Eve off that property so quickly—then he couldn't be hurting her.

"Take the expressway north, and we'll jog west from there," Finn advised. "I'm bringing up the route to get you to the expressway, Kell."

"The fastest way possible." Burke slid a glance toward Declan. "Don't worry, buddy. We're on his trail, and he thinks he's safe. We're gonna show him otherwise."

"Yeah." Gripping the phone so hard it hurt, Declan found himself praying that green dot on the screen stayed in motion. Because it was when it stopped that Eve would be in real danger.

Malsovic bent and hauled Eve up by one arm. "You. Why are you here? Who came with you?"

"I followed you. I came alone."

He shoved her violently to the floor again as the two women came into the small home with a struggling Royce Raiker.

Eve gave the boy a quick once over. Bound hand and foot, he looked tired and wan with dark circles beneath his eyes. His hair still bore the effects of the dye they'd use to lighten it for the passport picture. She'd told him her name while they were in the trunk. Assured him his mother was alive. She hadn't dared to tell him more. Not then.

She tried to catch his eye now, give him a reassuring smile. But he was bucking and fighting, trying to twist away from the two women.

"This one is a problem," the older of the two said in Chinese. She let go of the boy and signaled for the younger woman to do the same. "A good beating would make him behave."

"He is not the one to worry about now," Malsovic said

in English. He approached Eve, and she got to her feet, warily keeping an eye on the two women who came to circle her. "You lie. You are not alone. There were others there inside the house."

"Men I paid to follow you."

"It is not possible." He looked at the younger woman. "You have a bathtub?"

"We have large tub. We fill and bathe in it."

"Fill it." He never took this gaze off Eve. "You are here with your husband. You both deceived Shuang. I know this already." He waved a hand at Royce. "He was not taken from Raiker's property. So you lie now, too, I think. You and your husband came to find the boy."

There was a clatter and then a scrape as the younger woman rolled in a large metal washing tub. She placed it in the kitchen, turned on the faucet and began filling a pitcher.

"Is my mom really okay?"

Eve's gaze went to Royce, who had stilled and was watching her. It was unsurprising that Malsovic had figured out her and Declan's charade. He must also suspect that Declan's whole scheme with Shuang was a trap. "She really is." He looked like he was afraid to believe her. She hoped she was telling the boy the truth. Jaid was still alive, as far as she knew. They needed to cling to that.

Staying alive until Declan and the others got there was uppermost in her mind. Stalling was the best strategy. The GPS pin was still clipped under her hair at her nape. How long had the car ride been? It was difficult to tell since she'd been unconscious for part of it. She just needed to keep Malsovic talking long enough for Declan and the other men to follow them here.

"Help me search her." He motioned to the graying older woman. "She had a knife earlier. Strip her." Eve waited for the two to converge on her before aiming a vicious kick at Malsovic. It didn't hit him where she most wanted to injure him, but he muttered a curse when it connected with his thigh with enough force to have the contact eddying up her leg.

The woman's slap had her seeing stars. Both she and Malsovic grabbed Eve and wrestled her to the floor.

She'd worn the long skirt Declan had bought that day, the cotton shirt and hijab. She struggled violently against them, striking out with fists and nails. The female pinched her and yanked her hair as she wrested her clothes from her.

"No bruises!" Malsovic barked as the skirt was pulled down her legs. The two battled to unbutton her blouse.

The woman in the kitchen chided the other one in Chinese. "He will sell her, too, Mama. She must be in good condition." Translating the words had Eve fighting even harder for her freedom. They were to be sold? She could understand bin Osman's interest in the boy. But his only interest in Eve would be if he were still involved in human trafficking.

Declan. She winged the plea on a mental prayer. *Come soon.*

The older woman was panting now, Eve's outer garments in a pile on the floor.

"Bath ready."

She was dragged, struggling and kicking to the metal tub. Eve doubted very much that a bath was what Malsovic had in mind. He forced her to kneel by the container, grasped a handful of her hair and yanked her head back painfully. "Gallagher is with you?"

Tears stung her eyes at his painful grip. "Yes." The man suspected that much already, so she'd save her lies for something more important.

"How many other men?"

"None."

He shoved her head forward, over the rim of the tub, submerging her in the water. Her body exploded into a frantic battle for freedom. Water was in her mouth, her nose. She choked. Gagged. More water rushed in. A moment later, he pulled her head up.

She gasped and coughed. His voice seemed to come from a distance. "How many others?"

"Just...my...husband."

This time she managed to fill her lungs before he pushed her head under water again. There was yelling in the background, but she couldn't hear it for the roaring in her ears. Her chest was full and tight, razor blades slashing her lungs. She stopped fighting. Saved every bit of effort for holding her breath.

When he raised her head, she was panting. Desperate for oxygen, she tried to haul in great gulps of air, found she couldn't fill her lungs enough. "How many men?"

"He...hired two." Her mind was fogged. It was difficult to think. "We came...for...the boy."

"Your husband...he still works for Raiker?"

Something told her to admit that would seal Declan's death sentence if the two came face to face. "No." She braced herself as the pressure on the back of her head increased. Her forehead touched the water. "He was fired. He just...wanted money. Now...he intends...to sell him back to Raiker."

Something inside her wept for the boy who surely was hearing all this. He'd feel confused. Even more alone. But she'd worry about that later. And she was done talking. Because it occurred to her that the more time Malsovic spent torturing her, the more time the men had to follow them to the small farm where they'd been brought.

But her words had satisfied him for the moment. He looked at the woman in the kitchen. "I need to go now. You get me in early."

"I can't do that! You must wait. The auction starts at two. Buyers come to browse at noon. Sellers at ten AM. I told you this!"

"Then I will stay here." Forgetting Eve for the moment, he straightened and took a gun from his waistband. His smile was slow and ugly. "You will hide me today."

The younger female slid a look at her mother whose eyes were wide and frightened.

"Towel!" Malsovic barked, gesturing to Eve's hair. The older woman hurried to obey.

"Maybe I can help," the daughter said. "For more money."

His mouth twisted. "Of course, Huan. Always more money. I need someone to watch these two. I have much to do."

Now that she'd agreed, Huan seemed in a hurry to get them out of the house. "We go now." Her mother had returned with a thin cotton towel. She began to roughly dry her dripping head. When Eve raised her hands to take over the task, they were slapped away.

Malsovic and Huan were arguing over payment. Eve went back on her haunches, grabbing the towel from the other woman, who began combing her fingers through her wet hair, pulling at the snarls. "What is this?" she murmured in Chinese.

A cold bolt of fear twisted through Eve when she felt the woman's fingers on the GPS clip. Ducking away, she shoved her aside. Saw the woman's hand rear back but didn't dodge quickly enough to avoid the slap.

"Bitch," the older woman hissed in her native tongue as she undid the clip and examined it. A pleased expression crossed her face when she looked at the ornately worked 'G' in the center of it. "You will not have need for jewelry where you are going."

Eve leaped at her, desperation fueling the move. As long as they remained here, Declan would find them. She had no doubts about that. But the conversation between Huan and Malsovic made it clear they would soon be on the move again.

She couldn't leave without that pin. Tackling the woman, she took her down to the floor. Rolled. Eve pressed a thumb in her eye. Her free hand went to the woman's neck. When she screeched, Eve grabbed for the hand still clutched around the pin. Was prying her fingers open when she was yanked back and then thrown across the room.

"Mama, are you all right?" Huan's voice was shocked.

"She has something of mine!"

Malsovic reached down and grabbed Eve's throat. Hauled her upright. "You have nothing." He spoke in English. "You *are* nothing. Soon you will learn that." His smile had a quick shudder working down her spine. "I would give a great deal to teach you myself. But it will give me pleasure knowing someone else is showing you a woman's place in this world." He looked over to where Huan had gone to comfort her mother. "What does she have? Bring it to me."

With a slight push from her daughter, the older woman shuffled forward. Showed him the pin. Malsovic picked it up, looked at it closely.

"It was a gift from my husband," Eve said in English.

"Please." The word nearly choked her. "Let me keep something to remember him by."

"He will soon be dead. And you will have a new life." Malsovic looked at Huan. "She may keep it." The younger woman repeated the words in Chinese. With a crow of delight, the older woman fixed it in her hair, turning to show it off to her daughter.

"I will be gone all day and most of the night," Huan told her mother, her voice heavy with meaning. "You know what to do."

Nodding, the older woman sent a triumphant look in Eve's direction. "Yes, I will. I keep her clothes, too?"

"Not the hijab." Malsovic looked at Huan. "Bring her something that covers her completely." The woman disappeared through a door leading off the room.

Eve spared a glance at Royce. He wouldn't look at her. There was a set to his jaw that for a moment reminded her of the boy's stepfather. *Just hold on a while longer,* she told him mentally. The agents had to be close.

Huan returned with a black abaya, a loose-fitting robe-like dress and a niqab, a veil to cover the face. She produced them with a flourish, and Malsovic looked impressed. "Yes, good. You may have them back after she goes on auction." He turned to Eve. "Put them on. Unless you want me to do it for you."

She crossed slowly to take the garments from Huan. She tried stalling, as if unfamiliar with how they were worn. She'd actually donned similar garments twice, both times when she'd traveled on a job for the State Department. But despite her slowness, the other woman had them on her in minutes.

"Get the boy." Malsovic grabbed a handful of Eve's robe and was pulling her toward the door. Opening it. He'd put her in the trunk again. And she wouldn't have another chance at escape until they reached their next destination.

She purposefully tripped, falling into him. Her hands went to his shirt. To the weapon he'd shoved in the waist-band beneath it. She actually got a hand on it. Started to pull it out. His mighty shove sent her sprawling. The gun landed in the mud with a light thud. Eve dove for it. His shoe came down on the back of her neck, exerting enough pressure that she feared he'd break it.

"So much trouble." His voice was low and ugly. "I do not wish to bruise you before the auction. But maybe you need more water before you learn." Just the thought of the near drowning experience had her catching her breath. "Get used to your position. You will be at the mercy of men the rest of your life. Many, many men." His foot lifted. He pulled her up with a hand in the folds of her abaya, gath-ering the weapon as he rose.

Huan had joined them with the boy, supporting him as he hopped toward the car. "Put him in the back seat and bring me the duct tape from the bag in the front." The woman did as she was bid, rejoining them with a roll in her hand. "Bind her," he ordered. "And gag her. It will do her good to start learning how to be silent."

"They're on the move again."

"What?" Kell's head swiveled toward Declan. "After stopping for nearly fifteen minutes? What direction?"

"North." Declan and Finn's voices answered simultane-ously. Kell's mouth flattened. "Then we go north. At least if he's moving, no one is being hurt."

He'd meant the words as comfort, but Declan knew that

the time Malsovic had stopped had been long enough to inflict a great deal of suffering.

Another thought niggled at the back of his skull. One he couldn't quite dislodge no matter how hard he tried.

The GPS worked whether the body it was on was alive or not.

And because thinking that way was the surest way to insanity, he shoved the thought aside. Buried it. And concentrated on everything they could do to find Eve and the boy.

"Stillions is en route," Finn said quietly. "He and another fed, and two from DOS."

Declan nodded. The FBI agent had coordinated contacting the State Department and the US Embassy when the search for Royce had gone international. But they hadn't left the US until the passports had shown up, undeniable evidence that the boy was in the country, in Malsovic's custody.

His mouth tightened. They had no evidence right now that the man had Eve. But nothing else made sense.

The vehicle moved steadily on the expressway toward Kuala Lumpur, which was just over three hours to the north. Because of the lateness of the hour, the traffic was light. The vehicle they were following was making good time, as well. Malsovic had stopped for fifteen minutes, but they'd gotten turned around a few times on the country roads before the GPS locator had shown the other car was on the move again.

The distance on the device indicated that they were now only ten minutes away from the other car. Ten minutes. His fist clenched around the phone in his hand. They'd been too late last night to stop the shooting. Too late to catch Malsovic before he'd taken Eve. The man was always one step ahead. "As close as we are to the vehicle, the next time he stops, we'll have him." Declan said the words and tried to believe them.

"Damn straight," Kell replied. "And when we do, you can have first crack at the guy."

He didn't answer. Couldn't. Because if the man had hurt Eve—or the boy—only God could save him.

They were heading west of Kuala Lumpur when the GPS locator stopped. Declan stared at the screen of his phone, willing the green dot to stay motionless. He'd gotten his hopes up before when it had halted briefly—likely for a traffic light—before advancing again. It did start to progress again, but slowly. As if the car remained still. But the person wearing it was still moving.

"We might have a destination." Hope, a sudden spear of it, stabbed through him.

"How far away?"

Declan turned on a reading light to check the coordinates on the map. "Seven miles, thereabouts."

As he flipped off the light, Finn said, "Close enough for us to begin strategizing about how we're going to take him out." They spent the rest of the trip doing exactly that, as Kell drove more slowly, moving in the outskirts of the capital city. The homes here were nearly identical boxes set down close to each other with brightly-colored trim and roofs to individualize them. Dawn was smudging the sky beneath angry splinters of clouds when they drove to the location indicated by the coordinates. "Right there," Declan murmured. "Red roof and door."

Kell kept driving. Turned at the nearest corner and coasted to mid-way down the block. Finn passed out the weapons again before the men got out of the vehicle, falling into a synchronized step. At that moment, they looked more alike than not, Declan thought grimly as they made their way silently between the houses to the one they sought. All of them had mud crusted on their shoes, knee high on their pants. Unshaven. They shared a single, deadly purpose.

When they came to the house, they split up to predetermined posts. They'd each try an entry into the home, and whoever found a way inside first would summon the others. Kell had a special magic with locks and alarms, so he went to work on the back-door. Finn would take a window on one side. Declan detoured to the front. At the corner of the structure, he dropped to his belly and crawled to the car. Empty of course, he saw when he risked a glance in. But the hood was warm to the touch.

Staying low, he went to the other side of the house and used his knife to pry off the old aluminum combination window. It was a type that had been popular in the States decades earlier. Access could be made here, but it would be slow.

His cell signaled an incoming text. Kell. Declan moved toward the back, keeping his weapon ready.

There was a narrow, overgrown walk leading from the back door. Ignoring it, Finn and Declan fanned out on either side of the other man. Kell held up one finger. Two. On three, he eased the door open, and they rushed inside. Spread out, weapons ready.

And froze as a girl in the kitchen area stared at them, sleepy eyes wide in the act of pouring a glass of milk. The carton dropped from her hand, and she turned her head to give an earsplitting scream.

Giving them a perfect view of the clip in her dark hair with an oval bearing an ornately-worked 'G' in the center of it.

~

"I need to go to my own work now." When Malsovic looked ready to object, Huan waved to another girl who had followed her into the room. "This is Kim. She will watch your possessions if you need to go out for a while. Take them on regular bathroom breaks. Water them. They will be safe."

Royce and Eve were housed in large, wire dog kennels with padlocks on the doors. Both of them were still bound.

The space looked like a regular hotel room. Eve hadn't had a chance to see the front of the building. Hadn't realized that one of their stops was to buy the kennels. They'd stopped again for a long time before the trunk had opened. It had still been dark. She'd been dragged out and folded into the cage before being lifted onto a luggage cart. Malsovic had spread a blanket over her. And then she'd been in the dark again.

Her other senses had filled in the voids. The cart moving. The ding of an elevator. Its rise. And then her arrival here. The blanket had been removed before Malsovic had gone to the door with Huan. And apparently repeated the process with Royce.

"How do I know this place is secure?" The man sounded more than a little paranoid. And he was as antsy as Eve had ever seen him. Going to the window to peek behind the aluminum blinds. Pacing the area.

"This floor is only for sellers," Huan replied in a tone that said she was repeating herself. "Buyers staying at the hotel are on another floor and do not have the papers to access this level. Armed guards are posted up and down the hall. Just as they will be on the ballroom level. There is very valuable merchandise being held in these rooms. Trettin does not maintain the integrity of his auctions by taking security lightly."

"All right then, go."

Huan didn't turn to leave. "You owe me more money."

His expression turned ugly. "I paid you yesterday. And more tonight, at your house."

"The money yesterday not for me. That was for getting your first item listed in the final auction catalog. And for sending out an alert of the addition to our top customers. The woman..." Huan shrugged. "You will have to take your chances on her. Surely a blonde will get noticed. You paid for me getting you in early. For helping you this morning. But you owe for the cost of the room." She named a price, and Malsovic looked like he wanted to argue. Instead, he pulled out his wallet and walked over to shove some bills at her.

As she folded the cash and walked out of the room, he switched his attention to Kim. "Remove the tape from their mouths. I do not want marks visible at the auction. If you have problems with them, gag them another way. And get the boy to the bathroom first." He pushed by her and left the room.

Eve looked at Royce, but he skirted her gaze. Kim went to his cage and worked the key into the padlock. Swinging the door open, he crawled out of the enclosure before she helped him to his feet and half dragged him to the bathroom.

A suffocating sense of desolation was spreading over her, through her, and the feeling was a trap. She couldn't allow herself to sink into depression, any more than she could bank on false hopes. Declan would have found the GPS device at the farmhouse long ago. The men would know there was no way to track them to their new location.

Which meant that Eve had to figure something out herself, and quickly. Before they were taken to the ballroom for the auction.

∼

"*Nuer is daughter*," Finn said. It had been slow going. The older woman would release a spate of Chinese, and he'd try to pick out words to look up on his smart phone. "I think she's saying the girl belongs to her daughter. Just like the house she left hours ago belonged to her daughter."

Declan surged to his feet. The thought of how much time they'd spent had his patience shredding. His frustration mounting. And the pace of this interrogation was excruciating. They didn't have time to waste. He pointed at the girl again, seated on the couch next to her grandmother. "Mama," he tried. "Where is your mama?"

The girl appeared to be nine or ten. She looked uncertainly at her grandmother. "Mama. Work."

The three men stared at the child, then at each other, each mirroring an expression of shock. Slowly, Declan went to his knees before the girl. He pointed to the clip in her hair. "Where did you get that? Pretty." The child pointed to her grandmother. No help there. Pulling his phone from his pocket, Declan held it up. "Does your mama have a cell?"

Enthusiastically the girl nodded. He turned on the camera and aimed it at her. Shot a picture. Finding it in the gallery, he showed it to the child and she smiled.

"Mama's number?"

When she frowned, Finn brought up the keypad on his phone and showed it to her. "Numbers."

The girl's face brightened. She pointed out a sequence on his cell, and Declan tapped the numbers into the screen for the recipient. Then he added a text to the photo. *"I have something of yours. You have something of mine. Call."* He pressed send and rose. Glanced at Kell.

The man looked as frayed as Declan felt. Both paced, nearly bumping into each other in the small area. He'd give the mother ten minutes for a response, Declan thought. Before he'd follow it up with a phone call and voice message.

It took eight minutes for his cell to ring. Seeing the number, he nodded at Kell, and answered it. "We have a problem."

There was a moment of silence. Then a woman's voice exploded. "You have a problem if you have hurt An! I called the police! They are on their way to my mother's house."

"Good," he said tightly. "Then you can explain to them why your daughter is wearing my wife's hair clip."

There was a hesitation. Then, "Just take it. Take it and go away."

"I'll be glad to. As soon as you tell me where I can find my wife."

"Ah...a man took her. They went to Singapore."

"We will take An with us while we look. When we find my wife, you get your daughter back." The girl was staring at him from the couch, and he wondered how much English she understood. She was as much a victim in this mess as Royce was. Although they'd make sure no harm came to her, he wasn't exactly proud of his tactics. He could only imagine what FBI Agent Stillions would have to say about them.

But the girl was leverage. And Royce's and Eve's situations were desperate.

"He will kill me." The woman's voice was low.

"Who?" Declan searched his memory for the name on Malsovic's most recent passport. "Simic?"

"Not him. He has brought them to auction." Her voice was so hushed, he had to strain to hear it.

"Tell me where."

"I told my mother to leave my home immediately with my daughter with the money I'd made today. To keep it safe in case Simic returned there." The woman's voice went sly. "There is enough to pay you for my daughter. Name your price."

Urgency sprinted up his spine. "Don't waste my time. My price is my wife. Is your daughter worth it?"

"The Corus Hotel in JB." The woman sounded defeated. It took him a moment to realize she was talking about Johor Bahru. His stomach plummeted. Three and a half hours back. More if the traffic was bad. "The auction takes place on the ballroom floor. There is high security. Special papers needed. I work for Trettin, but I don't know how to get you on the list of customers. It is too late."

"You better hope that's not true," Declan replied looking at Kell and Finn. "Because that will mean it's too late for your daughter, as well." He was hoping like hell that the woman wouldn't call his bluff. They held no real advantage when they had no intention of hurting the old woman or girl.

"I will think of something by the time you get here." He heard the resignation in her words. "Call again when you are thirty miles out. Now let me talk to my mother. I have to explain to her why she will send my daughter with you."

～

Eve waited for her turn at the restroom. Royce had been returned to the cage. Kim flicked her a glance and went to the TV. Turned it on and settled into a chair to watch.

She turned to Royce and whispered, "*¿Hablas español?*"

Surprised, he rolled to look at her. "*Un poco.*"

Eve smiled, relief filling her. Even if Kim heard them talking, she would be unlikely to understand. Continuing in Spanish, she said, "If you have the chance, run."

He frowned, and she raised her feet a ways in the air. Wiggled them to mime running. He nodded. "Don't wait for me. Understand? Just go."

"*Bì zuì!*" Kim scowled over at them. Obediently, Eve went quiet until the woman returned to the TV.

"Did you really want to ransom me to my dad?" Royce's words were in English, and so low they were barely audible.

"No. I am working for him." The impassive look the boy gave her was heartbreaking. He'd likely heard plenty of lies in the course of the past few days. "There are others here. Declan and Kellan and Finn. All looking for us."

"You promise?"

She nodded. A part of her was happy to see the hope in the boy's expression. But there was a darker side that worried about putting it there. She had no doubt that the agents would have found the location device by now. But none of them spoke Chinese, and the old woman hadn't seemed to speak English. She wouldn't have been able to tell them where Malsovic had taken his prisoners.

It was over an hour before Kim got up and came to let Eve out of the cage. It wasn't totally an act when, after being pulled to her feet, she had to lean heavily on the woman. Her legs were numb. She could only shuffle across the room.

Afterwards, as she walked back toward the kennel, she

pretended to stumble. When Kim moved closer, Eve rammed her elbow into the woman's chest with all her strength. Once. Twice. Then lowered her shoulder and drove it into her, knocking Kim violently against the door-jamb. She had a moment's satisfaction when the woman's head rapped hard against the jamb.

If she could knock her out, maybe she could get the key to the padlock. Maybe... Eve threw her weight against the woman again, but this time Kim was ready for her. She gave Eve a huge shove, her foot swiping in front of hers. With no way to catch herself, she landed flat on the floor with enough force to drive the breath from her lungs.

Fighting for air, she was dimly aware of the woman's voice. "She is a troublemaker, that one. I should get more pay to watch her."

A pair of dark, men's shoes straddled either side of Eve's face. She closed her eyes in defeat as she heard a familiar voice say, "Fill the bathtub."

CHAPTER FIFTEEN

SHE'D WORN the abaya and niqab on the private ball-room elevator. Kim pushed the luggage cart on which Royce's kennel had been loaded. Malsovic had brought him a suit with shiny black shoes and a white shirt. Kim had been charged with showering and dressing the boy, a fact Royce had been vocally unhappy about.

It was the woman's turn to be unhappy when she had to tend Eve. She'd taken far more pleasure in the torture Malsovic had engaged in first. He forced Kim to make up Eve's face to minimize her cuts and bruises and to work on her hair. She'd then been dressed in the clothes he'd chosen for her to wear beneath the robe.

The elevator pinged. The doors opened with a quiet swoosh. They moved into the hall, a silent quartet, before he stopped them. "Remove the robe and veil."

A flush of embarrassment heated her skin, but slowly she did as she was told. Dropped them to the floor. The fishnet body suit left nothing to the imagination, with the scrap of black panties and bra beneath. Red stilettos and a matching collar and leash completed the outfit he'd brought for her. Looping his hand through the handle of the leash, he pulled her after him.

"She looks like a whore," Kim said

"All women are whores." His flat, obsidian gaze flicked over her, and the woman drew back. "After today, she will never forget it."

Armed guards dotted the hallway. Huan met them at the only open door into the room, her gaze cool and professional. Consulting the electronic tablet she carried, she said, "Items 162and 163. Let me show you to your spots." She'd changed clothes since this morning, Eve noted. She wore a suit in coral, the skirt hitting her mid-thigh, and her hair was twisted into a chignon at her nape.

The area they crossed was vast. The ballroom and surrounding hallways took up the entire top floor. Windows lined one wall, showing a breathtaking view of the city. The room was already full of people. Paintings. Sculptures. Some of the glass cases they passed displayed jewels. Coins. Stamps. One man was setting up a video that showed a magnificent stallion. Eve saw a few other women in the room, scantily clad. None made eye contact. There was a full-size cell with three small Asian girls in it, all wearing fluffy white dresses. The sight of them had Eve's stomach twisting in nausea. My God, what was this place?

"This will be your exhibition area." Huan waved a hand. The item numbers she'd mentioned hung on the wall behind her. "The table you asked for." It was set squarely in the center of the spaced reserved for them, with another electronic tablet on a stand. "Silent bidding is allowed prior to the auction." She indicated the tablet. "If you have a bid, it will appear before you, and it is your choice whether to accept it or wait for the auction. Please finish unloading. I will need photos for the video that will start soon. Customers who don't wish to browse will rely on the digital viewing before the auction." She waited impatiently for Kim and Malsovic to unload the boy and then took several pictures of Eve and Royce with her phone.

Nodding toward another woman making her way toward them, she said, "Cheng will be handing out catalogs. You will see I included your items."

Another woman gestured to her from across the room, and Huan hurried away. Kim and Malsovic lifted Royce's cage and set it on one side of the table. Eve had to follow closely or risk having the collar yanked tight on her throat when Malsovic moved beyond the length of the leash.

He dismissed the other woman, and she rolled the cart away and out of the room. Digging into a bag he carried with him, he withdrew several documents and spread them across the table. Then he turned his dark, flat gaze on Eve. "You already have an admirer."

A portly man with slicked-back, thinning hair was approaching them. His brown gaze painted Eve with a long, lecherous look. In Italian he said, "That hair. Like a blond princess. I would use you well. Perhaps give you to my friends to enjoy."

"If you buy me, my husband will hunt you down and cut out your heart," she responded in the same language. And had a brief moment of satisfaction when the man's expression went shocked, before hardening. Turning on his heel, he marched away. A forceful yank on the leash had her staggering back a few steps.

"What did you say to him?" demanded Malsovic in a furious voice. She felt a surprising lack of fear when she faced him. He could do nothing to her now. There was no bathtub in sight.

"I told him he should make a bid quickly. Before more men came."

"Liar." He leaned closer, breathed into her ear. "You need to be in one piece to fetch the best price. The boy does not." The fear that had been absent earlier was back, a jagged blade of it. "Each time you disobey...each time you send someone away, the boy loses part of a finger. Do you understand?"

Swallowing, she nodded, a wave of desolation sweeping over her. Eve understood completely. She understood their situation here had passed desperate and was edging on hopeless.

And she understood that she'd failed Royce Raiker.

"Does anyone else have the feeling that Huan is about to screw us over big time?" Kellan muttered.

There were back at their hotel, taking turns watching the girl in one room, which involved showing her how to work the television. In the other, they changed into the suits Huan insisted they buy. The auction, the woman had insisted, had a dress code.

They'd used most of the trip back to Johor Bahru consulting with Stillions by email. His team's flight should be landing soon. But the Bureau, the State Department or both were tagging the proper officials in Malaysia about the auction. While the FBI consulted on international kidnappings, they had no arrest power in foreign countries, necessitating a coordinated effort. Despite the Malaysian government's efforts at improvement, corruption remained in both their local law enforcement and politics, which was hardly comforting.

They'd developed an alternate plan, and it depended on the three of them attending the auction. Paulie had transferred the money out of Malsovic's account to the one the first half of Shuang's payment had been diverted to. Plenty of money to bid, if that was what it took to rescue Eve and Royce. The strategy wouldn't be necessary if Stillions was coordinating a raid with local law enforcement, but the fed had been out of contact for hours. And time was running out.

"Auction starts in an hour," Finn said quietly from the girl's side. An and Finn had developed an easy relationship on the trip back to Johor Bahru. He'd shown her how to work the camera on his phone, and they'd taken turns taking silly pictures of each other, much to the child's delight. Now she was surrounded with soft drinks, candy and snacks in preparation for the time when they'd have to leave her alone.

But for the men in the room, that time wasn't coming fast enough. "We have to get in the ballroom soon." Despite Stillions' strict orders to wait to hear from him, Declan could feel each passing minute like a physical wound. Elmont Trettin was a high-profile international criminal, who no doubt had friends in very high places. Had to have in order to have remained free all these years despite his sheet of crimes. Malaysian officials had insisted on photo evidence that Eve and Royce were in the Corus Hotel. Huan had promised to deliver it to the FBI agent's cell number. But the silence from the feds involved made him wonder if she ever had.

He was beginning to think Kell's fear was prophetic.

"Stillions told us to wait until we heard from him." Finn looked at Declan and Kell. "Who thinks we should follow his orders?"

Relief flickered in Declan when the three men looked at each other. Simultaneously they uttered, "Hell, no."

Fifteen minutes later, the taxi dropped them off at the Corus. "I'll go to the counter," Kell volunteered. "You guys stay out here until we make sure we aren't being set up."

The other two nodded. Declan was the only one Malsovic would recognize. Knowing that, he wasn't clean-shaven as the other two were, and he'd bought a fedora that he wore low on his forehead. It wouldn't be enough to prevent him from being identified. But by the time they drew close enough for Malsovic to do so, it would be too late.

They loitered in front of the hotel while Kell went inside. It wasn't raining today—not yet—but the dark ugly clouds scudding across the sky indicated that more precipitation was imminent. Declan's gut was coiled so tightly it was all he could do to remain still. Huan had explained the way the auction worked. They couldn't be sure Malsovic wouldn't accept early bids and skip the auction all together. They couldn't be certain that Royce and Eve were still inside the ballroom of the hotel.

He didn't want to consider the possibility. Couldn't. When Kell came to the front doors, waved them inside, he and Finn joined the man silently. All Declan could do at this point was hope like hell the two were here. And that the rescue plan they'd concocted would succeed.

~

"Congratulations." One of the hostesses smiled prettily at Malsovic as she poured him water from a crystal pitcher. "Your items are bringing much interest, even the one that didn't get placed in the catalog. You must be pleased."

"Very pleased."

She moved away, and he looked at Eve. "Soon now," he said in English. "I hope you are ready for your new life."

"And what of the boy?" she asked in Serbian. Saw the shock on his expression, quickly followed by rage. "What will become of him?"

"You are full of secrets." He wound the leash around his hand, tightening it until her head was pulled back painfully. "The boy does not matter once he is sold." He shrugged. "His father had his chance, but his people betrayed me. So, someone else will buy him. One of his enemies, likely. Perhaps they will send proof of his parentage before sending pieces of him to the man. For ransom or revenge. He will be the lucky one. He will probably die." His smile was ugly. "You will spend your life wishing you were dead."

Eve was silent. She wondered if he knew that the prospect of the fates he described for them served to eliminate fear, rather than instill it. There was nothing more dangerous than a person with nothing to lose.

Scanning the crowded ballroom, she knew there was no chance she'd get away with what she would do next. But it wasn't her that she was worried about.

The key to the padlock on Royce's kennel was on the table. She eyed it now.

She waited long minutes, until the leash loosened as he was busy trying to communicate with a crowd of five prospective buyers who had come up to ask questions. She moved one hand slowly up to the collar she wore. The hook that the leash attached to was at the back of it. She unsnapped it. Held her breath. But Malsovic didn't appear to notice.

He would, she knew, within seconds.

"Royce." The boy looked up at her. She continued in Spanish. "Get ready to run."

She dove for the key on the table and then to his cage, half falling to her knees. Fumbled to fit the key in the padlock and yank open the door. "Bitch!" A hand fisted in her hair. Pulled her backwards. Malsovic's slap snapped her head to the side. He half dragged her with him as he began shouldering his way through the crowd. It was several more moments before Eve realized that the boy had been swallowed up in the human wall of people.

DECLAN RAISED his arms for the guard to pass the metal detecting wand over him before following up with a frisk. "What's all the commotion inside?"

The man blinked uncomprehendingly, then shrugged. "No English."

The three of them had split up. Finn and Kell were being searched by different guards at another doorway that led into the room. Huan had left papers for them at the registration desk that allowed them access to the ballroom elevator and had passed perusal by security. But the place inside was a madhouse, with people jostling forward in a crushing rush. He wondered if the auction was beginning.

He checked the time on his cell. It was still fifteen minutes before it was due to start.

"What is happening?" he asked the men closest to him. All shrugged, but an older gentleman on his other side answered in a British accent. "One of the items got loose.

The woman who let him out got quite a beating from her owner. Shame, that. Pretty little blonde. Fancied her for myself, but she's too wild for my taste." He winked. "I like them inventive, but obedient."

Everything stilled inside him. A blonde. There couldn't be more than one here, could there? An *item*? Fury surged inside him, dark and lethal. Like a possession. A thing. And everyone in this room was here to buy or sell, with no regard for human life.

"I don't mind a bit of a wild streak." It took effort to keep the rage from his voice. "Where can I get a look?"

"Front of the room, toward the left corner." The man began to drift away. "Or the digital display is playing on the wall behind you. 163. Lots of interest in that one. Maybe less now after that outburst."

Declan turned. There were no fewer than three digital displays playing on large screens mounted on the wall. Each item bore a number. His gaze focused on the middle screen, depicting image 155. He waited for what seemed an interminable time for the images to change. There was a wide array of offerings. Antiquities. Artwork. Historic documents. And people. He caught his breath when 162 was shown. Royce. And the next image showed Eve, in what could only be termed a porn fantasy outfit.

He thought about taking pictures of the images, sending them to Stillions for the proof he was required to show the Malaysian authorities. But it was too late for that now. With the auction ready to begin, they were out of time. He took out his cell and texted Royce's and Eve's location in the room to Kell and Finn. The British man had indicated there had been an escape, and the blonde had instigated it. If he'd been talking about Eve, did that mean she'd successfully released Royce?

He made his way toward the corner the Brit had indicated. His progress was slowed by the crowd. Apparently, there would be no chairs arranged in rows for the sale. Most of the people held an electronic tablet. Online bidding system, he deduced grimly. Which would make it extremely difficult to discover the identity of the buyers.

His cell vibrated in his hand. The text was from Kell. *I have a tablet. Just put in a pre-bid on Eve. Finn did the same on Royce.*

Ruthlessly, Declan shoved through the people. He had to stay back to avoid Malsovic seeing him, but nothing would prevent him from getting a glimpse of Eve. The British man's words played on an endless loop in his mind. *Got quite a beating from her owner..."* First they'd get the two away to safety. Then Malsovic would pay for every minute of suffering he'd inflicted on Royce Raiker and Eve.

He hung back when he got close to the corner in question. Craning his neck, he could see Eve, head held high, sporting a red mark on her cheekbone that showed promise of blooming into a vicious bruise. So, she had been the blonde the British man had mentioned. Malsovic had her restrained. A rope. No. He shifted his position so he could see more clearly. A leash. His chest went tight with anger. But there was a small body next to her huddled in a dog cage. And he knew that her efforts had been in vain. Royce had been recaptured.

The vibration in his hand signaled another text. *Bidding closed on Eve. Bastard isn't waiting for auction.*

He texted Kell back. *I'm ready.*

Turning, he moved toward a set of the double doors leading to the hallway. There was only one elevator located in an isolated hall on the lobby level that went to the ballroom. There must be a stairway exit somewhere, but Declan was betting the buyer would elect for the privacy of the elevator.

A man's amplified voice boomed out from behind him. "Good afternoon to all of our guests. I trust you find today's offerings intriguing." The greeting was repeated in several other languages, each time to appreciative applause from the crowd. "Please get your tablets ready. The first item is up for bid."

Declan stopped listening. Because Eve was being led from the ballroom through another set of doors by a hulk of a man. Bearded. Not particularly tall, but wide. His suit strained across his massive shoulders as he tugged her toward the elevator. With a purposeful stride, Declan went out the doors closest to him, headed in the same direction, several yards ahead of them. There was only one button to press, for lobby floor. He reached out a finger to stab at it.

He didn't look at the couple who stopped a little behind him. Not until the elevator doors opened and he stepped in. The man followed, positioning Eve on his other side. Which suited Declan perfectly. He reached forward and pressed the button to begin the descent. They had twelve floors to reach the lobby.

"When I rush him, stop the elevator," he said in Scottish Gaelic, smiling at the man as if the words were addressed to him. He just frowned and didn't answer. Crouching to the floor, Declan did a deft sleight of hand and picked up the pen he'd just laid there. Rising, he offered it to her captor. "Is this yours?"

The man wouldn't understand the language any better this time around, but his meaning was clear. His gaze dropped to the outstretched pen. Even as he shook his head, Declan closed in to knee him violently in the balls.

He let out a high-pitched, keening moan. His grip on

the leash slackened. Eve surged forward and pressed the button that would stop the elevator. Then her captor's hands came up, and with a roar, he wrapped them around Declan's throat. Took him down.

Declan was outweighed by a hundred pounds, give or take. So, he had to be sneaky. Fast. And he had no qualms about fighting dirty. He brought the pen up, narrowly dodging the ham-like fist that grazed his cheek and jammed it into the man's neck. Blood spurted from the wound. But it didn't stop the stranger from wrapping his hands around Declan's throat. Squeezing.

He used the pen to stab at the man's hands, trying to loosen his grip. But his vision was graying. His strength ebbing. His movements grew weaker. Then the stranger above him screamed. Rolled to the side. Howled again.

Declan rose. Took a moment to make sense of the scene. Eve had taken off a stiletto and was grinding its sharp heel into her buyer's temple. Her captor reached up to grab her wrist. And Declan took the opportunity to raise his foot and stomp violently on the stranger's balls again. And this time the man cried out and curled to a fetal position, the fight streaming out of him.

Eve released a long shuddering breath as she reached for the elevator button again. "Going down?"

"I think that would be wise." As he kept a careful eye on the man on the floor, Declan reached out to take her hand. Tug her forward. And had time for one frustratingly short kiss before he glanced at Eve's would-be owner stirring on the floor. With a quick move he gave the guy a kick where he had to already be throbbing. And didn't much mind the misery-filled moan that filled the space.

Slipping out of his suit jacket, he wrapped it around Eve's shoulders. "Royce." Her voice was worried. "He's still up there, and Malsovic bragged that there was a lot of interest. We have to get back before he's sold."

Rewrapping an arm around her waist, he hugged her close. The relief that came from touching her nearly made him weak. "Kell and Finn are there. Inside the ballroom." Which reminded him that he needed to send a message that Eve was safe. "We've got a plan." Much like the one that had just been enacted. "But first, we have to get you somewhere secure."

"No, I can..."

He shot her a look, and she quieted. "You're right. Give me money for a cab and go do what needs to be done. The only thing that matters now is Royce."

His arm squeezed her tighter. "You matter, Evie. You matter plenty. When this is over, we're going to talk about that." And because she did matter—too damn much—he wanted her somewhere out of harm's way before the final scene with Malsovic went down.

When the elevator doors opened, they left the man lying inside the car and swiftly headed toward the nearest exit. Declan summoned a cab and gave her a short rundown on what she'd find in the hotel room when she got there. "We've already texted the girl's mother her location. Huan is still upstairs, but she may arrive for her daughter before we get there."

"Yes, I'm acquainted with Huan, although I didn't know she had a daughter." A taxi rolled slowly up to where they stood. "She provided the tub of water for Malsovic to try his hand at waterboarding."

His organs went to ice. His hand rose to cup her face. "He...tortured you?" Every dark fear he'd had while they searched for her congealed in his chest. Searching her gaze, he asked, "What else did he do?" Cold, deadly fury spread through him.

"Nothing." Her hand came up to cover his reassuringly. "We were never alone. And I want you to promise to be careful when you return to the ballroom. I didn't come through this to lose you now. Don't let your hatred of him blind you to the fact that he's still dangerous."

He reached behind her to open the cab door and then pulled out some bills so she could pay the driver. Once she was seated inside, he leaned down for a lingering kiss. "Don't worry about me." He straightened, his smile grim. "I'm dangerous, too."

"THE PAYMENT IS COMPLETE." Finn Carstens didn't give Royce much more than a glance. The boy would recognize him, and hopefully not be too traumatized to play along with the final act. He pretended to peruse the documentation Malsovic had on Royce's parentage with a critical eye. Finally, he collected it into a pile and looked up at the man. "Everything seems to be in order."

"I wish you luck with your future transactions." Malsovic's voice was heavy with meaning.

Finn offered him a small smile. "I have been waiting a long time for such an opportunity. The boy is quite a prize. It's too bad Trettin takes such a large percentage from each transaction for himself." He could tell by the man's grimace that he'd struck a nerve. He looked around, lowered his voice. "I think perhaps you and I could do further business together, but there's no need to discuss it here. Too many ears. But I have a small job I need done, and I would pay well. No transaction fees."

Shrugging, Malsovic said, "It never hurts to discuss business."

"My philosophy exactly." He drew out his phone to text Kell. "I'll have my associate come to take care of the kid. Valuable merchandise requires close monitoring."

Malsovic stared at Royce. "He is a troublemaker, that one. He will take supervision."

Finn shrugged. "I won't have him long." When Kell approached, he said, "You may take him out of the cage, but don't let go of him. If he escapes, your life will be worth nothing." Malsovic handed Kell the key, and the man bent to unlock the door of the kennel, grabbing Royce by the arm and drawing him out. Finn gave him the receipt he'd received to prove he'd made payment and the documentation on the boy.

"I'll guard him with my life." Kell led Royce toward the door.

Finn watched them go then turned to Malsovic again. "Let's step outside the ballroom and find a quiet corner." He was somewhat surprised when the other man followed him but probably shouldn't have been. Every person there had been searched for weapons. Armed guards dotted each of the doorways. Malsovic probably thought he was safer here than he'd be anywhere else.

They walked across the plush lobby outside the ballroom, with its scattered couches and chairs grouped for intimate conversation. Finn pretended to look around and be unhappy with the smattering of people there. "Follow me. Our business is too sensitive to discuss out here." He led the man toward the men's restroom in the far corner. Ushered him inside.

There was a sitting area outside the restroom itself. The

place appeared to be deserted. Finn turned to Malsovic. "There is someone I want you to meet."

"I meet no one without hearing of your needs. And payment must be made first."

Declan appeared from around a corner. "I agree. Payment definitely needs to be made. By you."

Finn moved to block the door should Malsovic decide to flee. But the man showed no fear. "Gallagher. It is a pity I missed you with the rifle." The two men circled each other warily. "Not a pity that your wife was unharmed, however. She earned me fifty thousand dollars tonight and is already on her way to an Indonesian brothel." He bared his teeth. "She will spend her life cursing you for not rescuing her."

A quick feint had Malsovic dodging. Declan followed up with a wicked cross jab that rocked the man's head back. "She is safe in my hotel room. Have you checked your overseas account lately?" The other man wiggled his jaw and spat blood at Declan's feet. "The fee paid for the boy came from the money you stole from Shuang."

His face suffused with fury, Malsovic charged, head butting Declan in the gut and taking him down. Finn settled against the door, arms folded across his chest to watch the show. Malsovic had a thumb gouging Declan's eye, which was dislodged a moment later when Declan kneed the man in the balls, before plowing his fist into the man's face. Malsovic wrapped his hands around his throat. Squeezed. Bucking beneath him, he dislodged Declan and the two men rolled, a tangle of limbs and flying fists. Malsovic grasped Declan's head in his hands and rapped it hard against the floor. Declan's hands came up to lock around one of the man's wrists and gave it a quick vicious twist. The sickening crack had Malsovic screaming in pain.

"That," Declan said as he brought his head up to crack

it against the other man's, "was for Royce Raiker." Giving a mighty heave, he unseated him and rolled quickly on top of him. "This," he drew his fist back, "is for what you did to Eve." Blood sprayed when his blow landed. Followed with a second. And then a third. Malsovic's struggles were growing weaker. And the fury raging through Declan showed no signs of dissipating.

"Gallagher." Finn's voice was mild. "C'mon, man, that's enough."

"It's not nearly enough."

"He's got a lifetime behind bars ahead of him. You don't want to deprive him of that."

Reason returned in increments. Declan gave his head a quick shake to dislodge the temper that still pulsed inside him. "Okay. Let's get this piece of shit handed over to the authorities. The sooner he starts that life sentence, the better."

Declan got up, hauling Malsovic to his feet, shoving him toward the door. He and Finn flanked the man, one on each arm, but they provided more support than restraint.

They moved to the lone elevator, shared it with a corpulent man in an ill-fitting suit. He held a length of rope, and it entwined the three small Asian girls who had been held in a cell in the ballroom. With a pudgy finger, the man reached out to press the button for lobby floor. Finn and Declan exchanged a meaningful glance.

"How much for the girls?" Declan asked. Malsovic picked that moment to ram his elbow hard into his gut, and Declan slammed the man's head against the side of the elevator twice in quick succession.

The man frowned at them, sidling away to the corner. "No English."

Finn pulled out his wallet. "US dollars."

Shaking his head, the man clutched the rope more tightly. Stared at the floor numbers as they descended. Declan reached into his pocket and brought out a pen, handed it to Finn. "Go for the eye," he advised.

It wasn't necessary. The elevator settled on the lobby floor, and the doors slid open to frame a half dozen cops in full riot gear, weapons ready, shouting commands in Malay. Another dozen were running through an exit that must lead to the stairwell.

Declan raised his voice above the chaos. "Take us to US Federal Agent Stillions."

"Your mom is going to be pretty mad that she slept through this." Adam Raiker's voice was gruffer than usual. His jaw was tight. But no one could mistake the raw joy in his eyes as he gazed at Royce on video chat.

"Is she going to be all right?" Eve saw the boy looking past his stepfather to where Jaid was hooked up to a serious number of machines.

"Yes. The doctors upgraded her condition this morning. The medicine makes her sleep a lot, though. Don't worry. As soon as she wakes up and hears the news, she'll make me call you back."

"Promise?" The boy had been a trooper, but Eve wondered if he was about to crash. He'd been through more —far more—than any kid should ever experience.

"Are you kidding? If I don't, she's liable to crawl out of that bed, order her own plane and fly to get you herself."

That drew a smile from the boy. "Bet she would, too." He was silent for a moment. "Eve and me talked in Spanish. She said to be ready to run when she said run. And I did. As fast as I could. But there were too many people. They caught me again."

Adam's throat worked. It took a moment for him to reply. "You used your head. That's what counts. Go on and eat." Room service had been delivered next door minutes ago. "You're going to need your strength for the trip back to the States."

Royce beamed. Heaved a sigh. "First place I'm going is to the hospital to see Mom. Then I'm ready to go home. Our place, not the one in Virginia Beach."

"I'm pretty sure that can be arranged."

"Okay, Royce. Kell and I have got the weirdest meal ever laid out on the desk in the next room." Finn popped his head in the door. "You have no idea how hard it was to get pancakes, a hamburger and french-fries, a chocolate malt and popcorn."

"Have them come get me if Mom wakes up, Adam."

"Think she won't make me?"

The silence in the room lasted until the door closed behind Royce. Then the man heaved a sigh and muttered, "That situation was much too close."

"There were some dicey moments," Eve allowed. She slid a glance to Declan. "I was pretty happy to see this guy in the elevator. From the looks of Malsovic, the rounds he went with Declan did real damage." She had no sympathy for the monster. Though the bruises on Declan's face and knuckles still had her stomach clutching with worry for him.

"Good. Stillions sent me updates throughout the hours of debriefing after the raid, and I got the texts from all of you. Paulie has kept me apprised. But there are still details missing. Start from the time you met Pascal and fill me in."

They took turns doing so, not glossing over any of it,

because he'd have their heads if they did. When they finished, Declan said, "You probably already know that Stillions and the State Department people are pretty pissed that we went to the hotel without their okay. They were trying to cut us out of that end of things, I guess by leaving us completely out of the loop. We had no idea if they'd gotten the photos to convince the Malaysian authorities to mount the raid. And we couldn't wait any longer. So, we went with our own plan."

"If you'd waited for them, Eve would have been gone. And if they hadn't showed up, you wouldn't have been there to rescue Royce. Stillions isn't getting any sympathy from me. Although, he wasn't a fan of your tactics. What you call leverage, he insists on referring to as kidnapping."

"Declan smoothed that over with Huan, the mother," Eve put in quickly.

He shrugged. "I pointed out that she was in a unique position to mitigate any charges leveled against her for participating in the auctions by turning evidence against Trettin. First one who flips usually gets the best deal, and there's a pretty substantial international reward out on the guy."

"In the interest of expediency, Stillions prevailed on the police to allow me to interpret at Malsovic's interview." A quick shudder worked through Eve at the memory of the hatred in the man's eyes. "He spoke freely, because he was blaming everything on Zupan. When he wasn't accusing the man, he was throwing Shuang under the bus. I...uh... added some of my own inquiries. According to his answers to my questions, Lexie Walker was a runaway who had come looking for work and was eventually caught in bin Osman's web. She was a favorite of his. He kept her for himself at the Kaula—what's now the Latifma—while renting out the other women. This made the other females bitter, but none as much as Shuang, who, according to Malsovic, wasn't one of the enslaved women, but bin Osman's right hand in the operation. Then Lexie got pregnant. We saw the paternity report and birth certificate. She was terrified bin Osman would take the baby."

"He probably would have," Declan murmured. "The local police seem to think he would have gladly paid Malsovic for the boy. But no one can get through the layers around him. And we learned that Pascal, the man Eve met with, is known to have a close working relationship with bin Osman's two oldest daughters, who are suspected of being part of their father's criminal network."

Raiker seemed to digest that for a moment. "When Royce is old enough, he'll have to be told the whole story. How did Jaid's father end up with the baby? He was only weeks old when Royce Benning took him to Jaid."

"Malsovic claims he found texts between the two of them on Benning's phone. Jaid's father and Lexie had hatched a plan to get her and the child out of the hotel. Malsovic claims he doesn't know how it went down, but he got called to the scene afterwards. The baby was gone, and Walker was dead. Stabbed several times in the chest. He said Shuang admitted to killing the woman in a fit of jealousy, but she swore the child had been there when she'd left the room. So, bin Osman ordered Malsovic to find his son and the killer."

"And he kept Shuang's secret. Blaming Lexie's murder on whoever had stolen the child," Adam guessed.

"Yes. Benning stopped coming to work, so suspicion eventually fell on him. Malsovic said the truth came out about Shuang killing Walker after bin Osman fled to Malaysia. That's why the man hated her. On Malsovic's phone, he had pictures of a lot of the evidence he used to prove Royce's parentage. He had more documents in a bag at the auction. There were copies of the text messages between Benning and Walker. And six copies of framed photos of the same girl/woman he found in Benning's apartment."

"You mean Jaid." Raiker's voice was as soft as she'd ever heard it. "You know he abandoned her when she was eleven."

Eve could only imagine what that had done to the woman. And the forgiveness it must have taken to heed her father's wishes and adopt Royce as her own. "Maybe he was trying to keep his family safe. He surely knew how dangerous bin Osman was, and he was in debt to the man. Malsovic had a more recent photo of Jaid from a tabloid when the two of you got married, and then he had a name to go with a face."

"Who...are...you...talking to?"

Raiker turned away from the screen to look at his wife. Her eyes were open. "The question is, who are you going to be talking to. Your son has been waiting to speak with you."

"Royce! You...found him!"

The man nodded at the computer. "Well, my people did. He's good, Jaid." His tone was gentle. "He's okay. Worried about you."

"Just a minute. You can talk to him yourself." Eve and Declan rose. She carried the computer and he opened the door to the adjoining room. Finn glanced up when they entered, a broad smile on his face. "Looks like someone's awake."

Royce abruptly forgot food he was shoveling into his mouth. He'd made serious inroads into the meal. His mouth full, he yelled, "Mom!"

Eve set the computer down next to him. The picture on the screen jiggled as Adam moved his laptop to a table that swung out over his wife's bed. And the tears running down Jaid Raiker's face had Eve swallowing hard and turning away. "Maybe we can give them some privacy," she murmured to the men in the room.

"Of course." Finn surged to his feet, followed her and Declan to the door. "C'mon, Kell."

The four of them had no sooner gotten in the other room than Declan surveyed them grimly. "Lexie Walker's family could never have a claim on Royce, even if they knew of his existence. But bin Osman is a loose end."

Eve crossed to one of the beds, sat on the corner. "Too many people here know about Malsovic's claims of Royce's parentage. Although neither Pascal nor Megat seemed eager to share the information with their boss."

"Have to wonder if their relationship with bin Osman's daughters means they don't want a male heir showing up," Kell suggested. He leaned a shoulder against the wall.

"We can't count on that." Declan's expression was sober. "It's too much risk for the boy."

"If you've got a plan," Finn put in, "now is the time to share it."

"Declan got access to Pascal's computer through some Trojan horse thing," Eve said, never taking her eyes off the man. He had something up his sleeve, she could tell, and it had to involve Pascal's files and communications they'd gone through.

"Our best bet is to thoroughly discredit the men who were contacted by Malsovic and Shuang regarding Royce." Declan moved to the laptop on the desk. Sat down in front of it. "If we destroy their credibility with bin Osman, he'll never believe anything they say."

"So, you're going to send the man damning communication from Pascal's computer?"

Declan threw Finn a wicked grin. "He's going to get a passel of email copies, showing just how closely aligned Megat and Pascal are with the bin Osman daughters. And maybe a couple of emails I add that disparage bin Osman's leadership ability. That should be enough to have the man cutting ties with both of them. And the beauty of it is that all of the communication will appear to be coming from Ahmed Pascal's computer."

"What are you waiting for?" Kell drawled.

He was fast. Eve had known that from the other occasions when Declan had worked his magic on the computer. She helped when it came time to composing the phony messages in Malay, but the task was finished in less than an hour. When he finally leaned back in his chair, Kell pushed away from the wall.

"The heroics of the day have me famished. Let's get something to eat."

"Maybe you could go downstairs, get something from the dining room." Declan suggested.

"Why?" Kell frowned. "They've got room service. We'll just order something."

"I wouldn't mind a drink with my meal." Carstens crossed the room, opened the door and steered the other man through it. "Sure you two don't want anything?"

Eve should have been embarrassed by the speed with which Declan was getting rid of the other two. Would have been, if she didn't have an overwhelming desire to be alone with him. Finally. "Bring me something back," she called over her shoulder. Then Declan had the door shut behind them. Strode to where she was sitting and tugged her to her feet, into his arms.

His kiss was explosive, fueled by a flood of pent up desperation. Eve recognized the response. Returned it. Her fingers raked through his hair as her mouth twisted against his, pouring everything into the contact. His presence at her side had steadied her during the endless hours of the debriefing, when she'd needed to keep a tight rein on her emotions. But the desire to feel Declan against her again had simmered for hours, gathering heat and strength until she'd felt as though she'd combust from it.

Her fingers danced up his shirt, releasing buttons until she could slip a hand inside and rest it against his warm skin. Nipping at his bottom lip, she took a long shuddering breath and could feel something inside her calm at the strong steady thud of his heart beneath her palm. His hand skated under the back of her tee, and her bones went to water.

A haunting thought had the breath shuddering out of her, and she tore her mouth from his. A little lightheaded. More than a bit weak. The possibilities she'd refused to let herself consider when Malsovic held her captive remained at the hem of her mind like determined ghosts. But somehow, being in Declan's arms took a step toward banishing them. She could have lost him. So easily. They could have lost each other.

His hand stroked up and down her spine in long velvet glides that had the remaining strength streaming out of her. "You gave me some bad moments for a while there, Evie."

"There were one or two," she admitted. Because they were there, she slipped the rest of the buttons on his shirt out of the buttonholes to rest her cheek against his chest. Flesh to flesh. The contact was soothing. "I was a big fan of the hat," she said suddenly, as she brushed her fingers along his ribs. "Reminded me of Indiana Jones."

"First Dirty Harry and now Indiana Jones." She could hear the smile in his voice. "I think you have a thing for iconic action heroes."

"I appear to have a thing for *heroes*. Or one in particular." Slipping her arms around his waist, she leaned a bit away so she could look up at him. "I've been remiss for not thanking you for the rescue you mounted. I'm bloodthirsty enough to have relished seeing my buyer writhing in pain on the floor of the elevator. And glad you were able to have a few minutes with Malsovic before the authorities swooped in."

"You and me both. That intention actually got me through some rough patches...thinking of what I'd do to him when I had the chance. Guess we'll have to be satisfied thinking about him spending the rest of his miserable life rotting in a Malaysian cell as the various countries fight for the right to try him."

She tilted her head as she surveyed him. The whiskers on his jaw gave him a slightly dangerous look. Certainly, he'd been dangerous to her equilibrium ever since she'd known him.

"We'll be home in a day or two." His gray gaze was focused on hers, the look in them intent. "This part will be over. But you and me...we're not. I've never been in love." His hand rose to cup her cheek. "At least not the death-do-us-part kind. But that's how it is for me, Evie. The whole time you were missing...it was like someone carved a hollow through my chest. I don't want to think about how close I came to losing you. I'm not about to risk it now. I love you." There was something in his eyes that might have been surprise. "Wasn't looking for it. But you sort of sneak up on a person. And damned if I'm going to let go of this—or you— once we get back to the States."

Her heart stuttered hard once, before doing a slow easy spin. "I come from practical stock. I know that love grows over time." Shared interests. Common goals. That's how it had been for her parents. Her siblings. But then, she'd never had all that much in common with her family. "It's not supposed to happen like a lightning bolt, is it? Because that's what it feels like with you. You pack a helluva punch, Declan. I've loved you since the first time you apologized, for real. The first time you kissed me." Her smile went a bit misty at the memory. The man saw too much, despite the smokescreen she'd put up to prevent exactly that.

"It'll be a different sort of Christmas this year. For both of us." He trailed a finger down her cheek. "I'll have to teach you the intricacies of gift buying without links involved." His smile was indulgent. Then it faded, as he sobered. "You'll be the first woman I've ever introduced to my family. I think that alone will have Gran considering you the best present I've ever given her. And then there's New Year's Eve to consider." His eyes glinted. "I already know what you're going to wear."

Yesterday, she'd feared she'd never see this man again. And now...now she was in his arms, talking about a future she'd never dared contemplate. And that would be the real blessing of the season. "You're just full of plans," she teased.

"As a matter of fact..." His head lowered, and this time when their lips touched, it was less urgent and more of a promise. After a long moment, he said, "Since we've been pretending to be married for over a week already, I'm thinking we should just..." The panic she felt then must have shown in her expression. Being a wise man, he just smiled. "I'm Scottish. We're a pretty romantic lot. Irresistible, really."

The flare of panic had ebbed, to be replaced with amusement. "Is that so?"

"We'll take it slow," he decided. "But I feel the need to warn you that my powers of persuasion are legendary."

She didn't doubt it. Just as she didn't doubt this utter certainty of what she wanted. Her lips brushing his, she murmured, "I look forward to being persuaded."

Kylie Brant is the author of forty romantic suspense and thriller novels. She's garnered numerous industry nomination and awards, including twice winning the overall Daphne du Maurier for excellence in mystery and suspense, as well as a career achievement award from Romantic Times. Kylie is a three-time Rita nominee and has been nominated for five RT awards. Her novel, PRETTY GIRLS DANCING, was a #1 Amazon bestseller. She's the mother of five, a former elementary special education teacher and an accomplished multi-tasker. Her books have been published in twenty-nine countries and translated into eighteen languages. You can find Kylie at www.kyliebrant.com

ALSO BY KYLIE BRANT

THE MINDHUNTERS

Waking Nightmare

Waking Evil

Waking the Dead

Deadly Intent

Deadly Dreams

Deadly Sins

Secrets of the Dead

What the Dead Know

CIRCLE OF EVIL TRILOGY

Chasing Evil

Touching Evil

Facing Evil

STAND ALONE NOVELS

Pretty Girls Dancing

OTHER BOOKS BY KYLIE BRANT

McCain's Law

Rancher's Choice

An Irresistible Man

Guarding Raine

Bringing Benjy Home